SOUL COGS

EVEN IF YOUR SOUL BREAKS

MICHELLE R YOUNG

*I am terribly broken
and know darkness well
but the light inside of me
has a story to tell.*

~Christy Ann Martine

YOUR EXCLUSIVE ART AND STORIES ARE WAITING!

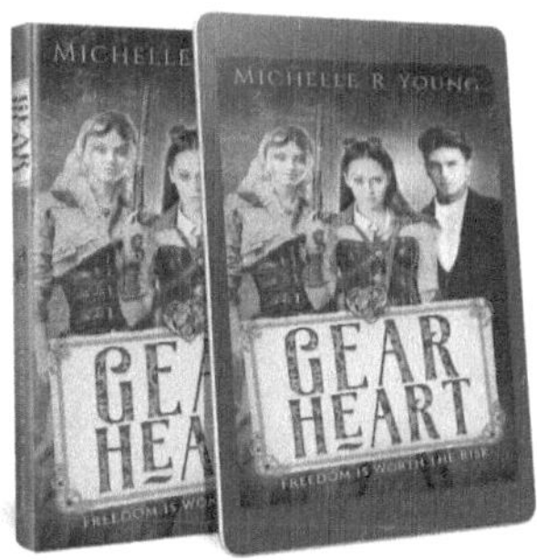

Gear Heart received so much praise, there is no way the story could stop there!

In *Soul Cogs* the adventure continues. New secrets and stories will be available here! Click the link to receive exclusive content such as the official art of the characters, favorite scenes, the cities' perspectives and Aspen's inventions. And that's just the beginning!

Click the link for exclusive content or scan the QR code.

www.mypureart.com

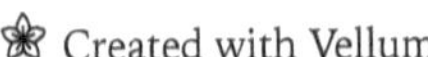 Created with Vellum

REVIVAL

ASPEN

Currlion Western Abbey
January 1, 1887

I open my eyes to see a palely lit room with round stone walls. Even the air has a blue mood to it, as if the world had just experienced a great catastrophe and melancholy is the new normal. Turning my head, I quickly feel how sore I am, just from that simple movement. There are hospital beds all around me with steel-barred head- and footboards. I'm on one too, I see, and there is a basin on the bedside table next to my bed. It appears that someone's bandages were recently changed, due to the gauze left behind.

Looking around the small, six-bed room, I see a short doorway with a simple white curtain blocking the opening. *What lies behind that curtain? I have to find out where I am, and where Sissy, Thomas, and Keagan are as well.* I toss off my sheets and begin to get out of bed, but my back feels like it's on fire. I scream from the sensations that course through my torso as I try to move, instead landing flat back on the bed. As the mattress's squeaky bounces settle, I hear a scuffling sound coming from the curtained doorway.

Great, someone's coming! Quick, Aspen, think! What's the last thing you remember? How did you get here? Images of the fight on the ship flood my vision, as I recall Keagan and myself jumping off the boat's edge and that same feeling of fire running across my back right before we broke through the freezing water.

The shuffling curtain interrupts my memory as a nurse and my team of troublemakers come running into the room. Lori is already in tears as Keagan runs straight to my bedside, taking my hand in his. He looks terrified, or at least I think he does. I can't see too well with my eyes tearing up.

"Aspen!" my team cries out, each with a different emotion. Thomas, unlike Lori and Keagan, looks relieved and rather happy as he reaches my bedside, whilst the nurse and Keagan begin to examine me from front to back.

"My name is Nurse Hudson, Miss Wolfe," the woman says to me. "I'll need to do a thorough examination of you to make sure you're all right." She ushers the boys behind the curtain once more before removing the hospital gown I'm wearing.

She is slight in figure and must be in her mid-fifties, though she lacks even one grey hair in the dark brown bangs that hang out from under her wimple. She starts with my senses and then checks my bandages that I now realise are wrapped around my upper chest and shoulders. As she cleans my back with a cold wet rag, I can feel the room becoming even chillier, and I brace myself to keep from shivering. *This place isn't well insulated, I guess, but I'm in no position to complain, as long as we're safe.*

As Nurse Hudson continues to work, Lori fills me in on what's been going on.

"You've been sleeping a great deal. We're currently in an abbey that has a small hospital ward connected to it." *This must be a place where the poor and homeless come when they need a hospital,* I think. "Keagan and his father often helped in repairs around here whenever they were needed. Everyone here was more than willing to help and hide us, especially when they saw the condition we were in." She dabs her eyes. "Keagan said that when you and he both jumped ship, a dimie bot cut your back just as you were going over the edge. He didn't find out about your wounds till you made it to the shore and he tried to pull you out of the water. He said that neither of you would've made it if it weren't for the two dimies who swam you there from the ship." Lori looks away from my bed as the nurse applies something to my back that stings so bitterly, it makes me sit straight up in a flash. I nod my head as the memories come barreling back to me.

"Miss Wolfe, I'm going to have to stitch your back up again; one of the cuts has reopened," Nurse Hudson says, laying a lithe hand on my shoulder.

I nod my head in approval. "Go right ahead. I am quite at my leisure."

The stitches are quite painful, stinging with each prick and pull of the sutures and thread through the skin of my back. However, they're still nothing compared to the pain of the open wounds themselves. "What—ow—what about Damon?" I continue. "And the police? Do they—"

"No, they have no idea where we are," Lori reassures me. "And as for you and Keagan, they don't know if you're even alive. Thomas was out at the market with the nuns earlier this morning. He overheard from the fisherman that the constables and Damon's dimie watchmen are searching every inch of the bay for your bodies. All the remaining officers in the city are just beginning to search the town."

"We're afraid that they will make their way here soon," Keagan hollers from behind the curtain.

"Oh, you need not worry about that," my nurse says with ease as she ties off my stitches. *That was a long stitch. How far did that blasted bot cut me?* "We have quite a good number of places to hide you rascals." I can feel a slight smile curl at the edge of my mouth whilst she helps me back into my hospital gown and sits me up in bed. "The doctor will come see you in a short while, but for the most part I will be your caregiver until you're back up to snuff. I'll be right back with your breakfast and I expect you to eat every bite of it. We need to get you on your feet as soon as possible with your current situation." When she flashes me a warm smile, I recognise who she reminds me of, which leads me to yet another question.

She leaves the room with her supplies and parts the curtain, allowing Keagan and Thomas to enter in again. "Where is Winona?" I ask immediately. Keagan stops mid-step through the doorway as I say her name. The room's blue essence turns darker now; their faces become pale and sombre.

"Aspen...Winona was killed on the ship during the fighting," Lori responds meekly.

"Keagan held her in his arms as she died," Thomas adds. "He even killed the man who shot her."

"Don't tell her that!" Lori snaps sternly before sighing and fidgeting with her hands. Thomas looks down and messes with the pageboy cap in his hands. I can tell they're trying not to cry. My attention shifts to Keagan, though his eyes avoid mine, instead downcast and bolted to the floor. His jaw is clenched as he sucks in air through his teeth, and his knuckles are white, bunched in fists. The sight frightens me.

"Keagan," I say almost unintelligibly, but he is gone in a flash through the curtain. An immense crack rumbles through my heart and lungs as my breathing begins to quicken. The cracks open up to black empty pits as my tears begin to fall. All I feel is pain. Just like when we lost Papa and Mum. Lori and Thomas are by my side, and through my tears I can see their sorrow as well. *They feel it too.* Somehow, this gives me a small feeling of comfort. People always say that misery loves company, so I cry and let out the pain as best I can with Lori and Thomas. The only problem is that it won't stop flowing. Lori holds my hand, and Thomas turns away completely. I wish so badly to hug Lori, but she holds my hand as if it may break at any moment. Why do I get the feeling that they think I'm a frail porcelain doll with my wounds now? The feelings flow like a never ending waterfall when I need it to be a small jug that will soon be empty.

Nurse Hudson comes by and leaves the breakfast for me as I continue to weep, yet it feels like mere moments have passed when she comes back and not one bit of food has been eaten. I can't. I'm not hungry anymore.

Finally, the tears lessen, leaving my lungs completely exhausted. In an instant, I feel as if all the remaining energy I have disappears. Nurse Hudson decides to feed me whilst constantly nudging me and shaking my hands to keep me awake. She doesn't stop until all the food is gone, but I can barely feel it in my stomach. I couldn't even taste it, whatever it was. She gently lays me back down on the bed before ushering Thomas and Lori back out of the room.

Things are so different now without a house, or soft beds to lay our heads. I especially miss the lavatory accessibility.

And...Winona. Gosh, now I remember this feeling from when I stayed awake those three nights—the hunger, the exhaustion. I guess for people like me, and frankly our whole group, it's so important to have someone there to care for you and keep your house in order. When one works as hard as we do, one barely has any time to take care of oneself, mending clothes or cooking like she did. Not to mention how it was her love and kindness that made the manor feel like home. Without her, it would have been a stuffy old house with no warmth or merriment. She really was the heart of that home, and our family. I now know that there was no way we could have made it this far without Winona taking care of us and loving us. Good Lord, she did so much and went above and beyond when the house was filled with her own kind as well. I see those days as a golden memory right now. They were our reality less than a day ago, yet I can't touch them anymore. Just remember.

As exhausted as I feel right now, my mind won't let me fall asleep, swirling with thoughts of Winona and Keagan. *Keagan.* He left the room without a word. I can't help but blame myself for that. *How could I possibly forget what happened to Winona? How could I have let any of this happen in the first place? This isn't how things should have turned out. Winona was supposed to go home with Thatcher, she told me her—*

"Thatcher!" I squeak out through my ragged throat. I've cried so hard, my voice is raspy now. Just the thought of Thatcher fighting off that second wave of men and dimie bots makes my eyes burn. *We lost the best of us that night. And there was nothing I could do to prevent it. All we did was run.*

When I wake back up, Nurse Hudson lets me know it's already afternoon. The abbey's personal doctor, Dr Doyle, gives me a full checkup, then declares in a serious tone,"You were very lucky, Miss Wolfe. The blades were very close to cutting some very important nerves along your spine. What you need to do for a full and quick recovery is to keep those cuts clean and put as little strain on them as possible. So, try to not involve your upper back and arms in stretches or heavy physical movement. You are to remain here as a patient until we remove those stitches, which should be in about a week or two. Do you understand, Miss Wolfe?"

"I understand, Doctor," I say through my thin voice.

After a nod of his head he begins to play with his stethoscope, which has a watch attached to the back of it. "Miss Wolfe...I promise that you and your party will be safe here during your recoveries," he starts as he takes a seat on the bed adjacent to mine. "We are aware of what all of you did for the dimies, and what lengths you took to make it possible. A dimie named Daniel once saved me when I had nearly drowned in a freezing river, reviving me and bandaging up my broken arm. If it hadn't been for him, I wouldn't be here talking to you, Miss Wolfe, nor would I have become a doctor. I had a good future ahead of me; he did not. So I want to thank you on his behalf for what you did to free those enslaved in the city."

"You're welcome, and thank you for helping us as well." It's then that I realise something. "Is—is this the hospital where the townspeople send their sick and hurt dimies?"

"You guessed it. It's the only place in town that will properly care for them," he says before leaving through the curtain. I'm tempted to get up and see what lies beyond that veil. It seems everyone but me is allowed to go beyond its cloth.

Maybe tonight, whilst everyone is asleep, I can try to walk though it.

As if he could sense my scheming, Keagan comes through the doorway with not a single emotion evident on his face as he looks at me. *Did the room just become cooler?* Next to join in are Lori and Thomas, along with Nurse Hudson with more bowls of steaming food. Lori and Thomas take a seat on the bed to my right as Keagan stands at the foot of my own, and I realise they are still wearing their night-running gear. Well, it's not like they had a change of clothes with them. We weren't that prepared.

Something else that gives me a twinge of guilt is that everyone has a patch or a bit of gauze wrapped around a wounded area that I hadn't taken much notice of earlier. For Lori, it's her cheek and upper left arm, whilst Thomas has bandages around his little dark fingers. Keagan, however, also has a fresh cut through his eyebrow and a long wrap of gauze on his left arm. His temple has a new bandage around it, as does his wrist. Those weren't there this morning or when he ran out of the room. *Where did those come from?*

After proving to Nurse Hudson that I can feed myself, she leaves the four of us alone to eat our dinner together. "Alright," I begin to them, "so I've been thinking about where we should go from here."

"What do you mean?" Thomas asks before taking a loud slurp of his soup.

"I mean our only plan right now is if Damon's men come around, the nurses will just hide us. But once I get better, we can't just leave town empty-handed. We have to go back to the house to get supplies for our journey to London."

"You mean *we* have to," Keagan corrects me as he points to himself, Lori and Thomas. "You're not to leave this abbey until the doctor certifies you and your cuts are healed." From the stern look on his face, he doesn't seem to be willing to negotiate the matter.

"But what about the things I need to get? I know what and where they are."

"Lori can find them, and between the three of us we can carry whatever you need," Keagan replies without missing a beat.

"But what if they're too heavy once you add the rest of the supplies?"

"Aspen, you're heavily wounded, and stitches on the back break easily. Hell, you can barely lift yourself off that bed without breaking them. What makes you think you're going to make it up the hills in the snow and back down with loads of supplies? You're staying here, and that's all there is to it."

A silence fills the room as we become awestruck at his new assertiveness. The way he talks to me now reminds me of when Lori and I were sneaking back into the house. He was so angry when he caught us; his energy seems similar to that night, but there's something different this time...I sense fear in his words.

"You know you currently don't exactly look like Adonis yourself," I snap back. "What makes you think you can do it alone?"

Keagan looks hurt slightly as he straightens back up before he replies. "I never said I did."

"You didn't need to."

I look away as he continues. "I don't even like the idea of going back to the manor now that we're wanted by Damon and the police. It could already be under watch or crawling with bobbies."

"There are things we can't leave behind." Lori gestures her hand at me in agreement.

"I agree with them, Keagan," Thomas adds. "There's something I need to take as well. It's a gift my grandfather gave me. It's the last thing I have to remember him by." Thomas stares quietly into his bowl of soup.

Keagan's put-out demeanour changes to regretful as his jaw unclenches. "We three will go tonight then, in just a few hours," he says. "From what you told us earlier, Thomas, the bobbies haven't made their way to the estates in the hills yet. So we should be fine if we hurry. They don't even know if we're alive or not, except you, Lori. As far as Damon knows, you've abandoned us and are on the run somewhere."

"Where did he get that idea?" Sissy asks, confused.

"Because you weren't with us the day we were caught in the warehouse trying to open the portal," I explain. "I acted the part to make it seem like you were supposed to be there and then abandoned us."

"She was pretty convincing as well," Keagan adds with a half-smile. "She nearly cried." It feels good to see that smile again, even if it's directed at Lori instead of me.

"So, once we come back with our supplies, then what?" Thomas sets aside his empty bowl.

"We'll make our way to London after my stitches are taken out," I continue. "Seems like it'll take a week or two, from what the doctor's told me. I'm still working out the plan on how we get to London safely, but now we at least have time to prepare. Thomas, I don't think it'd be good if you go out to the traders market again. Someone may recognise and follow you to find out why you've been missing. Same for the rest of us, of course. We have to keep a low profile."

"Maybe we should put some of our clothes in the water for the bobbies to find," Thomas suggests.

"That's not a bad idea," Lori says with a lighter tone. "We should tear them up a bit, too, so it seems as if sharks attacked you. But the clothes have to be black, since it's our night running gear that Damon caught us in."

"How about my cloak? That'd be discernible," Keagan says nonchalantly.

"Yes, and one of my corsets," I offer. "We can even put some wine on it before tearing it up, to make it look bloody." Keagan seems to blush a little, so I add, "Lori can be in charge of that, of course."

To this, both Thomas and Keagan give a sigh of relief. We have our plan; now we just need to prepare and wait for nightfall.

HEADLINERS

KEAGAN

"Everything looks clear," Lori says.

I suppose most of the policemen were on that ship last night, so they never made it back to port, and the rest of the officers are still searching the beach, docks and water for our bodies. *I bet they don't have many officers left inside the city, since they're busy close to the water. Or perhaps they're waiting inside for us. Is that even allowed for constables?*

We flip over our capes and hoods to the white side and wrap them close to our bodies to blend in with the snow as best as possible. I may have some trouble with this, however, due to my cloak being very dirty from the fight on the ship and the sand on the shore. The closer we track through the snow towards my home, the bigger and tighter the knot in my stomach gets. I just can't shake the feeling that someone is waiting for us in the manor.

We sneak up to the windows at the back doors so we can check inside. Each of us takes a different window, belonging to a different room. Lori puts two flat hands together near the sides of her face as she peers inside. After a few seconds, she turns to face me with both hands coming softly together, our sign for curtains closed. Thomas sends me the same signal. At my window, though, the curtains that go to the mudroom are thin lace and semi-transparent. But even with this, it's still hard to see. Everything is still so dark. It looks like the house is dead empty.

I give the thumbs up, and Lori immediately comes over to unlock the door. But just as she inserts the key into the lock, a lantern comes around the corner and runs to the door. "Lori!" is all I have time to say before the door is opened, revealing bright light and what lies behind it.

When the light lowers and our eyes begin to adjust, we hear a familiar voice from its holder. "We were wondering when you were going to come home, old boy."

"Good Lord, James! You nearly stopped my heart!" I snap at my friend in a hoarse tone. "What are you doing in my house?"

"I and a good friend have been guarding the house ever since this morning's paper came out. You made the front page again, Keagan." James tosses me the paper.

A band of thieves and menaces to society, otherwise known as the Night Phantoms, were caught by Governor Damon and the local constabulary on New Year's Eve. The good samaritan's dimie, Gertrude of Damon House, as well as Charles Farthington, found damning evidence against playboy Keagan Myrack and sisters Aspen and Lori Wolfe. The three have been extracting and stealing confidential information, precious gems, dimies from multiple cities, and even innocent children to try and eradicate our way of life and the entire working class. The trio is charged with kidnapping, larceny, breaking and entering, manslaughter, along with cruel and unusual punishment towards their victims, as well as the felony charge of stealing and releasing slaves. Their capture is now being rewarded with 100,000 pounds, dead or alive. These criminals are dangerous. If spotted, notify the police or kill on sight.

"Well, doesn't that just top it all," I say after reading the paper aloud. "How could it get worse than this?"

"Keagan, we have paddy waggons coming," Lori says, pointing down the snowy slopes as the lanterns on the carriages shine through the trees. They are not ten minutes away from where we are.

I shove the newspaper back at James angrily. "Did you—"

"No, I didn't call them," James responds defensively, "but please hurry. We packed a few sacks of food, money and other things you can use for your journey."

"How'd you know I'd come back?" I ask, lowering my arms.

"Call it a hunch. You always were well-packed when you travelled."

"My sister's tools...and my photo album, are they packed too?" asks Lori.

"Not yet." James pulls my arm, giving Lori and Thomas space to get inside the doorway. "I made arrangements with my family in London. My great uncle will take you in. There's a carriage filled with other things that I will personally mail to his house."

"Thank you, brother, but...is this the same great Uncle George I remember when we were kids?" I ponder hesitantly.

"...Yes."

I take a long inhale, knowing what's to come with his

insane great uncle. Last time we stayed with him, he burned half of my hair off and used my best clothes as colour-dye testers.

"When did you get here?" I ask.

"Four hours before you did. Miss Masie came to me knowing that if there was anyone who would help, it would be me." This makes me smile, knowing how lucky I am to have such loyal people still in my life.

Step by step, I follow James back into my ancestral home. But something is wrong. It's dark, and cold. Like something is missing. *Winona.* The heart of this manor has stopped beating, leaving the house dead, stabbed by a man I once trusted with my life. What a foolish thing to do. *How could this place ever feel like home again? What is a home without the people you love, anyway?*

"Keagan." I hear James's voice forcing me to focus back on the present task. I look at him as he hands me a lit candle. I look over my shoulder to see Lori and Thomas going to their rooms to get their things. I should probably pack all the money I can carry and check Aspen's workspace, though Lori is probably doing that now. "Come on, old boy, let's get you packed and ready." He places a hand on my shoulder and pushes me forward.

Just keep moving.

Warm clothes, old trinkets from my fondest travels, and even the one rare picture of my mother with Winona laughing together at what looks like a picnic. *Winona never did tell me what they were laughing about.*

For the first time in a long time, I realise that the house is silent. Makes me wonder who will take care of it whilst I'm away. It's not like I'm off to study in Morocco whilst Charles and Winona keep the house tidy. Who would when rumours are spreading that Aspen and I are dead?

Wait...if I'm to be assumed dead, which is what we are needing people to believe, then it seems we have an issue. If I'm dead along with Aspen, then Lori and Thomas are not kin and are also *gone*. Winona and Charles never had the chance to possess the will, or at least they shouldn't have. Then the house will be taken by the government, and everything will be put up for sale. *The will!* I toss the vests and shoes I'm holding into the rucksack, take James's arm, and bolt to the library, where I fumble with the hidden catch inside the devil at the base of one of the shelves, and open the secret door. The door slides open, and I immediately get to work at the podium with the deed to the estate.

"I'm sorry that Mary isn't here to help as well," James explains, "but she was quite peeved when she learned that all the dimies in the house suddenly vanished. When we heard the news this morning, she refused to come help. Said she now has to ready the house to find new butlers and maids. Sorry to say, Keagan, but my wife is quite angry with you and the Wolfe sisters for stealing our help."

"I'm sorry, I truly am, to be on opposing sides from Mary, but I will not apologise for what I believe to be the right cause. Besides, we only provided the means; it was the dimies' choice to leave," I reply sombrely, trying my best not to sound arrogant.

"Hmmm. I'm still trying to figure out how I feel about the whole thing. It's a noble cause, but it's just so dangerous. You always were more daring than I." At that remark, I look down at the deed to the estate that I just temporarily signed over to him. *James is my best friend. He may not be willing to protect the dimies, or even Aspen, Lori or Thomas, but he's always protected me, just like I've protected him.* James catches me glancing at the deed on the pillar and with a bittersweet smile says, "This is one thing you need not worry about whilst you are gone to who knows where. You just need to promise me that you'll come back one day so I can give it back to you. That way I can add a good sucker-punch on behalf of my entire household." *I'll miss you too, James.*

"James, you are now the newest manager of the Myrack estate; you must watch over it and keep it safe in my absence. This allows you a simple ownership title and monthly allowance. By law, it cannot be taken from you when signed over. The government will not be able to confiscate it on your watch, as long as all expenses are always paid in a timely manner. Will you agree to these terms?" I hand him a quill.

"I will," he says, looking at me as though I were laying on my deathbed. Once the document is signed, he takes it in his pocket, ready to show the bobbies when they come. "Keagan? I fear this might be the last time I can get you out of trouble like this, since I will have to focus on my family's future very soon. Mary is expecting, and you are the first to know, brother."

"Congratulations. And you have already helped us more than you know. I understand that your future child and wife must come first. I'm just grateful that you still chose to aid us."

"But I'm serious, you better come back. I can't possibly take care of two households at once forever. Especially when one of them belongs to my future child's godfather!" We grab the rest of my things and then head to the back door. If we weren't running for our lives, it would be easier to truly smile and pop open a bottle of champagne for James.

When we make it to the door, Miss Masie rushes towards me in a plain dress with no frills, which I never thought I'd live to see her wear. She gives me a strong hug and a kiss on the cheek before handing me one sack of money and one sack of food. "Now ya promise me I will see ya again, along with the rest of ya new family. Promise me, Keagan." She points a skinny finger at me like a mother would as I nod my head earnestly. Satisfied, she hugs the rest of us once more before ushering us out the door. But as the four of us say sorrowful and fast farewells to our friends, I don't feel relieved or grateful, only heavy-hearted.

The police will be at the house any second now, and we are at least ten metres away from the cover of the trees. Rushing through the snow as fast as we possibly can, we make it to the edge of the thick firs, where I stop to glance back once more. This might be my last time seeing my ancestral home or my friends waving to us. I wave back once before being pulled gently into the snowy branches by Lori and Thomas. They have the same pleading and scared looks on their faces as Aspen did before we jumped off the boat together. *I knew damn well what I was getting myself into and so did the rest of us. Nothing in that agreement changes.*

"We're sorry, Keagan," Lori says so softly I barely hear it.

"Well, I am too, but I put James in charge of the estate. It'll take a lot for the governor to try it and take it now."

"I say, well done, old boy," Lori calls back as she starts walking, mimicking James, which makes me laugh. I needed a good laugh.

~

As we make our way back down the snow-covered hills near the abbey, we discuss where to plant the fake clothes. Thomas suggests the easternmost strip of the beach, since that's where he last heard the bobbies would be searching. We decide to look around first for policemen before tossing our clothes in the current, which will hopefully send the clothes towards them down the beach. By the time we agree on the plan, we can see the abbey in the distance.

Aspen is fast asleep when we return, so Nurse Hudson helps us stain the clothes with potent red wine and currant berries. I'll have to repay them for the wine someday, since theirs is specifically for Communion. Lori and Thomas are given the honour of tearing apart the cloak and corset as they please. Between the giggles and tug-of-war game between the two, I'd say they quite enjoyed it despite staining their hands red in the process.

Once the clothes have been thoroughly dishevelled beyond repair, it truly does appear as if a sea monster had attacked us. Thomas and I clean our hands and bundle up once again before we set out towards the beach to plant the decoy clothes. Lori agrees to stay behind to help Nurse Hudson clean up the mess we all made, and so she can stay close to Aspen. Thanks to our friends who prepared our luggage in advance for our journey, we now have our day clothes and coats to walk around in society as normal people once again. However, we still keep our hats low and our scarves covering half our faces. It's a good thing it's winter, so we have a reason to hide ourselves like we do.

Even though the time is nearing ten o'clock at night, there are still a large number of people roaming the streets. I start to feel very uncomfortable; someone could bump into us and knock our hats off at any second. We have to take the next alleyway that comes around to get out of the streetlights. I don't care if we need to take a detour to get to the beach from where we are; we have to do it. I tap Thomas on the shoulder and nod my head towards the next alley's opening. We smoothly change our course, and, as we are turning in, I look behind my shoulder from under the brim of my hat. It appears that a man on the opposite side of the road is looking our way from just a short distance behind us. This is a long alleyway, filled with crates and huge blocks of ice. *That's right, the ice cutters are on the left—which means Bill's butcher shop is on our right. The ice men seem to always forget to lock up their doors, which could save us if we need to hide now.*

Placing my black gloved hand on Thomas's upper back, I move us behind the cold insulated crates filled with ice. Thanks to the help of the streetlight, I have the advantage of looking through the ice to see if a figure is coming our way without being detected. A man close to my height, but with a rather thick frame, pokes his head down the alleyway. My hunch about being followed is correct. Surprisingly, I can feel the cold coming off the icy window in front of me, despite the already freezing temperatures. Through the ice block, I can make out that he is taking a few steps in; but since there are no sounds or movement going on through the stretched divide, the man slowly reenters the streets and back into society.

"Looks like that bounty for our arrest has really gotten people suspicious, huh?" Thomas whispers as we near the voices of the bobbies on the pebbled beach.

"Yeah, even if the *night phantoms* were reported dead and

missing, not everyone believes it, I would say," I reply, hoping that he gets the hint to use our given names in third person. We don't know who could be listening. *He's right, though. That man was very suspicious of us. I doubt he recognised us, but I can't help but wonder. One thing is for sure: Currlion is no longer safe for us on the streets in any way. We need to leave as soon as Aspen heals.*

We take off our coats and wade knee-deep in the icy water as we disperse a few of the decoy fragments.

As we wait to see if the bobbies are coming our way, we can already tell that the current will bring the clothes to the shore by the time they arrive. So, we don our coats and take the rest of the clothes further up the dark beach to a clear area. This time, we strew the clothes across the beach itself, where high tide would have brought them in just an hour before. By the time we do this, we can hear the calls of the excited men. They must have found Aspen's destroyed bloody half-corset. *Keep coming this way, gents; there's even more gifts waiting for you.*

Laying ourselves behind a sand dune, we watch the bobbies crowd around and examine the tattered clothing piece. We are happy when we see a few of the constables staying where they found the corset and the remaining ten men come our way. Satisfied with our work, we make our way through the dark and back into the maze of alleyways. I know he's trying to stay as quiet as possible, but I can still hear Thomas giggling as we dash down the darkened streets and backways. I can't help but wear a mischievous smile of my own as we run. *It'll feel good to go to sleep tonight knowing we helped the police with their jobs and saved our necks at the same time.*

HIDEOUT

LORI

It's been twelve days since Aspen woke up and was restricted to fiddling with her gadgets, including Gear Heart, whilst she recovered per the orders of Nurse Hudson. It may or may not have been my fault, since I might have gabbed about Aspen's bad habits of staying up till all hours and disregarding her personal health. So we've been keeping her busy with mind games, books, and riddles.

Something she has enjoyed the most, though, is teaching Thomas how to build a few gadgets. She loves to see how he fixes a machine. It always amused her when she would sketch out half a machine's schematics and tear the remaining pieces apart for him to build the rest, without fail every time. It felt as if their lessons would drag on for hours. However, I wish she had spent more time with Keagan, or rather that he felt open enough to spend time with her alone. There's still a conversation barrier between the two that I so wish I knew how to fix; but to be honest, a similar one still exists between Keagan and myself after the things we practically screamed at him in the library.

But today, Aspen's stitches are to come out, and Dr Doyle assures our whole lot that her wounds have healed wonderfully. However, due to them reopening as they did, there will be a few scars visible. When Aspen hears this, she doesn't appear to be too dismayed, although I don't know why I was expecting her to be, what with all the scars she currently carries. She tries to convince us that she doesn't care—*"What's a few more scars?"* she says—but I know it annoys her, even if it's just the slightest bit. She doesn't deserve more of them, that much I know to be true.

Sissy makes funny faces each time the threads are pulled out, as she sits on the examining table in her backless white gown. The boys stay behind the curtain since they aren't allowed in, but they still want to be nearby in case she wants people to talk to. "Does it hurt very much?" I ask meekly as I sit facing her. I don't particularly like watching stitches applied or taken out.

"Not too much. It just feels really awkward. It's hard to describe. It feels disgusting."

"That's one," Nurse Hudson says. "Now we only have two more sets to go, all right? The awkwardness will be over soon." She tries to assure Aspen, but I can tell she wants it to be over now. I look at the area where the stitches were just removed and see a jagged line of red lacing Aspen's back, the area around it looking a little purple still. It must be having a hard time healing properly even under these conditions. We'll have to make sure those scars are covered by her dresses in the future, or she could be recognised and tagged by those markings alone.

When the last stitch is taken out, Nurse Hudson begins cleaning the area and applying a salve. "You still need to take it easy, since the skin of those scars are still thin. I recommend you stay another day or two so we can continue to monitor them. It will also help you plan your escape from Currlion," she says loud enough for the gents behind the curtain to hear us. "Aspen, you'll be happy to hear that you can now start tinkering again, just nothing that makes you stay up too late. You still need your proper rest each night."

"Yes, ma'am," Aspen says happily as we help her dress in normal day clothes for the first time since she arrived here, though we're leaving out the corset for now per Dr Doyle's orders. Once she's dressed, I help in repinning her hair as the boys are ushered in by Nurse Hudson whilst carrying Gear Heart and the generator. I tap Aspen on her right shoulder, causing her to look in the direction of the approaching company and exclaim, "Oh, thank goodness we still have Gear Heart and the generator. Just the thought of Governor Damon presenting it to the Queen in his name makes me see red. I must record how you and Thomas were able to connect it to the lighthouse to make it work. That was a stellar job you two did."

"Don't look at *me*," I reply, putting up my hands and gesturing to Thomas. "That was all him. I just made sure no thugs distracted him as he worked."

"It must have been an adventure in itself, eh, Thomas?" Aspen smiles.

"You're right about that; I've never worked and thought so fast in my life," Thomas says energetically.

"I can't wait to write it all down. Lori, do you know where my work journal is?"

"Yes, it should be...Thomas, have you seen Aspen's work journal, the one with our father's sketches of Gear Heart on the first pages?"

"I haven't seen that since we left the house the night of New Year's Eve."

"Damon took the journal! Damn it all, I just remembered that he had frisked us and taken everything. But didn't you say that you raided the case that had everything they took in it?" Keagan rubs his temple.

"Yes, but we—we," I stammer, thinking back to what happened as we were opening the locked trunk. There was a lot going on, and the sounds of angry and hurt men were filling the air. *I remember seeing other things in the trunk but my mind only processed that we needed Gear Heart and the generator. And now Damon...Damon still has Aspen's journal with all the necessary details to create more bi-dimensional teleporter machines. And I have to tell her that, even though I can already tell she's guessed it herself.* "... We didn't get it," I finish as timidly as a mouse.

Aspen doesn't say anything at first; she just hunches over, groaning with her head in her hands. "You must be joking! Lori, please tell me this is a cruel joke, because it's not funny at all."

"It's not," Thomas replies for me as my stomach performs acrobatics.

"He also has your journal, our weapons and the radio transmitter," Keagan adds.

"Oh, well, this is just splendid now, isn't it?" Aspen says, flinging her arms in the air sarcastically before wincing. "We cannot let him make more transporters or else the slave trade is back on, and I have a feeling he'll make it happen with or without the queen's blessing."

"How's that?" Thomas asks.

"The black market. Slaves sell for high prices, receive unfair treatment, and suffer through terrible labour. It would be the perfect place to do his work. Frankly, I'd be surprised if he wasn't already a part of the black market and the underground rings from when the slave trade originally opened up."

"You know, I think you're right. He has more connections than I do, and he used to make multiple trips a year to France with large amounts of dimies when I was a kid. France has the largest black market for the trading and selling of dimies now. It's easy to buy off the bobbies there with a cut of the profit. That's how they keep the major rings safely protected and hidden." Keagan leans on Aspen's footboard.

"And how do you know so much about the underground, Mr World Traveller?" I ask sceptically.

Keagan just stares at me, slightly peeved. "Damon and my father used to discuss matters like this when I was younger, and I would listen in through the door."

"Great, so then Damon probably knows the underground of London as well," I say. "We're going to need eyes in the back of our heads to just walk through the streets. Keagan, do you know any safe hotels or places we could stay whilst we're there?"

"Actually, that's already been taken care of thanks to James," Keagan says reassuringly, although looking somewhat worried still.

"Really? That's so kind of him. What are the arrangements?"

"Welllll—" Keagan draws out as he rubs the back of his neck.

"Everyone, quickly follow me!" Nurse Hudson says, coming in and going straight to Aspen's bed to help her up.

"What's going on?" Keagan asks.

"The police are here to search the grounds. They've come with dogs. I'm going to take you four to our hidden cellar. I'm warning you now to inhale through your mouth, not your nose. We make perfume oils, and they're stored in the cellar. It will take a miracle for the dogs to sniff out your scent down there." She wraps a blanket around Aspen's shoulders and gets her up on her feet.

We all follow her through the small stone abbey towards an even colder area, as if that was even possible with the blankets of snow laying over the entire city. The closer we get to the hiding place, the easier it is to smell the sickly sweet scent. Sadly, as we make the last turn towards the wooden doors ahead of us, the aroma mixes with the smell of fish and meat. When Nurse Hudson opens the old wooden door, we see that it is well stocked with fish, dried herbs, and Communion wine. On the floor is a stone cellar door that has a round metal handle on top of it.

"The lid to the cellar has to be this bloody heavy stone, because a wooden lid would only soak up the oil's scent and fill the pantry and food with it as well," Nurse Hudson explains as we head down into the cellar. "However, due to this urgent matter of hiding you, we made it so no animal could track your scent through to this spot or even to this room, due to the amount of perfume we used."

Keagan enters first, so that he and I can aid Aspen down the steep, stone steps if she needs us, Thomas following. This tactic reminds me of when Aspen splashed me with that scent-blocking liquid as I ran through the woods with Lucy from the tracking dogs. Winona helped create that mixture. It's like Nurse Hudson is playing the part of Winona now that it's time to run and hide again without her present.

It's already hard to breathe in from the perfume-saturated air. The further down we go into the stone-lined walls of the cellar, the dimmer the light becomes. I can just make out the lined shelves of large and tiny bottles that must be filled with a million different marinating scents. When we reach the bottom we have to watch our heads so as to not disturb some of the low-hanging dried herbs and flowers. Thomas looks up at them and the shelves in curiosity, despite how dull the light is. In a way, he reminds me of Aspen when we were kids, always curious about new things no matter how earthy or oily they were, whilst I only seemed interested in flowery and shiny things. What can I say? I was a little lady even then.

There is but one short stool in this cramped cellar, so we give it to Aspen, carefully sitting her down before taking a seat on the chilling pebbled floor ourselves. Thomas sits close to me on my right, though Keagan sits across from the three of us instead of the place I expect him, next to Aspen. *It will take time. We all just need to be patient with one another from now on.* To think that we're about to be trapped down here is rather frightening, since there are no windows. We shouldn't use candles either, since that will only take away more air. Nurse Hudson doesn't even warn us before she puts the lid back in its place, trapping us in darkness. There are tiny shreds of light rays poking around the stone lid opening.

For the longest stretch of time we remain as silent as we can, although I still cling to Aspen's arm and try to convince myself that anyone above cannot hear our subtle breathing. Thomas keeps a tight hold on the hem of my skirts. I try to give him a reassuring squeeze on his shoulder, but I end up bumping him in the cheek instead. After a slight grunt, I can feel that he has released his grip on my skirt. *I didn't mean it. I'm sorry!* To my dismay, Aspen abruptly lets go of my hand as well, but it lasts only a second before the back of her hand gently finds my forehead and works its way up to my scalp. As my head rests on her knee, she continues to stroke my hair, soothing my anxious nerves.

A few minutes later, we hear faint voices and clattering footsteps coming our way. My heart skips a beat, and I fear it will forget to start again. Then, the sound of sniffing noses is the only thing we hear. The dogs are right at the opening of our hiding place. What if they insist on looking down here too? The sounds of a heated conversation follows after the whining of dogs. They must be convincing the bobbies to move on. The sound of chaos fades into silence as the men and the dogs move away from the opening of the cellar. I allow myself to inhale again, along with everyone else. *Well, at least it's nice to know that I wasn't the only worried one here.*

We wait in the dark for quite some time, actually, the pique of my fear beginning to diminish when we hear rather rushed footsteps above pounding towards us. As quick as a flash, Nurse Hudson and Doctor Doyle pull the lid off our hideout. The light makes all of us squint as we begin to get up from the floor.

"Fancy meeting you four here," Doctor Doyle says, pulling out a handkerchief to cover his nose and mouth as he comes down the steps and reaches behind Keagan for a blue bottle before rushing back up.

"What was that he took out?" I ask Nurse Hudson as we walk up the steps ourselves.

"A special tonic we use from the herbs in our gardens. We like to make our medicine ourselves, and since the apothecaries here can be low in stock for specialty items, we like to keep them in the same place as the perfume oils, although on a completely different shelf. The doctor is using it for a dimie who came in last night; poor chap had a nasty time, it seems. He was malnourished and had some terrible cuts. "

"Oof, that doesn't sound good," I say. He must have been

one of the few that escaped from their homes but didn't make it to the warehouse in time. I wonder who hurt him, though?

"Indeed, but that tonic should make him right as rain after some bedrest and a few good meals."

"Well, I'm ashamed to say that there is little that we can do for him unless you happen to have a large lens we could use," Aspen says. "That's the only way any dimie could fit through the portal we made using Gear Heart. Unless they were a baby, of course."

"We planned for it to be compact, but we may have overshot it with the lens," Thomas grumbles.

"What if you just move it further back than you had before, to create a larger opening onto whatever it was projected on?" Keagan suggests.

"We can't. It's a lot like magic lanterns. Unless they're the right distance away to have a clear or at least mostly clear show of the dimension being projected, it will be too fuzzy for the portal to properly allow anything to pass through it. It'd be like talking to ghosts; they're there and yet not at the same time. The portal wouldn't be usable. And the lens size also changes up the distance the projection can go. With ours being so small, it gives only a very tiny window to the dimies' dimension. That's why the lens on the original machine was a godsend, since it was already the perfect size and distance away from the wall." By this point we've made our way back into the recovery room.

"Sounds like a complicated matter." Nurse Hudson pulls in our dinner cart.

"Not always. It's sometimes just a matter of dumb luck, finding the right size and angle to make things work," Thomas replies, to which Aspen gives him a proud smile as she sits back down on her bed with me beside her. The gents sit parallel to us on the other unmade bed as we take our bowl of porridge from the dinner cart. We even ask Nurse Hudson to join us, but she waves her hand, pulls away the cart, and tells us she must tend to the new patient.

Now, we just need to come up with a plan to get out of Currlion unseen. But every outgoing train and carriage is being checked before they leave town. Looking over at Aspen, I see her playing at the bits of food floating in the creamy soup with the tip of her spoon. Whenever she starts to get crafty notions, she always ends up absently playing around with her food, though it doesn't put my worries at ease with her current condition. And by the devilish smile on her face, whatever she is planning can't be good.

ALL ABOARD

KEAGAN

How am I going to explain James's crazy great uncle? He's been diagnosed as partly insane and partly diluted; he's been in and out of mental wards for years, yet he's the last surviving member of James's family in London. *It's probably because he scared the rest of them all to death. Let's just hope he won't scare us to death.*

We wait in the woods, hidden with our white cloaks in the snow-covered forest. The dim light of dawn is beginning to grow as the blue tint of the world is slowly fading away to the sun rising higher with each passing second. The brighter it gets, the easier it is to tell which train cars are still being checked by the police now that all of the passengers have boarded.

"You need to start running when you see the icebox car," I explain. "Then when the train's caboose comes into view, jump on and pull the brakes. We'll be running for the icebox car and heading inside. Once you pull the brakes, run like bloody hell to catch up to our car and, when you get inside, hide in any open crate you can find. You should have a good amount of time before the men on the train find out what's going on. They'll probably blame some child who felt grabby with the brake cord."

"Got it," Aspen says, trying to stifle a yawn from her hiding place behind low-hanging fir branches.

"Just out of curiosity, Keagan, have you ever jumped a train before?" Thomas asks with curious eyes.

"Actually, I have, but in much easier conditions than this. I'll have to tell you the story when we're safe on the train to London."

To think, we have to do this twice in one day. But we can't take any risks of someone tracking us. Besides our reversible cloaks, we are all wearing normal day clothes, warm coats, and gloves. The ladies are wearing their split skirts due to the amount of running we are about to do today whilst still needing to blend in with crowds. Lori is in charge of carrying Gear Heart and the generator, whilst Thomas and I take care of the heavier baggage.

Thanks to the training we've been putting Thomas through, he's become quite the strong little lad. From the looks of it, the train car the bobbies are checking right now is the icebox car. Third stop, exactly two hours to York. I have to be right about our route. Nurse Hudson and Dr Doyle were helping us memorise the train routes and stops for hours last night. Dear Lord, they were saints themselves for helping us like they did.

It was cold when we left at four in the morning, and we were all trembling as we said our goodbyes to the abbey. These past two weeks have made me and the rest of us feel like we are the dimies we were once hiding back at home.

Constantly being hidden and kept quiet, barely let outside, and tended to regularly with tender regard. *We treated them as kindly as the abbey treated and cared for us, right?* I want to say yes, but something squeezing my heart tells me that we could've done more.

I truly wish there was something anyone could have done for that poor dimie who came into the abbey the day we were hiding. The poor fellow was cut and battered worse than a fish at the market. I remember Nurse Hudson telling me that his wounds were deeper than expected, and that he was bleeding internally to the point that even surgery couldn't save him. I feel like he deserved a better burial as well than what he got. It was just us and the members of the abbey—strangers, no one he knew or loved. It makes me pray for the safe return of the dimies who jumped ship on New Year's Eve. *Please, God, tell me that they made it. At least most of them. They had to have made it.*

Looking back through the binoculars, I see the bobbies searching the train for us. They seem satisfied and move back onto the platform and out of our line of sight before they hop aboard the train next to ours to begin searching again. "Coast is clear," I announce. "We should be safe by the time our train comes to us."

"Perfect. Now, let's move closer to the break in the woods; we need to be closer to the tracks," Aspen orders, and we follow suit with our luggage and Gear Heart packed away in a hatbox. Sadly, it was the only thing from the abbey's lost and found that would work. Still, we were able to add enough padding that the machine should be safe even when running with it.

Aspen should make it to the train no problem since she has nothing to carry. The doctor said the scars should be fine as long as she doesn't rub it or do any serious stretching. And yet I can't help feeling wary about her condition. If she were to get hurt again like she did, I don't know what I'd do. Especially since this time we'll be hiding on a train for hours, unable to reveal ourselves to get a doctor without risking death or imprisonment.

The train's whistle shrieks through the breaking light of dawn just as the sun begins to paint the snowy trees in hues of yellow and orange. Hiding in the deep periwinkle shadows of the brush and trees, I have to squint now as the train slowly heads our way. I can hear the crunch of snow nearby being made from just one person, and know it's Aspen preparing to run after the train. Here it comes—the train quickens in pace, now a safe distance away from the station and still at running speed.

I look back to see Aspen standing behind the tree, looking beyond the snow-covered branch. The expression on her face resembles that of a cat about to pounce. She is so eager to get back into the swing of things that it's hard to contain her. Though after being practically chained to her bed by the orders of Dr Doyle, it's no wonder.

With a quick whisper of godspeed to Aspen, we begin running through the thick frosted woods. Luckily, we still have a good enough line of sight to the tracks between the trees. We can hear it coming, but the burst of sound it gives off as it rolls beside us still shocks us. Cars rush along the tracks next to us, the train's wheels and clicks growing louder each second, speeding up until...the icebox car.

Through a clearing in the trees, I look back along the curved path and see Aspen tearing out from her hiding spot in a gust of fresh powdery snow, running alongside the train as the cars are now gradually passing her. Just a few more cars till the caboose comes.

The three of us make our way in a rush through the coverage of the woods as well, trying to keep up with the train, though running through the snow with the amount of parcels we have to carry is quite exhausting. Running after staying dormant for two weeks is one thing, but in the snow with added weight? That would be a trip for anyone, yet Aspen is still keeping up a good amount of speed with the train just as the caboose comes in from behind. With one quick look over her shoulder, she takes a leap, catching the railing of the train she pulls the brakes. Aspen is off the train by the time we're halfway to the icebox car.

"Perfect timing or what?" Aspen asks as we load up the last of our luggage.

"Couldn't have performed it better myself." I smile whilst expelling heaving puffs of steam from my mouth as I help her aboard. Closing the door as quietly as possible, we pause for a second then split off. Lori and Aspen go to the other set of doors on the right side of the car, and Thomas and I stay behind the one we just closed, listening closely for the sounds of anyone approaching us. After thirty seconds of waiting, the train starts back up again with a slight jolt. Since there are no other doors to this car than the ones directly on the side of the train, we are safe for the time being.

We rest for some time and try to open a few of the crates to snoop around. But as luck would have it, none of them will open. They are nailed tight, no matter how hard the four of us try to open them, which gets us talking about the next train. "We didn't have to hide in the crates this time because they never went searching for us, but what if we're not so lucky next time?" Lori asks, putting a spotlight on the elephant in the room. "What if on the next train they don't just start back up? What if they do come looking for us and we have the same problem with the crates?"

"Got any of those sleeping darts left, Aspen?" Thomas asks, and I am unable to contain my laughter at such a remark. Even with the seriousness of the situation, we all can't help but laugh a little.

"If I may say something," I speak out when the giggles have subsided. "I think that we just have to cross that bridge when we get to it. However, it wouldn't hurt to look around for something that could pry off the lid to one of these stubborn boxes."

"Agreed." Aspen begins looking around with the rest of us in different parts of the car, though we eventually give up and instead examine our luggage until the train slows to a halt. It seems we've made it to our first stop.

After the second stop, we begin to prepare to hop off the train at the next station. The feeling of anxiety is crisp in the air, much like the wind that still whistles through the cracks in the boards of the traincar walls. We still don't know what we will do if workers come to check the cars after the second stop, besides hiding behind crates. We'll be at the third stop soon. *I can't believe we pulled this off once already.*

The second the train's brakes hiss out steam, we crack the doors open slowly and Thomas pops his head out to check down the length of the train. Giving us the thumbs-up as he keeps his head out the doors, we pick up our luggage and shuffle ourselves out of the car. Thomas keeps a lookout and occasionally glances in between the train cars to check things on the other side. *That should be the side where they'll unload all of the luggage, so we should have a good chance to sneak away and onto the next train fairly easily.*

"When's the train to London set to leave again?" Thomas asks, glancing back at us as we unpack the last of the bags.

"Ten o'clock sharp, and right now it's..."

"Two minutes till ten," Aspen calls out hoarsely after checking her wrist-bound pocketwatch.

"Yeah, I think it's the one in front of us.." And sure enough, we hear the ticket man on the platform yell, "York to London! All aboard to London! All aboard!"My heart freezes for a moment before all of us start running towards the sound of the ticketmaster. We dart our way over the rough gravel behind the parked trains, trying to make it to the end of ours in time.

"Where did the time go? We were supposed to arrive at *twenty* minutes till ten, not *two* minutes," I groan.

"It must have been the police checks through the train at Currlion and York that changed the time enough to make us late," Aspen explains in huffs. "Not to mention the other two stops could have been prolonged for the same reason without us knowing." *That does make sense, but I really wish this time that she was wrong.*

"Here!" Thomas calls over to us from ahead, right as we hear the sounds of the wheels beginning to push forwards with a resounding chug. We are already at the end of our old train and, just as we pass the conductor's car, we see that the station is also behind us. But the icebox car is gaining speed and height as the steep hill along our side of the tracks begins to grow. As much as our stiff legs are begging us to stop, we can't slow down for a second. Running far behind the sleeping and dining cars, we are nearing the caboose.

Aspen quickly hands over the hatbox with our most valued item to Lori, dashes at breakneck speed up the ever-growing sloping hill to the tracks, and jumps onto the caboose just as before. As the train begins to stop, we make our way to our "privately reserved" car first as Aspen tries to catch up. Each of us pile inside, and after I'm done lifting Lori and Thomas into the car, Lori pushes me towards the crates, saying, "See if you can find any that can open."

Thomas looks out of the car towards the head of the train. Jumping from one crate to the next, I attempt to get a grip on each lid, but every single one is closed shut until I find a few that are so terribly nailed down that half of their sides are open just enough for me to reach my fingers under. The creaking sound of wood and torn nails never sounded so good. I find three more that open with ease and start to transfer the smaller boxed contents into the other, lesser filled crates. Right as I am pulling our luggage into the now totally empty crate, I hear Aspen's voice from behind me. Turning to make sure everything is okay, she makes it inside.

"Quick, there are men coming this way," Thomas says as he starts pushing the door on his side closed again with a soft roll this time.

"Over here, there are two crates left for us," I call over.

"Will there be enough room?" Lori asks.

"There'll have to be," Aspen says, looking into the crate next to me. "Lori, Thomas, take this one; you two are the smallest, and that one has the smallest amount of room left."

Without another word, they pile in and hug each other tightly to save space inside. Just as Aspen is making sure Lori's lid is closed enough, she and I both turn to the doors where we hear the men right outside saying, "I thought I told you to lock up this door!" In a bolt of fear, I grab hold of Aspen's waist to lift her, but she pushes my hands away and climbs in herself. I feel slightly dejected but carefully step inside myself right above her and close the lid back up as best

I can. I wrap myself around her like I did the night of our first mission, only this time the quickened heartbeat that I hear is not hers, but mine.

The loud rolling of the car doors causes Aspen to inhale sharply. We can hear the men's heavy footsteps along the wood boards. They must be big if they're making that much noise just from walking. Our crates are located on the very back wall, catty-corner from the doors we entered, so perhaps they won't even bother looking around in this area. However, as I hear their stomping footfalls come closer our way, I begin to doubt myself. They walk so close to us that I can hear them breathing heavily.

"Remind me to fire that new carpenter," I hear one of them say. "The nail work on this line right here is atrocious. They're practically half-open already." I hear a hammering thud. I think it's his fist atop the lid of Lori and Thomas' crate. My hand flies up to cover Aspen's head as I squeeze us together even more, making us smaller. The second the giant slam hits our crate, I can make out the slightest squeak. It's hard to tell if it came from Lori or Aspen, but I think it sounded close enough like nails in wood for the men to dismiss it. I can't take in any more air; my lungs have frozen as we huddle together, waiting for what might come next.

The giant's steps fade away until we hear the loud slam of the sliding doors, along with the latch of the lock being put in place from outside the train car. After waiting a few moments more to make sure they've walked some distance away from where we are, Aspen writes a checkmark on my hand with her finger that's still over her head.

"Okay," I whisper as I put my hands on the top of our lid and push hard enough for it to come right off once again. We get out immediately, just as Lori and Thomas are lifting their lid off as well.

"Oh my goodness, that was a tight squeeze, wasn't it?" Lori breathes out.

"I don't know about you, but that was a real thrill. Was that you that squeaked when the man hid our lid?" Aspen asks, walking away.

"Guilty," Lori replies sheepishly.

"Well, I'm just glad it's over for now," I say. "Thank goodness he didn't renail the lids shut himself. Based on how big and strong he sounded, I think we would have had some real trouble getting away," I lift the lid on the box with our belongings hidden in it, handing a bag filled solely with blankets to Thomas before checking to make sure everything else is situated safely. I never had a chance to make sure things were okay for our bags, since we were in such a hurry.

"You know, sissy, Cousin Harry would sure be proud to hear that we hopped not one but two trains in one day just to get to London," Lori says, looking over my shoulder. I see the two sisters have made themselves comfortable, sitting on a blanket and covered by another, as they lay back on the boarded wall. Thomas takes a seat close to them.

"I think you're right on the money," Aspen replies, "and Aunt Mae would turn stone dead. What a lovely sight that would be."

"Cousin Harry?" Thomas asks.

"Oh, he's one of our cousins that taught us acrobatics; he and his sister were in the circus. They were in an act together." Lori lays her head on Aspen's shoulder.

"*Were?* Did they retire?"

"Well, only one of them did. Harry got injured during one of their practices two years back, and he hasn't been able to perform properly as an acrobat since. His sister, Monica, is still with the circus last we've heard, but poor Harry has become somewhat of a gypsy." Aspen avoids my eyes.

"Poor chap," I say. "I hope nothing like the ones in the Jonothan Blu tale?"

"Harry, oh no. Only if he went completely mad," Lori says.

"If the rumours are true about him, then he hops trains as well, just for fun, to see how many he can get on in a day." Aspen laughs.

"Rather funny notion, don't you think?" Lori adds on.

"Indeed. Honestly, it sounds like something we would do if we ever got bored," Thomas chimes in, which puts a smile on our faces.

We've been on the train all day, and now night has fallen. *We've got to be close to London by now.* I look at my pocketwatch, which projects the time at ten after six in the evening. Looking through the crack in the boards, all I see is dark countryside with a city in the distance. *I bet that's London. It shouldn't be long now.* I turn back around to see Aspen and Lori fast asleep, bundled up tightly to each other. *I'll wake them up once I know we're closer.*

"Keagan?" a small voice says, making me turn around to see Thomas awake but still wrapped in his blanket on the floor.

"Hey, Thomas. Can't sleep?" I whisper tenderly as I kneel down to his level.

Nodding his head, he yawns. "I wanted to ask you something without the ladies around. Do you think it's okay now?" He looks at the dozing dames in the corner.

"Those two are fast asleep. You should be fine to ask me anything," I say, getting back up, taking my blanket off of a crate, and wrapping it around myself.

Finding a place away from the girls behind the crates in front of the doors, I motion for him to come my way. Taking a seat, he fidgets with his fingers a bit before posing his question. "What was it like growing up in the manor with all that land and space to explore and have fun?"

That wasn't what I was expecting to be asked. I know the sight of such a home and the size of land my family owns must look like heaven for anyone, child and adult alike. However, aside from the times I would sneak around without getting caught, the thought of my childhood only reminds me of all the fun I couldn't have at home due to Father's strict rules.

"It was outside the walls of my home that I could truly have fun, actually. That's not to say that I didn't have any good memories of life in my home, but it was always elsewhere that life was more enjoyable. I learned that during boarding school and my travels. Sorry if that wasn't what you were hoping to hear."

"That's okay, but I'm guessing what made the trips and being away from home more enjoyable were all the girls you met along the way."

That sentence makes me feel like I've been put under a microscope. "Aha, so that's what you're trying to get at then, huh? Ladies," I say, a bit jolly from the sudden nerves that are getting to me as I dodge his question. Now it's his turn to look rather sheepish, as his eyes immediately avert to the floor. Time ticks away and it appears that I've made him more than a little uncomfortable, judging by his silence. "I do admit to my past of being a bit of a ladies man; however, if we're being honest here," I say, grabbing his attention once more to where his eyes are looking back at mine. "Of all the women I've ever seen, met or courted, none—not a single one—could hold a candle to Aspen. That's the kind of woman you need to find in life for yourself if you ever get so lucky as to find one like her."

He needs to know that I'm not the same man I was when I was travelling the world. And that there is no life worth living if there is no purpose or stability in it, which I did not have. I feel like he needs to know that I'm in it until the end of the line when it comes to Aspen. That way he'll know what the right way of pursuing a woman is. There's no one else to teach him this stuff but me and the ladies now anyway.

"So, tell me why you asked me about the girls I've met? Did you have your eye on a young lady back in Currlion?"

"No! I—"

"Shhh." I hush him before his little outburst wakes the girls.

"I just...does it matter much that you two are a bit different in age?"

"Heh, not really. I actually prefer slightly younger women. They're often more amiable to me. Why? Your girl isn't too young, right?" I ask now, curious and slightly concerned.

"She's a little older, actually, but she doesn't seem to see me the same way I see her."

"Maybe not now, but just wait. It's possible that you'll be old enough and much more strapping in her eyes by the time we get back to Currlion." I nudge him in the arm, which makes him smile at the thought of such a scene.

"That's another thing. How long do you think we'll be gone?"

"Now that's a hard question to answer. Besides, I don't think I'm the person you should be asking. I'm guessing a few months, but who's to say? A week, half a year, two years or more even. If there's anyone you should be asking, it's Aspen." I feel slightly dejected as I watch her sleep so peacefully against her sister.

I promise to try and make things right between us, Aspen. I just hope that you will let me.

UNCLE GEORGE

ASPEN

Luckily, we're able to lift Thomas up through the roof hatch window when we arrive in London, so he can climb out and unlock the doors from the outside for us to make our escape. However, it's just our luck that we arrive in the middle of winter during a cold downpour. The rain is so thick that it's hard to see where the next set of train tracks starts in front of us, or if there's even one at all.

"Okay, first things first, we have to get a carriage," I say. "Keagan, you and Lori go and get one. Thomas and I will follow behind at a safe distance, in case anyone is watching for a group of four like us."

"On it. Lori, shall we?"

We all flip up the hoods of our coats and open our umbrellas with our luggage in hand. We are ready to go. Keagan hops off the train first, lending a hand to Lori once on the ground. When they're gone, I stick my head out from under the umbrella to look around. Nobody is coming out in either direction, and even if they were, they would still have trouble spotting us.

Waiting a moment longer to prepare ourselves, Thomas and I hop out of the train, me first then helping him down with the rest of his parcels before I grab hold of the case with Gear Heart. Keeping it safely tucked under my umbrella close to myself, we head out. Walking in the same direction that Keagan and Lori did to the next platform we finally find through the rain, we see that it's packed with people awaiting their train. Luckily this platform has a sturdy green metal awning to keep the crowd sheltered; however, what Thomas and I are in need of is a walkway to the...*there it is!* Nudging him with my umbrella, I nod upwards in the direction of the covered bridge that goes to the platform to enter into London.

We scurry our way around the coming passengers, not bothering to close our umbrellas. Walking down the slippery steps is an all too unpleasant experience since Thomas and I both slip nearly three times. We manage to catch ourselves on the next step down, though I do land on my knee, which hurts like the devil. Once we finally clear the stairs of despair, we look for the departure gate as we pass by the air train's port. Looks like they are currently out of commission for the night due to the horrid weather. Knowing how terrible the weather tends to be in London, I'm surprised they would invest in the air trains at all.

Stopping at the opening of the gate, we try to spot our party; but because of everyone being under the already crowded cover and the lines of carriages getting picked off one by one, it's clear we need to head to the very front to see if we can find them. As we near the middle of the departure gate area, a familiar voice catches my ear. "Gerald, Lucinda, there you are! Come with me or we shall be late." I turn in time, as does Thomas, to see Lori approaching us with her hair covered in a scarf and Keagan's hat under her umbrella. To be honest, I have to take a second glance to make sure it's my sister when I first see her. But then again, with nightfall and the storm already blocking out most of the streetlights, who can blame me? Following her to a hansom cab with the driver opening the door for us, Lori and I take his helping hand as we step in but keep our heads as low as possible so he can't get a good look at us. After we three step inside with our bags, we take our seats across from Keagan and Thomas.

"Where was it again, sir?" the driver yells over the deafening rain.

"Waterloo, Fifteen B, please," Keagan yells back. When the driver echoes exactly what Keagan said, he gives him the thumbs up. The driver closes the door and promptly begins the trip from his driver's seat in the rain.

"Really, Lori, you had to use my middle name? And *Gerald?*"

"Those were the only ones that I could think of that would get your attention." Well, I have to hand it to her there, it did get my attention. "I feel sorry for the bloke," Keagan says as we shake the rainwater from our clothes and bags. "Whilst we were awaiting you two, he explained that all the cabs were taken for the night. Pity to any man who would have to work in this storm.".

"Pity to us as well for having to travel in it. At least now we'll soon be someplace safe," Lori says, handing back Keagan's navy-blue bowler hat.

"Right...safe," Keagan says, looking out the window with his fist to his mouth.

"Is there something you might have left out of conversation, Keagan, that concerns our safety?" I ask, knowing his mannerisms all too well by now.

"Well, we aren't going directly to Uncle George's house.

Once we arrive at our detour and pay our way, we'll wait for our contact to leave, then walk the rest of the way, which isn't too far."

"That is actually—" I begin.

"Inconvenient?" Lori interjects.

"Smart, I was going to say. What if Damon has men checking every train station for us by now? It's best to throw them off the trail."

"Precisely." Keagan smiles.

"I think we've rubbed off on him quite well. What do you think, sissy?"

"Quite well indeed," Lori says.

Both of us are slightly more cheerful than before, even in our dripping, dishevelled appearance. Luckily for us, we're warmer now and beginning to dry off on our long drive up to our decoy address. "Just how far from the station is Waterloo?" I ask.

"From Hampstead Heath where we started, about another thirty minutes, maybe more due to the rain."

"Judas! We're going to catch our death from being about in this weather," Lori whines.

"A nice warm bath and clean dry clothes, and we'll be right as rain in the morning," Keagan reassures her.

"Please don't say rain," Lori says, glancing out the window, which makes me snicker a bit, along with Thomas. Keagan looks at her from the corner of his eye whilst keeping his head forward at the water-swept window. I can tell that her banter and complaining is getting to him, yet he's trying to stay polite. However, after being pent up in the abbey for two weeks with limited access to even stepping outdoors, it's no wonder he's getting rather peeved. Can't say I feel completely cheerful myself.

Just as Keagan said, the ride takes about thirty minutes. *Thirty five minutes to be exact, but who's counting?* Stopping at 15B Waterloo, the driver gets down and opens the door for us as we are still picking up our luggage. By the time we open our umbrellas, we're even more drenched than before. After Keagan pays the cabby and we start to walk up the white stone steps to the lovely little flat, we hear the trotting of horses as the carriage begins to pull away. Once it disappears, we all turn around and walk two blocks, until Keagan directs us to St Georges Road.

"George Adlene lives on St Georges Road?" I ponder aloud.

"He used to say it was once named Carter's Road till he came along, and then they named it after him. I *think* that was a joke. He's lived in this area longer than anyone, so if anyone could say that was true, it'd be him."

"While this conversation is delightful, please tell me we're getting close," Lori huffs, looking tired, cold and put out, just like the rest of us.

"There," he says curtly, pointing with his umbrella. The building he indicates is quite a sight compared to the lovely flats on the rest of Waterloo Street. Uncle George's house has a patched hole in the broken chimney at the top of a three-story roof. The plaster is chipping so badly on the outside that the brick underneath is showing. And, if I'm not mistaken, I spy a window so terribly shattered that at first glance it appears to be an elaborate spiderweb.

"Now, Uncle George is a very eclectic inventor, and his house will be filled with gadgets and contraptions," Keagan announces. "Not quite like yours, Aspen, so we need to ask about all of them before messing with them. The last time I didn't ask, half of my hair was singed off; I had to shave my whole head to make it even. Also, he has a housekeeper who last I heard is still around." He walks up the first of the dirty stone steps. I'm glad that he's in front of us, so that he can't see Lori and me smile at the thought of Keagan with a smoking half-head of hair. "Her name is Miss Pauline, and the poor lady is always on the verge of an anxiety attack. Her job is to keep the old man from killing himself and destroying the house, other than the normal housekeeper duties, that is. George is also a retired veteran of Her Majesty's weapons and espionage division, but he was forced into retirement due to… well, insanity," he adds, setting down one of his suitcases.

"He's insane?" Lori asks, fear in her voice.

"No. Well, yes. It's hard for me to explain properly, but it's why he's the perfect person for us to stay with. If he were to say anything to anyone, they would take it with a grain of salt. He says delusional things all the time, so why should swash-buckling underground slave napping vigilantes be any less weird than the other stories he's made up in the past?" Keagan laughs.

"Wait, you mean he could be lying about knowing the queen? Did he actually work for her?" Thomas asks, confused.

"Well, that part is true; he was even her top engineer. But he didn't last long, since he was a bit fanatical. Even now, he seems to have a knack for catching things on fire." He gives a big inhale and exhale before knocking twice on the door and, after waiting three seconds, adding a third knock, to which the door swings wide open. But there is no one behind it. Keagan doesn't move an inch; he doesn't even flinch when the door opens abruptly, unlike us. I open my mouth to ask what we're waiting for, but it's answered before I can speak. A series of thuds come from the next room, a drawn curtain in front of its arched doorway. *That sounded like books falling.* What comes next is a man shooting through the curtain and trotting to the open doorway, clearly in his early elderly years. "My, my, what have we here?"he says in a clear jolly voice. "Only special friends of mine know that particular knock to open the door,"

So, this is crazy Mr George Adlene then? Greying, receding hair sticking straight out of the sides of his head like crinkled wires, peppered handlebar moustache, and clad in a grease-stained white undershirt, paired with a green and silver embroidered vest and back pants that reach the centre of his little round belly. But it's the childlike wonder in his cool blue eyes that gives me the strange reassuring feeling that he isn't completely mad. *This man is a good one, even if Keagan deems otherwise. He's probably just a little eccentric. I know something about what that's like.*

"Uncle George, good to see you again," Keagan says with a nervous smile. Few things make Keagan visibly nervous like this. Whatever happened between them must have been something huge compared to what we've put him through. At least he still treats us the same, for the most part, without much fear. Well, he treats Lori and Thomas the same, that is.

"Keagan Myrack!" he bellows with open arms. We quickly rush in with the rest of our belongings into the parlour, bringing a burst of rainwater with us, and swiftly close the front door.

"Uncle George, now is not the best time to be screaming our names in the night to the neighbourhood!" Keagan half-whispers, half-exclaims.

"Well, how about tomorrow morning then?" he asks innocently.

"No. No yelling of our names outside of the house of any kind. Or inside, for that matter, just to be safe. Only whistling, whispering, and normal voices. It's imperative that we don't attract attention."

"Well, where's the fun in that?" Uncle George calls out with a laugh. "And if you were looking for a place to not attract attention, I'm afraid you've chosen the wrong household, my boy." He claps a large hand on Keagan's shoulder. Now I have a sinking feeling that this man will be a barrel of laughs mixed with a nightmare. "So, who are these young people you've smuggled into my abode? Last time you did something like this, you were seventeen—"

"Uncle—" Keagan tries to stop him, but I interject as well. "Oh, really?" I ask with a cocked eyebrow as I give Keagan a sideways glance. Keagan himself grows bright red, with a fearful look in his eyes.

"George, I swear—"

"Tut tut, boy. Don't go threatening me when I haven't even had a chance to set your hair on fire," George playfully scolds whilst wagging a finger in his face with a warm smile. "Now, who might you be, my dears?"

"This is Miss Aspen and Lori Wolfe, and this lad here is Thomas Brimstone." Keagan gestures to each of us, one by one. "I'm currently the acting guardian of the three of them...in a way."

"What luck to be a guardian of such lovely young ladies and lads. Come—you must have tea and meat pies with me!" He jubilously flings open the curtain to the next room. The walls appear to be strung with train tracks, whilst fizzing test tubes threaten to overflow an overcrowded desk by a drawn curtained window.

"It's almost eight o'clock at night," Lori says. "Shouldn't he be having dinner just about now?"

"No, he usually eats dinner at nine or later. Besides, he'll always stop for tea and meat pies," We leave our things in the parlour, happy to be rid of the extra weight. "George, we're quite exhausted. I think perhaps we should just—"

"Nonsense, my boy, I insist!" He waves to us as he pulls a cord three times that's hanging from the pastel-blue-painted ceiling.

"That's what I'm worried about," Keagan mutters to Thomas, making him smile.

Pushing back a crowded bookshelf on wheels, Uncle George reveals a hidden alcove with a small but quaint table, surrounded by shelves filled with inventions of various kinds, books, and knickknacks. As Uncle George clears off a space for us, I stroll by the crowded desk and notice that the papers covering it are plans for what appears to be a dirigible of some kind. However, my attention is quickly stopped short by the whistling of a locomotive, then the sight of a tiny locomotive barreling down tracks over our heads.

A white china teapot, teacups of multiple styles and sizes, cream, sugar, biscuits, and steaming meat pies are being carried in on its little cars, precisely stopping right where Uncle George is sitting. *What a curious display and ingenious idea.* I can already hear the teasing that will be waiting for me later from Lori. *Aspen's found a new tinkering buddy.*

"The Darjeeling Express, right on time," George says proudly, flicking open his pocketwatch.

He holds it very far from his face and just stares at it as we all stare at him, confused in our seats. Suddenly, a little cuckoo bird on a spring comes shooting out of his watch, extending until just a few centimetres away from his face and even chirping each time. Each time it nears his nose, he looks at it in a comically cross-eyed way.

"What was that?" Thomas asks.

"My little friend the cuckoo bird," he says cheerfully. "One of my many inventions, or as my housekeeper calls them, 'mad contraptions.'"

"So, you do have a housekeeper," I say, trying to sound innocent.

"Yes, she's the one who made this spread before you, of course. I'm sure she's heard all of ye coming in by now, so she should be out any sec—"

"George!" comes a woman's low yell from across the house. "Meat pies and Darjeeling tea right before your dinner? Isn't it enough that I'm constantly putting out your fires..." A stout little woman in her early fifties suddenly emerges, brandishing a dirty wooden spoon and berating George all the way down the hall till she catches sight of us. "Oh, guests? You didn't tell me we had guests."

I have to cover my mouth from laughing at such a display, and I see I'm not the only one. For such a short woman, she certainly exudes a lot of confidence.

"Let me please introduce to you my charming and industrious housekeeper, Miss Pauline. Pauline, these are our guests for as long as they need to stay. You remember Keagan Myrack." He gestures to Keagan who is still grinning, as he stands and gives a short bow.

"Keagan, is that really you?" she replies with astonishment. "Why, just look at you! You've grown into a fine young man. I hope you act like one as well. What say you, ah—" Pauline says, looking at the rest of us and then Uncle George expectantly.

"Ah, forgive me. This is Miss Aspen and her sister, Miss Lori Wolfe. And this is Mr Thomas Brimstone."

"What lovely names. It's a pleasure to make your acquaintance. Please forgive me for my little outburst. I am nonplussed at the moment from the thought of all the food in need of cooking. I was wondering why you wanted such a large amount tonight."

"Quite all right, Miss Pauline," I respond. "And to answer your question, yes, Keagan can be quite a gentleman." Keagan beams with pride as he takes a sip of tea and I add, "He's always giving the ladies the most *considerate* attention," causing Keagan to cough up his drink.

Miss Pauline and Uncle George begin to laugh uproariously.

Keagan isn't having the best night, or few weeks for that matter, I think as my mind goes through the events that have led up to us getting here safely. From saying goodbye to his few true friends, to losing everything he owned in less than twenty-four hours—his home, his good name, Winona, his freedom in polite society. And Lori and I were the cause of that. *How will we ever repay a debt like this to him?* I suddenly feel an aching regret in my stomach for my easy joke at his expense. After all, he's been nothing but loyal to us and our mission ever since he pledged his allegiance. Though he could work on what he chooses to keep secret from us.

After tea, we move directly to the dining room, which has a glorious chandelier that moves slowly up and down its cord, the arms on the lights spinning gradually like a top as the stagnant teardrop crystals dangle from the bottom of the kinetic fixture. I've never seen anything quite like it—it's almost hypnotic to watch. Unlike the tea party we just had, the food is carted in by Pauline. "She refuses to allow a train to bring dinner to the table," Uncle George explains in a mocking tone. "She can only allow *so much ridiculousness.*"

Once Pauline has laid the dishes of tantalising food down, she excuses herself to prepare the guest rooms as we eat. "Pauline loves to remind me that the reason we live on St George's Road is because we are so conveniently close to the asylum across the way." Uncle George laughs as he takes another bite of the herbed chicken. "She says that they are just waiting for the day that I slip completely into madness. Though I must remind her we are here because it's been named after myself, of course."

"Mr Adlene?" I start.

"Uncle George, if you please, no need for formalities when you're my guests."

"Yes, uh, Uncle George, are you indeed partially insane as you joke about?" I ask boldly, to which Keagan gets a look on his face as if he just bit his tongue.

Uncle George takes a quick sip of tea before responding. "But of course, my dear. The most brilliant of us inventors usually are in some capacity," he says proudly, which earns a gentle smile from me.

I raise my purple-flowered glass. "Well, I can't argue with that now, can I, since I'm one myself." Raising his glass up with mine from across the red-stained wood table, I can tell how happy he is to have us here. We're probably the first visitors he's had lately who aren't openly afraid or confused by him.

Uncle George asks us all about how we got to London and what brought us here. We let Keagan lead the conversation, since he knows George the best. But instead of lying about hopping a train, he explained everything in detail, even the scary parts about us hiding in the crates from the men. The thought of being pressed up to Keagan once again enters my mind, and bittersweet memories of the first time he did that in the old warehouse resurge, bringing back those old butterfly feelings that I thought were lost. *Try not to think about that right now.*

Uncle George asks the rest of us about our stories, so we explain everything that happened in Currlion, from our arrival to hiding the dimies, even the fighting on the ship. Thomas speaks about how we saved him from the men burning his family's store; he even mentions poor Gerald, much to our surprise. We do, however, leave out the more painful detail of losing Winona from our tale. It's almost like her name is forbidden to say now since we've begun to mourn for her. I don't want that, though, as painful as it is. I still want to remember her and keep her name alive. However, I can't bring myself to speak of her. I wonder if the others feel the same way.

SETTLE DOWN

KEAGAN

Full from the mouth-watering dinner, we finally trudge our way up the stairs to the third floor where the guest rooms are kept. Both Pauline and Uncle George aid us in bringing the luggage that we aren't already carrying. "My word, it feels like you are packed to stay forever; not that I wouldn't mind it, actually," Uncle George says flatly.

When we finally make it up to the third floor of the house, we split off. The girls are down the hall from us and are ushered to their new room by Pauline. Uncle George shows us to ours, now dragging my suitcase there along the white wooden floorboards. I'm too tired at this point to be angry about something like that. As he and Thomas enter first, I look over my shoulder and see Pauline leading the ladies into their quarters. I've known Pauline for as long as I've known Uncle George, but I definitely don't know her as well as I do him. "Can we trust Miss Pauline, Uncle George?" I ask. "We understand that maids and housekeepers love to gab, and it seems they can practically hear through the walls."

"Miss Pauline? Ha, you need not worry about her. When

an inventor and worker of the queen's Espionage Division earns enough for a housekeeper, the queen herself employs them and makes sure that they're in the strictest confidence, just as the inventors are about the business conducted in and outside Her Majesty's walls. Once I went into retirement, the queen unemployed her to me, but I hired her back on when she refused to work for anyone else. Said it right to Queen Victoria herself. So, to answer your question, yes, you can trust Pauline with your very lives and all your secrets."

We set our bags down and look about the long room. There are two beds on opposite walls right next to the door when we walk in. The two windows for the room rest on the left side wall, one right above one bed and the other next to the only large dresser in the room. There is a small writing desk against the back wall in between the white marble vanity and a simple white bureau that towers in the right corner of the room.

"Well, that's a relief," I respond to Uncle George's previous statement. "You now know that we've had a troublesome history with moles within our operation. They nearly ruined everything for us. Miss Pauline must care a great deal for your well-being if she chooses to stay even after everything she's been through."

"What do you mean, boy?" he asks, straightening up his back after setting down my bag.

"This may come as a shock to you, but not every household has toy trains that bring them their tea and meat pies. Or their own laboratory with dyes and explosives that *the help* are specially trained to handle. I've also seen Pauline handle a semi- automatic Edison bolt rifle; an extremely low number of people in general know how to handle such a weapon, let alone housekeepers."

"Well, in my opinion, every household deserves a tea train, Keagan, whilst the idea that she worries about my well-being is probably true. Did you ever think that perhaps living in any other household might be dull compared to one such as this?" Uncle George gives me a thoughtful look before stepping out of the room. Thomas and I share a look of surprised agreement. *I must admit, he's got a point.*

Getting back on my feet, I peek my head into the hallway and see he's making his way to the ladies' room just as Pauline leaves. Motioning for Thomas to follow, we head our way to Aspen and Lori's room ourselves. When we get there, we see that Lori has made herself comfortable on the bed, sitting back against its plush white embroidered pillows. Aspen, however, is stretching her arms out as she takes in the room around her, just before closing both sets of curtains on their set of windows. Their room is a mirrored set-up of ours, except the mouldings on the walls are much more ornate, and the bedding appears to be more feminine in style by its lace and embroidery, compared to our darker coloured sheets and pillows. Pauline definitely prepared our rooms specially for our two pairings.

I remember these rooms from those holidays during boarding school with James. We often decided to stay in one room, though, so each night could be a sleepover, unlike at school where it was always one person to a room. Gosh, did we put Uncle George and Pauline through hell back then. But then again, they easily got us back for our shenanigans.

I fidget with the cuff of my sleeve and imagine it to be the brightest shade of green ever seen before laughing bitterly at the memory. Uncle George is going on about the living situation and apologising that the dumbwaiter is broken, so Pauline will be unable to send up morning and midnight tea to their room until it's fixed. Something tells me it's not broken and that Pauline was just tired of performing such a silly task for other guests. "Miss Aspen, have you ever fired a semi-automatic Edison bolt rifle before?" he asks just as we enter the room.

"Can't say I have, sir. I once had the chance to fire a Tesla pistol," she answers rather bluntly with a tired grin on her face. "Pistols are more my style anyway. So much easier to be hidden and surprise someone with than a rifle."

Uncle George's belly bounces from laughing before taking a seat at their table in the centre of the long room. I walk forward towards Lori, who is trying to pull the largest and heaviest of our luggage towards the dresser, and say while helping her, "Uncle George wishes to disprove my earlier comment about this house not being normal, including Miss Pauline and her odd housekeeping tasks."

"I'm afraid you're losing the battle on that one, Uncle George."

"Well, I don't know. The way you detailed your latest living arrangement with Keagan here doesn't exactly sound normal to me. Who's to say that all households aren't as odd as either of ours?"

"The majority of England does, George." I leave Lori with Thomas to help her unpack as I plan on how to bring up a rather sensitive topic.

"So the normal plan, then?" Lori asks as she helps Thomas take out the inventions and inspect them for any damage. "Find and free dimies and bring them home with us?" *Well, she's just pulling out all the stops tonight, now isn't she?*

"Right. Uncle George, there's something we should probably ask you right away. Would it be okay with you if we were to bring dimies here—"

"No, we can't do that this time." Aspen interrupts me, much to my surprise. "The governor knows our history with that, and he and his men will be on the alert for any signs of activity from us. We can't make the same mistakes we made last time."

"Well, then where can we take them?" Thomas calls out as he wipes off a few of the grenades. "Uncle George, you wouldn't possibly own an empty building or house we could use, would you?"

"We need to take them somewhere where they won't be heard or found, but can survive comfortably," I elaborate, more to hear myself think. "They aren't objects; they need to move, eat and communicate just like humans, so how are we going to make this possible?".

"May I suggest finding or making a new lens for Gear Heart first, before you go galavanting over London at night to liberate dimies? You did say it was an important piece you needed to find. If you start spiriting away dimies without one, they'll start piling up with nowhere to go. Although, people might think Jack the Riveter has found a new taste in victims. So we could spread that around as a rumour to help your case."

"Jack the Riveter...who's that?" Thomas asks.

I've heard enough rumours over the past year to know how gruesome of a thing Jack is. How do we explain him to Thomas? Uncle George looks at me for approval across the table, since even he knows it's not exactly a pleasant topic for children to hear about. I mouth to him, *Don't scare him*. He nods his head once before addressing the question. He better have some level of tact in his mouth. "Jack the Riveter is a failed invention for Queen Victoria's militia. As they were building him and testing him out, something went wrong and they weren't able to stabilise him. Now he roams London and is very volatile, so if you see a metal man with red glowing eyes, run to a more public area and hide as best you can. He's able to identify and pick out people when they're alone in quiet places, like alleys and sometimes dark bedrooms with open windows. He's attacked mainly street women at night, since they're often alone. You shouldn't need to worry, though, Thomas; there has never been a case of a child being hurt by him. My thinking is that they programmed him to attack beings of a certain size relative to an average adult's height."

"Then I guess little people are in the clear as well, despite being adults or not."

"Let's hope so, for their sake. As for the placement of the dimies, no, I do not own an open house or building for which to house them, aside from my own. However, I wish I did. What fun we could have with all that extra space."

"Maybe we should just sleep on it for now and get used to the layout of the town first," Lori suggests as she puts a gauntlet along with a pile of nets and cubes in one of the drawers.

"I second that. I'm exhausted," Aspen says, looking along the wall for something. My guess is the light switch, except there isn't one. Both her eyes and mine land on the bright lantern that hangs on a hook above the night table. *How dazed are we to not even notice where the light in the room is coming from? That scares me a bit, actually.*

"Uncle George, wasn't the first and second storeys powered by electricity?" I ask, now trying to remember if this floor was powered as well when I stayed here during school.

"Actually, we were only able to afford the two levels downstairs, but each room is well illuminated by both the sun and moon. Not to mention, we store a good amount of matches, candles and lantern oil in the nightstands up here. There are also the sconces on the walls if you truly need more light at night up here."

Well, perhaps it's for the best, since it'll make it harder for Aspen to use this room to work on inventions at night. And if her sister realises that she hasn't gone to bed at a certain hour, she'll know she's most likely in the laboratory. "All right, then, we can handle that," I say for the lot of us, as I look over to see Thomas closing the trunk and Lori putting away the last of our limited armoury. "Thomas, we better turn in. We'll see you ladies in the morning."

"I'm off too," Uncle George says, looking from Aspen to Lori as he stands up from his seat. "There's something I want to look into before I go to bed that might interest you all tomorrow. Here's to a new day." Uncle George earns a smile from each of them, but Aspen doesn't lay an eye on me when I try to give her a smile as well. Even as we were saying goodnight, neither of the girls would look our way. Perhaps we're all more tired than expected.

TAKING FLIGHT

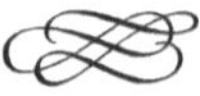

ASPEN

I usually never sleep well the first night in a new place. Even when Lori and I would stay with our extended family, the first night was always the hardest. But last night made me feel so refreshed that I wake right up naturally, feeling warm and cosy in my thick sheets. The cool blue light grows brighter from the windows before dawn floods into the room. I realise there is a smile on my face as my mind begins to clear. Last night, I had a lot of anxiety about what staying here could mean for us. I think back to the little discussion Lori and I had before we turned in.

"What are we doing here? He's loony."

"I know. But that's what makes our position perfect. As long as we stay here, we'll be safe from people finding our location."

"How are you so sure?"

"Lori, the man believes the street he lives on is named after him. He obviously has eccentric tendencies, just by his actions alone. So if he does tell anyone about us, it'll be discredited, because no one will be able to take him seriously."

"You really think we're going to be okay here, though? I'm more worried that if he were to have a violent spell, he could seriously harm one or more of us."

"Miss Pauline has lived and served him for how many years? If there was anything like that going on, they would've chucked him into an asylum and thrown away the key. If it makes you feel better, we can lock the door to our room at night, and the windows as well. We don't want Jack the Riveter coming in."

"Please don't even mention him. Just the rumours of how he kills his victims is gruesome enough. I'd rather not think that we have a possible killer inside *or* outside this house." I gave her a tender side hug to try and help ease her nerves.

Now, looking up at the sunlight that paints the ceiling in light yellow and rich orange, I think back to all the talk we've overheard from mainly men conversing about this notorious killer. Lurking in the dark with red glowing eyes, faster than any human. Rumours say he can even beat a train's speed if he wished. Taking his screaming victims to a piece of metal and riveting it through their skin, pinning them as they bleed to death. *What kind of war is the queen expecting if she had her inventors create such a horrendous machine? A horrendous monster is more like it.*

Lori lays fast asleep in her bed, so I have to tip-toe my way around the room as I get ready for the day. After donning my dark green skirt and cream day shirt, I manage to pin my hair half-up and half-down without much fuss or noise. By the time I'm making my way down the stairs, I can hear Thomas' voice coming from an open room on the second floor. Curious, I walk over to see that inside is a large plain brick room, inexpertly covered in chipped white plaster, filled with tables overflowing with open books, and with a pile of sketches near the window.

Test tubes and chemicals continue to bubble and crackle as they make their way up and down curled glass pipes, or simmer over burners that rest in the very back of the room. The amount of light shining in that area makes their jewel-toned colours pop even more. In the front of the room closer to me is a sitting area with beat-up and slightly singed red and blue reading chairs, in front of a currently dead simple brick fireplace. But where I spot Thomas is in the centre of the room, where Uncle George is sketching out something on a large chalkboard. The table in the middle of the room blocking part of my view of the board is filled with little flying machines of different shapes and styles.

"What a curious place this is," I say, announcing my presence.

"Morning, Aspen," Thomas says cheerfully, the smile on his face telling me that Uncle George has been quite entertaining, especially when I can see what they've been talking about.

"Miss Aspen, I was hoping you would wake up soon. I was just about to send Thomas to get you. I mentioned last night that I wanted to show you something." Uncle George spins around to me with glee.

"Well, I'm glad you hadn't, or you would've woken up Lori. She was sleeping so peacefully, I'd rather her wake up naturally today."

"Very well. You're the ones I truly wanted to talk to, anyway, since from what you told me last night, I gathered that Keagan and your sister are not the inventive type."

"You would be right in that sense. They're better at being

suppliers and intel gatherers. Thomas and I are the brains, but Keagan and Lori are the faces of the operation."

"You would do well working in Victoria's espionage or engineering divisions."

"Victoria?" Thomas echoes.

"Her Majesty, the Queen."

"You just seem to refer to Her Majesty by her Christian name quite often whenever she comes up. Did you know her at all?" I ask, now curious about this old man's history.

"Ah, let's leave that for a later conversation. I'd like to see how much experience you have in your trade as inventors and craftsmen. I want to hear about what your teachers were like and what they specialised in themselves."

"Well, my grandfather was a gearmaster back in Currlion," Thomas says, fidgeting with the cap in his hands as he sits politely on a burn-marked wooden stool. "He made all types of pyrotechnic mechanisms, though most were toys."

"Very nice. You were lucky to have a family member like your grandfather to learn from. What about you, Aspen?"

"I'm usually making weapons and gadgets for our missions, or for defensive purposes—besides the multidimensional transporter Thomas and I finished together."

"Oh, yes, that was mentioned the other day. You had a name for it, did you not?" Uncle George ponders with curiosity in his eyes.

"Yes, it's Gear Heart. My...father had named it when we first built it together. He's the one who taught me engineering," I explain, slightly choking on my words. I need not let my feelings get in the way during a simple conversation.

"That's very exceptional of your father, allowing his daughter to help him and learn to become an inventor instead of just a tinkerer," Uncle George says exuberantly.

"You would deem me an inventor?" I ask earnestly.

"Well, of course. Someone with your amount of ability would easily be considered an engineer-level inventor among the Royal Society crowd. Didn't your father think so?"

"Uh, yes, indeed." That was all I could say on the matter. One day, I hope to understand how Papa could do what he did to Lori and me—and maybe one day I can forgive him. Just not today.

"Now, I bet these creations of yours are marvellous in their own ways, and I would very much like to see Gear Heart one day if you would let me. That said, my dear, have you thought of experimenting in a different direction? Have you ever considered air travel?" Uncle George becomes more excited the more he speaks.

"You mean like the air trains?" Thomas asks.

"Precisely, except no man has been able to correctly invent a vessel large enough to fly farther than ten kilometres or transport over twenty people. The air trains are the largest aircraft we have; and what's worse, they don't get good mileage. They last for forty-five minutes in the air at most. That's enough to transport people to two towns away at most, if they're lucky. And they cannot be refuelled in the air mid-flight, unlike the land trains that are fueled with coal as they run," Uncle George scribbles down explanatory notes and numbers on the dusty chalkboard as he talks. "With our combined efforts, we may be able to create a flying machine you could sell to the Crown as a war and transportation aircraft. It would be quite hard for Victoria to pass up such a treasured need."

The cobwebs of my tired brain are swept away by his words, and my fingertips tingle with golden opportunity. But is such a creation possible? And how would we keep something as on grand a scale as this a secret? As if reading my mind, Thomas asks, "Where would we hide a machine that large in such an elaborate and dangerous city as London?"

"I hate to say it, but he's right," I add. "Besides, I've heard a few rumours about the gangs in the city's underground, not to mention Her Majesty's secret police."

"No, that's not right. There aren't any secret police." George wags a piece of chalk at me.

"No?"

"Her Majesty has a group of spies, but they're hidden in broad daylight throughout the city. The rumours surrounding them, though few, are mostly true. They're said to be the shadows of the entire city and report regularly to Victoria about what goes on with the people—mainly about the levels of crime and if there is any talk of rebellion." George relays this all with a surprisingly grim expression, like he's reliving a dark memory.

"You sound like you're familiar with them. You used to work for the Crown. Did you know some of her secret service-men?" I ask hesitantly.

"I did...because before I was discharged from Queen Victoria's service, I was one of them."

"You were one of Her Majesty's secret spies?" Thomas asks with wide eyes and an open mouth.

"Aye, but I hated the work I had to do. I felt like the biggest snitch. I much preferred my work in Victoria's armoury division, where I could create gadgets all day. I was ordered to be a spy when talk of war and rebels in the city began. The queen needed extra eyes and ears, what with all the new immigrants and growing population of poor once the slave trade had ended. One of my mates was wrongfully accused of treason and was to be hunted down for his trial and execution. I knew he had been framed, but there would be no way to convince the Crown and Parliament it wasn't him."

"What happened to him?" I urge him on.

"I still had contact with him as he was being hunted. I, along with twelve other agents, were assigned to bring him in. However, when I found him, I tried to get him out of the country so he would be safe from the Crown. But the night we planned to have him disappear, something went wrong. I was certain he was safe. He was five feet from the loading dock, five feet from the ship to Spain and to his rightful freedom." George takes a big exhale before continuing. "They shot him one metre and a half away, and I could do nothing for him. If I had run out to save his body or just to weep by his side, I'd have been shot too, for conspiring with the enemy."

"And that's what made you go mad then? That's what caused you to be discharged from the queen's service?" I say, feeling terrible for Uncle George. I feel we have much more in common than expected.

"That's only half-true. I was caught that night, charged with seeing him before he left, and with watching from afar without attempting to stop him from leaving England. I was arrested and tried before the queen but found not guilty. Take my word, children. Do not cross those men and women if you meet them or if they find you. Don't take anything they offer you. They'll only twist it against you." George has a terrified look in his eyes, his hands shaking before him.

"So, wait, how were you found not guilty?" Thomas asks with an expression that's exploding with questions and *what if's*. Lori says I have that expression at least once a day.

"I was charged with aiding a guilty party that had radical intentions and had committed malicious crimes against the Crown. My mates and students on the inside served as witnesses, and all backed me up with a solid alibi. I was deemed not guilty, but a day later I was given an honourable discharge from Her Majesty's services and was deemed functionally insane. Anyone accused of insanity of any kind is deemed incompetent and uneligible for service to the Crown, even though she's practically mad herself now."

"So, were you trying to create an airship for Her Majesty, then? Is that why you want to create one for her, to have a clean slate with her again?" I ask thoughtfully, walking over to the chalkboard.

Uncle George clears his throat before speaking again. "No, I wasn't working on an airship, but my sources tell me that the queen desperately wants one."

"I see," I reply. *He truly respects the queen; he sure wants to be back on her good side.* If I didn't know better, I'd say they were once good friends. It must have been terrible to have to be judged in court by someone you considered your friend. Then again, looking at it from the queen's point of view, it must be terrible to have to judge someone you trusted, when there are so few you can truly trust.

"The idea of making the aircraft is one thing, but the real problem is keeping it hidden and getting it to the queen herself, instead of her advisors," George explains. "You have to get clearance through them or the captain of the armoury, who can be very hard to persuade as of late."

"You said you had sources. Do you still keep in contact with your old co-workers?" I ask as I look over his sketches of different airships sketched in white chalk on the blackboard.

"Actually, yes, especially a young man named Timothy Pembroke. I trained him when he was an apprentice. He's very loyal and keeps me up to date with the goings on in the weapons division."

Why does that name sound so familiar to me? I know I've met a Pembroke in Currlion who mentioned something like this, I think as Thomas hops off his bench and starts looking inside a few boxes in the corner near the table covered in books.

"You said no one has ever created a large-enough flying machine that works properly, right?" Thomas points out.

"Yes, but—"

"Then why do you have a stack of papers here that talk about all the different inventors bringing their ships or designs to the queen? It seems from what these newspapers say that there have already been at least ten people with their finished machines in front of the queen and her advisors. What chance do we have if they're stocked with this many designs?"

"Yet again, the newspaper is telling only part of the story," George says, puffing out a ring of smoke from his pipe.

"How so?" I ask after taking one of the papers from Thomas's stack, dated October 17th, 1886, not even three months ago. I begin reading out loud. "Brilliant new inventor claims he has done the impossible and created the impenetrable war aircraft for the queen's militia. Sir Humphrey Ravenport is to be transported by the queen's personal guards, along with his valuable new creation, to the queen's military training base." I pause to give Uncle George a questioning look.

"Yes, but what the papers aren't allowed to disclose is that each of those machines, if deemed stable, are tampered with and made unstable before demonstration," George says. "The queen is left out of the knowledge that the machines are sabotaged."

"How are you certain of this? Why would they even do that?" Thomas asks.

"I've been told it's due to the pride of the captains in the engineering and military divisions. They want someone already in service to the queen to create the machine instead of an outsider. And I know all of this because Timothy was assigned to aid in the tampering of the last aircraft before it was introduced to the queen. He told me in the strictest confidence. If word gets out, it will be his life and mine, possibly even yours…" George pauses, letting out a long stream of smoke before adding in a foreboding tone, "Do you understand?"

"Yes sir," Thomas and I say, keeping eye contact. Then I finally make the connection of who I've met that has the bond to Timothy. "This Timothy Pembroke. I believe I've had the pleasure of meeting an extended family member at a dinner in Currlion. Keagan is better acquainted than I with the family, but what else can you tell us right now about this man? Could he possibly help with our cause? Or even be willing?"

"Well—" George begins, but he's interrupted by Lori and Keagan bursting through the lab door, bickering back and forth. Lori wears a policeman's hat on her head, and they each carry in a pile of clothes of the same navy-blue colour. "Well, you could have at least told me you saw the bobbie," Lori spits out.

"How could I? I didn't see him until you did," Keagan counters.

"That's exactly what I mean. Where did all that training go, huh? Have you learned nothing from the past few months?"

"Hey!"

"What did you two do?" Uncle George and I ask in unison, though his voice sounds much more jovial than mine.

"Would you believe that we ransacked a local theatre for these costumes?" Lori asks, bright amber eyes beaming.

"No," I say flatly.

"Told you she'd know," she mutters to Keagan, though he says nothing. Both of them lay the clothes in a pile on one of the bare chairs in front of the fireplace.

"We got them from the Scotland Yard tailor," Lori explains. "He's the only tailor in London that works on both Scotland Yard's men and the queen's guard uniforms. Tomorrow there will be a few less uniforms for the tailor to mend."

"You robbed a tailor?" I walk over to inspect the uniforms, partially worried yet still impressed.

"I know the owner and his son; they owe me a huge favour," Keagan assures me.

"Keagan," I press on, putting my hands on my hips, but I can't stop the new smile that spreads across my face. Uncle George begins to laugh heartily, and my entire wall of disapproval comes crumbling down, though it wasn't that sturdy to begin with.

"When did you two go to get these?" Thomas asks with a furrowed brow.

"Just now. Keagan knew where they hid their extra key and everything. It was such a clever location. There was a hollow brick in the wall with a set of keys in it. You'd never know the difference between it and the other bricks."

"Yes, but it's a good thing that we needed only three uniforms, since we had to run off pretty quickly as well. The guards were right in the middle of patrolling the area when we were leaving."

"Three. Wait, do I not get a uniform?" Thomas asks.

"I'm sorry, love, but you're not tall enough to appear as an adult policeman. Very few adults are in the metre-and-a-half range."

"When I reach a hundred and fifty centimetres, then can I

go on more night runs? And wear costumes like these too? I'm tired of not getting to be a part of the excitement."

"That's for your own good, Thomas," Keagan starts. "We see things we don't want you to see yet on our night patrols. And with London being so much grander than Currlion, there are a whole lot more problems. Thieves, drinking…"

"Prostitutes and brothels…" Lori adds.

"Gambling dens that make stolen dimies fight one another. It's quite a city, isn't it?" I smile sarcastically.

"Not to mention we wouldn't want you to possibly come across Jack."

"Let's hope none of us do," Keagan says.

"Oh what, you think you can't take him? Don't worry, Keagan, you have us to protect you," I tease with a glaring smile as I fall into the remaining empty chair with my legs hanging over the arm. Keagan gives me a thin-lipped grin, like he wants to bite back with a remark but is holding it in. "You both came in at a good time actually," I say, getting back on topic. "Uncle George was just telling us about a certain inventor, a mister Timothy Pembrook. Do you know about him, Keagan?"

"Yes, he's the nephew of Mrs Pembrook back in Currlion. We were schoolmates for a time before he decided to become an apprentice. Timid personality but generally good-natured. Most of the time he seems a bit egotistical, however."

"You forgot inattentive and anxious," George chuckles as he puffs out more smoke. "That boy was a hopeless case when I first took him on; it took him six months to finally put something together correctly. Now he's in charge of repairs and electric weaponry. Hope he doesn't blow up one of the queen's naval ships."

"Didn't you do that to one of her ships?" Keagan points out in a smug voice as he side-eyes Uncle George.

"That explosion was never proven!" he snaps back, pointing a finger at Keagan. Keagan, however, can't help but smirk.

Thomas starts to ask more about what happened, and I can't help but smile at how close George really is like a crazy uncle to Keagan. What a strange relationship they have. Though the more I hear about his past, the more certain I am that he is quite mad. *Aren't we in for an interesting ride...*

THE NOTE

LORI

First things first. We need disguises. Aspen makes sure we won't use the police uniforms as we scour the city today, making the good point that we wouldn't blend into a crowd if we were to wear them, as constables were always standing out on the streets. Besides, what if other policemen come up to talk to us? If any of them recognise us from our wanted pictures, we'll be dead for sure. But we finally come to an agreement that we'll wear the uniforms tonight instead. I can just imagine the talk if we get spotted running the rooftops in those clothes. People will think the bobbies are trying to catch rooftop thieves now.

However, without the uniforms, we have to go about other means to create our disguises. Luckily, Uncle George has supplied us with an ample amount of things to use. I wrap my hair with a scarf as if I am about to go for a drive in a stage-coach. Aspen wears a conglomeration of old skirts that she ruins with grease and a few tears here and there. After teasing her hair and using a dark green shirt and moth-eaten purple shawl that Pauline was about to throw out, her outfit is complete.

I, on the other hand, don a light green-feathered cap along with ruffled mint skirts and my grey coat, looking like a common middle-to upper-class woman. The main difference with us now is our noses and eyebrows. We manage to use our powder to make Keagan's eyebrows nearly invisible, which was quite tedious since they were so dark to begin with. Thinning out mine is a much easier task, as is situating a crooked nose on me. Keagan and I rather enjoy giving Thomas bushier eyebrows and a pointier nose through adhesives, whilst we gave Aspen a thin unibrow, a large bulky nose, and freckles.

Aspen, by the end, has the appearance of a gypsy who has seen better days. It's very difficult for the lot of us to keep a straight face when looking at her. Aspen keeps trying to convince herself out loud that it's for the best to blend in with the crowds, but we can easily see the humorous grin on her face when she looks in the mirror.

Thomas is almost unrecognisable by his face alone, so is the perfect disguise. Keagan has a bit more trouble since there are no other clothing options left unless he were the one to wear the dress and I donned the suit. However, Uncle George manages to find a false moustache for Keagan to wear that almost covers his chin by how bushy it is.

All of us wearing disguises reminds me of when Aspen and I were children. I recall the few times we were able to have Father dress up as the queen and Mum was captain of the guards. Father would always make us laugh with the high-pitched voice he would use to imitate the queen. Mum loved to chase us around and tickle us when we would *storm the castle to kidnap Her Majesty*. Funny how we're in a similar situation now, but it's no game this time.

Before we leave, we sit down with Uncle George and a map of London with areas marked in red, black and gold. The black areas are dangerous places of impoverishment to stay away from as best we can. He even warns us of where the police stations are, so if we plan to check out those areas it may be better to observe them from the rooftops if at all.

Keagan is paired with me once we meet up at the roundabout of St George's Circus, to act as my *escort*. In Aspen's case, we're all satisfied in knowing that no man will want anything to do with her in her current guise. However, Keagan still gives her his cane with the hidden sword to aid in making her look older, and for protection. Each of us begins our journey of charting the city by exiting Uncle George's home at a different time and a different way. Thomas uses the back door whilst Keagan uses the front. Aspen climbs through our window to the rooftop, and I take the front door but go in the opposite direction than Keagan, to make my way to St George's Circus. Everyone's departure is divided into time intervals. Miss Pauline even peeks out the window to make sure no one is standing around or watching the house when each of us leave.

Each of us takes an intersection at St George's Circus, a roundabout where all the buildings converge to a circular plaza. We each take a moment to look down two streets that lead to the dangerous poor districts so we can remember what they look like. It's a good thing we're planning on swinging through the city a bit tonight as well. I remain where I am until Keagan comes to link arms with me, so we can begin our walk of the city. Looking across the crowded plaza of steam-powered cars, horse carriages and bustling passersby, we see Aspen and Thomas heading down Black Friars Road. At each intersection, we pause and examine it to remember the street names and the look of the brick or pastel buildings.

When we reach the bridge, we notice an increase in the number of children playing outside. Thomas even helps fetch the ball in a game, declining to join in since he has to keep up with us. I see him look back at them and a pain starts up in my stomach. It was there that I was slapped with the reality that he's still so young, and that staying with us takes away from him getting to be a kid or make friends his age anymore. *There has to be something we can do about that.*

After two hours of walking through the lower side of London with a glimpse every time, we near a bridge to see what lies on the other side, and Keagan and I realise it isn't just these two areas that are impoverished. Practically this entire side of London Bridge is a poor sector—I don't think Uncle George realises that.

"Do you remember many districts like these in the central part of London?" I ask Keagan.

"Only a few, and sometimes only a couple strips of buildings. This is definitely the more concentrated area of lower-class neighbourhoods."

"And this is where we plan on doing our jobs—brilliant," I grumble. "Nothing like desperate people catching us one night for a hefty sum."

"Well, at least we won't have to worry about anyone breaking into the house."

"Why do you say that?"

"Well, you see, there are trap doors all over Uncle's house. Since he knew we were coming, I'm guessing he made most of them dormant for the time being. There was one night, however, that one unlucky thief fell into a trap when I was staying there. The man ended up falling through a trapdoor in the floor and landed in restraining nets with tranquillising needles. He was paralysed in a matter of seconds, caught like a fly in a spiderweb. Bobbie took him away with ease, and ever since the word spread from that thief and his mates, everyone stays away from the house, whether they be a thief or a paperboy."

"I don't know whether I'm even more fearful or respectful of Uncle G—"

Keagan gives me a quick look and taps one finger to his closed mouth once. *No mentioning of his name? Right, people know him around here; we don't want nosy people listening in.* "Heh, even though I still have my moments of distrust or dislike of him, you can't blame him, after all of his years of service to the Crown. He still holds and remembers too many valuable secrets, so it's just a precaution. Just like the housekeeper; she's somewhat a protector of Uncle herself."

"She doesn't seem to act like it from the way she talks to him, but from what I've heard so far, it sure sounds like she's fiercely loyal to that man."

"Indeed she is," Keagan says, ending our conversation for the time being as we take in the names of the buildings to the left and right of us. Everything seems to be going well, and we've hit a very pleasant-looking street, it seems. The buildings are fresher and the bricks seem newer and cleaner than the past three streets we previously ventured on. Out of nowhere on the opposite sidewalk, a rather colourful woman and her simply dressed male companion stops Aspen and acts exuberantly when she speaks to her. She is donned in multi-coloured feathers lining her bustle and shoulders, along with a self-spinning gear and feather-embellished hat. Aspen's expression is rather taken aback that this woman seems to recognise her; I guess Aspen is accidentally impersonating another gypsy woman who this lady seems to know.

Keagan and I walk ahead a little farther until we end up at a cafe, and sit outside for a short spell as we watch over Aspen and her little friend. Thomas ends up just sitting on a porch step looking up and down the street, but mainly watching the spectacle this woman is creating. Thrusting her hands towards Aspen, she grins wildly. Aspen's entire demeanour has changed into a friendly but sly facade. She takes her right hand and looks hard at it, pointing at it with a knowing look on her face as she nods up and down.

"That lady wants a palm reading," I laugh.

"She looks the type to get them regularly too. This is like watching a sideshow at a circus." Keagan smiles under his moustache as we see Aspen flail her arms in the sky and then place a hand over her heart. The lady seems to gasp at the answer and then dance in place a little. People and their dimies still continue to pass us by as we watch my gypsy sister put on a show for her customer. For a brief moment it feels to me as if we aren't undercover, that everything we're doing today is mere sightseeing and merriment. This is how I wish things could be for us: no more hiding, just getting to go to a simple cafe and not have to look over our shoulders to see if we're being followed constantly.

I ponder the idea as I glance down at the table the exact moment a goldish-yellow-furred paw slips a note on the surface from behind Keagan and me. Nudging Keagan, he sees and opens it, his eyes widening just before he stands up in such a hurry, he knocks over his seat in the process. Searching the crowd, he spies something I cannot and suddenly bolts from the table, leaving me behind. I get up and try to follow him as best I can, but I quickly lose him since he darts and begins to push people and dimies out of the way.

I look back for an instant to see what's going on with Aspen, but she's still talking to the woman. *She'll be fine, so I can go catch up to Keagan now. What was on that little slip of paper? What could have caused him to dart off in such a way? That for sure caused more than one person's attention to focus on the two of us.*

Rushing around passing couples and dimies carrying filled baskets, I manage to catch up to him at an intersection. He looks around in each direction frantically as billows of steam puff out from his mouth. His hair is slightly unkempt now and the look on his face appears to be volatile. The sight of him makes me pause a second as I walk the rest of the way towards him. Who was it he thought he saw in the crowd? Charles? Gertrude? He wouldn't be so bold to hunt Damon down on foot in broad daylight like this, would he? "Kay?" I ask when I finally catch up to him. "What's going on? You look deranged right now. Calm down." But Keagan still looks around over the heads in the crowd frantically. "Tell me what that note said right now," I puff out, a little winded from the sudden run in my heavy skirts.

Pulling me over by my arm under the blue-and-white-striped awning of the nearest corner store, Keagan hands me the now crumpled slip of paper. "Read it for yourself, Lo." Taking it from his hand and pulling it taught, I can make out the scrawled words:

Thatcher is alive in the city, but not for long. Hurry!

· · ·

"What?" I breathe out. "Kay, that had to have been Gertude who slipped this to us. I saw her paw."

"I figured. I saw her face a little, though most of it was covered by a cowl. I tried to catch her but she's too slippery."

"Should have tried harder." I let the harsh words slip from my mouth without even trying to stop them. I know things are still unsteady between Keagan, Aspen and me, but I don't want to hold my tongue—I'm just angry. "Some things never change, eh?" I add, trying to lighten my tone a bit. Keagan doesn't respond so I just offer him my arm and nod my head back to the cafe we dashed from, now a whole block away. Right as we near the cafe, we get a glimpse across the street right as Aspen and the feathered peacock lady are waving goodbye to each other.

"You know, dear, I think I would very much like my fortune told as well. What say we go and see that gypsy woman there?" I say sweetly.

"Ah, Penelope, why must you indulge yourself in such queer things?" Keagan plays along.

"Please, dear, it's all for a laugh, I promise you."

"Oh...all right," Keagan says with a false smile under his moustache. We make it to the edge of the walk and wait for the two carriages to pass by. Taking my first step through the streets, I can feel the hem of my dress sweep up dust and litter. *How filthy are the streets here? Honestly, how does a woman walk around with roads like this?*

Aspen sees us coming and quickens her pace towards us. Thomas has left his place on the doorstep as well, and is jogging his way over to us. He probably thinks something's going on. I mean, yes, there *is* something going on, but we don't need him involved at this time; four is a crowd, and we don't want that attention right now.

"I say, I know that lady you gave a reading to just now, and I thought to myself, wouldn't that be fun?" I look over Aspen's shoulder and give Thomas a penetrating stare that actually stops him in his tracks. Pausing for a moment, he finally bends down to the ground to tie his boots.

"Oh, did you now? Is this really the right place for another reading?" Aspen says in a gypsy accent with a raised unibrow.

"Indeed I think it is," I say as I show her my open right-gloved hand that has the note wedged between two fingers.

"Well, all right, but that'll be a shilling," she says, playing along as she quickly takes my hand and unfolds the message along my palm. Her eyes open slightly, and instead of doing the fake exaggerated charade like she did earlier, Aspen simply looks up to me and Keagan from her slouched-over position and says, "Well, this is grave indeed, now isn't it?"

"I once tried to chase such things myself, but they soon became lost to me, disappearing in a golden yellow flash and leaving me at a crossroad," Keagan pipes in, and it seems that Aspen understands, but strangely enough does not look pleased.

"Did you perhaps try looking at the problem at a different angle—above, perhaps?"

"By the time I would have found a way to do so, the problem would have worked its way far out of reach, don't you think?" Keagan adds with that edge in his voice from earlier after losing Gertrude.

"Well, it's smart to remember to try and exhaust every resource when the stakes are as high as they are. That's something I thought you would know, sir, but I guess I was wrong."

"Asp—Miss, we have truly tried our best to fix this problem you see here," I say, slightly wiggling my hand she's holding to get her attention back. "Do you possibly see a solution to this situation we have?"

Aspen gives a long exhale as she looks at the note in my hand before speaking again. "Not at the moment. The best thing you can do is keep searching and hope the answer will turn up. Lovely gloves, Miss. *Be sure to save them.*" She walks around us and off in the direction we all were originally going. I pocket the note in my purse and take the rather flustered Keagan's arm once again as we walk a little farther in the opposite direction.

I give Thomas a little smile, and he reciprocates it before getting up and making his way towards us. "Eh, Govna, can you spare a farthing?" he says, lifting off his cap.

"How about a tip instead, boy?" Keagan replies. "Trouble is about, so keep your eyes open for *yellow*-bellied traitors. We don't want them running around too much—they seem to have the answers we need."

"Interesting advice, sir. Good day, I guess?" Thomas says with a quizzical look on his face as he replaces his cap and goes back to tailing Aspen. We, on the other hand, start to make our way back to the other side of the street from whence we came.

"Think he understood?" I say as I pick up the front of my skirts, even heavier now with the trailing dirt and grime.

"I may have made it too complicated, but he could just be really good at acting the part, you know."

"That's true. The problem is, though, he's told us he's seen us save that dimie in the alleyway one night, but that was in the dark of night and who knows how far away he was watching from, so—"

"...So he doesn't even know who to keep an eye out for,"

Keagan finishes for me with a sigh. "He probably thinks I was talking about Charles."

"You know you're right," I say, looking ahead at the black-smith's open workshop on a side street, whose furnace spews out a fountain of sparks every few seconds. Who knew Uncle George would live so deep in the working-class district? I guess it fits, though—if he needs something special to be created, he can ask the blacksmith and tinker shops. Also, no one in their right mind would break into George's house. Pauline already can shoot a gun, and Uncle George might end up paralysing the poor bloke for his audacity in breaking in, if he doesn't quickly get stuck in a trap first. Perhaps that's already happened in the past, and that's why they're okay with living in the area...

THE BRIDGE

KEAGAN

Making it back home near six thirty in the evening, we all rest a while and have a refreshing dinner with Uncle George and Pauline. We explain how after walking around our side of the bridge and the area of Belgravia, we decided to take a taxi carriage as a whole, to observe the rest of the surrounding city area while giving our feet a break. But after sitting in a carriage for so long, I think it would be good tonight to go for a run across the parts of the city that we just saw, and some we have yet to venture into. I just know we'll be exhausted after all is said and done. We decide as well that tonight Thomas is to come with us. Even if he cannot go with us on every night mission, it's important for him to know the layout of the city.

Donning our police uniforms over our night clothes, save Thomas, we take our time making our way towards the bridge, the same way we arrived on the ground this morning. However, this time we are running over the rooftops. If anyone sees us, they'll just think we're a group of bobbies chasing a cat burglar. *Maybe we should wear bobbie uniforms more often instead of our night running outfits? We would get away with much more, rather than when we're eerie black-clad phantoms.*

Making our way to the bridge, we find a nearby alley and hop to the ground. The bridge is just at the end of this street. Tonight we decide to observe the area across the bridge a bit better, since we should be able to remember our side of town. Making our way to the sidewalk with Thomas walking beside us, we should appear as if we are a couple of constables escorting a child back home.

"Stop that man! Police, police, stop him!" a man's voice yells out from behind us. But just as we turn around, a flash of a shadow runs right through us, pushing Aspen into me. Catching her, we all look in the direction the man ran and see the desperate look on the victim's face. My guess, a pick-pocket. "What are you doing? Catch that thief! Why are you letting him get away?" the large unhappy man yells at us. And then it hits me—I look down at our uniforms and realise the predicament I have put us in with them. *We look just like bobbies, but we sure aren't acting like them.*

Then the man's eyes narrow and a look of recognition flashes through them. More and more people on the sidewalk are starting to stare at us in curiosity at our lack of action. One glance at Aspen and Lori's faces tells me that we need to run now.

"Ah, yes, sorry about that, sir. Well go after him right now."

"Wait. You look very much like someone in the wanted papers." He gets uncomfortably close to me and I can't think of what to do next, then his eyes shift to Aspen and Lori. Jumping back with a start, he points his finger at us and yells out, "It's the night phantoms! They're in disguise! Don't let them get away! They're wanted criminals!"

As fast as a bullet, the entire population of the street seems to have their attention on us. *Fantastic—not twenty minutes into our run and we've been recognised.* "Freeze right there!" I hear more men call out, and when I look around the angry accuser, I see it's real bobbies that are gaining ground.

"Tom, Lo, flee now," Aspen orders, and without hesitation they run back down the alley we came from and shoot out their grappling hooks, making it to the rooftops before the police can even try to follow them. On our side, a circle of men begins to form as others lead women and children away from the scene. The second Lori and Thomas starts to run, the man who recognised us lunges for Aspen. Using his momentum, Aspen steps aside and lets him propel himself into the man who was coming towards me from behind, tackling him.

An opening in the men has formed and, taking Aspen's hand, we dart through it and head straight towards the bridge. The real bobbies are following us now, and we barely make it around an oncoming horse carriage in time, allowing us a chance to block off the bobbies for a few seconds. The sound of the mare's sharp whinny makes me even more unnerved about our situation. Still, we make our way safely to the opposite sidewalk, and what few people are strolling along instantly make way for us. Gents shield their ladies as we dash by, whilst others run to the sides of the walk, entirely getting out of range. We've made quite an impression on Londoners, haven't we? And with just a few wanted posters. The looks of horror and raised arms speak volumes to me. *How twisted rumours can become, from Currlion to London. What are we known as now, a band of murderers? Come to think of it, that might have been one of the crimes we were charged with in the newspaper.*

As we near the middle of the bridge, I begin to wonder where else the word has travelled, and to what proportions?

We are monsters now to anyone who recognises us, it seems. Now we are no better than the bloodthirsty gangs around the city. The bobbies are still behind us and, just as I start to think of a way to lose them, my heart sinks from the sight and ringing sound of the bell on the Scotland Yard paddywagon barreling up towards us on the bridge from the direction we're running.

Most everyone is still making a way for us, but at the sound of the bobbies coming near, it seems to strike a newfound courage in the few men nearby, who make a barricade with their arms outstretched towards us, halting us in our tracks. The paddywagon makes a stop and officers pile out. Jumping atop the stone railing of the bridge to give us advantage and distance from the men, we watch nervously as the officers close in on us.

"It's no wonder they arrived so suddenly," I mutter to Aspen. "Scotland Yard headquarters is just left of this street. Someone must have called their station."

"Honestly," she breathes out. All the hungry eyes on us makes me feel like a sheep cornered before a pack of wolves. Some look famished compared to others, and are probably relishing in the thought of capturing us for the reward bounty, or the thrill of fighting us perhaps. Others appear to be frightened; however, they still have their arms stretched out, ready to snatch us up.

"All right, you two, hold still," a loud booming voice from a megaphone calls at us. "Surrender. There's nowhere to go from here." The speaker's face is obstructed by the spotlights that are positioned on us; however, I can still make out the voice to be the chief of police. Guess I never learned my lesson in boarding school after all; he won't be all too happy to talk to me again. *If only these lights weren't so blinding we could see a way out,* I think as I shield my vision, and my ears pick up the tune of a boat chugging through the water. Glancing below, I see our saving grace nearing the entrance to the underside of the bridge. Looking back up at Aspen, I see how hard she is breathing and the paralysed expression on her face. Shots haven't even been fired yet and she already appears to be hit by one.

"Aspen, do you trust me?" I whisper in her ear as hope re-enters my system.

"Are you seriously bringing this up right now?" she whispers back hoarsely.

"No talking!" the guard yells at us whilst he cocks his gun. "Now come down from there one at a time, slowly."

I look over my shoulder one more time and see our ticket out is almost gone. "Do you trust me?" I say again, not bothering to whisper this time.

"Yes," she says. Before the words are out of her mouth I pull us over the edge of the bridge, where we soon find ourselves on a thick pile of ropes and tarps just as the boat heads under the bridge. The air in my lungs gets knocked out of me from the force of the landing, though we just make it. We hear the men shout as we continue clinging to each other.

"Check the other side of the bridge!" one of the men orders. Soon after, the water on the other side of the bridge is being illuminated as we near it. Coming our way is a small tugboat hauling in a fishing ship. They are a little ways off, but if we hang around a bit, we might be able to make it before the constables catch us with their searchlights.

My heart races as we frantically shuffle off of the pile.

Aspen, always one step ahead, has already pulled out her grappling hook shooter, and gestures for me to do the same. She points at the beams under the bridge before aiming her gun. Shooting up to the underside of the bridge, we tuck up our legs and pray the tugboat captain doesn't notice. It appears he hasn't seen anything, though, since his gaze remains ahead of him on the channel. The boat we just left now slips under the bobbies' lights whilst the oncoming boat nears the other side of the bridge. The voices of the men bounce off the walls of the underbridge as we hear their confused exclamations.

"They didn't drown, did they?"

"Of course not. Go check the banks of the river. You two go get the police boat, we need to check the water."

Things aren't looking too good. This tugboat doesn't have any good hiding places, but the fishing ship might. Nudging Aspen in the side with my boot, I point to the ship and wrap one of my arms over my head as the signal for "hide." After nodding her head, she immediately grabs hold of the metal beam with her free hand and shoots her grapple to the edge of the ship, flying off towards it.

I do the same, then we duck down low and sneak our way to the side of the ship. I keep my eyes towards the captain's area. Nothing out of the ordinary. Maybe they didn't notice us because of the dark cover from the bridge's shadow. Aspen pauses and puts her hand up, telling me to wait. As we do, I realise that the entire ship reeks worse than the smell of the channel, reminding me of beached fish and sun-cooked algae. Then we hear it, the sound of men's voices coming near us, but it's from the deck we're on. With a creak and slant of the ship, Aspen grabs my arm and pulls me to the nearest pile of crates, and then to a tarp on the ground behind them.

The second we lift the tarp over our heads, I feel the urge to throw up over the edge. The putrid smell of rotting fish has been amplified, and from the tears in Aspen's eyes I can tell she feels the same way. I never was good with rocking boats or the smell of fish, but this is a whole new level of discomfort. We begin taking out cloth, gauze, tissues, anything from our hip satchels to cover our noses and stop the smell. By the time we do, the darkness around us diminishes slightly. We must have passed under the bridge.

Remaining in our crouched position under the tarp, we keep one corner lifted to look out on the deck and breathe fresh air. The bobbies' beam lights are crawling all over the ship, and we can hear the confused shouts of the crew on deck. They're probably yelling at the constables, trying to figure out what's going on. This goes on for what feels like an eternity, the smell of fish becoming overwhelming. All of a sudden I feel something brush against my leg; looking down, I see it's a rat. *I hate rats.* Stifling my newfound level of disgust, I pull us both out from under the tarp and towards the nearest rope pile, just as the torches disappear around the corner.

On our way to the pile, we notice a few of the fishermen on deck with their backs to us as they puff their pipes. These are tall burly men who look like they eat rust and fish bones for breakfast. When we reach the rope pile, we quickly realise it's too small to hide the both of us, but we have to do as best we can now before anyone sees us. Sweat beads down my back whilst we crouch low behind the thick ropes. I can easily look over them and watch as smoke plumes from the fishermen's mouths.

Aspen and I begin to look around for a safe hiding place that does not involve putrid rat-riddled tarps. The bobbies are beginning to walk on the opposite sides of the river now that the tugboat is farther away from the bridge. Our boat, however, slows to a halt whilst searching lights are roving the deck again. I hold my breath as they near our spot. Just as I think we're going to be caught, a loud crash echoes through the area, coming from the right side of the bridge. The lights that were close to our hiding place are gone in a second, to instead uncover the cause of the ruckus, and in doing so they illuminate…us? Or at least two figures that resemble us remarkably, picking themselves up from a couple of trash bins. It appears that they had run into it and created even more of a clatter in the process. All of the constables chase after them as our doubles stumble off to the nearest street.

"I don't know who those two were, but thank the Lord they were around when they were," I whisper.

"I don't know. I don't like the idea of our doubles running around the city; they could cause some serious trouble for us," Aspen whispers back.

I put my hand up, pausing the conversation as one of the crew comes our way. Passing right in front of us on his way to the very end of the boat, he rests his thick arms on the railing and stares at the bridge as the boat begins to pick up speed again. I point to the shore, but she shakes her head and points to the railing where the street starts on the other side of the boat. Now that I think about it, that would be the safer bet, since the fishermen are mostly on this side of the boat.

Taking our grappling hook launchers, we ready them in our hands and check one last time for anyone coming. The coast is clear, however, so we run from our hiding place across the deck, aiming our guns to the stone railing that separates the road from the channel. We are three metres from the edge of the boat when a massive form obstructs our ticket to freedom. We both slam into the large man, causing the bucket of fish he was carrying to disperse everywhere.

The three of us just sit and stare at each other in shock for a second before Aspen jumps straight over the man's head. I run around him and meet her on the edge of the ship as she shoots out to the road's stone fence. The exasperated calls from the crew seem to grow, and once we are safe over the stone railing, I sneak a peek back at the ship. The crew is throwing different things our way, like trash or the fish we spilled. Others are shouting obscenities or calling for the constables to come back. Before matters can get any worse, we dart towards the nearest alleyway and check the corner to make sure it is clear.

"So what's the plan? Try and find our impersonators, or regroup with Thomas and Lori?" I huff out.

"We should regroup. If we do find our doubles, I'd rather our whole team be present in case we need our whole powerhouse. If anything, Lori and Thomas can remain on the rooftops in case we need eyes in the sky for an aerial attack."

"Apparently Thomas is wonderful at that style, from what Lori has told me about them getting Gear Heart back from Damon's men."

"That's right. Maybe we should keep him on that style of fighting for now when needed during missions, since he's already good at it."

"Makes you wonder what kind of trouble he and his friends used to get into back home," I add, making Aspen laugh slightly as we run off.

Two houses from our rendezvous point, we check to see if the area is clear for us to use our grappling hook to get over the great divide of the road. Waiting for the last carriage to turn the corner, the street is pretty cleared now. Looking over as we prepare our grappling hooks, I think I can make out

Lori and Thomas coming our way as well, from the other side.

"Mr Myrack, Miss Wolfe?" a rough male voice says from behind us. Whipping around, we both raise our grappling hooks to our unexpected visitor. We see that it is the two hooded figures from before on the bridge. Putting their arms up, they stand about two and a half metres from us. "We are friends," the female says. "We were the ones who posed as you on the bridge. We gave the bobbies a good run for their money, you can be sure about that."

"Friends show their faces," Aspen demands. The pair look at each other through their full-face masks and quickly pull them off, exposing themselves. I've never seen these people before in my life, and by the look on her face, neither has Aspen.

"We've been trying to catch up to you so we could properly introduce ourselves. You two sure are fast," the lady says, and by the quick rise and fall of their chests it does appear that they were following us instead of waiting for us. Still, we don't like to be tailed. *Are we really that easy to follow?* "Allow us to introduce ourselves. I'm Andrea and this is Ghedi." Andrea is of medium height but thicker build than Aspen. She has black wiry hair that is pulled back into a bun, and appears to be in her early thirties. The man named Ghedi has a handsome Egyptian face and rather dark complexion with curly dark hair. He doesn't smile when introduced, though, instead just giving a quick nod. I get a strange energy around this man, and it's not a good one.

"We were following you to guide you to the rest of our group. There's something we've been eager to talk to you about."

"Like?" I say.

"We wish to work with you," Ghedi finally says, speaking in a smooth voice. "If you will just follow us, Anthony will explain everything. He's better with words than we are."

Aspen looks at me and, to my surprise, nods yes. "Lead the way," she says easily. *What is she thinking? It could be a trap.* Aspen points towards them with a knowing look. She's obviously planning something.

"All right, well, let's get going then." I put my mask back on and our guides do the same before turning to the back of the building. "How far is this friend of yours, anyway?" I glance over my shoulder to see that Aspen is giving signals to Lori and Thomas across the way.

"Not too far. We got a tip from a taxi man that you were in the Waterloo area. One of our members works at the railway station where you came in. So we decided to group near there for the meeting."

"Really? All right, then. Aspen, ready to go?"

"Yes, sorry, I dropped something back there." She makes her way towards us. Ghedi eyes her as we start to run, but quickly focuses back on making the next jump from building to building. *Keep your eyes forward, Ghedi.* I look back every now and then to see that Lori and Thomas are indeed following us by two buildings' distance. When we make it to Waterloo, we climb our way back to the ground. Our guides lead us between the housing units where the clothes are hung in strands above us from window to window. The only light comes from the flame in a lantern at the edge of a pocket area in the left building.

I unsheath a dagger in one hand, and as I glance behind us, I notice Aspen reaching for her pistol on the spring net box on her hip, the newest invention she managed to come up with whilst she was in the hospital. None of us even knew about it at first, because Thomas was smuggling in all the pieces she needed when they were doing their lessons. No one seems to be following us from the ground in either direction, so that's good, but the moment we turn the corner we see that we are already outnumbered. There are five people here spread out, some of them sitting on crates and others standing in the open or leaning on a brick wall. Two figures are hiding in the darkness—I wouldn't have noticed them if one of them hadn't shifted their stance when we came around the corner.

A man comes up to us with short brown hair, a clean beard, and moustache, and rather tall in stature wearing a grey suit. "We've been eager to have the chance to talk to you," he says. "Ever since we saw you at the railway station, we've been trying to find you again. Your work as the night phantoms is truly amazing." It isn't until he turns his head to address Aspen that I see the long red scar that traces the left side of his face from his temple to his jaw. "I'm Anthony, by the way. I take it you've been introduced to Andrea and Ghedi—"

"You recognised us at the train station?" I say, rather alarmed. If someone who's never met us recognised us even in our soaked appearance, who else could have recognised us that night?

"Well, not me particularly. It was Samuel, actually. He works as a porter there. He has a magnificent memory for faces." Anthony gestures to the large blond-haired lad resting on the box on the adjacent wall, dressed in brown vest and pants.

"Does he now? Samuel, what station was it, and what was the weather like?" Aspen asks expectantly, standing with her arms crossed.

Samuel looks at Aspen rather sheepishly before hopping off his crate and making his way towards us. Standing in front of her, his hands fidget with his vest as he speaks. "Well, Miss, I work at Hampstead Heath Station. To be honest, I had to do a double take when I saw all of you together, due to the pouring rain. Pardon me for saying this, but at the time you were rather…dishevelled in appearance."

"Do you remember the day or what outfits we wore?"

He seems to have trouble keeping constant eye contact with her, and she's at least thirty centimetres smaller than he is. It would seem that this man is rather timid in contrast to his tough appearance. That or he finds authoritative women like Aspen intimidating. "Well, uh, I know that it was about three days ago. I remember that Mr Myrack here had on a long black coat. Your sister, the blonde one, had on a light blue coat, and if I recall she was actually wearing a tophat when I saw her. You, m'lady, were carrying a single hatbox—it was pink with florals on it—and you were wearing a dark-colored coat. There was also a young lad with you, wasn't there? Dark skin, pageboy cap, no more than twelve?"

"I'm thirteen! Why does everyone think I'm twelve?" Thomas's voice pipes up from our side of the alley. He and Lori come around the bend in time to see everyone's surprised and yet relieved faces. They probably thought they weren't going to come after all, but truth be told they've been here the whole time. Aspen had signalled earlier to check the area to make sure this wasn't a trap. They've been observing from the rooftops till she gave them the signal that it was safe.

"They can't help it, love. You just have a very young complexion," Lori tries assuring him.

"This is the boy you saw, Thomas Brimstone, and Aspen's sister, Miss Lori Wolfe," I say, introducing our latecomers to the party.

"I still can't believe you could tell who we were on that

rainy day when we all were a soggy mess." Aspen looks at Samuel in a rather sceptical manner. "Your story checks out, but you have yet to prove your authenticity to what you say you can do." I can tell she is analysing him to see if he is being honest with us or not. *We were already taking a great risk in coming here, but now…*

"Who are those hiding in the dark over there?" I ask, nodding my head at the two hooded figures peeking over the crates in the back. "Friends of yours, I presume?"

"Yes, actually, wait one moment, please. Isola, Issac, it's okay to come out," Anthony says reassuringly as he walks away towards the hooded couple. The two hiding figures reluctantly come forward from the dark, and as they approach us I notice they aren't walking with human feet, but long bird-like legs and fur-covered paws. These are dimies, but why would they want to hide from us if they identified us as the Night Phantoms? Maybe they were keeping them safe as their back-up crew if we weren't the real thing. *They think like us too.* Still standing a little ways away, they lower their hoods, and sure enough they're dimies; one is a horned-bill yellow-feathered bird, the other a purple-furred otter with a wide flat tail, similar to a beaver's.

"This is Issac and Isola." Samuel gestures from the bird dimie to the otter.

"It's a pleasure to meet you. Would you by chance know any dimies in or from Currlion?" Aspen asks, her tone now much more inviting.

"Well, I've known a few who have come from there or moved there with their owners over the years. Why do you ask, Miss Wolfe?" Issac asks curiously.

"Would you by chance be acquainted with two bear dimies,

Winona and Thatcher, or a yellow monkey dimie named Gertrude?"

"Thatcher, yes, he's the large brown-furred bear dimie. He's quite a tough character. If you were to meet him, you'd never realise how kind he can be."

"Oh, I believe we could. So you don't know the other two, then? Also, have you seen Thatcher in the city recently?"

"Can't say so, ma'am, haven't seen Thatcher for a few years now. As for the other two, I've never met dimies by those names in my life, actually. Have any of you?" Issac turns his back to us to address his partners, but none of them know.

"Now, Miss Wolfe," Anthony pipes up. "You mentioned earlier that we have yet to prove ourselves, and yet we already have. By helping you tonight and diverting the attention of the constables when you were on the ship, we proved that we are your allies. We risked being caught by the constables ourselves so that you could get away. However, the reason why we asked you to come here tonight is for something simple that we believe you will thoroughly enjoy. We would like to help you and be a part of your team, to be your guides through the city and fight alongside you as well."

"And how do you propose to help us, exactly?" I ask flatly. "Act as decoys when needed, like tonight?"

"Even better. Face it, London is a bit different than Currlion. But we can assure you that no one knows this city like we do. We have people of almost every class standing here."

Somehow knowing this makes me feel uneasy, the idea that the rich, the poor and the homeless are working together. Unless everyone is honest with each other, there will likely be a lot of trouble.

"And what if we already have someone who knows

London? And better than all of you since they've lived here all their lives, which is much longer than any of you have?"

"So that's why you almost got caught tonight?" the man named Ghedi asks smugly.

We just stand there in silence at his audacity till Anthony speaks again. "This person on your side, do they usually go on your runs about town with you? Perhaps they just weren't with you tonight and this was an accident?" Anthony's tone is much more reasonable and sounds like he's trying to ease the tension to better our favour on the matter.

"They can't physically keep up with us, so they're a part of our intelligence team. So is Keagan. He aids in intel from time to time," Lori says smoothly. Aspen seems to approve of this answer since she doesn't try to stop her from going on.

Our attention is quickly shifted to the opening of the alley. A man with a broad frame is coming our way, though it appears he has a slight limp. Each of us reach for and prepare a weapon, since we can't tell who is coming. Looking over at Anthony, he appears to be just as worried.

"Pardon me for being late again," the man says when he gets closer.

The girls immediately lower their guard and their weapons. "Do you ever arrive on time, Harry?" Andrea snaps as he enters the lantern light, exposing a scruffy face and honey-coloured hair that pokes out of his bowler hat. He appears to be down on his luck by the appearance of his clothes. "One of these days your lateness will be the death of us."

"Harry, is that really you?" Lori asks, as Aspen replaces the newest version of her bolt blaster.

"Hey, there are my cousins!" Harry says, finally seeing the girls as they rush towards him. "Gosh, I've missed you. Look at how beautiful the both of you have become. And so famous as well," he adds as they both rush into his arms for an embrace. They hold onto him for a while with big smiles on their faces. It makes me happy to see them smile that wide again. *I should try and make them smile like that more.*

"So the news really has spread that quickly about us, huh?" Lori pipes up, still clinging to his arm.

"Well, yeah. Otherwise none of us would be here tonight for our meeting." Harry smiles.

"We've been eager to meet you," Isola says. "To be honest, we were a bit sceptical when Harry said you were his family."

"Ah, yes, but just look at our attractive complexions. Anyone would mistake us for family." Harry smiles wider.

"Yeah, the two beauties and their dog—nice family right there," Samuel sneers, making the whole lot laugh. Thomas and Lori are snickering, but Aspen just pats Harry on the back as he gives Samuel an unamused look. Looks like we know who the butt of the joke is around here.

"Why didn't you send us a letter that you were in London the whole time we were in Currlion?" Aspen asks.

"I'm sorry. By the time I heard about you *Night Phantoms* and your adventures in the paper, it was near New Year's Eve. After New Year's, practically all of England was reading about you in the paper. So knowing how good you two are at running, I was sure that by the time the letter had arrived, you would be in Ireland or Scotland."

"Well, all right, I guess we can forgive you this time. But I'm with Andrea here on your tardiness. Do you know how suspicious we've been of this group?" Aspen scolds him.

"They nearly shot us," Andrea says dryly with her arms crossed.

"You what?" both Harry and Lori say.

"It's a grappling-hook launcher. Not a gun."

"But it can still do considerable damage," Lori warns.

"They were the ones to sneak up on us." Aspen flips her hand this way and that.

"So what do you think of our offer, to aid in helping you? Did they tell you about our safehouse?" Harry interrupts the banter.

"Uh, Harry—"

"No, they didn't actually. Where is this safehouse?" Aspen asks eagerly.

"Oh, it's hidden through a wine keg—"

"Harry!" The entire group scolds him, but Aspen just ignores them and keeps asking questions.

"Really? Any windows or other doors people could get in through?"

"There are a few windows here and there to aerate the place, but they're small. Think basement windows, the small rectangular type."

"Sounds optimal," Aspen says, giving Lori a look.

"But no, we haven't given our answer yet," Lori adds.

"Of course, we'll need to think this over after seeing the place itself," I pipe up, walking over to Harry and the girls along with Thomas. After introducing myself and Thomas to Cousin Harry, Anthony offers to show us the hideout immediately. I am completely against the idea of following them anywhere we don't know. Even though Aspen and Lori are cousins to Harry, hearing the rest of the group's animosity towards him does not bode well. Even if he is with them, how sure can we be that they're being honest with him and that they are who they say they are? "I think perhaps we should—"

"That sounds amazing; you have a safehouse of your

own?" Thomas interjects, walking closer to Isola who looks at him in a loving way.

"That's right, and no one would ever guess where it is either. The entrance is hidden."

"Is that so?" Aspen says with a serpent's smile. "Harry, how long have you been with this group? Do they seem like a nice bunch of people? I hope they let you practise your acrobatics." From what I can see between the cousins, it appears there is a silent code being observed between the two that only they are attuned to.

"Oh yes, whenever I wish, they allow me to stretch out and practice since there is so much space, though I don't always get a bite for dinner whenever it's a group meal."

"What? When have we ever done that?" Samuel objects, but the family unit under the lamplight seems to disregard his comment.

"Ah," Aspen says as she looks at Lori, nodding her head.

"We would love to catch a glimpse of your hideout," Lori says—guess she's in on the game as well.

Ghedi suddenly comes forth into the light and catches Lori's attention. "Before we leave, I feel I should introduce myself, Miss Wolfe. My name is Ghedi."

"Call me Lori, please. It's nice to meet you, Ghedi." At this point, everyone else comes forth and introduces themselves to both Lori and Thomas. However, Ghedi and Lori seem to have eyes only for each other for the remainder of the night. Even on our way to the safehouse, they sneak glances at each other. I know she's a romantic, but I wouldn't have picked this chap as her type. And I'm not particularly fond of the way his gaze looks over her figure when she isn't looking back at him. I'll need to keep an eye on this man.

ALLIES OR ENEMIES?

LORI

"I think we should give them a chance. I mean, they seem nice, and even cousin Harry is working with them," I say in a thoughtful tone.

"That's what worries me," Aspen sneers. "I love cousin Harry as much as you do, but he doesn't always make the smartest decisions, or ones with common sense. But besides that fact, you're just saying all of that because of that cute gypsy guy you were ogling."

"That is n—"

"Completely true and you know it," Keagan says dryly as he interrupts me with a knowing smile.

"Thomas, can you believe these two? Ganging up on me like this?" I ask.

"Kind of. I mean, you do have a history of being a flirt like Keagan."

"Who told you that?" I look at him, trying to hide my laughter as I speak. Thomas just glances in Aspen's direction. "Aha! And just what have you told him, sissy?"

"Nothing. Just how many romantic escapades and

gentleman callers you've had in the past. It came up in conversation as we were working one day." She removes her boots and weapons belt. I'm still feeling a little chagrined, though, for being judged. "Lori bird, you know you're a flirty person, and you know practically every trick of the trade to make almost any man you want to fall for you. Why are you suddenly taking offence to that?" Aspen takes hold of my hand.

"It's one thing to be seen as an amiable and social person who receives a lot of male attention, and quite another to be judged a flirt. Even if I know I'm a flirt, I'd rather not be called one. It's very rude."

"Even though you know you can be one and admit it to me every now and then?"

"Yes," I say matter-of-factly.

"What makes this gypsy guy so great, anyway?" Thomas asks out of the blue.

"Well, you saw him. He's tall, has midnight-black curly hair, and these beautifully warm chestnut eyes. On top of that, he was a gentleman the whole time we were there, not to mention he had quite a strapping physique."

"Which surprises me," Aspen says, "because you're usually drawn towards more light-haired gents like redheads and blonds."

"I am, but he's just so striking to me."

"Funny, that was the same way with me till I saw Aspen again," Keagan says more to himself than to the rest of us as he takes out the false bottom of the trunk where we hide our boots and weapons. He may not have meant for us to hear that, but I certainly did. As I look down, I catch a glimpse of Thomas playing with his dark coiled hair. "I'll say this," he continues. "If it weren't for our copycats tonight, Aspen and I could easily have been found by the bobbies."

"I don't like to admit it, but you're right, Keagan," Aspen huffs out. "They pulled off a good enough performance that allowed us to slip away."

"From what you've told me so far, I can deem that it's neither a gang nor the queen's agents," Uncle George assures us from the armchair by the fire. "She's never been known to employ dimies for such things."

"And their headquarters is in a safe and clever hiding spot," Keagan reminds us. "I doubt the owners will even find them or figure out the barrel is empty. It'll be pretty hard to top, too, since the price is free. We haven't found any other place better than this one." It's mainly Keagan taking care of our expenses these days, since he was able to take a good amount of money with him from the house. Aspen and I don't have all that much between us now, since our last allowance came in November. Since we are in hiding, we won't be receiving it unless we clear our names to the queen.

"It was a pretty spacious place, though, wasn't it?" I say. "The lighting was fairly good, and there were already extra couches and bedding down there, aside from where the group already sleeps. It must have been a storage area for furniture at some point." I notice Aspen is still thinking it over as she sits herself down by the fire on a footrest.

"And I didn't see one insect or rat in the whole place," Keagan adds. "Maybe we should give them a test. It worked for me, did it not?"

"Yes, but I don't think a fight or a game of catch will do justice with this group. What if they locate something that could be of aid to us?" Aspen muses as she stares at the tips of the dancing flames.

"What if they try to find Thatcher?" Thomas offers.

"No, that would take forever. We don't even have a clue where he is, only that he's alive. Also, we know him. Issac was the only one in their group who could identify him."

"Besides," I add, "even if we were to draw a likeness of him, there are probably hundreds of brown-bear dimies with ram horns in the city." We all ponder the situation for a second longer before a new idea hits me. "What if we have them locate where Damon and his men are, since we know they're somewhere in London?"

"Keagan, Uncle George, do you have any ideas of where the governor could be staying in London?" Aspen asks. "That way we would know if they found the right person."

"There are a few places that most elites go to stay when in London. The Charing Cross, Great Eastern and Great Northern hotels are all quite grand. That's where many people stay when they first enter the city at night, since they're all connected to the railway. However, you've mentioned that Damon has ordered the constables back in Currlion to continue to check all railcars and air trains. Damon or just his men could be staying there, since he's most likely still monitoring the railway system, and that's the perfect place to do it. That being said, there's also the Grosvenor Hotel, which is on Buckingham Palace Road. If he wants to stay in close proximity to the queen for a higher chance of seeing her sooner, or to stop you from seeing her, then that's the place for him to be."

"Keagan, anything to add on or rule out?" I ask.

"Other than what Uncle George has already given us, I vaguely recall the mention of the Langham, which is a very innovative hotel when it comes to luxury technology, something hard for Damon to pass up. However, there was also the...Land Hotel?"

"I believe you're thinking of the *Midland* Hotel," Uncle George corrects him.

"Yes, that's it! He would talk about those two when my father and he visited after the governor's trips to London."

"Great. We have a few possible locations, but I have a feeling that none of the members know what he looks like."

"Ah, I have just the thing!" Uncle George says, quickly exiting the room. A minute or two later, he comes back with a slightly crumpled newspaper in his hand. "I meant to show you earlier, but I was distracted. He made it in the *Star*. Read it for yourself."

Keagan takes the paper and searches the page for the article before reading it for everyone. "Governor Damon of Currlion comes to London with the business of meeting with Her Majesty the Queen, on a *revolutionary idea—one that could revitalise the age into its new era*. As described by the governor."

"One guess on what that will be about," Aspen grumbles.

"It doesn't give too many details about what exactly he'll be talking to the queen about, or when the meeting will be exactly, just that he'll be meeting with her in the coming months. And it shows a picture of him at the train station— can't tell which one, though. It does seem clear enough that our test group can use it to identify him."

"Perfect," I say as a faint giggle fills the room. It's George, laughing as he smokes his pipe. "What's so funny?" Thomas asks.

"Hehehe, ah, it's just that from what the paper has provided concerning the meeting time, it's clear he's on the waiting list to see the queen. She's a very busy woman and only has so many hours in the day to meet with visitors, regardless if they're governors or not. Besides, winter has always been a busy season for Her Majesty. Since food supplies have begun to shorten, there will be more operational planning in place of meeting visitors. Still, she may have it where he gets moved up to see her sooner." *He truly knows quite a lot about the goings-on of the queen and the royal court, even to the point of the daily schedule, it seems. How close was he to the queen? I must ask him another time for the details of their relationship; discreetly, of course.* "I have a feeling he's hiding a few aces up his sleeve other than just your journal, Aspen," he continues. "He very well could be biding his time until he's ready to see the queen."

"What are you thinking, Uncle George?" Keagan asks with a peculiar look on his face as he searches the newspaper further.

"I want to know what he's taking to show her. If he's as opportunistic as you've said, then it must be something special."

Aspen is the first to respond. "He did try to take Gear Heart with him to present to the queen, but we took it back. What if he's actually stalling for time so he can have someone recreate a new Gear Heart?"

"It's possible."

"Oh Lord," I exclaim. "If this is true, don't you think he'll have the machine made somewhere safer than a hotel? Somewhere he won't hurt people or himself if it blows up or gets stolen?"

"You're right, Lori," Keagan says. "However, there are quite a few places to have a machine like Gear Heart created, as well as a handful of freelance inventors who would gladly partake into whatever the governor's offering."

"Uncle George, do you know anyone who might be employed by Damon to recreate Gear Heart?" Aspen asks.

"A few, yes. I'll reach out to them. Hopefully they haven't been sworn to secrecy."

"Yes, let's hope indeed. And please do be discreet without giving away the actual name of my machine, or our names either. The main things we need to know are where they're working and what the governor has told them so far. That is, if they're willing to talk about such things."

"You can count on me, Captain Wolfe!" Uncle George salutes before promptly bidding us a goodnight.

"All right, so we have the test made out for the new group —we just need to present it to them," I say.

"Yes, but it's much too late tonight," Keagan says. "Let's go to bed for now, and meet up with them tomorrow to discuss the test. If they're truly willing to follow us and fight for the same cause, then they'll agree to do this. Besides, after we tell them why it's so important, they'll feel like they're already a part of the team."

"Yeah, if they actually manage to find him, or the places he's been," I say, thinking about that cute gypsy fellow. *I hope we all get the chance to better acquaint ourselves with our possible new partners— twould be a shame if we stayed in a strictly formal relationship with them.*

"Are you serious?" Samuel sits back in his chair from the table.

"Dead serious," Keagan says dryly. The other members, both dimie and human, begin to talk to one another as we sit and watch the mix of emotions flow across the table in discussion. Some of them look excited, and it's evident they're trying to win over the few who are sceptical and put out by the idea.

"Think of it this way," Aspen says calmly. "You get us this information and we know that we can trust each other, since that man is a common enemy of ours we need to locate. After that, we can rescue dimies to give them a chance at going home through the portal, as well as possibly sabotage the governor's plans."

"When can we see the machine?" Isola asks with an eager look on her face.

"Once we have enough dimies to send home. And that offer goes to you two as well." Aspen points to Isola and Issac, who appear a little more than intrigued in the idea of seeing their native dimension again.

"Once you provide an acceptable means of evidence that he's staying at a hotel or boarding house, or who knows where, along with notes of the night, then we'll determine if you're up to snuff," I say.

"What would you consider an acceptable piece of evidence?" Samuel asks, looking bewildered.

"A photograph, an accepted fake letter at the hotel, something that will mark his location as proof of him going and or residing there. And we will ask that all unaccepted letters, cameras and tracking bugs be returned to us. If you don't, we will find you."

"Also," Keagan adds in a respectful tone, "just so that you will indeed be working with your assigned team member, you are to meet us in three safe locations to give us your notes and evidence of his whereabouts. So don't give us fake evidence just to be accepted. If we find out he never was at any of the places you provide us, our deal is off. Remember, this is a game to test your agility, intelligence in the field, and trustability. Are you willing to try it? Because this is the regular type of thing we do."

"Some are more dangerous than others, and some are actually quite fun and easy," I add. "Are there any questions?"

"What if he goes under an alias?" Ghedi asks with a gleam in his eye.

"That's a possibility, but unlikely, since the places he would most likely be staying are safe for people of his class and status," Keagan answers. "However, if he were to use an alias, the only one I know is Balthazar De Gaulle. My father once went on a business trip many years ago with him, and met him where he was staying for dinner. He told my father to ask for that name. Though that was in France, so he shouldn't need to use it here, since we're considered dead and therefore not a threat to him." Everyone takes note of this information and nod their heads.

"So we'll be looking for one man with two or more possible names. This really is sounding more and more like a guessing game," Samuel says.

"Let's just call it a round of 'I Spy,'" I offer, making Ghedi and Samuel look my way. "Pair up with one other person, and make sure it's a person you work well with, not the person you're the most chummy with. Also, Isola and Issac, you must be paired up with one or more humans for safety purposes, since you'll be doing this at night."

The group decides to privately discuss the offer in another room, and we three sit waiting patiently.. While we wait, I inspect the quality of the room, and the thin, high-up windows, so filthy and fogged it'd be a miracle if anyone could see through them from the outside. And the lighting is better than I remembered, too. I hope Aspen notices these things so she can start feeling better about the decision to give this group a chance.

The metal door opens with a squeak as they pile back into the room. We rise out of our seats and meet them halfway.

"We're in," Samuel says. "And we've already decided on our pairings. Harry, Andrea and Issac are team one. Isola and Anthony are team two, whilst Ghedi and myself are team three."

"Fabulous," I say as all of us shake hands to seal the deal.

"When does our trial take place?"

"Tonight," Aspen announces. "We have the letters, trackers and cameras here for you. It's four o'clock right now, so we'll give you two hours to prepare. And remember, don't let him know about us or who you are. The best thing to do if you see him is to take his picture without him knowing and leave." The group just stands there with surprise and shock painting their faces.

Each of us sets down a satchel on the table, containing what they need."So you should probably start preparing and warming up," I add, which gets them flying around from room to room like a bunch of buzzing bees. We see ourselves out and make our way home.

After we don our night gear, we run over the rooftops back to the group's hiding place just before sunset begins. It is five-fifty at night when they exit the cellar and split up into their designated groups. Only one group is clad in black night running clothes similar to ours; the other two are wearing civilian clothes. Well, so far so good. If anything, it'll be easier to track them whilst we are on the rooftops. Each of us have already chosen a different team to follow for the night. I'm with Cousin Harry's group.

It's a good thing Keagan and I agreed that Aspen shouldn't

take the team with Ghedi or Cousin Harry, since I know Aspen can be a bit swayed when it comes to judging. He and I agreed to make sure she watched over the most competent seeming team of the group, Isola and Anthony. They appear to be the leaders of the group by how they carry themselves. However, I didn't think that Keagan and Aspen would just as quickly make sure I wouldn't be in charge of watching Ghedi's group. I thought I had made it clear to Keagan that he should take the group with Cousin Harry, and yet I was blindsided by the scheming couple. Regardless, I'll be able to make up for lost time with Ghedi later, I hope.

Issac is wearing a butler's uniform as he follows close behind Harry and Andrea, who have hooked their arms around each other as if they were on a nightly stroll with their dimie slave. We specifically told them to also pick out the hotels that their team wants to check out, so that they all don't end up at the same ones with nobody monitoring the others. After failed attempts at both the Langham and the Grosvenor to give the fake letter to the front counter, the little trio begins to make their way back towards the bridges.

The Grosvenor Hotel is so close to Buckingham Palace that I can see it clearly from the rooftops. *I can only imagine how beautiful it must be inside.* I dream a little along the way as I follow the team, not back to their hideout but to the Charing Cross Hotel. They make their way inside, but go too far for me to keep an eye on them. After five minutes have passed, I decide that I need to get to a better level than the rooftops to see what's going on.

They already passed the check-in counter and are now somewhere in the hotel. But where could they go? Once I make it to the ground in a sparse alleyway behind the building, I lower my mask and wrap my cloak tightly around me to hide my clothes. After managing to keep my eyes on the building's doors whilst crossing the busy street, I make my way over to the window near another side street, lest I need to make a clean getaway. As I gaze into the building, my eyes finally catch who I'm looking for; except they're not working, but rather sitting in the lounge area conversing amongst themselves.

What's this? They can't be exhausted this soon. Minutes roll by and they don't seem to move from their spots; however, someone dangerously familiar to me does. The sight of him causes a chill to run up my spine, and I reach for my bladed fan. Governor Damon has just stepped off the lift with two other men, who part ways as soon as they exit. Strolling through the lounge area towards the front of the building, the governor catches the attention of the trio on the couches. Andrea promptly pulls out the tiny one-handed camera.

I hope for their sake that they're actually able to get a picture that shows his face. Andrea appears to be waiting for something to happen. And indeed, when the governor makes it to the front desk where he needs to turn, facing Andrea's direction, that's when she takes the chance and raises the metal strip up to her left eye, as a disk flips open to expose a camera lens but no light bulb to make the flash. Aspen made sure not to include that part, so they wouldn't blow their cover. Just as quickly as Andrea makes this move, the lens cover closes back up, and she replaces the camera in her hand-purse. I actually think that they're close enough to get a good photograph of him. They succeed wonderfully in their mission, and it seems like Governor Damon wasn't even the wiser. However, I now see that he's on his way to the revolving front doors himself in such a hurry that I just barely have time to leave.

What if he saw me? Or what if his men did and alerted him? I hear footsteps coming my way, and I grip my fan tightly. The governor passes right before me without so much as a backwards glance, donning his navy fur coat and blue feathered hat as he heads straight for the railroad gate connected to the hotel. The further away he goes, the more I can finally feel my lungs open again for air. I glance back inside the hotel and see that Cousin Harry is giving one of the phoney envelopes to the man at the front desk. He happily takes it and puts it into the air tube that shoots it straight up into Damon's room. Once the letter is gone, so am I. Going all the way around the building to the back, where I can make my way back up to the top of the hotel to spy on Damon, I notice that he's not at the station. I look back down at the street at the front of the hotels and see that my team is already on their way back to the checkpoint where they're to meet me. *I guess I can't follow Damon any longer.* I mull the idea over in my mind to keep following him, and ponder whether Aspen would approve of it or not. But then I think about the respect we are trying to earn from this group, and that punctuality and keeping promises is an important part of earning that respect. So, very begrudgingly, I make my way back across the rooftops to our meeting place in Hyde Park.

THE MAN OF THE HOUR

ASPEN

Isola and Anthony had already made their way to the Great Eastern Hotel with no luck after much persistence, even after Isola tried to dress as a maid and check the registry. That was such an act she and Anthony put on to get the desk clerk to leave his position that I must give them extra points for it. I do feel sorry for the bellhop boys Anthony nearly fought with; however, they must have been so confused when he accused them of fraternising with his wife.

I'm just glad I brought along a disguise for myself to wear under my cloak. They didn't even recognise me amongst the members in the crowd, though they've never seen me in my normal day clothes yet so I probably blended in quite well amongst the excitement, I think to myself whilst lifting my outer lightweight purple skirt and black day shirt over my head before replacing them back into my rucksack and exposing my black running clothes underneath. As I change, I keep my eye on my team as they talk to each other on a side street away from the Great Eastern Railway Hotel. *I know that they're supposed to go to the Charrings Cross Hotel, but perhaps they have already forgotten? That'll mean a point deduction if they get lost. Then again, perhaps they are coming up with an idea of what their next act should be?* Anthony suddenly hails a taxi carriage that takes them in the direction of Charrings Cross once they seat themselves inside.

Racing over the shadowed rooftops as the world below glows in a warm haze, I feel the rush of adrenaline running through my veins once again, a feeling I love so dearly. I've done these runs a hundred times by now in different villages and cities, and yet I've never followed someone by myself. It's odd to be watching a team work together alone when you're used to being a part of one. *I guess it just means that we all will need to be extra careful of where we're going and what we're doing tonight,* I think just as I my foot slips down the slanted metal roofing.

Must have hit a wet spot, but I can't stay down for long or I'll miss their carriage on the congested street. It takes us around twenty minutes to get to Charrings Cross, at the end where the train enters the station. Though my heart still pounds ready for more action, a small break is still nice to be had, I must admit. As my team exits the carriage and heads for the hotel's railway side entrance, lo and behold, right in front of them comes walking from the front of the building with a quick stride none other than Governor Damon himself. *That was far too easy to find him; there must be a catch to this.*

And yet he walks right past my team and straight to the station where a train is approaching. Once Damon passes my team, they almost immediately stop in their tracks and do a double-take at him. With one look at each other, they noncha-lantly turn around and stroll slowly back towards the end of the station where a few benches rest. By the time the train has stopped at the station completely and let out its steam brakes, my team has situated themselves on a bench not too far or too close to where the governor is waiting where he stands. *Just look at him in his navy fur coat and blue feathered tophat. I wonder who the poor dimie was who had to die to make that ensemble? Must say, blue suits him; it matches the colour of his blood.*

The train's few passengers begin to exit and make their way to the hotel, all while Governor Damon tips his hat and gives a nod to the gents and ladies who exit the train cars as he awaits his expectant passenger. The second they enter the doorway of the train's car, I can tell they're there for Damon. A man with a grease-stained brown suede coat with a gear-bezeled vest and a tophat with multifaceted goggles that shake around a bit, proving that they are for actual use and not a mere accessory.

Other than this bloke with a young chocolate-brown whiskery face, another man steps onto the platform who dons a black coat that appears to have been singed extensively at the right side. He also wears large spectacles on his slender face, looks to be about fifty, and appears to have been taking notes quite scatteredly, considering the number of papers sticking and drifting out of the notebook he clutches at his chest.

The moment they spot the governor, they rush over and join in a quick embrace, first with the man wearing the gear vest then the slim bloke with spectacles. *So the governor is importing inventors now. How interesting.* My team seems to be acting as if they are looking for someone to get off the train as well, but Isola is taking great care to take notes of everything on the side of the bench that cannot be seen from the governor's place whilst facing forward still. That takes skill right there, not to mention she actually knows how to write. That's quite rare for dimies. I wonder if the rest of their group taught her and possibly Issac how to write. Anthony, on the other hand, is sneaking pictures of Damon every now and then. Those will be good to examine later to see if Keagan or Uncle George possibly knows either of the inventors.

Damon talks to the baggage boy for a bit and then back to his guests for a short while, wrapping his arms around their shoulders as he continues to lead his friends to the front of the hotel. Isola and Anthony will need to be very careful in how they make their next move. My team waits ten seconds until the governor is already halfway back to the front of the hotel with the luggage boy in tow. They seem giddy by how they jump out of their seats to follow, but they quickly recompose themselves when they get to the corner of the building, where I lose sight of them.

By the time I make it back to the hotel itself, I see that the governor's group is entering a taxi carriage as my team is hailing one. The next thing I know, we are flying down past Waterloo and Black Friars bridges, eventually heading back down towards the Thames. *Where is Damon taking these men, the wharf?* When my team sees that the governor's car made it to the wharf area, they promptly pay the fare and run after the car that just turned the corner.

After passing a few of the waterfront warehouses, Damon's car finally stops. The governor and his friends walk a few steps towards the docks as their car remains in place. *He must have told his driver to keep the motor running. He won't be in this location for too long, then.* I crawl my way across the top of the warehouse roof, staying in pace with the men below. *Where is my team? Perhaps they're afraid of being seen by the driver.*

They pause for a quick moment with the inventors laughing for a second at a comment I can't hear clearly enough. *I hope Damon laughs himself to death one of these days.* I take a look back down the way and I can faintly see two figures hiding in the shadows just behind the view of the car. They press themselves against the brick wall of the building before the one I'm on. *Are they just waiting now?*

The men's voices fade away as the sound of rolling doors slide open and soon shut again with a resounding clank. *I see that my second targets have made their way inside the building; now if only I could look inside myself,* I think, making my way towards the waterfront of the building where four elevated glass skylights await me. It's normal for warehouses to have skylights, since it's a safety regulation and needed for proper ventilation in the summer months. But what is not normal is that little scanning robot. Multiple lights are strobing out in four directions from the centre of the roof between the windows. *Motion sensors? Is that really a good idea with all the birds and cats that make their way up here day and night?*

I make it to the floor of the rooftop and crawl my way over to the first window I can peer into, careful not to catch the sensors. Damon is there, all right, and so are half a dozen worktables of partially created inventions. One is the body of a mechanical four-legged animal around the size of a large dog who is currently being worked on by two inventors.

Okay, how can I use this to my advantage? Do I have a camera on me? Please tell me I have a camera. I move away from the window and look inside my hip bag for my extra toys. *Flame whistle? No, not yet. Fly on the wall? That could be useful. Spyder…perfect. And I do believe that I put a recorder in it also.* I crawl back over to the window and see that Damon and his new inventor friends are over at a lamp-lit desk going over some blueprints. I take this time to look at the hinges on the window; they are all rusty and will surely be loud if I try to open it.

I look through the window once more and see that a few

men are taking a large piece of metal to the table saw. Another man is going to the hammering table with a dented metal panel. Now is my chance. I wait for the men to start hammering and sawing and quickly open the window, which was louder than I expected, even with all the sound below. After propping it open, I wind up the amount of feet my little spyder needs to go before it should descend. It has six metres of wire thread on its strand, but I'll wind it up for only ten feet since I don't want it to be seen.

I place it atop one of the beams on the ceiling—which it quickly walks along for three metres, until its back legs extend to the edge of the beam and latch tightly around the metal. Going over the side slowly, it lowers down on its thread and opens its spinnerette. Exposing a camera lens, it takes five pictures of the room, each time spinning ninety degrees and taking one picture from the front of its head. The men notice nothing out of the ordinary and go on with their work. I know my spyder is finished taking pictures when it begins winding itself back up to the beam. So far, so good; it's a shame I didn't get a good recording out of this one, since it's so loud. Still, at least we have these pictures.

But by the time my spyder comes back to me, I'm looking around on the ground floor with my magnifying and binocular goggles. I see that the work table is bare and there is no one around it now. I close up my spyder and put it back in my pouch before searching the floor again for Damon. I see his two inventor friends talking to the man working on the animal machine whilst holding up the blueprints from earlier. But Damon is not around. However, I do hear the doors to the building begin to roll out. *He's leaving!* I prepare to close the window and wait for the loud clank to do so.

With the window shut, I crawl away and back to the top of

the metal roof to see that Damon's car is already going down the street by the flash of its headlights on the buildings. He couldn't have gotten back in his car that fast. Someone else must have entered the building, then. I look over to the corner of where my team was, and see them running at top speed back in the direction of our meeting area.

Now I feel so torn. I have an aching desire to follow Damon and find out where else he is going. But at the same time, I can't be late to meet our new possible team members. We already know two important locations of his whereabouts just from tonight. *But what if there's more?* The fatigue in my back and legs tell me that it's enough for one night, but my mind races with the possibility that there could be more he's hiding from us. Something important that I could find out tonight if only I followed him.

I curse myself with every step I take, walking in the festival gardens towards St Paul's Cathedral. Maybe I should go in for Confession—Lord knows I've done more than my share of dirty deeds, not to mention all the curses I just threw at myself and Damon. However, it would take all night to list all the sins I've committed in recent months. *Forgive me, Father, for I have stolen a city's worth of slaves and set them free, but it took a massacre to do so.* Bet the priest never heard that one before.

Putting up my hood, I crouch down and sit on the steps, wrapping the sides of my cloak around myself and trying to appear as much a vagabond as possible. After waiting just a minute, footsteps begin to approach the stairs. I hope it's not a cop telling me I should leave the grounds.

"Forgive us, sister, but we've succeeded," a male voice says that I can only place as Anthony. I look up slightly and see Isola's smiling face at my level as she crouches down. I return the smile and stand straight up before taking a slow walk with them.

"I take it that things went well tonight?" I say, keeping my mask on and my hood.

"Yes, it was so thrilling to be apart of a real espio—"

"Hush!" I command, placing a finger to my mouth. "You never know who's listening. Now did you take notes and bring back everything?" I quiet Isola.

"Yes, we have everything detailed, photographed, and then some," Anthony says proudly as he hands over the pouch. I flip it open and see that everything wc gave them is all there. I nod my head in approval and latch it onto my belt.

"So what happens now?" Isola asks eagerly before blowing a steamed breath on her paws.

"Now you wait. My team and I will go over your notes and photos as a whole to determine if we can work with you. You might know sooner, but give us two days starting in the morning to get back to you."

"All right, fair enough. So this is it for the night then, Miss?"

"Yes, I believe that you've done more than your share for the night."

"Sounds good to me. Goodnight, Miss, we look forward to hearing back from you."

"Goodnight. Also, I loved the bit when you nearly decked the bellhop, by the way—you were really in character!" I say before walking quickly to the corner of the cathedral.

"Oh, thank you—but wait," Anthony says, looking baffled right as I give them a knowing grin before disappearing around the corner. I only hope that the rest of the teams did half as well as mine did, and stayed on their best behaviour. Well, as long as they weren't needing to act, that is.

"Eight o'clock, Aspen's team arrives at Charing Cross Hotel and spots Damon heading to the railway; they follow inconspicuously. Eight-fifteen, Isola's group sees Damon meet two men at the Charing Cross railway station." As Keagan details the inventor's descriptions to a tee, I take everyone's gear belts and bring them to the trunk we store them in. Lori brings over everyone's boots, and once everything is situated we put the false bottom back on.

"Leaving the station by car at eight-thirty, Aspen's group follows Damon and company in their car for twenty minutes by carriage to the wharf near Queens Street. The governor's car is parked, and they walk into a warehouse at eight fifty-two. They do not follow any further and wait outside, due to the chance of being seen by the driver of the car. They wait twenty-two minutes before only Damon leaves the warehouse and drives away. Aspen's team then runs to the meeting location in the festival gardens at St Paul's Cathedral and meets her at nine-thirteen. Does all that check out, Aspen?"

"It does indeed. And I give them five points for tonight."

"Wow, and I thought I was being generous," Lori says.

"Yeah, well, I get ten from all the pictures I took inside the warehouse," I say proudly.

"You didn't," Keagan says with surprise in his eyes.

"Yes. And this little guy was my partner in crime tonight," I say, pulling out my spyder. Lori still looks uncomfortable around it, however, so I place it on the table next to the pouches of cameras and notes that were used tonight.

"Brilliant as always, Aspen. And no one noticed?"

"Not one; they were making too much noise when it all happened to hear or focus on anything else, anyway. So what about your team, Keagan? We haven't heard about your adventure tonight."

"Oh, it wasn't all that exciting. Ghedi and Samuel checked out four of the six hotels, including the Langham, the Great Northern, Midland and the Great Eastern, from the time of seven to eight forty to no avail. However, whilst they were on their way to the Charing Cross from the Great Eastern Hotel, they noticed Damon go into a pub called the Viaduct Tavern. At nine twenty, they entered the pub and saw him at the bar, so they sat one seat away from him and ordered themselves a pint. They tried to listen in on the conversation that Damon was having with the bartender, but didn't hear much since the pub was rather popular and rowdy that night.

"However, they did manage to snap a picture of him talking to the pub owner. The governor had his drink and left the pub at nine forty. When he left, the boys tried to talk to the owner and get information, but the owner acted like he was a random visitor who just wanted to chat a bit. Their notes say here that 'That man has been here twice since he's come to town; he's not exactly a frequent visitor. But he sure likes a good conversation, which is why he comes here, I think'."

"If you ask me, Damon is probably just spouting off to anyone he can about his meeting with Her Majesty, including pub owners. So besides the picture they took, they received no other information about the governor; however, they completed the mission and found their target. I give them one point since that picture was all they have. And they were late to the meeting point."

"All right, so on our scale of one to fifteen, they scored a nine. That's not great, but that's not bad either," Lori says.

"And they did exactly as they were told. Some people could use more work than others, like Samuel and Ghedi, but for the most part they passed," I say.

"And we now know that Damon resides at Charing Cross Hotel. It really is the perfect place for him to stay at, you know. It's right next to Scotland Yard, it has its own railway station, it's next to the waterfront, and Buckingham Palace is nearby, whilst staying in an upper-class part of London. It truly is the perfect place for him if he wishes to feel protected and to have all his eggs in one basket," Keagan details.

"All of us were close to him tonight; we could have gotten him three times tonight, you know?"

"I didn't think that was in our job description," Keagan says, looking at me, slightly concerned.

"It's not, but for someone who could be as big a problem and danger as Damon, well, the *don't kill unless necessary* rule of ours may be required." I wait for their objections, but there aren't any. When I turn my head to look at everyone's faces, I see that everyone except Thomas has a questioning gaze. "It's just a thought. Doesn't mean I want to go through with it, though," I add to ease the silence in the room.

"So what are the next steps?" Thomas asks, curiosity in his eyes as always.

"Now, if we are all in agreement, we will develop the film they supplied us, along with mine, and then decide if we want to work with them. Are we in agreement?"

"Agreed. And what about this warehouse that Damon has all of his inventors at? Don't you think that it would be the perfect place to hold Thatcher? I bet he's in a cage somewhere for sure. Sometimes these places have basements, so he could easily be stored there," Keagan ponders aloud.

"That sounds probable. How about we go and check it out late tomorrow night? I know of two openings and exits already. We could easily make do, and at two or three in the morning they'll probably be going back to sleep."

"Time never stopped you when you were inventing, Aspen. What makes you think it'll stop them?" Lori laughs.

"True, but if they're working for Damon, they could easily have a curfew. I mean, anyone seen walking on the streets or in a carriage at three or four in the morning is seen as suspicious by Scotland Yard anyhow," Keagan adds.

"Even if we get there and one of the inventors is still working, we could easily dart him and it'll look like he fell asleep at his desk. I've done it enough times to know it's normal every now and then."

"Oh yes, I remember that night vividly when I found you asleep at your desk." Keagan smiles at me wolfishly as the fire paints him in a shade of red. A chill runs down my spine from the low tone of his voice as a blush warms my face. I shake it away before I can remember anymore from that night.

I look away; my eyes meet Lori's who has the same grin as Keagan. *I swear, those two are impossible.*

"But I'm up for it. If anything, we can see the warehouse for ourselves and get a good feel for the place," I say.

"Then it's set. Tonight and tomorrow we develop the film, tomorrow night we go to the warehouse and be ready to possibly find Thatcher, and then the next day we give the group our decision. Agreed?" Keagan says.

"Agreed!" Thomas, Lori and I respond in unison.

A GOOSE CHASE TO A RAT RACE

KEAGAN

We race each other to the warehouse on the other side of Black Friars Bridge. By the time we get there, it's around three thirty in the morning and I feel a long yawn coming on despite the run over here. Manoeuvring around the motion sensors awkwardly, we each find a place near the skylights. Just as I was afraid of, there is an inventor still at his station. After further inspection when we peer in from the dirty overhead windows, we see that he is cleaning up his station.

Sure enough, after sweeping up a few metal bits here and there from the floor, and putting away his small tools and wire, he turns out the light and leaves the warehouse through the tall sliding metal doors. Waiting a few moments longer, we hear the sounds of his light footsteps fading away in the night. The only lights we see are the moon and an emergency lamp that hangs by the doors the inventor just left through. Taking a chance, we move to the window Aspen points to and give it a good oiling before prying it wide open. However, even with the oil, it emits a long grinding noise. After waiting a few seconds to see if anyone comes around, we anchor onto the roof ledge one by one and slip down the rope into the dark building. The second we make it to the floor, we can see that there is a set of two small doors as well as large rolling doors located on the sides of the wooden wall that was at our back as we were coming in. Aspen points to the doors and then to our ears individually. Each of us takes a door to listen in on; I take the largest set in the middle. There are no sets of handles on this side, though the only way to know if it's locked shut would be to try and open it or stick my sword through the slit opening. We crouch by our doors in silence, trying to hear something—anything—to warn us of an incoming interference. After hearing a slight shuffle and the sound of metal clanking gently against itself, I get on my hands and knees and try my best to peer through the small gap. The floor appears to be lit by a pale light—moonlight, perhaps? I hear the sound of rattling chains once more, except this time I hear a grunt along with it. *Thatcher? Other dimies, perhaps?* My heart begins to pound with anticipation. *We have to get in there!*

I signal to where Aspen was, but looking around, I see she is now over at the desks looking over plans and ruffling through drawers like a cat burglar. When I finally get her and Lori to look my way, I stretch one arm to each lady and give them a thumbs-up. They rush over to my spot in the blink of an eye. I point to the ground and they in turn peek under the door like I had done earlier. I look behind us and see the eerie silhouettes of the metal skeletons and parts of machines lying on the tables in the dull lamp light. Just then I hear a loud clang, and the girls look at the front sliding doors with fear plastered on their faces. It's starting to jostle like someone else is unlocking it or trying to break in. Unsheathing my sword, I stick it through the sliver of an opening between our doors and thrust it upward. Just as I thought, it was locked, a wooden board that was easily thrown off. We rush ourselves inside with a heavy push on the left door before quickly closing it back behind us and replacing the wooden bar. Just as we do, we hear the main door to the inventors room roll open and footsteps shuffle in. *We must make haste.*

The tall and long tunnel-like room we are in has a vast amount of windows high on the walls that allow ample amounts of moonlight in, enabling us to see rather clearly what looks to be a horse stable. The clatter of chains comes from one of the stalls farther down the row. As we rush ourselves over, I smile under my mask, despite the high chance that we'll get caught and have to fight our way out. We look into each barred shadowy stall till we finally find it. The one stall in the whole room with a resident.

Unbolting the door, we make our way inside. Since the moonlight is on this side of the building coming in, there's an angle of shadow that the left side is cast under. We can see a form on the ground where the chains reach into the darkness and around their wrists. From the size of the shrunken form in the corner, I can tell that Thatcher has lost so much weight he's practically half his normal size.

"Hey, wake up, Thatcher, it's time to go now," Aspen whispers as we near him.

"Hmmm?" comes a confused voice, but it's not his. Thatcher has a deep baritone voice, not a feminine high-pitched one. All of us stop in our tracks; Aspen's hand, about to go into the shadows, jolts back to her side. Before I can touch my tinder box on my gauntlet, Lori has beat me to it with a sharp scratch and a burst of warm light. We can see the face of the shackled dimie we assumed was our lost friend.

We couldn't have been more wrong.

"Gertrude!" Aspen and I hiss out. I have half a mind to kill her where she lays, but by the looks of her, she is already a few steps from death. Bloody, fur-rumpled and stained with mud and lashes, she has nothing but rags to modestly cover herself . She looks drained as she squints at us from the bright match we push towards her. Taking a second for her eyes to adjust, they quickly gain a look of recognition in their filmy state. "You...you three came here?"

"What happened, Gertrude? Weren't you working with Damon and Charles?"

"*Was*. It was a double-cross from the beginning. Charles and Damon made a deal that they would be the only ones to see their plan through, since they are human; no Dimie could walk free, even if they helped them with their plans. My current state is the proof of it. Did you like my note about your friend?" Her voice cracks.

"So that was you who gave it to me in the street? You can surely run fast, I'll give you that," Lori says.

"Not fast enough. I gave that note to you because I had overheard the night before what they were planning on doing to both him and me. I was scared and tried to get away, and when I saw you in the crowd I had to let you know. But I was caught by one of his watchmen out in the crowd that day," she explains so quietly we crane our mask-covered ears forward so as not to miss one syllable.

"What are they planning? Where is Thatcher?"

"Skinning us. Now free me, then I'll talk more about Thatcher." Her voice raises a bit.

"Answer us first. Do you know where he is or not?" Aspen demands, holding up a pick lock in front of Gertrude's face.

"Get me out of here. Then you'll get Thatcher. You four will be as happy as ever if you just get me out of here," she cries with her eyes shut and her teeth bared. *She doesn't know where he is; she just wants out. What did they put her through to warrant this attitude from her?* The three of us exchange looks, an understanding passing between us. We have failed.

Now we have to decide to let this Judas of a dimie go or be left to die. I never thought I'd have to partake in a death trial for a dimie. I look from Aspen to Lori and neither of them seem to know what to do. We took an oath to help save dimies and free them from human oppression. This situation is running up that alley and yet we hesitate; but to be honest, after what she's done to us and her own race, I can't blame us. I know we're all thinking it, that this is a very selfish dimie who only looks after herself. I guess the saying is true, like master like slave. Since dimies are able to connect and read people through their eyes, they create stronger instant connections most of the time when they're being picked out and bought by their owners. Guess she and Damon must have had quite a connection when they first met.

"Help, please, help me." Her voice cracks with each word as she looks at us like she hadn't betrayed us not a month before. I can't believe the audacity of this monkey dimie. Is she truly this shameless to ask help from us after what she did?

"What are we going to do?" Lori asks Aspen finally, since none of us have really made any moves. But before she can answer, we hear voices from behind the large doors get louder as if they were right outside.

"Answer me right now. Do you know where Thatcher is or don't you?"

"Get me out of here!" Gertrude pops off, reaching for the pick locks, causing yet more of a commotion that will surely get the guards' attention. Not a moment later do we begin to hear the wood block sliding away from the bars. We look at Aspen with her eyes shut painfully tight and her brow furrowed. "Damit," she whispers as she takes her pick locks and works on Gertrude's shackles.

"Hurry, the guards will be here any moment," she snaps.

"You have no right to give orders right now," I say coldly, which causes her head to lower in shame. We all get to work on the restraints, and soon there is only one left. A loud click resounds through the stable, but it's not from the shackles. Aspen unlocks Gertrude's final lock and practically throws her at me. Aspen grabs hold of Lori and leads us out of the stall just as the doors on either side of the room begin to open. No doubt about it, they see us. But not for long. Each of us throws down a smoke bomb, one in the center and one for each side of the room. There are two pairs of rough-looking men coming our way through the smoke with the doors open. I half-run, half-carry Gertrude as we rush to the opposite side of the stalls through the smoke in a line, then to the opening as the roars from the confused men in the mist ring out through the whole warehouse.

The window we came through is still open, but it might take too much time to get up there one by one. Lori and Aspen grab hold of one another and shoot straight up. The second they make it over, I shoot up my grappling hook and tighten my grip on Gertrude, who is squealing as she looks behind us. I hear the calls of furious men coming closer through the clearing smoke. *They must see us.* Just as my feet lift off the ground I can hear a man yelling out as he runs towards me. I look down just in time to see a dark figure jump up at me while I am now halfway to the ceiling.

His fingertips just graze my boots, but make solid contact with Gertrude. With the weight of his body and hers,

Gertrude screams as she is swiftly yanked from my arms. As they fall, I reach back out to her in vain as they plummet to the ground. When they hit the hard floor she is atop the man, but the impact seems to have been too much for her. She appears to have fainted. Making it to the top, the girls are there to pull me over the rest of the way just before we run away from the open window, not bothering to dodge the motion detectors. How could we fail her a second time? *Even after everything that's happened.*

We run across London, far away from the river and the warehouses, for quite some time, till we find ourselves out of breath on a random rooftop with green metal slanted sides that curve where the windows were built in. "I guess we can rule out the warehouse now, can't we?" Lori says, taking her mask off as she slumps down on the gravel of the rooftop. The light from the streets shines up around the buildings in great beams of warm light as the sounds of the busy night and its Londoner inhabitants bustle about below. I wish they could all just shut up for once. All this noise is maddening to me right now.

"Well, this is a fine mess we've stumbled into, isn't it?" Aspen says, just before I start to spout off in a fit of anger.

"The guards have seen us. We couldn't find Thatcher, but instead found that yellow-bellied two-faced dimie, who we still couldn't save! And now Damon will know for certain that we're not dead, so he'll probably go hunting for us like he did in Currlion. I mean, I ask you, what else could go wrong?" I end my tirade and take a breath, waiting for a response from one of them. But the girls aren't looking at me anymore;

instead they've turned stark white as they stare with wide eyes at something behind me. I follow their gaze, turning my head to see what has stolen their attention—and I wish I hadn't. I find myself looking back at a metal man with glowing hellfire red eyes that dilate the second they focus on me. Rust patches cover his shoulders, elbows and knees. He looks like something out of a nightmare, with his claw-like hands dripping wet with a dark liquid silhouetted by the moonlight.

He's just as he was described in the rumours. Jack the Riveter. Brandishing my sword, he raises both arms to block, and when our metal connects, he immediately pushes me off of him with power I was unprepared for. I grunt at the force as my head whips back. *He's much stronger than a human.* I feel a push off my back, and I turn to see Aspen, who apparently used me as a lift to roundhouse Jack in the neck, knocking him off balance a tad before Lori does the exact same move, using me as a springboard once again. *I need to talk to them about that later.*

However, this time Lori's foot doesn't knock him down. Jack turns his head sharply to the right where Lori is coming towards him and catches her foot. He uses her momentum against her as he swings her in a half-circle, then flings her behind him. She tucks and tumbles over the rough roof before trying to get back up. Aspen and I both advance on him the moment he lets Lori go, but he projects two long blades from his arms, and his torso begins to spin around like a top before stopping and spinning back in reverse. Aspen and I jump back as fast as we possibly can from his deadly move. Leaving me to the side, he begins to go after Aspen, chasing so fast after her over the roof that she doesn't have time to prepare an attack. I have to act fast. *Think. What would slow him down or possibly...tangle him up?* Climbing to the top of a chimney, I think as I pull out my grappling hook. *Please God, let this work.*

"Bring him back over here quickly!" I yell at Aspen, and she manages to duck down just in time to miss his blades as she starts running back towards me. Waiting for them to be in better range, I prepare and aim my grapple launcher. Just as they begin to pass my perch, Jack stops spinning in one direction, and I see my opening. I shoot out the grapple, and it manages to catch his arm as he begins to spin the other way. *The grapple has a strong yet long wire cord, but if I stop it as he's partly wrapped—* Finishing my thought, I do just that right as I jump behind the chimney I was perched on, which pulls the tangled Jack straight into the wall with a clank. The chimney shakes and a puff of ash even comes out from the top.

I peek around the corner as the girls come running towards Jack with their weapons and arms raised to beat him down. And yet in a flash, he kicks off the wall and spins in the air, managing to untangle himself from my hook. Aspen tosses a metal box at him that explodes out into a net. Wrapping around him, the metal squares meet behind him, and the net constricts around his torso. Small sparks of electricity spark out here and there. *Aspen, what kind of weapon have you made?*

But the net doesn't seem to have any effect on Jack; in a mere moment he frees himself midair and lands flawlessly, jumping forward with his arms out straight into Aspen and Lori. Knocking down the girls in one blow, they hit the metal roof hard with their heads. Racing back out towards them from behind the chimney, I grip my arms around his cold metal body and tackle him away from the girls, but he quickly begins to struggle and tries to cut my arms with his bladed fingers. Grabbing hold of the blades, we slide farther down the edge of the green roof till something catches my foot. I can feel the wind from below blow up through the hairs on the back of my head.

We almost fell off the building, though the battle isn't over yet. I hold Jack's arms away from me as best I can, but he is stronger than I. He retracts his long blades into his palm to my surprise. But what he flips out as a replacement is even more terrifying, a spinning saw blade that comes closer and closer to my neck no matter how hard I try to push it away. Just then, the window next to us opens with a squeak and a Victrola begins to play jazz music. Jack's saw blade stops where it is, and his body goes rigid. I look straight into his glowing red eyes in confusion to see that they're slowly dimming. Then his entire being falls atop me, limp as old lettuce.

Still holding up his lifeless arms, I look over his head that feels like a bowling ball on my chest to see two battered girls holding my and Jack's legs from the top of the slanted roof. Aspen and Lori are shaking and appear to be holding us up with every ounce of strength they have. Trying to sit up with the heavy metal man still atop me, I see that Aspen is holding onto Jack, and Lori is holding onto me.

"All right, Keagan, slowly take Jack away from you, and then reach up as best you can. We'll get you over first and then him. Lori, do you have a good grip?"

"Like iron," she says through gritted teeth.

I do as instructed and reach up as best I can towards their hands. Holding onto my ankles, Lori lets go of one and reaches forward to meet my hand halfway, giving me the leverage to pull myself back to safety before the three of us carry Jack the Riveter to the flattened roof, so Aspen can inspect him further. But right as we are almost to the flat-topped roof, I hear a humming start up. We all pause and, as I look at the girls, Lori looks back at me in bewilderment. However, Aspen is the first to realise where it's coming from, as she stares down with a furrowed brow at the metal man we're carrying.

"His eyes are glowing again. Why are they glowing again?"

"He's turning back on!" I say.

"I know that, but why?"

"What made him turn off the first time?" Lori asks, making me go back to that heart-stopping moment of when my neck was almost cut off. The windows had opened, the music had begun to play, and he froze. Nothing else was different from before, other than the music.

"Music. He needs jazz music, quickly." I pull Jack, Aspen and Lori back towards the window that was playing the record.

"What?" they reply in unison.

"The jazz music made him turn off, I'm sure of it. He stopped trying to kill me when the music started playing."

"How can I get a good look at him on such a slanted rooftop?" Aspen argues.

"It's better than fighting him again and trying to do it that way."

"Fair enough," she says as Jack begins to move his arms around as if he were slowly warming up, though the closer we approach the open window, the less he struggles. Finally, after strapping ourselves to the wires of our grappling hooks that are secured to the top of the angled roof, we are able to sit right next to the window as before, this time however with Lori and myself at the base of the roof's ledge, holding up Jack and Aspen as she begins to inspect him further. Just as before, Jack's glowing eyes slowly dim till there is nothing.

"I guess music soothes more than just wild beasts, aye," I say.

"Indeed, and thank heavens it works. We like you better with your head on your shoulders," Aspen says, prying at his chest.

"You and me both," I grunt, as Aspen manages to open one side of Jack's head plate. Inside is a glowing blue trail of vein-like wires linked to two red bulbs. "So how do we turn him off safely?" I ask, rubbing my neck as I think again to what might happen if he were to wake up once more.

"Well, if he had an obvious switch or some wiring that led to this area in his skull, it'd be easier to do so. But this is a lot more advanced than I'm used to. It's no wonder whoever made him couldn't control him either," Aspen explains, pointing to his solid metal neck without one unnecessary wire showing that could easily be cut.

"What if it's in his chest instead?" I offer.

"What do you mean?" Lori says.

"Where he stores his energy. What if it's in his chest like how our hearts re-aerate blood?"

"Yet more brilliance; I was wondering the same thing," Aspen says, making me feel smart as she unbolts and pries open part of the bot's chest. And there, glowing before us, is a blue humming heart pulsating with sparks of energy.

"This is incredible, really," Aspen gasps. "He seems to have a regenerative fuel source through a reusable method. When triggered by jazz music, he falls asleep and begins to recharge through the stored energy he produced through the previous day and night's movement. It's essentially power through kinesis, which makes it no wonder he's able to keep going like he does. But when the music ends, he must power up again. He's definitely in need of a good oil job, though; he's been stalking far too much in the rain. Just look at these rust marks!" Aspen bickers like a mother to their child coming inside after playing in the mud.

She takes a long while to look over Jack's chest, neck, head and inner workings before she speaks up again. "If we try to disconnect any part that transfers energy to the different parts of his body, we'll most likely be electrocuted. So breaking the heart and clamping off the valves are out of the question, because that stored power is still being made, it seems. They designed him to work very closely to how humans work. It's incredible! Maybe if I can keep the energy valve that goes to his skull cut off, as well as making the trigger to turn him on inert, then we can take him with us."

"Take him with us? Why would we do that?" Lori asks, dumbfounded, and from the pressure in her voice I can tell that she's struggling to hold both the robot and her sister up on the slanted roof, despite having help with the cord attached to her.

I try to push on Jack more to help her out as Aspen goes on. "We could use him for trade or a peace offering. For the time being, we can store him in the cellar and keep him sedated with jazz music."

Aspen works fast, since we don't have a clue how long the tenants below us plan on keeping their phonograph playing. Pulling out pliers and a clamp, she works on an area obstructed from me by Jack's chest plate. "There, this should hold him safely enough until we get back to Uncle George. Perhaps he'll know of a better way to neutralise him if he deems this clamp to be unfit."

"Are you sure it'll be okay to take him away from the music?" Lori asks with an uncertain quiver in her voice.

"True," I add. "I mean, are you sure it'll work and we'll be safe transporting him back?" But right as I ask my question, the record reaches the end of its track, and we hear the windows below us click shut. Our attention goes to the direction of the once-opened windows, to each other, then to Jack. Waiting in anticipation to see if his eyes are about to turn red again, I prepare myself to crash open those windows if it means turning the music back on. We don't need to go through another fight like that tonight.

Every second that ticks by holds three heartbeats of mine in it, but the longer the seconds last, the more we can breathe and relax. Jack isn't waking up; his eyes stay unlit and his heavy metal body stays limp.

"All right, now, how are we going to get him home?"

Tied up in one of the wires of our extra grappling hooks, his limbs are strapped to his body as securely as we could make it. For us that was the easy part. Then there was the hour-and-a-half-long journey of getting him from building to building, having to jump in unison, and walking alongside one another since not one of us could carry him alone. I somewhat wish this could have been the test we gave to the new gang members, handing them the heavy work and leaving the espionage stuff to us. After all, us three individuals collected more information than they did as seven people in three groups. *Although they probably would have died if they had to fight Jack.*

By the time we make it to Uncle George's house and clammer down the stairs from the roof, Uncle George, Thomas and Pauline are at our sides helping us get Jack to George's lab. Strapped down to his work table, Uncle George, Thomas and Aspen all scrutinise the inner and outer workings of the robot as they sit on stools. Pauline accommodates us as we sit in the lounge chairs by the tiny fireplace, providing us foot basins with hot water to soothe our howling feet. We also make sure that a record is being played. Uncle George has made an extendable and flexible pavilion horn on the Victrola, extending seven feet and arching right over their heads above them and Jack.

"Aspen, come here, you should rest for a bit," Lori says. "At least soak your feet—they need it after tonight."

"Your sister is right, you know." I groan with my head leaned back and eyes closed.

"I will, trust me. We're just trying to see if I properly neutralised Jack."

"Aspen, what were you looking for in those drawers in the warehouse, anyway?" I ponder.

"I was looking in vain for my stolen journal. But I did skim a few pages that talked about a scheduled shipment to France. It didn't detail what it was, but I can guess it's more furs and pelts of the dimies."

"That's not good. That means he's expanding business at such a rapid rate it's now outside of the empire," I muse more to myself than Aspen. She groans before Uncle George diverts the conversation back to Jack.

"So, jazz music is 'soothing' to him in the sense that it switches on his sleep cycle. That must be why he stopped fighting when he did," Uncle George surmises, fixating his goggles on his face.

"That's right."

"Why would the queen want something like this?" Thomas holds up a rusty elbow. I get an uneasy feeling with Thomas holding his arm up, a vision of a knife at his throat held by that arm passing across my vision.

"He's a robot that was going to be used for war, similar to the dimie bots you're acquainted with back in Currlion. However, the inventors that made him didn't get the wiring right in his head, and they said that he became a rabid robot, killing at random. He even killed two of the three inventors who originally designed him. Now there's only one left that is in protective holding until Jack is found and can be destroyed by him alone. Bravo, children, you've made a very significant catch with this one," Uncle George commends us over the music. "However, I think we'll need to make some changes. It appears that if the clamp is administered for too long, there could be a build-up of energy when he's in sleep cycle. My theory is that if it builds up for too long and not released, he could become a bomb himself. If he manages to wake up with all that stored energy, he could be more dangerous than you can imagine, even more than tonight, I wager."

"That's hard to believe, considering how close we were to death during our fight."

"Actually, Timothy has seen Jack fight at full power. By his description, it makes your battle with him sound as if he was just toying around with you. He must've been at the last bits of his remaining energy from his last sleep cycle. Good Lord, when was the last time this thing was oiled?" He goes on as the clicks and metal clanging sounds of tinkering become synchronised with the jazz music. If it weren't for the tinkering noises, that music would put me right to sleep. A zap resonates through the room, causing me to jolt, and my vision blurs from light to dark. The spinning saw blade passes by my peripheral vision, but when I look around, Jack is still on the worktable.

"Aspen said the same thing."

"I did," Aspen confirms Lori's statement as I clench and unclench my fists.

"But to think that we fought him on low fuel makes me feel quite sorry for the poor blokes in the weapons division and royal military who were sent to try and catch him," Aspen continues, as the sight of Jack throwing the girls to the ground appears in front of me.

"Aye, those men were found in pieces. Terrible slaughter, it was. The only men able to speak could only identify who he was and how he attacked before they succumbed to their injuries."

At this, I see Jack's blades swinging again at Aspen, growing dangerously close. A tremor of fear rushes through my heart and lungs, making me jerk back. I shake my head, trying to clear it, praying my vision goes back to normal. But at the sound of a saw, I see Aspen leaping across my line of sight, sprinting as Jack the Riveter chases her across the roof, reaching closer and closer towards her exposed marred back. The whirring of his movements is deafening in my ears. He's about to grab her, but she's laying on her belly now, several long bleeding cuts covering her skin. On a shoreline, Jack is over her, raising his blades once more. My vision is blinded once again. *No, I can't take this.*

"No, Aspen. No. You cannot die like Winona!"

"Keagan!" someone shouts.

I'm back in George's lab, white-knuckle gripping the arms on the lounge chair I'm half-sitting half-crouching on. I look around and see everyone in the room staring at me with concerned expressions, even Uncle George. I can't seem to get my breathing under control as I feel the beads of sweat drip down my back. My hair hangs slightly over my left eye, now obstructing my vision of everyone.

"Are you all right, son? Be honest now," he asks me, starting to get off of his seat.

"I will be. Don't trouble yourselves. Just make sure that thing is secure. I just think I need some water." I point to the pitcher with a trembling hand.

"Here you go, dear. Now please lay back and calm yourself. You're safe here," Pauline reassures me as she hands me a cold cup of water. I try to lay back as everyone slowly goes back to what they were doing before I interrupted them, though I can still feel eyes on me from every corner of the room. *I'm safe here. So why don't I feel safe?*

SIDEKICKS

ASPEN

Just as we agreed, we are meeting back up with the gang, as we have come to call them, or as I like to say, our side-kicks. Tonight we are visiting them in their safehouse to discuss their roles in our operation. This time, though, we decided that Thomas won't come along, in case these people aren't who they say they are and try to double-cross us. We don't need him getting involved or hurt in a serious fight like that yet, despite how much better he's gotten at fighting during our training sessions.

Luckily for us, I supplied us with a new invention Uncle George and I perfected just last night. I'm so anxious to use it that I almost wish these people were double-crossers so I could use it on them. Regardless, we are planning on assessing their fighting abilities today, so I can use it on them anyway. I just hope that there's more metal around their cellar space than I remember.

Letting ourselves into the basement cellar of the winery, we walk through the rows of huge wooden kegs, as the sharp aroma of young wine fills our senses. The area is dimly lit only by the small blurred windows near the ceiling, giving the damp cellar an cave-like essence. Walking to the very back corner where the large empty wine keg sits, I glance back at Keagan and Lori. They give me a nod, letting me know they have their weapons hidden but at the ready if an ambush were to happen, just as I do. Rapping the door barrel lid of the keg, we lay in wait for a response. A few seconds later, we hear the echoes of voices and a door opening to footsteps right behind the barrel lid in front of me.

The lid creaks as it swings outward at first, then silently as it opens up wide to three familiar faces: Isola, Cousin Harry and Ghedi. We greet each other warmly and duck through the keg and into the doorway to their hideout. The entire group is there, waiting expectantly as they stand about the main room.

"Glad to see everyone could make it out today," I tell them.

"It's a pleasure, Miss Wolfe," Isola says at my side, and I regard her with a smile.

"Well, let's get down to it; you all passed the first phase of the test, though you still need to work on a few things."

"You're not joshing us? We're in?" Samuel asks.

"Yes, and we also have a job for you already," Keagan says, to which a small celebration erupts before us with everyone talking to each other.

"What is it we'll be doing? A heist? A raid of the dimies through the city?" Ghedi walks closer towards Samuel and rests his arm on his shoulder.

"What we need for you to do is keep a constant eye on Damon, as well as keep tabs on his whereabouts. If you can get the names of the people he sees, that would be wonderful, and we'll handle the research from there."

"Oh...yeah, I think we can do that." Samuel scratches his head.

"I should hope so. What you need to do is have one person per day be given the job of watching him, and if you need to take a half-day and switch out with someone, that's fine, but always keep a disguise with you. And make sure it's a different person each day. Since there are seven of you, you can each pick a day of the week to watch him."

"But what if we have day jobs?" Andrea looks rather worried. I now remember that she mentioned during our first meeting that she was a midwife and nurse to one of the local hospitals.

"Like I said, you can take shifts in the day. But for your case, Andrea, we would like you to care for the dimies, along with mending our injuries," Keagan replies.

"So does that mean I'm excused from keeping an eye on Governor Damon, Miss Wolfe?" Andrea looks at me.

"Only when we have dimies here for you to care for will you be taken off that job. Until then, we need all of you to help, understand?"

There came a series of yeses and yes ma'ams. Keagan picked it up from there. "As far as missions go, we'll be choosing who'll come with us and who'll stand by for help when we return. There'll be some missions where we may need everybody, and there may be a few where only humans are needed. We could be going into places where they keep or sell dimies off, so if you were to be caught during the action you could be chained up just like the rest of them."

"But we can still be of help." Issac stands up with hope in his dark eyes.

"Indeed you can. Once we're outside, you'll help us guide the dimies. In places where they've come to hate humans, you'll be needed most, to help sway their prejudice. The problem is that we have targets in the city we need to infiltrate where they hold dimies. Due to your safety, it's a hard matter to decide."

"Then don't decide. Let it be our choice to come in and help them. We chose to fight. Let us choose to follow you there as well."

"I admire your fire for this cause, Issac, and I respect you for it, but it's not that simple," Keagan gently elaborates. "The place we're looking at is very complex and dangerous; you could easily get lost or re-enslaved in it. We have to regard you just like the dimies we're trying to rescue when in such a place."

"Now for the rest of the assessment." Lori pipes up, stopping Issac from protesting further.

"Wait, there's more?" Samuel furrows his brow and opens his mouth; I can tell he's worried, to say the least.

"Yes, this will allow us to see everyone's fighting styles, prowess, and how much more training they might need. It will help us in choosing who goes on our missions with us."

Stripping off our night-running outfits, we reveal our sparing clothes underneath it all; me in my baggy pants and loose cream top, Lori in her leotard and wrap sweater along with her running trousers, and Keagan in simple trousers and his white button-up undershirt. Keagan takes one look at me when everyone is stretching and preparing to fight and says, "You know, you look like a pirate when you wear this. It suits you."

Strangely enough, this makes me smile. "I like to think that I am one myself, in a way," I say, making him smile back at me. That may be our first genuinely happy exchange we've had in weeks.

"All right, so who do we fight?" Anthony asks, diverting

our attention back to the group. Keagan simply smiles and starts to approach him for their match.

Ghedi, Anthony and Issac by far are the best fighters, which isn't saying much since both Keagan and myself still manage to subdue them in the test spar matches. Isola ranks the lowest for fighting, but she has great potential for grappling, due to the length of her arms and grip strength. Samuel only appears as if he would be a good fighter due to his size and foreboding aura, and yet we're finished with him in a matter of seconds. Andrea surprises the whole lot of us with how long she lasts. She even manages to land a punch on my arm as I block my ribs. Though, sadly, she still receives a lower score than Ghedi since she uses up all of her steam too quickly, and I'm able to overpower her with a simple pin move. We now know that endurance is her issue. Then of course there is cousin Harry; due to his limp, he is significantly slower than everyone else, but Keagan mentions to me that he can throw a hell of a powerful punch.

Overall, they aren't terrible fighters, but they aren't all too adept either. That'll need to change for sure if we're to take them with us. If we're going to build a following and a reputation as the terrifying night phantoms then we better have able and ready members. However, there's no way I'm going to leave them to practise with our weapons without us here. We don't want anyone pulling the pin on the wrong grenade again, like Keagan did during his training.

"Again!" Keagan calls out whilst giving a demonstration for boxing. Lori and I are going around and correcting everyone's form. Lori has spent a little too much time correcting Ghedi, again…so I make my way over to push her along.

"Augh, I feel as if my arms are about to fall off from my shoulders," Samuel groans with his sweat-drenched blond hair falling into his face. All the while he throws rather sloppy uppercuts into the air. I'm afraid that if he puts in too much force, he might punch himself by accident.

"Well, now we know who needs the most training and attention, don't we? Keep at it!" I say before adjusting his rather slinky arms. I hear two more groans fill the air above the sounds of laboured breathing. After an hour of training, we decided to let everyone take a break. Everyone begins talking about where they're from and what brought them to London. Then it goes off on what our favourite part about where we used to live is, and finally on the types of legends and stories that come with their hometowns.

"What was it like to be in the great battle on the ship this past New Year's Eve?" Ghedi asks with marvel in his eyes. He obviously has never been in a battle if he has the look of a child eager to play a game at the mention of it.

Resting on the ground a few feet from me, Keagan dries off his sweat from the back of his neck as he gives me a side glance to which I return a slight head shake in disapproval. "Sorry, but we prefer to leave that day in the past as best we can…what about you? Have you ever been in a battle?" Keagan says cooly at first before trying to add more levity into his voice.

"Myself? Oh plenty, I've been in plenty of street fights and battles in bars."

"I see." I can't help sounding sceptical; he doesn't seem to notice, though.

"Was it just you against one person?" Keagan asks.

"Well, I mean, usually, but there's almost always other people around."

"Classification, fights," I clarify. "Not battles. Battles are for wars, fights are for occasional uneasy disagreements." There's something about this guy that makes me want to put him in his place, away from his obvious lies.

"Ha, I knew I'd like you, Miss Aspen. I told you she'd see right through you—" Anthony laughs as he claps a hand on Ghedi's shoulder with a mug in the other hand. Taking a seat, he just continues to laugh.

"Aw, shut it, Anthony. I'm still a good fighter, probably even better than you." Ghedi's demeanour changes instantly from an excited child to a brawling bear. Time to cool this situation down again.

"Is that so? Well, why not have our next bit of practice be sparring against each other, then? Starting with you two. The winner will fight Keagan. And for the girls, the winner between the two of you will fight Aspen," Lori suggests.

"Actually, let's refrain from that for now, Lori. They still need to train. I don't think they're ready to fight like that just yet."

"So what do you know about battles, then, Ghedi, if you claim you've been in a few?" Lori asks instead, to which Ghedi instantly brightens up once more.

"Well, if anything, I do know the story of my great great grandfather Miro. He was in a battle against this small port town and the man who tried to take his love away."

"Ghedi, what was the name of the woman?" Lori asks.

"Florence, and the cursed man who tried to steal her away was named Jonathan Blu."

I nearly choke on my water when he mentions the name. Poor Isola and Andrea, though—Lori sprays water on them mid-conversation. I can't believe this is real; I never stopped to think that there would be another side to the story. Or the fact that we would even hear it. "My grandfather and my father would tell it to me all the time when I was little; it was my favourite to listen to."

"Is there a chance we could hear it? We've actually heard a similar tale, but from the side of Jonathan Blu."

"Well, this is perfect. Now you can hear what actually happened—the real story." He scoots closer to us with that same childish eager look in his eyes as everyone begins to sit on the floor around us.

"Miro and Florence had fallen in love through the years, growing up close to each other. One late fall when my great grandfather was back in town, he tried to propose to her during her courtship with Jonathan Blu. Both Florence's parents and Jonathan's wanted them to marry and detested Miro—a gypsy like me—and his family whenever they came near town. Florence would always sneak away from prior engagements and meetings with friends to visit with the gypsies, Miro especially.

Jonathan ridiculed Miro and fought him fist to fist for Florence's hand in the centre of town one day when Miro's clan came to sell their wares from their caravan. Miro was beaten badly and his family and friends were held back whilst Jonathan made a spectacle of him to the growing crowd. At some point, Florence came by and noticed the fighting. She was so angry at Jonathan for his behaviour.

She tried to reach out to Miro, as his friends were allowed to collect him, but Florence was restrained by her ladies maid from going any further. A few weeks later after the clan's elder and Miro had reached out to Jonathan and his family to make amends in person, they both were chased out of town by the townspeople and threatened with talk of war if they ever tried to enter the towns borders again.

For the rest of fall and early winter, Florence and Miro left letters to one another in a hollowed-out knot in an old tree close to the border of town. Miro would go get the letters at night, even though he almost got caught a handful of times. Then, late in the winter, Miro and his friends waited for the snow to come to town again. They were headed for Florence's house to help Miro in his proposal for her.

But in the middle of serenading Florence from her window, they were discovered. Someone managed to rally a group of men together that included Jonathan Blu. Before Miro and his friends knew what to do, a battle broke loose. The chief had heard about what they were up to and decided to stay in the woods that overlook the town, along with the other men and able women in their clan. When they saw the townsmen head to Florence's house followed by shouts, the forest began to bleed out the clan of battle-ready gypsies. At some point Florence's house caught fire, and as the inhabitants of her home evacuated she got separated from them amidst the chaos. Right when Florence was coming out of the house, Miro was fighting a man who lost quickly and turned cowardly at the end of Miro's blade. He begged him to spare his life. Miro granted him the wish only if the coward gave his note to Jonathan. When the man agreed, Miro quickly put the note in the man's vest pocket and turned to the forest with Florence as Jonathan Blu called out her name.

The chief was killed amidst the fighting but Miro didn't know it at the time. When Miro and Florence returned to the camp in the woods, she was received with open arms by the rest of the women who knew her well. Florence agreed to elope with Miro in front of the women in the clan, who were very excited to have her join them. However, as some of the men began to come back to camp, they were carrying women and goods they had stolen from their fighting back in town. Miro, his friends, and the gypsy women ordered that they give back what they had stolen." Ghedi breaks for a second to take a drink of water from a tin cup. The rest of us are listening intently with eager ears.

"In the story we heard, Jonathan ended up freezing on the top of a cliff with a note in his hand that read *'She was my woman first.'* Any idea how he obtained such a note?" Lori asks curiously.

"I can't say I know anything about that, sorry. But that does sound like something Miro would do. All I know is that I'm the product of a great love story that survived hellfire and prejudice," Ghedi says proudly. "Anyway, the men did eventually return the women and supplies, though I was told they just left them in the snowstorm wherever they heard the villagers' voices. After that, Miro and Florence were married and lived the rest of their lives together happily, as they should."

"Here here," Harry says, lifting his glass to Ghedi; all of us raise our cups in cheers before taking another sip. I wonder how much of Ghedi's story about Miro is true? Did they truly love one another? Or did he actually spirit Florence away as it was told in Jonathan Blu's telling? I guess there's no real way of knowing—just what we choose to believe.

"All right, now let's get back to our practice, eh?" I set down my glass and stand back up. A small groan emits through our group—one I don't take lightly. "Would you rather go out and run laps throughout the city for a few hours? Because we could work on your endurance instead. What do you say?"

"No, we can fight. Fighting is good," Isola says as everyone gets back on their feet immediately with rather unamused looks on their faces. As the group lines up against the wall as instructed, I whip out the new invention that's been hiding in plain sight this whole time.

"The bracelet you see on my arm before you is, as you can see, fashionable, well-made, and the perfect trap. Samuel, please approach me and prepare yourself."

Samuel does as he is told and readies himself a metre and a half away in a slightly bouncing boxing stance, all the while eyeing the bracelet I have on my outstretched arm. "Now attack me."

Without hesitation, Samuel takes two steps forward with pursed lips, reeling his arm back, preparing to strike me. The second he begins to come towards me, I rip off my bracelet and fling it at his arm. The bracelet stretches out wide in the air three times its size, and the second it meets Samuel's approaching arm it latches on and pulls his whole body back towards the metal pillar that stands near the edge of the room just behind him. With a loud *clang* he is stuck to the pillar by the bracelet he is trying desperately to pry off once he picks himself off the ground.

"As you can see, this magnetic restraint bracelet is very effective in a fight, and for subduing your opponent. This will be the first weapon you will practise with. Do not, however, unless you are in total life-threatening circumstances, aim for someone's throat. This could constrict them, and when their head hits whatever metal is nearby, it could cause major head trauma. So only aim for their limbs or waist. Do I make myself clear?"

"Yes, ma'am," our small crowd says.

"Very good. Now, it has a magnetic range of around ten

metres. Anything over that will just create a strong pull, but nothing that will completely subdue them."

Pausing, I see Andrea's hand in the air. "Why were you not affected by the magnet on your wrist since you were still close enough to the metal pillar?"

"Very good question," I say, going over to Samuels' caught forearm and pulling out the magnet release that looks like a small silver tube. I press into the clasp until it becomes limp. Samuel rubs his forearm as he stands back up and walks back to the rest of the group. "Here, you see how it's limp and no longer magnetic? When the piece is neutralised by this negative magnet, the ones inside the clasp here are separated. It's only when you break off the bracelet from your wrist as you throw it that the magnets inside are active once more. Throwing it causes the whole band itself to stretch out to its limit. And when it hits something, it immediately wraps itself around and the clasps meet magnetised, where they are drawn quite powerfully to the nearest metal. This can be very dangerous, so you must be aware of your surroundings when you're thinking of using them. For example, you could use this in a kitchen with many knives and pots around. With every weapon you use, you must take into account your surroundings."

"And tonight you get to practise with it," Keagan announces, nodding at Lori.

"At first we'll be using these to hit targets, then we'll practise on each other. You can pretend that these wooden rods are a weapon of your choice, like a knife or a pistol. Now, no beating each other with them; this is just for sparing," Lori says, passing out the wooden sticks that are about half an arm's length. Everyone takes a turn to hold out a stick a metre away from the metal pillar, as the rest of the group practises throwing the bracelets towards the stick.

Some miss completely, others manage to latch straight onto the pillar instead. Other times it even hits someone's chest and closes up with nothing, only to roll over the person and straight to the pillar. After a little more practice, we choose the three with the best scores at catching the rod. Anthony, Issac, and Andrea are quite happy with themselves until they hear that they have to fight us now using the bracelets. Anthony and Keagan step into the centre of the room and prepare themselves. Only Anthony has the bracelet on his arm, though.

Keagan advances first, far too quickly for Anthony to use the bracelet yet, and immediately blocks him. Before jumping back, I can tell that he is trying to keep distance from Keagan so he can try to use the bracelet. He is relying too much on it, since he doesn't try to attack Keagan with his own abilities. We'll need to touch on that problem after this. Keagan keeps closing in on him to where Anthony has to try and fight back. Finally, right before Keagan ends the match with a strong blow, Anthony takes off his bracelet and slaps Keagan's arm with it, as his fist is only a few centimetres from his face. Anthony is getting lots of points just from that move alone.

The second the restraint is clasped together, and Keagan is dragged back to the pillar. The moment Keagan hits the pillar, Anthony comes rushing at him with his wood rod. But something is wrong: Keagan's handsome face is overcome by a beastly expression as he quickly brings himself to his feet with a loud screech and sparks fly from the friction between the pillar and the restraints on his bicep. His teeth are bared and his intense eyes could start a fire. Just as Anthony swings at Keagan with his rod, Keagan blocks it with his own and in a fluid motion kicks Anthony to the ground. The wild look still lingers as Keagan tosses aside his stick and brandishes his sabre from his hip. Anthony starts to anxiously scoot away.

Stunned for a second by Keagan's rather violent state, I try to collect myself before speaking. "Now, what you see here is a great example and a caution to remember. Even though your enemy is restrained, it doesn't mean they can't fight back or hurt you. Remember that a cornered animal will almost always fight back, and so will a person." Gently placing my hand on Keagan's, I slowly have him lower his sabre and re-holster it before releasing him. He doesn't look at me directly. The moment he's free, he begins to rub his wrist and stare at the ground. Still facing the pillar and Keagan, I can feel the tension emanating from him and the rest of the room.

"I believe it is time for us to say goodnight now. We apologise if we may have made any of you uncomfortable tonight, but training will push you out of your comfort zone." I finally turn towards the group of worried faces pointed at both Keagan and myself.

"We're fine. Still in one piece, aren't we?" Anthony says, hand still over his chest from where Keagan kicked him. I nod in earnest, though I can tell my embarrassment is showing through. We end our session with them abruptly as we all clean up the area and do a quick stretch with everyone, letting them know what to do for their sore muscles to speed up their recovery. As Keagan and Lori head through the barrel, I tell them to go on ahead outside.

"I want to apologise again if Keagan frightened anyone here. Sometimes he forgets when to stop holding back during sparring. This will not be an easy or safe job, so if you wish to back out, do so now."

No one makes a sound; they just look at one another in

contemplation. Anthony looks back at me and finally speaks. "We're with you. I know what happens in bloody battles and what they do to a man. But I can tell Keagan can still keep control of himself."

"Thank you. We'll be back in a day or two to continue the training. Right now, stretch, rest and let your bodies heal."

"Yes, ma'am," Anthony says before I head back through the barrel door. Hearing it close behind me, I take a deep breath and hear it echo around me in the barrel, stilling me for a moment. *Lord, that was embarrassing.* Meeting up with Lori and Keagan outside, I can see he's still keeping his eyes down and taking deep breaths.

"Let's go home, shall we?" I say almost as a suggestion and less as an order.

Lori and Keagan look up at me and both nod their heads before we all shoot our grappling hooks to the rooftops. Our run on the way home is rather quiet, without much to speak about. But when we finally make it back to George's house and Pauline lets us in through the back, we erupt with conversation, telling Pauline and George all about what happened, though we fail to mention Keagan's outburst.

"Was I that badly prepared when I first joined you?" he asks.

"Not completely, but you at least had some redeeming qualities, like boxing and swordplay."

"Well, that's at least a little reassuring," he says, resting the back of his head on the chair. He acts as if nothing happened back there. I know something bad is going on because the same thing happened to me. But he just doesn't portray it. Then again, he's had years of hiding his true self just to get what he needs from others. I thought I was good at seeing through that guise, but perhaps I'm losing my touch.

Maybe I never was good at it after all. Father held up a mask that fooled me even after he was cold in his grave, so who's to say that Keagan hasn't done the same? Who's to say he isn't always hiding his true self from us...

Father, of all the things you showed me, I wish you had taught me more discernment. But then, I would've figured you out long ago if you had, huh?

RABBLE ROUSERS

LORI

February 4th, 1887

Dear Timothy Pembrook,

How are you, my boy? I must say, it has been far too long in between our visits and check-ins. You simply must come this Wednesday night to my house for dinner. My nieces and nephews your age are currently staying with me, so we will have some company to join us when you arrive. Oh, and due to the inability to accurately diagnose the issue with your inventions that need fixing. I propose that you bring them with you so I can take a good look at them in person.

Yours truly,

George Adlene

February 6th, 1887

Dear George Adlene,

Dinner sounds wonderful, I'll be there at eight sharp as usual. And I can't wait to meet your nieces and nephews, I only hope they are saner than you are. As for the machines, I am rather hesitant to bring them, not that I do not wish for your aid, but the sensitivity is quite grave with many of them. However, I shall try and bring a few that I need help with. More and more inventions seem to come in that are faulty, and they aren't all mine even, every inventor here thinks because I'm the youngest that I should handle all the grunt work and repair jobs. But there are so many that I fear I'm falling behind. So your help will be much appreciated as always.

See you Wednesday night at eight.

Your student,

Timothy Pembrook

Uncle George had sent Pauline up to Aspen and my room to help dress us for dinner. We weren't expecting to dress so lavishly, but Pauline insisted, saying that Timothy's greatest weakness is women. Ladies make him more coerced by just being in the room, due to him usually being unable to think straight when a pretty girl is around. I packed up only one fancy dress for each of us from the house, and since the rest of our items James was sending have yet to arrive, we are having to wear our best.

"What exactly do we need Timothy's help with, other than seeing the queen? I wanna know so I can give off the accurate amount of flirtation." I smile as Pauline pins the last strand of my hair back in an elaborate coiled bun. In the mirror, I see Aspen still in her under-bodice, looking over papers she holds above herself as she's sprawled along the bed. Rolling her eyes with a smile, she turns my way.

"There's a chance we'll need his help with the model for

the war balloon; other than that, he may need to help sneak us into the palace to speak with the queen. He could lose his job for what we're asking him to do, and if things go awry, possibly his life as well, if he's labelled as a conspirator with us."

"Understood. High-level flirting prepared and ready to fire, Captain." I salute her in the mirror as she gets up and walks over till she's right next to me. Pulling her loose hair before her chin like a beard and making her voice gravelly, she says, "Thank you, my beloved first mate."

Giggling, I stand so she may get her hair prepared by Pauline next. After we don our dresses and perfume, we make sure every hair is in place before we descend the stairs. Pauline has already beat us to it by way of the servants' passage. With Aspen in the lead, we descend the staircase, taking care to hit each step in our bouffant dresses. Halfway down, and in the direct line of sight, Keagan, Thomas and Uncle George come around the corner in the midst of a bitter bickering, by the sound of it. At the sight of Aspen's forest-green dress and my pink rose-embroidered one, the men stop midstep. Pausing for a second, Aspen winks at me and poses, and I follow in suit. We each put out a hand on the railing and a hand on our hip.

"You both look ravishing, ladies. Timothy will think he was hit by a train." Uncle George claps for us. Thomas applauds as well with a grin on his face. I notice now that even the gents have put on their best clothes for tonight. But when my eyes catch sight of Keagan, I feel my smile faltering. Keagan gazes at Aspen as if it pains him to see her in that dress, and yet he doesn't look away for even one second. *They still haven't talked things out, have they? Then again, when have they had a free moment alone to do so?*

"Now, we all know what to do?" Aspen asks. "Uncle George and Keagan, you're going to do your best to win him over to our side, of course. Think you can handle it after being out of action for a while?"

"I've been acting as a foreign diplomat for my father for so long, I know exactly how to play this game," Keagan scoffs as he pours himself a glass of brandy. "I could tell someone to go to hell and they would look forward to the trip."

"He's right, you know. Charisma opens doors," George offers.

Aspen ignores his comment and instead gives Keagan a worrisome look that he catches instantly as he looks back down at the alcohol in his hand. "Don't worry, I'm having only one glass, I promise," he responds. Aspen doesn't look fully convinced. Sissy and I have noticed recently that there's been a significant difference in the levels of alcohol filled in the glasses that are kept downstairs from one night and the next morning. With all of us going to bed around the same time as Uncle George does, Aspen has claimed that someone must be drinking late at night as the rest of us slumber. *He promises, but he's shown us before how cheap a promise can be.*

Thirty minutes later, a knock at the door causes Uncle George and Pauline to rush over as Keagan and Thomas take a seat in the cluttered study. Aspen and I rush into the drawing room for our dramatic entry that's soon to come.

"Timothy, my boy!" George exclaims as he opens the door. "So good of you to come, and right on time as usual."

"Punctuality is key, George. The day I show up late,

presume I was spirited away, or that a lovely lady has bewitched me into losing all sense of time."

"Right-o, my boy. Now come, I must introduce you to my family."

That's our cue to make our way to the study. When we reach the hall, we find Pauline at the door, hanging up a coat on an extended hook that juts out of the coat closet. Once the coat is on it, the hook shoots back into the closet and the door closes right behind it. Pauline doesn't look the least bit fazed by the invention; her attention is on us instead. With a huge smile on her face, she trots over to us and starts to fluff up our skirts a bit more, checking us over to make sure we're ready to leave Timothy starry-eyed. *I think Pauline would've made a good mother; she's certainly happy when she gets to doll us up.*

By this time, the boys have already been introduced to each other, and we suddenly hear George say, "I'd like to introduce you to two other guests tonight; Lori, Aspen, could you come here, please? This is Miss Aspen," he says as we enter the room.

Timothy begins to speak before he even sees us. "M'lady, it is a pleasure—"

"And Miss Lori."

"My...m'la—" Timothy's grip on his bag begins to tighten and a knot seems to form in his mouth, only incoherent sounds leaving his tongue. Timothy looks not too far from Keagan's age, possibly twenty-three, with a small build and rather thin, even in his black suit. Thick round glasses frame his sharp grey eyes, whilst his mob of sandy hair sticks out from the back of his head in frayed tips. A few strands even have black markings on them, as if they have been burnt. Clearly he attempted to slick back his hair for the evening but could not see the pointed fringe in the back, the poor bloke.

"Lovely ladies, are they not, Mr Pembrook?" Keagan says before taking a sip of brandy.

"Ah, yes, indeed." He looks away from me for a second and back to Keagan.

"Shall we take our seats for dinner? I don't know about you, but I for one am famished," Uncle George offers.

"Indeed, let's go eat." Thomas stands with perfect posture in his little suit, coiled hair pulled back slightly and much more manageable-looking than usual. Keagan must've helped preen him since Pauline was so busy with us. Making our way to the dining room, Keagan pulls out a seat for Aspen, and Timothy pulls out mine with a nervous smile. Once we're all seated, Pauline carts in roast duck with mushroom sauce, baked potatoes in rosemary, mixed cooked vegetables, and buttered rolls. Our conversation begins with praise for Pauline for such a meal and soon digresses into small talk.

"So what brings you to town, Miss Lori...and company?" Timothy asks, catching himself to include the rest of us.

"Well, you could say we're in town for business. But I'd like to hear more about *your* line of work," I say with longing in my gaze. "Uncle George has spoken about some of what you do, but I wish to know more."

His fork immediately clatters on his plate that has his next bite of food. "Well, Miss Lori, I can tell you that I work with some of the finest minds in the empire, who have the pleasure to be in service of the queen as I do. I both create and repair marvellous inventions for Her Majesty, and I've even brought along a few with me tonight."

"Oh my. Is there a chance that we could see them, please? They sound most fascinating."

"Oh, uh...well, of course. However, I promised Uncle George he could see them first. Once he's done, you can most certainly look at them yourself. Although, of course you must promise me you will speak to no one about this."

"Oh, my lips are sealed," I say, brushing my pinky over my lips lightly.

"Ah yes," Timothy mutters as he stares at my mouth for a second with a somewhat dream-filled expression. I can only think of what he might be imagining, and I steel myself from a shudder. At least we know my charm is working on him.

Whilst Timothy and I had been conversing at the end of the table, the rest of our party has been having their own discussions. Suddenly, Uncle George raises his voice and says, "Timothy, I'm so excited to see those inventions you've brought with you, and fret not—I'll get to the bottom of their issues and fix them quick as a whip." Timothy doesn't respond, though, just lifts his glass of wine to his ever-reddening face as Uncle George goes on eating like nothing he said was troublesome. I almost feel sorry for the boastful little liar who sits across from me. Lifting my own glass, I hide my smile beyond its brim from the funny chatter. "Oh, and Timothy, I have a new invention myself I'm very excited to show you. I can't give away any details right now, but I can say it'll leave you gobstruck."

"Oh, yes, wonderful. I can't wait to see it," Timothy says in a weak voice.

The rest of dinner is held in pleasantly shallow conversation, mainly concerning London and all its eccentricities. Luckily, we've dodged all questions of our last names and where we've come from. Obviously, he's been so out of society that he probably hasn't seen our wanted posters very closely. Once dinner is finished, we retire back into the drawing room, which is filled with Uncle George's model trains and other toy-like inventions. I've begun to wonder how many are actually toys and how many could be weapons, since he's known to make anything possible in this house.

"Why don't you give me the weapons now so I may work on them, and you talk to my nieces and nephews, eh?" Uncle George asks with a smile.

"Splendid idea. 'Twould give us a good chance to get better acquainted," Timothy says earnestly as he hands Uncle George the large black leather bag. The bag pulls down Uncle George's arm from the weight as he takes it from Timothy. As Pauline carts in the tea, Aspen rises to excuse herself for a moment. Now is her chance to fiddle with Timothy's machine. *Don't you worry; we'll keep him occupied.*

"So I am a little curious about something," Timothy says brightly, turning to all of us. Thomas, how do you fit into the picture?"

"Well, actually he was adopted," Keagan answers on Thomas' behalf. "We were helping out some friends of ours when we saw him alone at his family's abandoned home. We decided he needed a home of his own, so why not ours?"

"Are you happy with your new family, Thomas?"

"Yes," he finally speaks up himself. "They're so much more exciting, though I do still miss my old family at times."

"Well, that's understandable, but at least you're in good hands now. So I take it you're currently being homeschooled? Or are you on early holiday?"

"Actually I've never gone to school. My grandfather was a Gear Master, and he took me on as his apprentice when I was old enough. We would make the most stellar things: toy spiders and mechanical flying dragons, even jewellery. What I'm happy about is that I'm still able to make and invent things now with Asp—"

"We're currently searching for a good school for Thomas to

attend, of course," Keagan interrupts Thomas before he says too much. "But the task has become difficult for us. We don't know if we should choose a local school back in Bath or a trade school specifically for gifted inventors. What do you think?" Thomas looks at Keagan with a bewildered expression from interrupting him so suddenly, then his face seems to stiffen as he stares at his shoes. He seems to understand what he almost let slip out.

Something tells me Thomas rather likes our unprecedented lifestyle. Now, I know he's stayed with us for far too long already. He needs a mother, a father, and proper schooling. What life could he possibly have after being dragged through the mud along with us, anyhow? Best thing for him would be to find him a family that could actually offer him a future. I know we couldn't possibly do so, but perhaps Uncle George or Keagan know of a few families who would love a boy his age. The only problem would be convincing Thomas that the opportunity would give him a better life instead of feeling betrayed. Then there's saying goodbye...just the thought of doing so makes my eyes begin to well slightly. *Stop this train of thought this instant. You are in front of a guest and in the middle of a job.*

After some discussion of comparable schools and which might be the right fit for Thomas, Aspen and Uncle George come down the stairs, only without the machines that Timothy had handed over. My nerves are starting to get to me, and my hands are tingling all over with fear. *Will he help us at all? What if he betrays us? If we have to, would we even be able to blackmail him? Honestly, where do we draw the line for this mission? It really isn't all that clear.*

"Well, Timothy, the machine you gave me was a bit tricky, but Aspen here figured it out just fine," Uncle George says, earning a quizzical brow and squinted eyes from Timothy.

"I'm sorry, what? Aspen, you say?"

"Yes. She took one glance at it and immediately determined the problem. I was able to have a nice puff on my pipe as I watched her fix the infernal contraption. Would you like to see it? 'Tis still upstairs on the work table."

"You're pulling my leg, old man." Timothy gets up with a grin and shoves his hands in his trouser pockets as he walks towards George and Aspen. "I know she didn't fix it, so now let's see what you did. I want to make sure you didn't put another streamer popper in this one to prank me further like last time."

"I can assure you, *Mr. Pembrook,* that I did indeed fix your machine," Aspen exclaims in a purposely over-formal tone. "Look at my bare hands. You can still see the signs of grease and the scent of metal." Aspen's hands are almost always like that, it seems, so she should be true to her word.

Looking at them, Timothy's brows furrow in a rather unpleasant way. "All right, what are you playing at this time?" he says to Uncle George.

"Timothy Pembrook, I would like you to meet Aspen Wolfe. I'm sure you've heard all about her by now."

"You—you're the one the entire empire is on the lookout for! But what are—"

"After looking over the palace's guard layout and the security system, we decided it would be out of our favour, more than our circumstances usually are. So instead of a highly probable chance of being thrown into prison on the spot or shot, we decided it would be much less of a hassle for you to come and meet us here for a little help on both our parts. Understand?"

"And what makes you think I would even want to help you? Or even *could* for that matter?"

"Oh, but we knew if anyone could help us, it would be you," I say in my softest voice, coming out as sweet as marmalade. Timothy mumbles unintelligible words as his trembling eyes lock with mine.

"This is Miss Lori Wolfe, by the way, Aspen's younger sister and my ward," Keagan says, patting Timothy on the back, snapping him out of the trance from my gaze. "And I'm Keagan Myrack. Pleasure to see you again, my old schoolmate,"

"You all must be fools if you think I'll have anything to do with this," he says, pointing a finger at all of us in a sweeping motion.

"Timothy, I really must press that you come upstairs to see Aspen's handiwork on the machines. I think it will be worth the trouble."

"Fine, fine! I'll go and look at them," he says with a huff as he stomps his way up the stairs like a spoiled toddler whose dessert got taken away. The rest of us follow up right behind him, including Pauline. Truth be told, she's probably the most trustworthy person in the house right now, so if she were to confirm what we're doing is legitimate and less murderously revolutionary than rumours say, we may have a chance.

The lot of us fill the laboratory, but Pauline just stands in the doorway. The more inventive side of our party, however, forms around the Edison bulb-lit table holding the latest machine, which appears to be a large barrel gun of some type. Timothy takes several minutes to look over and inspect the piece, and with each new inside part he looks at, he becomes more and more astounded.

"So here is our proposal," Aspen says cooly, sitting on a

stool in perfect posture. "Myself and George can fix all the inventions that you cannot from the armoury, as well as throw in a new invention here and there. In return, all you have to do is keep our secret and get an appointment in two months exactly to show the queen a model of a proven-to-work aircraft battleship. After that, we just have to sneak in unseen as a part of your engineering team for the meeting. All you have is two steps—it's nothing."

"Oh, right, I'm sorry, those are completely non-problematic tasks for someone at my level of work under Her Majesty. I'll just waltz right up to Her Grace and say, 'Your Highness, I must see you in two months' time. Do you think you could fit me and my group of inventors in your schedule?' Do you have any idea how many aircrafts she has seen thus far? And knowing me and my record of handiwork, she wouldn't give me the light of day." Timothy flails about his arms as the sassy tone grows stronger in his voice.

"Ah, yes, but has she ever seen one like this?" Uncle George lays down a blueprint of what I assume to be the battleship designs he and Aspen have been working on for the past few nights and mornings.

Timothy bends down over the design and looks at the calculation and the measurements. "Have you checked the possibility of wind velocity and turbulence on a craft like this?

"Yes, and from what we've gathered so far, if we're able to get the exact amount of materials and perfect measurement of each wing and siding, then it shouldn't only fly like a dream but be quite sturdy in nearly any storm. We're currently preparing a test model. It'll have the exact measurements as this life-size version, except scaled down by one-thirtieth so to be only two metres."

"Give me one good reason why I should go along with any of this."

"Didn't you tell me in your last letter that the queen is becoming restless and will sack you if you don't come up with, or at least fix, three new inventions in one month's time? That was about two weeks ago, wasn't it? If we start making you look good and then even better, the queen will hear about it, making it easier to gain an audience with her." Timothy just grumbles in vague agreement.

"This is a sort of launching gun, is it not?" Aspen says, pointing to the left side of the double barrel. "The ammunition goes through this end of the long tube. Now, with the amount of launching force this holds, it should be able to shoot out a large piece of ammunition a pretty far distance, shouldn't it? It's almost like a handheld cannon but with almost no kick-back, due to the vibration absorption barrel at the other end."

"Yes, indeed. How, um, how did you go about fixing it? And what of the other two inventions?"

"Well, I'm sorry, but I just didn't have enough time for those other two at the moment. However, I could tell you how I fixed this one, if you were a bit more open to our offer, that is. Until then, I can't say I remember all too well how I fixed it."

"Obviously, we'll give you the time you need to think about such an offer," Keagan pipes up. "Within reason, of course. Unless you already have a decision. Since we weren't expecting you to jump aboard the idea right off the bat."

"Indeed, sir, and I must say I am against the entire idea of it. How dare you? You rogues try and convince me to aid you, even to use me to get to the queen, let alone help in the making of a war balloon. And by the means you did so as well! Wining and

dining me and surrounding me with flirtation from such a lady!"
he exclaims, not even able to look at me directly. I feel somewhat insulted. "I shall have nothing to do with this, a—and I
don't want or need your help, Miss Wolfe, or yours, Mr Adlene. I
am in service to Her Royal Majesty in her engineering armoury,
and as such I shall surely figure out my own inventions. Good
night to all of you." He huffs as his face grows even redder.

Starting to collect his belongings back in his bag, the lot of
us stand around, trying to remain as peaceful as possible. I
wonder about Aspen and what comments she could be biting
back at this moment. "And you, you clever shrews," he
suddenly continues, stopping his packing to point a finger and
sneer from me to Aspen. "I ought to have recognised you from
your ghastly pictures. It's amazing what a bit of face paint can
do these days. Best leave that flirtation out of your games
from now on, or a man might take you for what you really
are."

To say that was the straw that broke the camel's back is an
understatement. Aspen immediately rises up from her seat,
but before a word can be spoken, Keagan grabs ahold of Timothy's wrist and bends it back with such strength that the level
of pain is evident on his face. "You need to take those words
back before I make you eat them."

"Unhand me, Mr Myrack. Don't forget who I work for."

"Oh, no, Timmy. Remember where *you* stand right now. In
a room filled with highly dangerous and wanted criminals who
could do worse than break your arm for what you just said."
Keagan's face begins to redden; something is off about him
right now, much like the night we brought home Jack the
Riveter.

"Keagan, you've made your point," I say in earnest. Pauline

begins to walk closer to the two men, appearing as if she's ready to diffuse a bomb.

"Go on, Keagan, do as you're told." A smile curls at the edges of Timothy's lips. "You always were good at doing what your father commanded you to." And just like that, he's on the floor, a hand gripping his bleeding nose and lip whilst Aspen and Uncle George push Keagan back towards the drawn windows. But Keagan looks as if he wants more than what he just fleshed out on Timothy. It's almost as if I can see the red glow that fills his vision. Thomas backs away towards the fireplace with a face empty of emotion. As Pauline and I try to aid Timothy with a handkerchief over his bloody face and pull him back on his feet, Aspen tries consoling Keagan with one hand on his face and the other on his chest. Averting his gaze by turning him to face her instead of the now teetering Timothy, the slowing rise and fall of his chest assures me he is coming back to us.

Once Timothy loses the dazed look in his eyes, and Pauline cleans off most of the blood around his mouth, he goes on packing his bag with not so much as a word. Uncle George slips out of the room, rather uncharacteristically noiselessly at that. A few moments later, Timothy has his bag packed and immediately begins to stomp his way out of the laboratory and down the hall to the stairs with us in tow. Halfway down the stairs, the fifth and sixth steps suddenly give way to his weight, as he falls and a net suddenly shoots up from under him, and attaches to a large hook on the ceiling. It causes its captive to scream and struggle about, calling out for Uncle George. Thomas can't help but laugh at the sight of the frustrated man, and to be honest I can't help but smile a bit as well.

"Oh, my, Pauline, I do believe we forgot to make one of our

intruder traps dormant. Uncle George grips the ropes that contain Timothy as he holds up a handful of small photographs in his left hand far enough away that I can't make them out. "Must have slipped my mind. But seeing how I have your undivided attention now, Timothy Pembrook, I need you to remember who it was who fixed so many of your inventions for the past six years. Not to mention which young troublesome lady repaired and finished that difficult machine of yours tonight."

"Are you seriously blackmailing me?" Timothy spits out, now royally angry, hair and clothes completely dishevelled.

"You could call it that. I just want you to remember that you could go and tell your boss or even Queen Victoria herself about the whereabouts of my guests. However, you need to know that what proof we have against you would appear to the Crown as if you've been in on the game for quite some time. It would cost you your job and title, possibly even your head." We four stand at the railing at the top of the stairs, mouths agape to the smooth, almost rehearsed display that Uncle George is performing.

Finally, he backs away and kneels down at the base of the stairs. Pulling out a small knob in the moulding, he lowers the net back down into the floorboards. Uncle George and Pauline are there in a flash to help Timothy out of the snare, just before the net is completely hidden again and the steps are back in their original place. "Now, I wouldn't want that to happen to one of my own students. So why don't you go to bed and think things over, eh? Let us know what you choose in your own time." Uncle George gives a narrow-eyed serpent's smile as Pauline nimbly hops over the trick stairs and assists Timothy's with his coat and hat before showing him the door. Timothy's eyes are wide but his brow knit in frustration after hearing Uncle George's *suggestion*.

The moment he's out the door, Pauline immediately begins to bicker at Uncle George and follow him around like a squawking crow as he goes back into the study. "Really, George, do you not think that the net was a bit much? He was your student, bless his soul. You needn't pull such a move on him." We all carefully hop over the fifth and sixth stairs one by one, helping each other until we're all down on the ground and crowding back into the study.

"Pauline, I don't believe you realise how opportunistic that boy truly is. I had to let him know that we had information against him, just like he has on us, or else he would've just gone immediately to Scotland Yard and have us all thrown in jail awaiting trial. That boy cheated his way into his job and he would just as quickly turn our guests over to the bobbies if we didn't have a knife of our own at his back. And now that we've offered him something as grand as bettering his name in the queen's eyes, in return for helping us, there's no way he'll turn us down."

"He wasn't always like that, though," Keagan says. "In school he once witnessed a rather large bit of trouble that James and I got into. We made him promise to keep it a secret, and to my knowledge he still hasn't told a soul. We never got caught for it, either. Although that punch probably didn't help our chances now."

"And you, Mr Myrack, what has gotten into you? Punching the living daylights out of that man. Why, I have half a mind to slap you here and now for such a display. And in front of two ladies as well. But what he said about you ladies, now don't you heed one word of it! What he said was just a fit of lies tossed around from anger." Pauline rushes over to us and holds each of our hands tenderly.

"Don't you worry, Pauline, we're not unaccustomed to rumours and slanderous speech. We know which ones to worry about." I reassure Pauline with a calm smile; Keagan, however, still has the same peeved expression from when Timothy had first said those terrible things about us.

"Something's wrong with him, that much is for sure. He never acted like that when we were at the manor." I take out the last pin in my hair, letting it drape the length of my back as Aspen slips into her nightgown.

"I hate to admit it, but you're right. Do you remember when Damon came to the house for a surprise inspection?"

"How could I not? We were all nearly caught."

"Well, when he was alone with Keagan, and his men had left the house, I overheard them talking. Damon was saying awful things about you and me in the sense that we were merely there for Keagan's pleasure. And yet back then, Keagan only warned him politely to refrain from such talk about us. But now he's become so much more volatile, even in the way he warns someone."

Taking a moment in my seat to ponder her words, I eventually arise to allow Aspen to sit at the vanity and unpin her hair. "How can we help him? He must still be suffering from all his losses. I know I still am, what with all the nightmares we've been having lately."

"I know what you mean. I've been noticing we've all been a bit crabby to one another lately. Makes me wonder if..."

Aspen pauses, unpinning her hair and staring at herself in the mirror with a faraway look in her eyes.

"If what, Sissy?"

"Oh just a thought. Might be dangerous, actually, but I think it could be what we've been needing for some time, among other things. I'll explain tomorrow; right now I feel drained." She unpins the last strand of her hair and gives it a quick brushing all over.

"I'm right there with you. I certainly wasn't expecting even half of what happened tonight to occur."

"When are things ever perfectly expected with us?" I hear her say as we tuck ourselves into our beds.

"You're right—almost never, but...do you think that perhaps one day they will be? I mean, one day we each could find someone to spend our lives with in the way that society expects it?"

"It's possible, I suppose. I don't understand why one would want such a dull, monotonous way of living as a married woman in society, though," Aspen says sleepily as she shuffles around under her sheets.

"Yeah, right," I mutter as I pull the sheets higher over my shoulders. *I'd still like to think it's possible, though.*

CHAMELEON COSTUMES

KEAGAN

Dear Keagan,

I hope you and your party have found your stay in London to be comfortable and safe, concerning your host in residence. Things here have been progressing in a surprising way—not fully good or bad. Just surprising. The numbers of unemployed people have diminished exponentially since the dimies left. The majority of the lower class are able to find better jobs than what they had as well. One of the brothels in town actually closed down due to the women leaving for better positions like the laundromats, mills, and in a few instances the kitchens of mansions. Even though it's still winter here, the children are happier than ever when they play. They tell me all about how much more food their parents are able to bring home as of late.

And don't you worry about your estate; James still has custody over it, though Damon and the local government are surely trying to take it away. Your friend Nicholas Finley has been pulling the strings behind Damon's back to lessen the power they have on taking your home. He has been keeping us updated on what's to come if Damon stays in power here. He tried to go to London with Damon but was turned down due to his rank as a policeman. He has told us recently that Damon plans on using these metal robotic men to patrol the streets at night. It all seems so odd.

In more personal news, the reputations of James and myself have become a little worse for wear. After I was spotted in your house alone with James, it didn't remain a secret for long. Now very few if any customers have come to visit my shop. Everyone is spreading rumours about me being a Jezebel and about James's infidelity to his expectant wife. Who, by the way, is progressing at a healthy rate in her pregnancy. She knows her husband and the situation all too well to believe such slanderous gossip. She even made a point to come in and buy four new dresses from me as a large party of her friends accompanied her, showing there were no hard feelings.

Despite her good efforts, however, I fear I will soon need to reach into my savings to keep my shop open. I can't bear the thought of losing my business after you aided my brother and me a few years ago. Still, I can't shake the feeling that I will need to close up in the coming months. That being said, if there is any way I can help you, or you know of a place where I can begin again like my brother Tamrin has, I would be much obliged. After all, you've travelled the world; perhaps you would know of a place for a bouffant woman like myself.

With love,
Miss Masie

Morning comes with the most silent breakfast we have ever had. Not one person addresses anything that happened last night with Timothy, or my abrupt action. I keep my head down and mainly play with my food rather than eat it. I think about the letter Miss Masie sent me. I can't help but fear the worst for her and James in the future if they're found guilty for helping us escape. Uncle George, who always has something to say, minds his own business this morning.

Glancing at Aspen once after feeling her gaze linger for far too long, I can evidently see her grimaced lips and furrowed brows that are directed at me. Lowering her butter knife and scone, she gently clears her throat. "I think all of us could use a full day or two just to ourselves, in a safe manner, of course. Each of us needs to come up with a disguise and spend the day out by themselves and for themselves. Be it pampering alone in a warm tub in the house or out on the town seeing a play and eating a nice dinner in a tavern. I think we all have been caged together for quite some time with very little of it truly to ourselves. I've noticed us bickering with one another and getting angrier. So I believe we need to take a break for today and possibly even tomorrow for ourselves."

"I love this idea, but how hard must it be for you to come to terms with taking a break?" Lori pipes in with a snarky grin. "Usually you have to be broken first to finally have one yourself."

"Which is precisely why I want us to have one and continue to have them on the regular. This way we won't break down so easily. We work so hard each and every day with little rest. I believe it's time for just that. I see now how dangerous it can be if just one of us breaks as I did. But if we were all to fall like that and in different ways, who knows how long it could take for us to rebuild ourselves."

"So we can go anywhere and do anything we wish for two full days?" Thomas asks.

"Within reason. If you are to go about town, you must wear a disguise. And don't go anywhere dangerous, either, where you could get dragged into trouble. Just go to the park and stretch out under the trees. Go play with the other kids if you like. Visit a candy shop or a tinker store. You should be getting your monthly allowance by now, anyway, so you could treat yourself with that. Just do your best to not speak to many—or *any*—adults at all."

The light in Thomas's eyes seems to grow brighter than I've seen in a while. From what he's told me, he's been so excited to finally get out of this house. At least we're allowed to leave at night if we need to; poor Thomas is stuck here in this cage of a house day in and day out. We spend so much of our time being cooped up indoors just so we can break some rules for a greater good at night. Well, it's high time he gets a chance at some freedom of his own.

"What are you going to do, Lori?" Thomas asks.

"Oh, well, I want to do a million things right now, but I don't know which to choose. I could go to the dress shops across the bridges, or the oh-so-many pastry shops I've seen on our runs that I've been dying to go inside. Possibly even see a play if there's one showing I like. What about you, Keagan? What are you going to do?" Lori goes on with stars in her eyes as she clasps her hands together.

"Uhm, well..." Just then, there's a knock at the door that

causes my posture to shoot straight back up at attention. A few seconds later, Pauline is in the room, holding out a letter to Uncle George. "It comes from the armoury, signed from Timothy for Mr Adlene and household." Even from my seat I can see that it is half-blackened and charred. "Timothy is asking if the deal is still on the table, and letting us know he could easily pull some strings to make an appointment to see Her Majesty the Queen."

"How do you know it's from Timothy and not a fake from someone else?"

"Ah, look here. Timothy and I use this telltale seal in our letters." He laughs jubilously as he turns the parchment to show a stamp of a circle of gears with a crown in the centre. "We've done it now, children."

"We're going to meet the queen?" Lori squeals. "Oh my goodness, what do we do? What do we say? Now I know I will be going to that dress shop for sure; I can't see Her Majesty without a new dress."

"Not unless you'll be shopping in the men's section, because that's what we'll be dressed as when we meet her," Aspen says, diffusing her sister's excitement. "If we don't die then you'll hopefully have another chance to present yourself in a more Lori-ladylike manner," Lori lowers her utensils at the sound of this suggestion from her sister. "I know what you're thinking, and no, I don't care that this will be the first impression the queen has of you in person. You absolutely may not dress differently."

"But what if—"

"And no, you cannot come along as a member of her court. How would you get into the room with the rest of us for the special meeting?"

"Augh." Lori instantly crosses her arms and produces a pouty lip.

"However, you do still have the chance to get a new dress today. I'm sure there will be some occasion where you can wear it soon," Aspen says tenderly, still keeping her eyes on Lori. Her eyes begin to search the table wildly and her pout starts to diminish into a smirk. *What is that little minx thinking? She looks just like Aspen right now when she schemes.*

"So it's settled. Since today and tomorrow are the end of the week, we'll take two days off before having to get back into action."

"Let's do it!" Thomas is immediately out of his seat, leaving what's left of his scone and flying up the staircase. Lori and Aspen both finish their meals very quickly before heading back upstairs, discussing all the different ideas of what they could go do today.

What if I asked Aspen to spend a bit of the day with me? No, she said alone—we aren't to spend time together, though come to think of it, it'll be a bit of a breather to be alone for once after so long. The only other time was when we each watched over the teams during their testing. But that was only for a few hours at night. This will be a full two days. What am I even to do? I can't see the connections I have here due to present circumstances, so what then? Perhaps I should just go walking and play it all by ear.

Sitting there alone in the dining room, I manage to eat a third of the meal before going upstairs to don my disguise for the day. As I do, Thomas is running down the stairs looking like a paper boy with a new nose, even with a newspaper in his hands. Right behind him is Lori in her same costume as before, the upper-middle-class lady with the green dress and a lace parasol. They both pass me in haste and are in such an excited state they nearly forget to close the door. *Why can't I have some of that excitement?*

Uncle George suggested I go about as a coal miner today; that way most people wouldn't try to touch me or get near for fear of getting dirty. So after smudging my face with cinders from the fireplace and clothing myself in a miner's outfit, I fill my pockets with some spare money and head out for the day. Making my way over to Waterloo, I see the scene of bobbies entering into a home and a familiar-looking taxi driver nearby. The closer I walk, the better I recognize the location. That's the house we stopped at when we first arrived in London as the decoy location. And it's a good thing that we did—that household is crawling with police, one in particular holding up a wanted sign in the homeowner's face. Even though I can't see whose pictures are on it from my place on the other side of the road, I would bet anything it is ours. We are definitely not in the clear or safe in any way yet.

Taking a side alleyway just to get away from the scene, I head towards the bridge and find myself passing a tavern with the delicious aroma of fresh cooked fish and chips. The twinge in my stomach practically forces me to head inside, because it demands to have that meal. Was that ever a brilliant decision. I cannot remember the last time I even got to sit in a tavern for a simple mouth-watering meal. With every bite, my mood begins to change, and I start to realise how excited I am to have the free time for myself. My mind swims with all the people I know in the city. *How are they doing?* I wonder. *Would they even wish to see me again?* I wonder who is expecting children by now, and who is still single. There's got to be someone I can see again; most of the people I know in London are actual friends and past mentors of mine. *I've got to be able to see at least one of them, but would they even accept me now?* Especially if I come to them looking like a filthy coal miner. I guess we'll just have to find out.

Exiting the pub in my coal-miner attire, I begin my walk across the bridge and decide to head over to Hyde Park. I'm about a third of the way there, near the Belgravia townhomes, when I start to hear a familiar voice. *It can't be.* Turning the corner just as I approach it comes the Austrian baroness, Carina Von Trap, dressed in her everyday regalia just as she did when I was a schoolboy. The only thing different now are the few grey streaks in her deep red hair. She and her red-bird-dimie maid, Matilda, are strolling around the corner at the same time as me, now a metre away.

She steps back quickly with a start for a second. I tip the brim of my hat as I bow my head, an excuse to apologise low enough so she doesn't recognise me. Side-stepping the baroness, however, isn't an easy task. Taping her fan to my chest and resting it there, she stops me as she looks under my hat. Trying my best to look more gruff by pursing my mouth and raising my eyebrows to add a more wrinkled look to my face, I look back at the baroness. "You look just like a boy I used to tutor in language and foreign affairs," she says. "But of course you couldn't be him. Keagan would never pass me by without a proper greeting and a 'Good day, how are you, M'lady'."

"I'm sure any man who would be so honoured to know her ladyship would do just that," I answer in a gravelly voice as I try to walk away again, keeping my eyes forward.

But stopping me again with her fan once more, she continues. "You know, he always had this air about him as if he were wearing a mask, trying to hide his true face from most people. He eventually lowered his mask for me so I could see who he really was. But I know that he would never put that mask back up after being such a good mentor to him for so long...even if he is in hiding. Isn't that right, Mr Myrack?"

The hairs on my neck stand on end, and I know she means business when she speaks to me like that. Sliding my eyes towards her, but still facing forward, I see that knowing look on her face that says it all.

"Baroness Carina." I clear my throat and answer with my voice as I take a proper bow before her. "Please, forgive my rudeness at not addressing you properly before, but as you said, I am in hiding. It is best if no one were to recognise me."

"Yes, well, you nearly had me fooled; however, I was always able to see right through you, Keagan. Do not lose heart, though. I doubt anyone else would have recognised you."

"Thank you, m'lady. I am actually a little happy you did, because it gives me the opportunity to talk to you once again. How is the baron? Is he still acting as a business advisor to the owners of the mills around town?"

"Indeed. However, those matters are such a bore to me, and his business friends are always leaving their plans and papers with Hubert to look over. Causes such a mess in his office. You'll have to forgive me, however; we do not have long enough time right now to converse. Matilda and I were on our way to tea with the Van Burens, and we shall be late if we do not start walking again."

"Still refuse the aid of a carriage, I see."

"Well, my dear, I hate the idea of having to sit all the time every day. How else should I maintain my figure?"

"You haven't changed a bit, m'lady." I smile genuinely.

"No, but you have, my dear, and I propose a challenge for you."

"Oh?"

"Yes, I am inviting you and a guest of your choice to my costume ball coming up in a week. It will give you a chance to practise more on your disguises. I want to see if you can thoroughly fool me." Her Ladyship rifles through her purse before pulling out a stamped letter that I recognise all too well. "We will catch up more on all your recent endeavours there. I don't want to miss a single detail." She extends the lavender wax-sealed letter invitation to me, which I take without hesitation.

Tapping it on my fingernails for a second, I say, "I'll only come if I can bring two guests. There are two ladies under my guardianship I could not choose from if forced to do so."

"If they are the ladies in the wanted pictures next to yours, they better be on their best behaviour. I know you were made to look more like a ruffian in your wanted photo, so I can only assume that they did the same with those two ladies."

"Indeed. So I take it you don't believe what you hear about us, then?"

"Not all of it. After all, you always were a bit troublesome, despite having a good heart. However, if there is one thing I've learned, it is not to believe every string of gossip or word you read in the paper, but do believe there is a thread of truth in it somewhere. So yes, I believe you may be behind something rather dangerous and above the law. But no, I do not believe in the terrible things they have marked you as. Because I know who you really are, and I also know we will have much to discuss at my party." She ends as she taps her fan lightly to the letter in my hand. "Until then, Master Myrack," she says with a nod of her head.

"Until then, m'lady," I say with a nod and a smile as she

begins to walk off behind me. *Costume party, eh? I doubt it would be wise to come in constable uniforms. That already was a failed look for us. Where do I know that can supply us with real costumes? From what I remember of the baroness's past parties, it will be an extravagant occasion. And Aspen as an old gypsy woman and myself as a coal miner simply won't do.*

Pausing a second on the sidewalk, I lean against the pristine white stone walls of a Belgravian manor. Keeping my head down, people pass by me without a glance, keeping their distance. *Where oh where could there be costumes at our disposal in such a city as London?* Costumes these days are not exactly for the tight-pocketed, but surely there could be some place we could go to find some. I doubt that Uncle George has enough spare fabric in the house to aid us in making some. And the thought of him suddenly ripping off the curtains and bedsheets for our fabric makes me think of the heart attack that poor Pauline would have to endure.

No, there's someone I know…Tamrin! Of course, Miss Masie's brother would surely have access to tons of costumes for us to choose from. The only question now is if he will let us? Hopefully we could just rent them. Feeling confident in my old friends' loyalty, I make my way across town to the royal opera house. Now four in the afternoon, the sunlight is beginning to shine through streets in rosy rays of light speckled by dust that gives the world an ethereal feeling, as if time has stopped just for a moment. In that moment I feel as if I am not a wanted man anymore, that I can walk freely and see whom I wish without the fear of their betrayal. I never knew how much I would miss a simple luxury like this.

Taking the backway entrance, I rap on the plain wood door three times in different places, making a triangle, and then waiting two seconds, tap it lightly with my knuckle in the centre three times. The door opens and instead of my friend, an aged and very small woman stands there with a broom in her other hand, looking quite flustered.

"Quit rapping on that door! You'll get your money when it's due time and not a moment sooner!"

"M'lady, I think you are mistaking me with another."

"No I'm not, Fletcher Cummings. Now you just get back to the lumber yards and wait for the money to come!" The small woman begins swinging the ragged broom back and forth at my head, missing me by a few centimetres.

"Madame, please! Tamrin, are you here at all?" I call out, backing away.

"Don't you be calling for him. He doesn't want you here either, Fletcher."

"I'm not Fletcher!" I call out as her swinging starts to push me back towards the street I came from. Through her swings I notice a dark chestnut-coloured face peek out from the entrance of the backstage area. The next thing I register is that the broom has come too close to my face; but before I am struck, I backhand the bristles and twist my wrist to grab hold of the rod.

The little old lady does not like this and begins to thrash around even harder. "Fletcher Cummings, you let go of my broom this instant!"

At this time, Tamrin comes up right beside her with his tail-dreadlocks bouncing at his back. He peers at me for a second as he takes in this awkward scene. "Do I know you, sir?"

"Tamrin, your sister says hello, but she demands to be seen as the dominant twin. The fat lady may sing but she can never bend. There is a trap door beneath the stage where you store—"

"That's enough! That'll do, Keagan, thank you. I know it's you now," Tamrin snaps laughingly, looking quickly at the small woman. *I guess his hidden stash is still a secret.* He gently touches the angry woman on her shoulder and lowers the broom in her hand. I let go of my end and straighten back up. "That'll do, Mrs Anderson. This isn't Mr Cummings, this is an old friend of mine. Sorry about Mrs Anderson. She's the theatre's cleaning lady and self-proclaimed personal guard."

"She's a credit to her profession. How are you, Tamrin?" I say, opening my arms for an embrace that he gladly takes part in with a pat on my back.

"Come inside; I'd like to see if you can tell what's different with the opera house after you've been absent from London, and for so long, I might add. What's it been, three years?"

"Ah, yes, I'm sorry, my friend, that I've stayed away for so long with few letters supplied. Life has been quite eventful, to say the least, if you haven't heard recently." We stroll one by one back up the creaky wooden steps and into the opera house.

"Oh, believe me, nearly the entirety of the city knows about you and your lady friends."

"Yeah, but what about me being a criminal?" I say jokingly.

Laughing for a second, Tamrin crosses his arms over his chest before responding. "Masie sent me a letter dated New Year's Day. After comparing it to what's been spoken of you and your party to her letter, it's actually quite an appalling difference."

"But Miss Masie never helped us with anything."

"That young lad, Thomas, helped in catching her up a bit. Apparently he had Winona deliver a letter or two directly to my sister one day after he was living with you. It detailed that he was okay and not to worry about him. Also that he will be staying in a grand house with a bunch of people to play and invent new machines with every day. At first, she was worried and thought it was fake, but since it came from Winona's hand she knew he was okay."

"He what?" I breathe out. "He wrote a letter that could have been taken and had the whole lot of us found out and locked up without us knowing, and Winona took part in it!" *Oh, just wait until I get home, kid.*

"Hey, don't get mad at Thomas for this. She told me she has since burnt the letter and no one but her has laid eyes on it. It helped her piece together what was actually going on, and knowing your character like I do, we could rule out many of the grievances that were listed in the paper. I mean you, a murderer? Please, you would never."

"Heh, yeah, I wouldn't know how to even kill someone properly." *Why don't you just put a bullet through their heart like last time?* I rub my neck nervously. Technically each of those crimes were committed not directly by us, but still, we were the cause of most of them.

"Her knowing actually helps me be able to lend you a hand if you're in need."

"Oh now—"

"Don't say anything; you and your family saved both my sister and me when our businesses were about to go into ruin. Without you we'd be in the gutter."

"Well, who wouldn't have helped new immigrants with great talent?"

"Plenty of people, trust me. So were you just coming by to see me today, or are you in need of help, my runaway friend?"

"Well, it's actually to help me hide from the law in a way, but not in the way you're thinking. I need to borrow some costumes."

"Costumes...of what calibre?"

"Well, uhm, the baroness's costume party."

"Baroness Carina Von Trap's annual costume party? How did she even invite you to that when you're in hiding?"

"We just happened to bump into one another." I shrug my shoulders nonchalantly.

"Right, well, there are a few costumes in storage here I could let you borrow. Follow me." My friend looks at me with his golden eyes and a smirk before spinning towards the costume room at the back of the hall. Glad to know one thing about this place hasn't changed. Every step I take, I notice a new invention to aid in theatrics. A mechanical self-winding pulley machine with crank handles is right behind the back curtain that sees out onto the stage. Tamrin must have noticed my slowed steps since he points to the ceiling, saying, "Look there, see those cords?" I look up into the tall black painted ceiling, only to make out a few thin cords with gurneys on them. "Those are our new flying machines for our fairytale productions. Just came out this year. After lots of tests, it now runs very smoothly."

"Really," I say, knowing Aspen would absolutely love to look at something like this.

"And over there is our lift system." I gaze in the direction he mentions and see a very large metal structure that resembles a leg with a round foot and a railing at the base. "It's to help aid our performers and set designers when there's a large load that needs to go to the bridge over the stage, or the platform on the stage."

"Ingenious. And I take it those are part of your new props? They look very realistic indeed," I say, pointing in the direction of the prop room, where a cow and a few birds with large outstretched wings are acting as living statues. For a second I wonder if they're actually stuffed animals.

"Aha, you found our new animatronics. They still move a little shakily, but they have a recording of the actual animal sounds inside of them; the birds even sing if you want them to."

"I have a friend who will definitely want to see all of this for herself."

"A friend, eh? Is she a keeper this time, I hope, or just a passing fad like all the others?"

"Nope, not Aspen. If she'll have me then she's the only one." I smile proudly.

"Glad to hear it. Then I truly hope to meet her as well, and that she doesn't look like she does in her mugshot."

"Yeah, they did a terrible justice to us all in those photos."

"You said it. You looked manic in yours. The girls looked like witches crossed with bed warmers."

"Okay now, they didn't look *that* terrible," I say, starting to get a little unnerved at that statement about the ladies. Tamrin says nothing and just walks over to a nearby desk where they used to have piles of theatre scripts when I was younger. I used to come in and watch the plays right here from behind the stage. I look around and see that the crate near the curtain is still there; that was my special front-row seat that Tamrin used to let me and James have whenever we wanted to come. Tamrin comes back from the desk now with a yellowed paper in hand. Taking it from him, I see it's our wanted poster, and I hate to admit it but he's right, all of us look quite menacing. I guess I didn't see it as well as I thought when James showed us by the lantern light.

"Touche," is all I say, to which Tamrin supplies a smug grin, takes the parchment, and stuffs it in his pocket. Putting an arm around my shoulder, he pulls me forwards towards the costume room. "Many things have changed, my friend, but don't let this get to ya. There's nothing we can do about it now except help hide ya till ya can make things right again, yes?"

"Quite so."

SOUL COGS

ASPEN

My sister's words are ringing in my ears before they're even uttered. *You said we'd be taking a day off! Aspen, I thought you meant all of us, as in yourself as well!* Sorry, Sissy, but I just can't help myself. I need to make this aircraft prototype model. I know I'll hear every syllable of what she has to say later, and the worst part is that she'll be right about most of it. Who knows if Keagan will say anything, though; he barely even speaks to me now, let alone cares if I'm resting or not. He just seems so far away. When we were living at the manor, he always tried to tear me away from my work when I was pushing myself even the slightest bit too hard. Now he just pops out of the house without so much as a goodbye or a sideways glance.

Perhaps we really are just partners in this now...nothing more. My thoughts race and I misplace one of the steam tubes when it pops right off the engine. Shooting across the room with the steam fuming out like a whistling tea kettle as the sunlight strands glisten through it, my hands fly up into my hair, and I feel my frustration rising. I'm supposed to be relaxing, but all I know right now is uncertainty. I can't even get this engine built properly, despite the long hours of testing and diagrams of different engines between Thomas, Uncle George and myself. *What would Father think of me right now? Why do I still care about how he would see me? He's dead; and more than that, he betrayed us!* I have the sudden urge to scream, but it scares me; this is no time to act like a child.

I finally slump to the floor, and not a moment after, I hear footsteps coming from outside the laboratory. *I mustn't let anyone see me in this state.* I begin to crawl on my hands and knees, trying to find that missing piece that just flew off. Tears brim in my eyes the moment the door swings open and Uncle George comes in, muttering to himself. That is, until he sees me. "Aspen, what on earth are you doing here? Aren't you supposed to be enjoying yourself out in London on your day off? It's actually sunny out there for once. Why stay in here? At least sit by the fire with a nice read!"

"I know, I know, but—"

"You were the one to suggest it, and it sounded like you meant to include yourself in that. Did you not?"

"I did, but then I got to thinking that I really don't have much time for that. I mean...come here and look at this blasted thing."

"All right, I'll humour you, but only for a moment. Then I want you to actually go and have some fun for yourself. Deal?"

"Look at this side where the steam connects to the engine. It simply won't work with it. I've been testing it with a level of steam that will allow the airship engine to keep it afloat, but the tubes end up flying off and the whole thing just whistles like your toy train."

"I see." He goes to the blackboard to look over the engine's sketches and calculations, then back over to the books table where he looks over our old designs as well as our current one. I wait as patiently as I can, though I'm ready to jump out of my chair to look at them as well. Finally, he comes over with the blueprints, lays them down on the table, points to the engine valves, and says, "Unless we get this part exactly right, we'll need to start the designs from scratch. Even if it's one millimetre off of the gauge and length on the inside of the engine, it won't work." Hearing this, I lay my head on the desk. "Right now the only things I can think of that keeps it from working are the valves and the tube connectors, since they aren't the same gauge," he continues. "So they simply won't stay fit. We'll just have to measure and grind out the difference."

"Yes, and then what? Every time we make a change to this, something else breaks and we have to adjust it. I'm starting to wonder if we need to just stop and redo all the measurements and calculations."

"You're right, we should. But not today."

"Fine...one more thing, Uncle George. What if we were to replicate the same type of energy power supply from Jack and use it for the airship?"

"Oh, Aspen, I can tell he has a very sensitive type of power source, and though it's probably a superbly efficient type, as opposed to steam or fuel, it'll be quite hard to duplicate since it's so advanced."

"Oh, well, then never—"

"I like the way you think, though. We better start taking notes and doing our research on it if we're going to replicate it, huh?"

"Wait, you're really up for this?" I say with wide eyes.

"Of course. I love a good challenge when it comes to

inventing. But not today. Today you rest like you said you would earlier."

"Argh." I walk over to the fireside chairs and fall into one with my legs hanging over the arm. After a few moments of silence, I feel a pull in the fabric above my head. Looking up, I see Uncle George gazing down at me smiling though his moustache. "You know that for the most part, there haven't been all that many troubles. This design has been very good despite the handful of hiccups we've had."

"You say that, but whenever I go over our notes, I see only mistakes."

"Maybe that's because that's all you let yourself see, instead of all the good progress you've made."

"*We've* made."

"Let's be honest—I'm here as an assistant, just a bit higher ranking than Thomas. You've done the most work out of us all. Which brings me to an even more important matter I've been meaning to discuss with you."

"I'm listening."

"Word to the wise, my dear. You would be smart to patent your inventions and blueprints before the queen's men get their greedy hands on them, claiming them as their own. Especially since you're a female, it would be easy for the men to take the credit in making the airship, whether or not they're your plans." He winds up his sticky-footed mechanical frog.

"Am I even allowed to present them to Her Majesty?"

"But of course. I used to patent a bunch of my inventions and present them to Victoria. She bought the patents for many of them, which helped me make plenty of extra money on the side. That's how I'm able to afford a three-level home in London. Half of the queen's inventors would be lucky to afford a two-bedroom flat. The heads of the engineering and service departments would easily steal the credit from a lady, even one like yourself, Aspen, and the queen wouldn't do much about it either." He places the frog on the work table and allows it to bounce around the room, its cogs turning and cranking with each flip and bounce.

"But she's a woman too; wouldn't she—"

"If the Crown can take credit for the invention of the century, then it will by any means necessary. All the other aircrafts were sabotaged because well-known and even lesser-known inventors had made it to the paper before the Crown could. Not to mention that the majority of the inventors who claimed their inventions as their own before the Crown could were foreign. Her Majesty is the Crown, and any one person who works for her helps in representing the Crown and its achievements for the empire."

"Hmph, well then, wouldn't I need to get the patent in my name for it to work? They would need to see me and my birth certificate or something, right? That's a recipe for disaster with our current relationship with society," I say, reaching for the frog before he jumps onto the tea table.

"Leave it to me. I know just the place to get it done safely. I'll fill everything out in your name—"

"Actually, Uncle George, I'd like to go in this three ways, please. Both you and Thomas are helping me make this, so you both should get a share of the patent. Especially Thomas, since this will help a certain money and education issue we're currently in concerning him."

"Ah, yes, Lori informed me of that situation. And if you have a male name next to your own, you'd have a better chance of keeping the credit anyway. Allow me to take care of the details in person, since they know me at the patent and copyright office. I'll make a stop there this early afternoon and we'll get the approval for it by the time we present the model to Her Majesty."

"But what if she doesn't buy the patent?" I say, toying with the frog's spinning gears and sticky feet.

"Then that's her choice. She's a very prideful woman, after all. It won't be our fault if she ignores the fact that you've made the impossible possible more than once."

"Ha! How do you know she won't just throw me and the rest of us in jail, regardless of the airship?" I say, letting the toy frog jump out of my hand.

"My dear, even if she chose to imprison you, she'd still buy the patent to the airship from you, I'm certain of that. On the matter of impossibilities, however, you re-engineered a bi-dimensional transporter practically from scratch with your father, and then again on your own after it was smashed to bits. It functions three times better and longer than the origi-nals. You and your family have escaped death at incredibly high stakes and managed to free captured dimies despite the odds. You found, caught and neutralised Jack the Riveter, whom Her Majesty's secret service couldn't even apprehend. And to top it all off, you're creating an airship no other inventor has successfully managed to do yet. Did I miss anything?"

"Tish-tosh. Anyone could've done the same things if they had the drive. Besides, I wouldn't call those impossibilities." I slump in my chair farther.

"Well, all of what you just said I believe to be wrong. I understand you're a humble person, Aspen, and use pride as a mask when you need to be in society; but when it's just you and those you trust, you need to give yourself more credit, as well as a break from time to time."

"Why does everybody think I need a break? I can't afford a

break! I don't have the time to rest, regardless if I want it or not." I feel more flustered than ever, since I'm contradicting everything I said at breakfast this morning.

"I see now," Uncle George says as he slumps down in the seat next to mine. "It's your soul cogs."

"My what?" I sniffle out.

"Hum, let me explain." He pauses. "My soul cogs are a bit rusty. They need to be oiled and maintained carefully; however, I'm terrible at cleaning and taking care of the fine-tuning. That's why I need and depend on Pauline so much. She takes care of my cogs and makes sure I'm resting and refined, at least the parts of me that aren't already broken." He tenderly reaches for the scar on his scalp. "Your soul cogs, Aspen, are so overworked and ungreased that they're smoking from grinding against each other for so long. My dear, when was the last time you had a day for yourself? Or a chance to prop your feet up by the fire with a full kettle of tea and a good book?"

"I'm afraid I just can't afford that right now."

"My dear, if you don't spend the labour to tend to your soul cogs, the machine which is you will die or explode, whichever comes first. None of us wish to see such a fate befall you. I know only too well the consequences." I've seen where his current madness lies in him, but the man he was before is still very present and alive. I just wonder how much more is hiding beneath the surface. Whether it will be madness or who he once was.

"You know, it's funny," I say as he gets up and walks towards the window. "It's amazing how quickly our entire reputations have fallen in one evening. I normally don't care, but concerning Thomas, Lori and Keagan…well, it matters to them. And now I wonder if even after all this work and with the possibility of the queen's pardon, will we have a good reputation after this? Will we be able to walk through the streets again? A reputation is so hard to build and yet so easy to shatter."

"Ah, just like Rome. It wasn't built in a day, but it can surely be burned down in one."

"Indeed it can," I mull, looking back at Uncle George. He carries a faraway gaze in his eyes as he stares out into the bright day.

Heart-wrenching cries through the dark bring me from my slumber, but for once they're not mine. Fumbling around in the dark, I finally find the matches on my nightstand. The cries still call out, muffled through the walls as I strike the match with my first scratch and light the lantern in a flash, Lori scuttling out of bed to don her shawl and slippers. But I don't mind my time with such frivolous matters the second I hear Thomas's voice outside our door. "Aspen, Lori, come quick. It's Keagan—I can't wake him up!"

That was all I needed to hear to bolt out of the room and bound across the old rickety boards. I pass Pauline in her bonnet and night dress, scampering up the steps as I race past the railing. "Go get a pail of water and some rags," I say over my shoulder. The further I run down the dark halls with the light in my hand, Keagan's wailing filling the air, the more it feels as if I'm in one of my own nightmares. Except this time, I do reach the door to his room, and when I open it, the real nightmare begins. I can see Keagan's form convulsing on his bed. The wailing has stopped for now, but his breathing is desperate.

Setting down the light, I call out his name and crouch down to take his hand. This usually is the best tactic for me when I have my worst terrors. But this may not have been the best first choice for Keagan. Much to my dismay, he reels and hits his back on the wall, still kicking his feet out on the mattress to push himself farther away. In doing so, he manages to kick the bed off of its frame. As I stand and put up my hands to where my face can be illuminated by the lantern, the look on his face turns from horror to recognition. Just then, Pauline and the rest of the household rush into the doorway, each carrying a candle or lantern. The fuss makes Keagan flinch where he sits, back still pressed up against the wall, one leg on the mattress whilst the rest of him is sitting on the hard metal spring frame of the bed.

I can hear the fuss of everyone in the room, but it sounds muffled as I gaze at Keagan. He looks from the bed to his hands, to the group who are wetting rags in a basin for him, and then to me. His gaze remains on me with that greatly pained look on his face. Is this what I look like when Lori wakes me from my nightmares? Do I look so desperately terrified that I would want the darkness and everyone around me to disappear? Does my face carry that much sweat on it, expressing such a high level of pain, as if my heart could turn to stone at any second? I wouldn't know; I can never see in those moments, only feel. And what I felt then I know that Keagan is feeling now. His gaze doesn't break from mine for a second, until everyone starts to close in on him. All this tedious talk and rushing around isn't good for him. It'd be better to be one-on-one, keeping the rest of them nearby outside the door if needed.

Pauline reaches for his arm, probably to bring him closer so she can wipe his sweat off. Gently placing my hand on her forearm I push it down and away from Keagan. "I'll take it from here."

"But, Miss Wolfe—"

"It's fine. Lori can explain to you that a solitary helper will be better. Right, Lori?" I look to my sister with a false smile.

"Right. Yes, everyone, we need not crowd him, it won't do any good. Come, let's just wait in the hall for a moment. They'll let us know when things are better." She half-pulls and half-leads the way out of the room, with Miss Pauline and Thomas's nightgown sleeves in her hands. Uncle George takes a quick glance back at Keagan with a knowing look in his eyes before closing the door behind him. Everyone but Thomas left their lights in here—two on the nightstand and two on the table—allowing the room to be fully illuminated.

When the door closes, I don't make eye contact with Keagan again until after I have one of the small bowls filled with a clean rag and water in my hands. Walking over, I see he's stopped looking at me and has started to put himself back onto the part of the mattress still atop its frame. His breathing and shaking limbs, however, remain. The second I near him with the rags, he recoils slightly, looking at me almost as if I were a stranger. *Where is that face coming from? He's never looked at me like that before.*

"C'mon, let's get you to cool down a bit," I say. "You need to take a few deep breaths. That will help." I dip the rag in the bowl of water, but before I can even squeeze out the extra water, Keagan reaches his hand in and takes it himself. Droplets of water hit the mattress in muffled thuds as he brings the wet rag to his forehead, eyes and back of his neck. I can properly see now that his shirt is soaked with sweat, reminding me of the few times I had to change nightdresses because I had a similar experience. "Don't worry, you'll be fine," I continue. "Just breathe with me."

"I *am* fine," he says, dropping the rag back in the bowl before covering up his face again with one hand to block his view of my gaze.

Getting off the bed, I walk back to the table, staying quiet. But he's not okay. I can tell because just being around him with this level of tension in the air makes me almost nauseous with each passing second. "I don't think you are, Keagan," I spit out as I place the bowl on the table, a little harsher than I intended, actually.

"I am!"

"Quit lying and let me help you," I blurt out, walking away from the bed and towards the dresser. "You helped me; why can't I do the same to you? Is it because you don't want me to? Do I not deserve to help you now?" Everything I've pent up from the night of Homecoming till now is coming out, and I'm unable to stop one word of it.

"No, that's not—"

"Then what? What's different now from before? I'm sorry I was the one who messed everything up; if it weren't for me and my stupid ideas, Winona would be here, and you wouldn't be hurting like me." I look at the floor, keeping a white-knuckled grip on the dresser behind me.

"What are you going on about? I'm the one who ruined things between us, and for everyone else! I kept the biggest, most damning secret from the whole lot of you. And Charles, damn that man, I should have seen something—anything— that would've led me to believe he would betray us like that. And it's my fault that Winona died on the ship that night! I was right in reach of her. I saw the man with the gun; I could have taken him down. I should have pushed her out of the way. I could have done *anything*! But I didn't...I just stood there. I didn't move or yell or warn her. I didn't do anything! I just watched with every means to prevent her from dying, and yet I was an idiot and did absolutely *nothing*!" He yells louder than ever before, covering his eyes with his hands as I slink down to the wood floor against the dresser. I can hear soft taps of water hitting the cloth of my nightgown on my lap as the burning of my cheeks grows hotter. "I freeze when things get too hard. I—I did—it to you and Lo—Lori, to eve—everyone! I'm just not cut out for this, I'm sorry. I'm s—so sorry. I hate myself for what happened so wh—why is it you don't hate me as well?" he says, raking his hands through his hair as his breathing becomes rapid to the edge of hyperventilation.

"I could never hate you. I'm sorry, too, that I made you feel that way. That it's taken us this long to apologise to one another after it all. I know I said it on the boat, but I think it needs to be said again. I can't bear to lose you. I was angry with you, but I don't think I could ever come to hate you." We sit there in silence and allow ourselves to take in all that just transpired. *Are we truly this broken?* We just remain where we are, each looking at the other, eyes overflowing with tears. "Just take one step forward, and I'll do the same."

"What if we break again?"

"Then we'll just have to pick up the pieces and start over. We'll fix it again."

Slowly, Keagan lowers one of his legs to the floor and stands up. I pull myself up from the floor and take a step forward as well. Each step forward is matched with the others until we stand face to face. Taking a lock of my hair in his hands and nesting it behind my ear, he holds my tear-stained, red-eyed face in his hand and leans his temple down till it's on mine. I reach my arms up and wrap both hands around his forearm as we stand there in silence, waiting for each other to breathe again.

"I'll keep taking steps forward to build things up again if you will, and if you wish for me to do so."

"I do, and I'll help alongside you as well," I say without hesitation, to which he gently takes his forehead from mine and pulls me in for a hug. I cling to him, now realising just how much I've missed him. He tenderly rubs the small of my back like he once did, making me tear up as I smile. We hold on to each other for dear life.

"I miss her, Aspen. I miss her so much it hurts my heart."

"I miss her too. I promised myself they'd be safe and free. I promised them and yet I failed. I don't even know if the ones who made it through the portal survived."

Keagan doesn't say a word but just holds me tighter. His wet clothes have become cold. Finally letting go of him, I turn back to the drawers and ruffle through them to dig out a clean shirt he can wear. The moment I turn around with a fresh cream-coloured cotton shirt, Keagan already has half of his shirt off, exposing himself to me in a state I was not yet prepared for. Keagan hands me the bowl of water, and I absently take it from his hands, giving him his shirt in return. Walking behind him, I run the wet cloth over his glistening back, gently feeling my fingers brush over his muscles. When I walk to the front of him, he begins to slip into his new shirt right before me without the slightest bit of hesitancy. The candlelight that paints warm hues over the contours of his chest and shoulders causes the walls to dance with shadows of his form. The movements are as hypnotising as the candles burning around us. I find myself unable to look away, and the room becomes increasingly warmer.

Keagan focuses only on changing his clothes until he looks at me as I clean off the front of his chest. But the smile and feelings I can't hide become too much for me as I feel his gaze digging into me. Buttoning up his new shirt, he keeps his gaze on me, calm and expressionless, though the only thing that comes to my mind from such a look is a wolf eying a lamb. At the third button, he smiles back at me, to which I stiffen and then turn around, realising I've been staring far too much. A moment later, I hear his footsteps approach me and I feel a shiver run up my back. He wraps his hands around my shoulders and places his cheek next to mine, with his chest flat up against my back. Only our nightclothes separate us now. "Did I surprise you just now?" he whispers deeply.

"Well, I...hmph, time for bed," I say abruptly, putting the bowl down, my face now burning.

"Aspen, I never knew you to be so eager. But if you insist," he says with a smile in his voice.

"I'm serious," I say, turning back towards him.

"Then why are you smiling like that?" He inches closer still with tired eyes and shaking limbs.

"I can't help it."

"The sight of my strong bare chest was just too much for you, I see." He bends back his head and puts the back of his hand to his temple dramatically, like a lady about to faint.

Taking the bowl, I chuck the water at him, hitting his head directly, then throw the rag which lands square in his face. I know I could've answered better than I did, but I couldn't help myself. Bending back over, he starts laughing as the rag falls to the floor. I blush and snicker at his reaction till he takes slow steps towards me. He doesn't stop until he is but a mere inch away from my face. A familiar heat creeps up my neck as his fingers lace into my loose hair. Brushing his nose on mine, he stares down into my glistening eyes.

"There's my Aspen," Keagan whispers before kissing my cheek, causing my smile to broaden. *Finally we are starting to heal.*

VALENTINE'S DAY

ASPEN

"Aspen, how do I look? Are the earrings too much? How about the dress? I don't know about the colour." Lori has been preening herself for the last hour to prepare herself for her Valentine's outing with Ghedi.

"Don't you worry about anything. I've never seen you glow this brightly, Lori. When Ghedi sees you, he'll hit the floor, out cold just from the sight of you."

Lori smiles in her new violet dress and starts to look over herself once more in the mirror. I hate it when I have to milk out praise for my sister, but at least it gets her to stop worrying about her appearance. I'm worried about Lori going out even with a disguise. Apparently during the second rest day, Ghedi and she had spent the entire day together, and now they're going to spend Valentine's Day together. Keagan told me he doesn't like Ghedi; it's in his eyes, he said. I didn't have the time to notice Ghedi's eyes or mannerisms all that much, what with everything else that's occupying my thoughts these days.

Grabbing her shawl and purse, we head downstairs where

the rest of the household is chatting with Ghedi and Cousin Harry. *What might he be doing here?* Wearing a black suit and a black bowler hat, Ghedi looks a little more decent than usual, though he still isn't anywhere close to Lori's level of dress. I pity the fellow for having to wait. I heard the front door open over twenty minutes ago, so he must have begun to wonder if Lori would ever come down. *I worry we may have dolled her up a bit too much,* I think as I go downstairs before Lori, since she loves a proper entrance.

"Lady and gents, Miss Lori Wolfe," I announce before the room, causing everyone to turn my way abruptly. Lori slowly walks into the opening of the room from behind me. I made sure to wear one of my plain shirts and split skirts with no adornments, so she would look even more dazzling by comparison. Although I was expecting an awed look from Ghedi, instead he just lowers his eyes and licks his lips. I now know what Keagan means when he says he doesn't like Ghedi.

"Oh Lori, look at you. You're positively radiant," Pauline says when she walks in the room.

"Very beautiful, Lori." Harry smiles as he holds his cane under his chin.

Pauline fawns over Lori, and Uncle George asks her what their plans are for tonight. I look towards Ghedi again and notice his eyes roving over Lori and constantly shifting towards the door. He's beginning to unnerve me. Keagan notices it too, but acts before I do. Tapping Ghedi on the shoulder, his attention on Lori has broken. Gesturing to the dining room with a rather serious face, Ghedi hesitantly follows after one last look back at her. *Looks like I won't have to play the older scary sibling role tonight, but I'd still like to.*

After sidetracking them, Keagan finally finishes talking to Ghedi. Arm in arm, the little couple heads out the door with smiles and giggles. Immediately after the door closes, Keagan heads back up the stairs in a rush. He hasn't said one word about doing anything for Valentine's Day. Perhaps he's just trying to give me space so we can start things slowly once again.

"Harry, why are you here tonight?"

"Oh, um, I'm here to—"

"See if I can make a corrector for his leg so that I can lessen his limp," George pipes in excitedly with a broad smile.

"I didn't know you delved into such medical practices, Uncle George. Will you be in need of an assistant?" I smile.

"No, but there is something you can do for me. Stay by the fire with a hot pot of tea and a good book. You should treat yourself today by loving yourself." Uncle George gently nudges me over to the dancing fire just before pulling the curtain shut behind him.

I decide to do exactly what Uncle George told me to do. I find a good book and curl up in the chair by the fireplace. Using the tea-train express. Every now and then the little train pulls up with a full teapot and fresh biscuits, and occasionally I hear a loud thud or two from upstairs, but I quickly disregard it since I know it's Harry and Uncle George.

However, after two chapters of Mr Hawkins' adventures on the high seas, I'm interrupted by a frantic Pauline. "Aspen, quick, we need to get you ready. One of George's important connections will be here for dinner tonight. He's on his way as we speak."

"Who is it?"

"Someone who will be very beneficial to you and your job. Now come, don't dawdle." Pauline takes the book out of my hands and practically drags me up the stairs, causing me to stumble along the way. Like clockwork, she dresses me up in my green ball gown and pins up my hair in a new style that enhances the swirls of my curly hair. In less than ten minutes I appear to be ready to meet the queen herself. With but a moment to look in the mirror, Pauline promptly puts a warm black fur wrap over my shoulders and leads me out the door. However, instead of going down the stairs like I expected, we walk past them and straight to the end of the hallway, where she places a palm on a plank of wood and flips it inward. The indentation of a door appears, which opens up to a drafty staircase.

"Pauline, what's going on? Is our guest coming by an air train on the roof? And why am I not wearing a disguise?"

"All good questions that will be answered exactly when you open the door at the top." She smiles knowingly at me, yet I still hesitate. "Oh, Aspen, come now," she huffs as she pushes me all the way to the top of the hidden stairs.

"Pauline, honestly, you are acting—"

With the opening of the door I lose my voice all together. The rooftop is lit with candles on the ground and boxes whilst lanterns are strung up overhead. Uncle George holds open the door with a grand smile and slender eyes, like he knows something I don't. I can't help but give him back a smirk. The moment I walk through the doorway, I see what's really going on. There is an old satin couch close to a standing fire pit that Harry is lighting near a few vases of flowers. Thomas is by the phonograph, playing a tune. Keagan is standing by a candlelit table, looking directly at me in his best suit. "Happy Valentine's Day, Aspen," he says, to which everyone else wishes me one as well. I am so gobstruck at the entire layout that I don't know what to do but walk further in.

"If you need anything at all, feel free to knock on the door," Uncle George says from behind me.

"Don't count on it, but we will if we need you," Keagan says. And with that, everyone walks out the door, leaving Keagan and me alone. The last time we were alone like this was when I woke up in his room, and here I am caught off-guard once again.

I'm still facing the closed door when I hear footsteps come up from behind me. "Shall we, Miss Wolfe?" Keagan's deep voice catches me off-guard; I have to take a deep breath before turning towards him. When I do, he is slightly bowing to me with a smile, and has his hand outstretched, awaiting mine.

"Yes, we shall." I give him my hand as calmly as I can. Once taken, he leads us to the table and pulls out my seat for me. Pushing me in, he takes his own seat across from me and lifts the metal lids off of our dishes. Roasted duck dusted in herbs with boiled potatoes, and red wine already poured.

"You know the wine may not be the best idea, seeing as what happened the last time we drank together," I say before taking a sip.

"Don't worry, I'll make sure you make it to bed just like always," he assures me, making me abruptly spit the wine back in the glass. Keagan doesn't look the slightest bit deterred at my actions; he even appears as if he enjoys it.

"Wait, what...what do you mean 'like always'?"

"I only put you in *my* bed that one time. Lori helped you to bed the night you were drunk. I just carried you to your room."

"You did?"

"Aspen, what's the last thing you remember about the night we drank the bottles of sherry?"

Thinking back, I remember dancing, a lit fire in a fireplace, and someone holding me gently. Anything could have happened that night for all I know. I've never really tried to think too hard about it, since I had such a hangover the next day. "Not all that much, I suppose," I say, trying to take a drink of wine for real this time. After a few moments of silence I can't hold back my feeling of guilt anymore. "I feel terrible. You set all of this up, and I realised only this morning that today was Valentine's Day. I have nothing ready to offer you."

"Yes, you do. You're here, aren't you? We're finally beginning to talk and act like we used to, which is the biggest gift I've been wishing for ever since we had our falling-out. Things between us have been like walking on thin ice ever since."

"I still feel like I need to make it up to you somehow."

"Oh, you can certainly try as much as you wish, my dear." He eyes me with a smooth smile.

"Keagan!" I say, trying to sound insulted; but I can't help but smile and laugh.

He continues to look at me with the same unwavering gaze. I feel my cheeks redden from the intensity till finally he takes my hand and says, "You leave me breathless, Aspen. I hope you realise how beautiful you are."

"Hmm, thank you. You know, this dish really does look scrumptious. We should eat before it gets cold."

"I'm sorry, did I make you feel uncomfortable?" Keagan's brow knits.

"No—no it's not that, I just…"

"Haven't you ever been told you are beautiful? Other than by me, of course." Keagan sits back with a questioning gaze.

"Besides family and strangers on the streets, no. Only when I'm around Lori, then it's plural; beautiful *ladies*."

"And you can't see it for yourself when you look in the mirror, or when men look at you?"

"No," I say flatly.

"May I ask why?"

"Well, you remember my aunt, don't you?"

"From what you've told me, how could I forget a witch like that?"

"Well, she had a hand in it, I can tell you that. Because of my aunt constantly berating me and my sister's close proximity, my experience with men has not been enjoyable as yours has been with women."

"Why would your sister being around you hurt your chances with men?"

"Well, think. Have you ever had someone more amiable around you to steal the attention at all times? Most of the time without even trying?" I say, playing with a sliver of duck meat before taking a bite.

"It sounds like you blame your sister for it."

"I'd be lying if I said I didn't, but I don't hold malice against her for it, since it's something she never means to do when it pertains to men I may be interested in. She's just naturally more pleasing to listen to or gawk at...at least that's what I've gathered from experience with other men."

"There's something you're not telling me. What happened to you, Aspen?" Keagan puts down his knife.

"What do you mean 'what happened?'"

"Aha! Now I know something is wrong," he says triumphantly. "You often try to deter a question by asking one of your own." I, on the other hand, feel rather annoyed by his smugness tonight. "C'mon, just tell me."

"Well, I think you should have asked *who* happened... "

"All right, then, who do I need to kill?" Keagan asks nonchalantly as he stands up, rubbing his knuckles.

"Keagan!"

Keagan looks at me with raised eyebrows and pressed lips.

I know he'll keep asking and get it out of me eventually—he always does in the end. Damn him for that.

"His name was Paul and we met when I was 16. He was new to Bath so he hadn't known my family long, and he had never seen Lori. She went to spend a few weeks visiting our cousins who were much closer to her than I. But when Lori returned from our cousin's home, she had caught a high fever. It lasted around two weeks before she was allowed to go through the garden or see her friends around town. Paul and I were becoming close and would go around town together, he often remarked on how lovely I was. Then one day he came over for dinner, and here comes my now healthy rosy-cheeked sister down the stairs, in her dining dress and pearls."

I pause to take a sip of wine again. "He couldn't take his eyes off of her the whole night. He barely even spoke to me the whole evening. Not a day later, he had the gall to come back to the house, asking for Lori to have a stroll with him. Lori later informed me that at the dinner table he told her how gorgeous she was, and how she was a radiant light he felt so lucky to behold."

"So she was boasting?"

"No...she was warning me. I had told her of the Paul I had come to know, and how he was interested in me. She declined his offer and told me the boy she had met was interested in physical attractiveness alone. 'Don't waste your time on blind fools like him; get someone who can see your inner and outer beauty,' she told me."

"Lori really said that?"

"She was quoting our mum." I rub my arms.

"I'm sorry you were treated so poorly, Aspen."

"Don't be. I've learned not to waste my time on blind fools, or my words on deaf ears."

"That's why I'm sorry. I never wanted you to feel like you were wasting your time with me, and I know my track record with women didn't help put you at ease...probably the opposite, quite frankly. But I just want you to know that there has not been one moment where I haven't been sincere when it comes to my feelings for you."

"Well, rest assured, I do realise that now. I mean, this whole setup helped most definitely, but it's more the fact that you've chosen to stay loyal to us through this time, despite the secrets we've both hidden from each other. That's something I'd like to apologise for as well. Lori and I both tried to keep you in the dark about a lot of things, and I think we can now let you in on them."

As we ate, we discussed more secrets than I think either Keagan or I had ever planned on sharing. He told me about the deals he would make with foreign ambassadors, how he nearly gambled away half his inheritance in Morocco, his other addictions, and how he finally became clean of them. I discussed nearly all the secrets my family held, like how my aunt was trying to get rid of Lori and me so she could inherit our father's estate and money, a battle we're still fighting along with Harry, her own son. "Harry and his sister ran away actually to join a circus," I say before taking a sip of wine. "Just because of that, Aunt Mae disowned them both without a second thought."

"She really is a charmer, isn't she?" Keagan remarks, finishing off his buttered bread.

"Yes, a real snake if there ever was one. Well, a few years into their careers as trapeze acrobats, poor Harry fell one night and somehow missed the net. He was fine mentally, but he messed up his leg and back to the point that he will never be able to perform again. Broke his heart too, since he and his sister had planned on being a duo act for as long as possible. As he was recovering, he and his sister stayed with our uncle. During our stay all together, his sister took care of him. She would also train us, and Harry would act as spotter. That's where we learned how to be more acrobatic ourselves, among other things."

"So tell me, Aspen. You're adept in acrobatics, fighting, and even ballet. And yet when we were dancing at the Governor's Ball, you were so tense and nervous that I thought we would have to stop just so you could calm down mid-dance. Not to mention ease the increasing pain in my feet."

Taking the last bite of duck, I wince a bit as the painful memory of trampling Keagan's poor feet at the governor's ball. "That's because whenever I fight or run at night, I'm not doing it in front of a crowd in a setting where gossip is king and everyone sees everything. Also, I never dance ballet in front of anybody, not even Lori. I prefer to do my performing in the shadows."

"Hmm, well, there's a certain ball coming up in a few days, a costume-themed one to be exact, held by an old mentor and friend of mine. Her husband has connections to mills that own a rather large portion of dimie-slave workers in the city. Could be a very prosperous occasion. But, of course, at a party being hosted by a baroness and all, you'll need to learn how to dance better in front of crowds." He stands and offers his hand to me. "Dance with me."

I can't help but smile at his gesture, and I gladly take his hand. Leading me over to the phonograph, he flips the record over to play a different tune. It's slow and romantic, a song I've never heard. He guides me through the steps one by one until I get the hang of it, then we dance faster and faster to the tempo of the quickening tune.

We don't speak all that much through the dance, aside from small encouragement he gives me every now and then. At the end of the song, he dips me, staying close to me the whole time. I let my hand rest on his cheek as he closes the distance between us and gives me a tender kiss. I feel as if I've been in a desert for so long without him near me; and now here he is, this beautiful oasis with fresh water that I've been needing for too long but could never find till now. I had it once, till I started to journey on. I had even begun to fear I had lost him forever. And yet here he is, pulling me into his kiss more than ever before, to the point I can feel my legs giving out.

He must feel my weakening knees as well, since he ends our kiss there and helps me to the couch. Watching all the fire flicker from the pit, they seem to float where they are as Keagan draws circles on my face, studying me closer. This time, however, I don't hold back; lacing my fingers in his hair, I bring him to me. I can even feel myself smiling as I try to kiss him. I can't believe how much I've missed this. I can taste the wine on his soft lips, and how they practically bruise my own as he pulls my waist closer to his. I can feel the air thicken around us, making it so much harder to breathe between each long kiss.

Keagan pins me to the back of the couch as he bites my neck, just before giving it a powerful kiss. Sucking the nipped area with his tongue makes me lose all memory of how we came to this. I find myself thankful for the cool breeze as I note the vapour trails from my mouth with each exhale. Every touch, every place his mouth lands, he makes me even warmer and excited than before. We keep going until I feel I may get overheated.

Reaching under my dress, he pulls my leg up and brushes

his lips across my knee. I know just from that alone that my face is as red as a tomato now. Lowering my leg, but not letting go of it, his hand rakes my bare skin whilst laying back towards me slightly. "Ha, perhaps I overdid it. But I guess that's not completely bad, eh?" Just hearing him say this makes my hands fly up to my cheeks in my habitual attempt to hide my embarrassment. Gathering my thoughts, I remember who I'm with and start to feel at ease again. We have seen the worst of each other and the best of each other.

"I think it's exactly what I've wanted all along, wouldn't you agree?" I say, placing my right hand on his cheek.

"No." He slides his lips onto my palm before gently kissing it. A pulsating feeling flows through me. I never realised it was such a sensitive area, and I find myself wishing he would kiss me more. "This is what I've been needing all along."

And just like that, my heart begins to melt all over again, for he is mine and I am his.

THE GEISHA

LORI

Draped in red silks, my face is white as snow now as Keagan, Aspen and I exit our carriage, pausing to gaze up at the grand white-painted homes in Belgravia. What a spotless line of townhomes; not a speck of dirt or trash lines the sidewalks or streets. The trail of carriages behind us wait whilst the faces of guests inside each are aglow in jubilation as the lanterns of the streets illuminate their masked faces. I open up my bracelet compact to check my black geisha wig to make sure it's situated and no blond hairs are showing. Pauline did such a splendid job fixing the wig on. I'm glad she knew what to do, since Aspen and I hadn't the slightest clue. Despite all our missions and tricks, we never once had to wear wigs; they were always for decoys hidden in our sheets. Pleased with my disguised appearance, I shift the mirror's view over to Aspen, who is fidgeting with the pink bodice of her gown. "What's the matter, Little Bo Peep? You lose your sheep already?" I tease.

"You know I could've gone as the Grim Reaper and traded my cane for a sickle." Aspen stares me down, spinning her cane in her hand. Shutting my compact on my wrist, I clear my throat and help hide one remaining brown curl that pokes out of Aspen's blonde bouncy wig.

"Why do wigs have to be so itchy?" Sissy asks Keagan before giving her desperate scalp a scratch.

"Beauty is pain, you know," he mockingly replies as he offers his arms to us so we may properly approach the host's home. "It could be worse; you could've been a French aristocrat, and then you would've also had to balance a tower of hair on your head."

"You forget, that *is* one of my costume choices tonight,"Aspen sneers through gritted teeth as we pass by a couple in jester costumes.

"Who said I forgot?" Keagan smiles bravely. I can already tell by the fumes and sparks in the air that Aspen is thinking of a way to get back at him or embarrass him later. Better watch my step, in case she wishes to hit two birds with one stone.

"Whether you're Bo Peep or not, I'd be your follower any day all the way to the very end, no matter what," Keagan whispers to her, but I can still hear it. And, my oh my, the look in Aspen's eyes when she gazes back at Keagan...I hadn't realised how long it'd been since she's looked at him like that, her eyes wide and full of yearning, completely speechless. *It's time for you to realise you are worthy of love, Sissy.*

And then I hear her say it. "I don't want to have only a follower. I want a partner."

"Then that's what I'll become."

The open door allows us to walk in along with a wave of couples behind us down the steps. The scent of perfume and cologne seasoned with sugary delights wafts towards us as we enter the glittering marble parlour. As we wait to greet our hostess, I hear the sharp pop of a cork sailing off in the air from its bottle. When I turn to its sound, I see a current of golden champagne fizzing just before a bunch of cheering guests raise their glasses.

"What a wonderful place of frivolity," I murmur, catching the attention of the man standing in front of me. Olive-skinned and dressed as a Renaissance noble, I wonder if he's an Italian diplomat. Giving a smile and a tip of his plush red hat, I bat my eyes and hide half of my face behind my Oriental fan. *I'll make sure to enjoy myself this time no matter what happens. I'd almost like to see Damon try and ruin this party for me. That way I can stop him dead cold myself,* I think as I finger the switch on my fan that extracts the blades. The one thing I wish Aspen hadn't insisted we do tonight, which was bring weapons, is actually making me feel more empowered and ready for the evening.

Approaching the hostess catches me by surprise; just one look at her makes me feel afraid, as if we are approaching a queen. The Baroness Carina Von Trapp is as ornate and elegant in appearance as where she lives. Draped in a viridian-green Grecian-goddess dress, her costume fits her aura and manner so well, it makes me even more nervous at what to say, or if I should say anything at all. However, after we're introduced, Keagan gives her a signal almost like a salute; the second she sees this signal, she puts on a smile like she did with the last guests, as if nothing were out of the ordinary, and simply nods her head. Coily hair is quaffed high atop her head in beads and combs, its red tresses shining much like the burgundy velvet curtains drawn behind her. With them drawn, it allows us to peek into the next room, buzzing with delight and delectable scents. *That must be where the goodies are.*

Tonight we go by fake names, as if the entire event were a piece of theatre; "Tabitha" for myself, "Amelia" for Aspen, and "Theo" for Keagan. Before we excuse ourselves to enjoy the merriment, Keagan leans in to ask something of the baroness, to which she happily replies in a whisper too quiet for my ears over the cheer of the guests. As we walk away down the hall to peek into the different rooms, we see there are jugglers and fire breathers in one large room where people can come in and out as they please, an area sectioned off for the performers. Such an act they put on! I was sure the jugglers would get burned by the pillar of fire shooting right over their heads; but they effortlessly toss their pins around the fire from one hand into the other, not one catching flame.

Another room is filled with several small, upholstered, cherrywood silk seats, where people converse and pick at their food on their plated laps. One room is entirely for tea and cake, though it only holds three tables. It is still filled with many people, each nibbling pastel frosted cakes of all different flavours in a heavy aroma of jasmine and rose-petal tea. Close to this room is the gallery and statuary room at the end of the hall, adjoining the large dance ballroom through double doors. Glimpses of each room are not enough to curb my curiosity. I want my fill of each and every room tonight.

"I believe there are a few plates of *petit fours*, and an empty dance card with my name on it awaiting me, so I shall bid you two adieu for the moment," I swiftly say as I slip my arm out of Keagan's crook and head back towards the room with the aroma of frosting and marzipan chocolate. Aspen—or, I mean Amelia—and Theo don't even try to come after me; I already know that, for them, tonight is business first and party second. But it's of little consequence to me, since they both know how to handle themselves in these situations, and where to find what they're looking for at any time.

Piling up chocolates and *petit fours* on my plate, each dotted with pink and blue frosting flowers, I feel my stomach ache to be filled. My nose is in a newfound heaven with fresh tarts just now being brought in from the kitchen. *Now I know my favourite room,* I think as I see bowls and platters filled with fresh fruit and cubed cheese of every shade of the rainbow come out to be placed right in front of me on the buffet table. I may never leave.

Fresh fruits of all kinds are in abundance, strawberries and raspberries so fragrant, I feel like I can already taste them as I pass by. Exotic pomegranate seeds appear to be little rubies next to the golden pineapple slices. Such an incredible spread makes everything appear as if it were a pirate's treasure. Every bite that enters my mouth takes me to a new location of bliss, a new paradise to explore just from the tips of my taste buds. However, after filling a considerable amount of food onto my plate and sampling even more around the length of the long table, I remind myself that it's not polite for a lady to gorge herself at a party like this. Aunt Mae would have been appalled at the amount on my plate or to even see me in this room. No matter; she isn't here, so I can eat without worrying about her from now on.

Satisfied with my plate, I move on to browse the rooms. The thought of getting to brush elbows with some of the highest classes in London and abroad makes me feel zealous. All that glitters tonight might as well be gold and diamonds. When I look to the ceilings, there are dazzling mobile crystal chandeliers that move and shift like kaleidoscopes, never in the same form more than once. Not to mention all the jewellery for the night; with each wave of a hand or turn of a neck, my eyes catch a new ornate bobble. The conversation's a bit dull, nothing pertaining to the dimies that I can listen in on yet. The ballroom is filled to the brim with dancers and eager onlookers waiting for an opening to step in. I nearly miss the French Rococo pastel style of the room with gilded mirrors and fantastic paintings. There are pieces with scenes of merriment and parties, Greek nymphs and gods, picnics in the French countryside, all strewn across the candlelit walls.

The grand crystal chandelier looks like a downpour of dazzling raindrops suspended in time, as they begin to fall from a cloud made of light. So many people are packed inside the room that I can barely even enter, but no matter, I still have half a plate of goodies with me, so I won't be able to dance yet anyway. The few chaps who catch a glimpse of me and are starting to make their way over will just have to wait a little longer for a dance. I wonder what Ghedi would think if he saw me dancing with another gentleman? It's just dancing, not courtship; I'll be fine. Though I do wish I could be dancing with him again instead.

The way we swayed to the music last night in the back of that cabaret was unlike any other style of dance I ever had the pleasure to try out. So quick in tempo, he made me feel as if we were dancing on the stars. But it's the kiss he stole that lingers the most in my memory. The soft brush of his warm lips on mine makes my heart flutter. What am I to do? I'm falling madly for a penniless gypsy when I'm in such an opportune place to find a rich husband of good standing. Another glance at the falling crystal drops of the chandelier takes me back to how we had to run through the rain to the nearest gazebo in the park. I do wish that he had lent me his jacket, though; it had gotten rather cold. Still, the night was a wonderfully romantic adventure. I hope he still wants to go on the next one this Friday night.

The tea room smells of jasmine and rich lemon cookies. Bowls of rose petals lay in the centre of each table, radiating the delicate scent of potpourri. I see that this room has half the level of loudness of the other rooms, and after sitting in silence for a moment preparing my cup of rosehip tea, I hear a rather tantalising conversation.

"Well, when does the new shipment come in? We can't wait forever or else profits will drop."

"Soon, Godfred, soon. There was a delay in the shipment, since all slaves being transported are now under special security. Blame it on those blasted night phantoms. They've created quite a number of barriers for us these days." A man with a high-pitched voice says.

"But how long? The mills can't work at full capacity with only fifty slaves working them. We need over a hundred, and soon."

"You'll get your fifty slaves as promised. They should be here in two weeks' time."

"Ugh, two weeks! My buyers will have my hide by that time. but all right, I'll see what I can do to sway them."

Peeking over my shoulder, I see the one named Godfred getting up and leaving the room, along with his associate. Standing from my seat and placing myself closer to the couple who are taking a sip of tea, I ask, "Pardon me, but do you know who those two gentlemen are, leaving the room? I thought I heard the name 'Godfred.' I'm looking for someone with that name."

"Ah, yes, miss, that's Mr Godfred Smith. Word to the wise, m'lady, unless you are wanting to discuss business regarding the mills around town, don't talk to him. He doesn't wish to discuss anything else tonight," a man with a black bird mask warns me kindly.

"Especially his most successful one, the Smith and Kipling Mill," the lady in a white swan outfit adds, rolling her eyes. "You'd think he was talking about his favourite child, the way he goes on about it."

"Oh dear—perhaps I won't chat with him, then. Thank you very much." I curtsy before excusing myself.

"You're welcome, my dear," the lady says before continuing her conversation with her partner.

I feel refreshed enough for ten dances now, I muse aimlessly as I walk through the gallery, saving my last *petit four* till I reach the end of the room. The gallery is filled with miniature statues on white pedestals in the centre and sides of the room, and between the white marble and bronze statuary there are vibrant oil paintings. Each is different; they don't seem to be of the same artist, either. There's one painting of Athena and Arachne duelling each other, a statue of Perseus holding Medusa's head, even biblical figures like Daniel in the lion's den.

What's the pattern here, though? Most lords and ladies who are art patrons keep to a theme, but here it all seems random. *Such an odd collection*, I think as I turn the corner to a smaller pocket-gallery area where fewer pieces are on display. Here I see one door guarded by a blue silky-furred bear dimie with extended wings. When he catches my eye, I give him a quick nod and smile before I circle back into the previous gallery, only to notice a man dressed as a Crusader in a dark corner by the door. One could easily miss him when walking in the room, but he doesn't appear to be the same Crusader I saw earlier on. Perhaps it was just a common costume to find; these things happen.

Now that I've seen each room, I believe, I am in need of one last chocolate tart before I let some gent sweep me off my feet in the dance hall. As I'm walking out of the gallery doors, however, the Crusader just remains where he is, acting like he's observing the sculpture of Cassiopeia and the sea monster. I can feel his lingering gaze on me, his stare different from other men tonight; it isn't warm, inviting or curious. It isn't even predatory, it's just...dangerous. Like he's not to be bothered as he's searching for something.

Strolling down the plush red carpet hall that connects all the rooms, I make my way toward the buffet room. The baroness has left her place beside the front doors. *I guess all her expected guests have arrived.* I grow closer to the buffet room and notice there is yet another man dressed with the red cross on his chest and chainmail underneath his cover. He stands just outside the banquet room in the hall, enjoying a plate of hors d'oeuvres. When I step inside the buffet parlour of dazzling food, I can't help but look around, only to see yet another man wearing the same costume, chatting with two gentlemen dressed as harlequin clowns. *Four men dressed as Crusaders? Something doesn't feel quite right with this.* I decide I'm not up for that chocolate tart anymore, and instead grab a quick glass of punch.

I promised myself I wouldn't let anything ruin my night, but I can't help but feel like we're all being watched and picked apart by these men. Making my way back out into the hallway, I decide to peek into the other rooms once again. I was too enthralled the first time around to even think about possible spies. *For a person in the reconnaissance business like myself, I am really doing a disservice to my profession.* Peeking into each room, I see now that there is a Crusader in all of them. *The baroness has dimies to serve the food, guard the doors, and wait on people. What would she need human guards for? It's more than mere coincidence that there are at least eight crusaders here, if not more.* There's a chance that the men dressed as harlequins might be their accomplices as well. My face begins to flush from my nerves, and I have to fan myself even harder to cool down and properly breathe.

A light tap on my shoulder causes a jolt to run through me, startling a couple walking by. Not knowing if it's Keagan, Aspen, or one of the Crusaders, I slowly turn around with my face partially covered by my fan. When I see the man that the hand is connected to, I quickly recompose myself; it's the Renaissance noble from before. *What a beautiful white smile he has.*

"Would you honour me with a dance, *signorina?* My name is Sir Leonard of Florence.."

"Yes...yes, you may, Sir Leonard," I reply with a gentle smile as I lower my fan.

"Pray, what is your name, *signorina?*"

"You may call me Tabitha, Sir Leonard."

With a nod and a smile, he whisks me away into the ballroom. I try my best to put my mind at ease and enjoy the dancing, but how can I, now that I feel as if there are people searching the crowds? It may not even be us being targeted, but with our bounty being so high, I find that hard to believe. I haven't seen hide nor tail of Damon, but perhaps he's one of the men in a mask. Whatever the case, once this dance is over I must see Aspen and Keagan to warn them. *Wait...I haven't seen either of them since we arrived here. Not in one room did I pass them by or see one of their costume changes.*

As the dance quickens, the room begins to spin like a top, and I begin to suspect it could be more than just the dancing that's making me feel so dizzy. Fear heightening, my mind conjures images of Aspen and Keagan being tied up and beaten into submission somewhere far away from the party. I keep trying to convince myself that they're probably doing some unseen work at the moment, but I can't. They've been absent from the party for more than an hour. I just know they've run into trouble, and I'm not there to help them. *I don't even know where to look!*

"Tabitha?" I hear Sir Leonard ask, seemingly from a distance although he continues to stand right next to me.

"Aspen, where are you?" I mumble.

"Lady Tabitha!" Those are the last words I hear as my swirling world turns silent and my vision goes dark.

THE BARONESS

KEAGAN

Soon after Lori takes her leave, Aspen too splits off from me, after I gave her a kiss on the hand. Between the note and the directions I gave her beforehand on how to get into the baron's study, she should be just fine. Seeing as how my previously discussed need for a private meeting with the baroness will have to wait a bit longer, due to the current influx of guests arriving to greet Her Ladyship, I decide to make my way to the banquet table. I just hope I won't need to restrain Lori from the morsels at her mercy. However, as I walk in I see her coming my way around the grand table, overflowing with flower vases and food displays. Her Ladyship has truly outdone herself this time. When I was in school, the spreads weren't nearly this marvellous. It's no wonder Lori walks right past me without any notice, since all her attention is on the glistening food awaiting her greedy hands to pick over. I really hate to stop her since it would be an embarrassment; but if she keeps going, she will soon create a leaning tower of food for any guests to notice and point at. Luckily she rethinks that last chocolate eclair and heads out of the dining room. Doesn't even look up from her plate—she really is amazed by this party, isn't she?

I pick out a few treats myself; whether they be covered in butter or icing makes no difference to me. Looking around, I've been able to spot a few familiar faces, but none of them seem to recognise me. Many just give me side glances or pay very little attention at all—luckily for me, since one of the women from Germany I once courted just passed by in an Egyptian costume. *Strange; in my memory she was much prettier. I suppose it's just time that's changed my view.* Dancing around the room to survey the faces of the passing partygoers, I notice some with masks and some with makeup, while others are easily discernible.

I pop another mouthwatering morsel of buttered crumpet into my mouth as I spot two men in the opposite corner from me across the room, dressed as Crusaders. They seem to be surveying the area as well, but by the tight knot in their furrowed brows I can tell that their conversation is anything other than pleasant. Though their eyes are mainly on the partygoers, they lie and watch from the shadows, like apparitions plotting to haunt one of the living. However, it appears they haven't chosen who to haunt yet. I wonder who they're looking for. Most of the couples are in matching costumes. *So what would be the matching costume of a Crusader? Joan of Arc, perhaps? Maybe an angel, even though that might be far-fetched?* Whoever it is, I hope they find them soon so that their scowls can diminish.

Taking my leave of the banquet room, I pass into the hallway, only to quickly be caught by the arm. "What do you think of the party, Keagan?" the baroness asks. "Can you honestly say you've been to any like it?" She's always had a habit of comparing her soirees to others.

"I can honestly say that I have never before seen one quite like this with so many delicacies and variety of entertainment."

"Oh, you still have the same silver tongue as you always did, my dear. I'm glad to see that hasn't changed. At least I know you still have the quality of getting yourself out of trouble. From what I know about your adventures, I hope it's been sufficient enough."

She leads me towards the end of the hall where two dimies stand, guarding closed double doors. I remember these doors; they lead to the library, where we used to do our foreign-language lessons. Entering into the long room with a few bright Tesla bulbs to light the place up, it feels more like a spacious hallway with a desk in the centre. The windows are drawn for the night, but with a faint blue glow behind them from the moonlight. The doors close behind her, and her entire energy changes from jolly hostess to my former motherly tutor.

"I must admit, Keagan, I never would have expected a bull-fighter as one of the disguises in your arsenal. Although it wouldn't surprise me to find out you participate in the running of the bulls in Spain."

"It is indeed a possibility," I smirk childishly, to which she hits me with her fan on the arm.

"Now, Keagan, I want to hear about everything you've been up to so far. I hope you haven't become too rusty in your languages."

"Not to worry, I've had more than plenty of trips to keep my skills in tune. France, Morocco, Spain, Germany, Poland, you name it. I've ventured far for my father's business affairs. Though you must forgive me, your ladyship, since we have scarcely spoken since I graduated university. There are many things that have changed about my life since our last meeting."

We sit down at the small red-velvet round pouffe near the fiction side of the book shelves. "Why don't you catch me up?" she asks, so I do just that. I tell her all about my travels, my father's passing, Lori and Aspen coming to live with me. I even tell her about Thomas and Uncle George. But I decided to only talk about our public appearances, nothing about our crimes against society. I've never been certain on how she feels about the treatment of the dimies; she's always treated hers quite well, giving them good clothes to wear, plenty of food, and servants' quarters to live in. But there have been times where I've heard her snap at them, not to mention how none of them look her in the eye or show much emotion if any towards her or her husband. That's generally not a good sign. "You would've loved the last party I went to. It was simple compared to your own; however, my wards and I are currently in somewhat of a feud with the host. You remember the governor of Currlion, yes?"

"Governor Damon?" she asks with a look of recognition in her eye. "I more than simply remember him, Keagan. My husband is friends with him. He's even been invited to this party tonight, since it's public knowledge that he's come to London. I believe he's here right now amongst the other guests."

The sound of a gun going off rings through my mind. *Governor Damon is here in this house, and the three of us are separated from one another. I have to find the girls and warn them. He can't know we are here. But what if he already knows and that's why he's here?* Memories of him and his party ambushing us on New Year's Eve take over my thoughts, along with the fiery pain of electrocution. All the blood and oil covering the deck and my hands. *The horror that was the fight on the ship cannot happen again. I never want to go through that much killing all at once.*

I find myself standing back up and feeling incredibly warm. "Keagan, are you alright?" The baroness asks alarmingly. "You just started to hyperventilate and I thought you were about to go into a frenzy." She pulls me gently back down into my seat before offering me her handkerchief.

Dabbing my brow and trying to take steadier breaths, I pretend to write it off as nothing. "I'm fine. I just remembered something he once said that I wasn't too pleased about. It's one of the reasons we're feuding currently. By any chance, do you know what the governor is dressed up as?"

"Yes, he came in as a Crusader. He even has real chainmail and a working sword he showed me."

"Does he now?" I say, trying my best not to let my voice crack under pressure. *Bugger, we're dead if he finds us.* "Do you by any chance remember where you last saw him? Also, I know he lost his wife some time ago, but did he by any chance bring a guest?"

"Oh, he brought quite a few guests with him tonight. Any Crusader you spot is a part of his group. Now, I know you're going to say that I shouldn't have allowed it, since this is much larger than the two-person guest limit, but you know how hard it is for me to turn people away. Besides, now there are more people to enjoy the party."

"Exactly how many came with him?" I ask gently as the baroness grips and fidgets with her fan, looking rather sheepish. "Baroness Carina, how many Crusaders are in your house right now?"

"Ten, I believe?" she says sheepishly.

"You allowed ten men in as a group?"

"It'd be an insult to turn him and his party away when they've all worked so hard on their costumes."

"Ah, I see." I rub my neck nervously.

"Is your feud with one another truly so great as to not attend the same parties?"

"Well, if we're being honest with each other, our little fight is one of the reasons we left Currlion."

"And the reason you're also in hiding?" When she sees the horrified look on my face, she continues, "Oh, come now, Keagan, quit beating around the bush. You need help in your cause. It's all the dimies talk about these days."

"What...what do they talk about?"

"That you're looking for people to join you and your *wards* in your cause to free the dimies. They wonder if they can trust you, after rumours of a massacre on a ship a few weeks back. They're in a real tizzy about everything concerning you...uhm, *night spirits,* is it?"

"Night Phantoms is what people have been calling us. So do your dimies explicitly tell you this, or do you simply overhear it?"

"Yes," she says matter-of-factly with a smug grin. She must sense my unease in the whole matter; taking my hand, her demeanour goes back to a thoughtful one. "As I said before, my dear, you need not worry about a thing. Your secrets are safe with me. What would I have to gain by informing on you, anyway?"

"Besides a huge lump of money?"

"At what cost, hmm? Your life and the lives of those ladies you care for? No, I won't have it."

"Thank you, Baroness Carina," I say with genuine gratitude.

"Now, enough of this. I want to hear more about this

newfound family you're acting as guardian for. I hope you won't feel too embarrassed to introduce me to them later."

"Not at all. If we can find the girls then I will most definitely introduce you."

So you can just as quickly sneak us out of here and away from Governor Damon and his men. Why did I not think he could have been invited? The governess always invites British leaders, aristocracy and foreign diplomats to her gatherings. However, I must admit, not even *she* was expecting him to bring along *ten men*! If Charles is one of them, I don't think I'll be able to restrain myself from throttling him, after the treacherous deed he dished out on us all. I must find the girls before it's too late. I can't let him take any more people away from me.

THE CRUSADER

ASPEN

Time to get to work, I think as I bid Keagan a goodbye for now; however, before he leaves me, he gives me a kiss on my hand, a gesture that makes me smile as we part for the time being. I know I've promised him a dance later tonight, but I'm still as nervous as ever about formal dancing despite the practice we've been doing daily. Taking a quick peek into the room with the lingering sweet smell of rose water and lemon cookies, I find myself convinced that this is the place where I shall be for the majority of the party once I'm done with business matters. It's the perfect place to be, anyway; all the tea I can drink whilst surrounded by people who only wish to have meaningless small talk. I can think up new ideas for the airship, or how our next mission should be executed. *Brilliant!*

I will say, though, even if I don't get what I'm looking for tonight, at least today wasn't a total waste. It was rather fun teaching the team how to get out of restraints and pick locks, not to mention how to escape after being captured. Does my heart good to have seen Issac and Isola mastering those techniques. Now I know that if they get caught, they'll be able to free themselves.

I stroll over towards the last room in the hallway, where the gallery is. Keagan told me to look into the smaller room for the door. Taking my time to look around at the art display, I find myself quite amused at seeing that each piece illustrates a different tale, myth or legend. *How entertaining,* I think as I gaze at a painting of Eros and Psyche, depicting the moment she sees Eros's wings for the first time. Waiting for the last couple in the room to finally leave, I peek my head into the corner room where a lone blue-bear dimie is standing in front of a wooden door. The door looks like oak and is covered in carved ornate designs of kings and castles, though I can only see bits and pieces since his blue bat-like wings are extended, fully blocking the entrance I need.

Walking up to the bear dimie, I catch his attention with my persistent staring. With a smile, I extend the small scroll containing the special message that was coded by Isola and Issac. It takes him a moment, but soon his eyes grow wide and he quickly closes the parchment back up and pockets it. "It's a pleasure to meet and be of aid to you, Miss Wolfe. My name is Peter." His voice booms and echoes off the walls of the small room as he bows with his left paw fisted over his heart and lowers his wings.

"The pleasure is all mine."

Taking a quick look over my shoulder to make sure the coast is clear, he goes ahead and unlocks the door that leads to a short hallway with two closed doors. "The first is the master's study, the second is a lavatory. But please don't take anything with you; I don't wish to get in trouble with the baron or baroness."

"You needn't worry, I only wish to look around. I promise not to steal a single item."

I extend my arm to him as I walk inside. He takes it without hesitation, and though he towers a full head over me, he still seems so small just in his bittersweet expression alone. "Thank you," he says just before he gives a quick smile and shuts the door on me, leaving me alone in the tiny wood-sided hallway.

I open the plain black door to the baron's study, only to see a room with no windows yet again. Now I know the baron has special information, if he has a bank vault-like room just for his study. Guess he should've checked on the loyalty of his household as well. A smile spreads across my face as I start looking over the desk, its drawers, and the bureau in the corner. Rifling through page after page of different deals, insurance papers, finances, even personal letters, I find nothing on his affiliation with the mills or his business associates who own them, and not a stitch of the most impor-tant information, their blueprints. There must be someplace where he keeps the documents of his most expensive asset. However, I don't see any kind of safe in the room, and there are very few rugs, if any, so I can dismiss the idea of a trap-door. After carefully sneaking a peek behind the few canvases that hang on the tan walls, I find myself with no options again.

Stepping back to take in the whole room at once to see if anything possibly looks the slightest bit out of place or fake, I decide to move back to the desk. It's decorated just as ornately as the door that Peter is guarding. Running my gloved hand smoothly over the edges of the desk, I feel no divot or wobbly piece that could give away the placement of a secret drawer. My last hope lies on the right side, and as I brush my fingers over it, I feel the slightest give and suddenly notice a cracked edge on the tree that's carved into the desk. Pressing it into the ornate rough surface, a piece of the thick moulding right near my head juts out from the desk. Jolting back slightly when it pops out of place, I carefully slide it out, and lo, there they are: the business-ownership papers, blueprints, and spare maps of the largest mill in London. Every last bit of information I could have asked for seems to be right here.

Laying out and pinning down the blueprints, I take one picture with my cameo brooch and, after placing it back on my dress, I reach up for my hair comb that Uncle George gifted me. Sliding out the film slot, I angle it high above the prints and shut it back into its slot with a snap. A bright flash illuminates practically the entire room to my surprise and fright. I know Uncle George told me to look out for the flash, but Great Scott, that was bloody blinding. I nimbly tuck the comb tightly back into my wig's coils as the black spots fade from my vision.

I take a moment to listen if anyone might be coming my way, after I hear a scatter behind the doors. Satisfied no one is there, I go back to the secret compartment. As I put the papers back, my eyes skim over the rest of the blueprints, and I discover papers entailing a new security protocol. Setting aside the blueprints, I take pictures of all ten pages without a chance to read any of it myself, only picking up words here and there as I document them. Satisfied, I put back the papers exactly as I found them, and slide the drawer back into place with a light click. *All is as it was.*

Cracking open the door to the study, I listen first before slipping out and tapping once on the door that my comrade is still guarding. There's a pause of a few seconds till I hear a lady's voice slowly fading away, and then the door opens back up. Pulling on my spring-loaded beaded belt, my outfit changes from a pink Little Bo Peep costume to a blue-ruffled-bouffant French aristocrat dress.

The fur of the dimie who holds the door before me matches the blue of my dress, as the shock from my outfit change makes his fur stand on end in bristly patches. Seeing the expression on Peter's face, I simply smile, give him a deep curtsy, and say a kind thank-you before heading back into the main gallery area. *My job and costume are complete. Now perhaps I can enjoy some of that tea before Keagan finds me for the dance.* Strolling along, I see a small statue on a bright pedestal that I hadn't noticed earlier. It's small and bronze, turning green with oxidisation, depicting a woman in a flowing dress who sits on a stone with a parchment unfurled in her hands. There's only one thing wrong with her: her neck is broken, exposing a large breakage of metal and a hole through the back of her neck to where she is looking far down. One could peer inside the hollow statue if they wished. *Strange. If this piece is broken as it is, why is it still on display? Maybe someone knocked it over and broke the neck but didn't bother to hide it.*

"The baron and baroness enjoy works of art and items that carry stories with them. They fill the entire house," a figure in a Crusader costume says with his back to me as he gazes at a painting of Jael impaling Sisera with a tent stake. "The one you're looking at there is a replica of the original in the queen's garden." It's hard to see him clearly since the light is so much darker where he is down the hall, but that voice...I know that voice. I know for sure that I don't have a good feeling when I hear it, either.

"Is that so, Mr...pray tell, what is your name, sir?" I respond.

"Miss Wolfe, I'm insulted you've forgotten me so soon,"

Governor Damon says, stepping towards me in the light where I can fully see his black eyes and half-twisted smile under his peppered beard. I feel my heart jump into my throat as the entire room suddenly becomes very cold. The pain in my arm and the scars on my back begin to flare up as he gets closer, stopping a respectable distance from me before turning to the small statue between us. I take notice of the sword he is carrying on his hip. By the looks of it, it's real. "I didn't believe the police back in Currlion for one minute when they told me you and Mr Myrack had been eaten by sharks or drowned in the icy water. You both are far too slippery and clever. However, something like that would be the perfect cover-up for the likes of you. Seeing you here tonight, popping in and out of rooms, only confirms my suspicions at how cunning you are."

My throat tightens. I feel like we are two dogs in a fight. Whoever moves first will cause a quick counterattack. I don't even know what to say at the moment. I finally mutter, "I see you are here, obviously, but I've failed to see your dimie bots roaming the streets like they did in Currlion. Or Charles, for that matter."

"Indeed, they are not here, which is a small blessing. Although, they're doing a marvellous job of finding the strays you left behind back in Currlion from that exciting New Year's Eve party you hosted. But fear not, I have a new toy you may play with, since you so easily bested my original bots. As for Charles, I have no need to kill my fellow man, especially one who has been so helpful to me. He's been paid handsomely to stay quiet, but I must tell you I've not a clue as to where he is. Probably traversing across Europe, living comfortably. Be my guest and try to find him if you wish; it wouldn't make a difference to me."

How fantastic. "What new toy did you bring for me and my team, then?"

"Now, now, dear, I don't want to ruin the whole surprise, though I know you've already tried to. You know how I knew for certain that your little sister must have been around? That machine of yours was taken from my possession. However, I must thank you for leaving me the details of your precious Gear Heart. I never would have come this far without your journal, you know."

"Damon, I demand you give me back my journal; it was my father's before it was mine. You have no right to keep it." I clench my jaw.

"True, but I think I'll hold onto it for a while nonetheless. Your party obviously wasn't concerned enough to take it when they raided my trunk. I just assumed you left it behind as a gift for me to remember you by."

He teases me unashamedly, and my anger is beginning to reach its limits. *He thinks he can just steal this away from me as well? My father's journal...my journal? I think not.* I slip out a knife, and I can feel the heat start to consume my head until he talks once more. I thought for sure that if he uttered one more sound I would pin him to the wall with my blade. But his next words tickle my shameless curiosity further.

"Now let's get down to the brass tacks, shall we? You recall that bear dimie slave. His name is Thatcher, yes?"

"How could I forget?"

"Have you missed him much? I've heard there were a few intruders one night in a warehouse where I do business, three intruders to be exact, fraternizing with a different slave. A rather scrupulous one at that, which makes me curious as to why on earth you would stick your neck out for the one slave who betrayed you and handed you over to me?" I remain silent, trying to piece together a way to get out of this less-than-amiable conversation. "Woe to the man who leaves the ninety-nine to go after the one. Or perhaps you were trying to get information about the whereabouts of a certain lost friend of yours? Would you like to hear about him?" Governor Damon eyes me knowingly, and though I try to fight it, I can't stop the sneer my face makes. Gertrude must have ratted us out yet again. I'm beginning to wonder if that whole mission was a set-up in the first place. It would be a bit elaborate if it was, on the off-chance that we even found the place. Not to mention the rumours that we were not even alive anymore. Damon's paranoia is starting to scare me a bit since he has so many pawns in play for his side.

"I don't care to hear your empty threats. If you have nothing more of value to say, pray leave me be."

"My dear, I simply wished to fill you in on the condition your slave is in."

"Friend, Damon, not slave. Though I know you can't come to swallow the possibility of a dimie and a human being friends."

"Yes, well, regardless, you will be happy to know that he's alive and being held quite well. The chances for his freedom, however, can only be determined by you. Turn yourself in along with your party, and he'll walk free wherever he may wish."

"And how do I know you aren't bluffing?"

"Oh, yes, I had almost forgotten. This is from him; he says to give it to Keagan specifically, but seeing as I've had no luck in finding him, I guess you can be my messenger." Even before he shows it, a nauseating fear washes over me. He pulls out the lily that Thatcher gave to Winona for Christmas. Taking the flower quickly from his hand, I hold it close to me as

Damon continues to speak. "You have three days to decide. Each day will become harder for him. I can't promise that by the third day he may be alive at all."

"Noted," I say curtly through my barred teeth.

"Miss Wolfe, do you know the story behind this piece in particular? It is quite a tale."

"I can't say I do, sir." I try to sound as cordial as possible as I put the flower in my wristlet.

"They say the artist's wife was found with a broken neck not long after the statue was found the same way. Both were suspected of foul play; they never found the culprits, however. Unlike her body, the killers never left a trace of evidence. She was a spy for England in the war of Austrian succession; during the war she managed to fall in love with an artist in Austria. It wasn't till a year after the war that King George the Second commissioned her husband to create the statue as a monument for his wife's service. It was positioned in the garden at Windsor Castle, in a location for guests to view and enjoy. One night, just a month after it was brought to the garden, the neck was bashed in, causing the cavity you see now. What a feat to get away with."

Damon gives me a sideways look, but I don't give him the satisfaction of returning his gaze. "Indeed," is all I say.

"When she was still alive, and the war was coming to an end, she began to get sloppy and gained too many enemies. She and her husband had to flee Austria just as the war was ending. Be careful that you don't stick your neck out too far as well, Miss Wolfe."

"Why? Would I meet the same fate as Thatcher?"

"Oh, my dear Aspen...if only you would be so lucky. "

A giggle rumbles in my throat. Damon, hearing it, gives me a peculiar glance. *Probably trying to figure out why I see his story so amusing, the twit.* "You know, Governor, you've reminded me of a story as well. Once there was a king and queen who lived in the lap of luxury in a palace that was golden, both literally and metaphorically. They and their court would gorge themselves on lavish foods and cakes of all kinds, and entertain themselves with new creations from the greatest inventors around the world. But their subjects, the lower classes, had been forgotten. The rulers didn't know the true meaning of the word 'poor.' So when the queen was told one day that the people did not have enough grain to make bread, and was asked what they should do, the queen replied, 'Let them eat cake.' Soon there was a great revolt and the aristocracy was hunted down, beheaded and ostracised, including the rich king and queen..." I pause to take in the governor's consternated expression. He *knows* where I'm going with this. I can't help but smile a bit before going on. "So here's the moral of my story, Governor—don't lose your head. Food for thought," I say over my shoulder as I keep my hand to my throat, walking back to the party. I don't hear footsteps following me, but I can surely feel his eyes burning into the scars on my back. For once, I don't mind the burning sensation; in fact, it gives me a giddy feeling and some satisfaction.

The moment I step into the room where the refreshments are, I see Keagan walking briskly with a look in his eye like a man on a mission. I need to warn him who's here, but now I'm worried about what's eating him. The second he turns his head to my side of the room, we make eye contact. Keagan jumps, and as we rush towards each other we manage to say in unison, "I must speak with you." A brief pause of surprise passes before I take his extended arm and we walk into the dancing hall.

"Governor Damon has decided to grace us with his presence tonight," I whisper in his ear.

"What? I was about to warn you of the same thing. Apparently he's told the baroness about his scheduled date to meet with the queen. It's quite soon as well."

"What's the day? Did she tell you?"

"The eighth of April." We try to blend into the crowd, but as I take a look over my shoulder, I see that Damon and a few men in Crusader costumes are looking around the room. He must have gotten a few of his men to come to the party. The thicker we mesh into the crowd, the safer I feel from Damon's gaze, and yet it's so much harder to breathe now.

"Any idea where Tabitha is?" I say just as I feel a tug on my arm. I flip out my fan to cover half of my face and turn my head to see a harlequin tugging on my hand slightly. "May I have the next dance, m'lady?" he asks, smiling. *Think fast, Aspen!*

"I'm terribly sorry, chap, but she's saved the next dance for *me,*" Keagan says, coming behind me and holding both of my arms so the man can't touch me anymore.

"Why don't you let the lady choose, now that there is actual competition around?" the harlequin says with a suffocating amount of pride in his voice. Keagan's face betrays him as it grows red. The man ignores his expression and leans in closer to me. But before he can say a word, the music starts up again, and I pull Keagan with me onto the dance floor. Starting up the song, Keagan leads me through each step, and I try my best to keep up regardless of how fast the tempo is.

"Some guests were attempting to revive Lori last I saw her," Keagan informs me as he leads me through the steps. "Apparently she fainted during a dance."

"She what?"

"Don't worry, she's safe, and none of Damon's men were involved in helping her. Listen, in the final verse there will be a hand bridge that everyone makes and has to go under."

I focus on the steps and glance around the room every now and then. "There are harlequins and Crusaders all over the room, watching us. Wait...how many people are dancing with us? Would they make a long enough bridge to stay under for five seconds?" I ask, mid-spin.

"I suppose so. Why does it matter?"

"I think it's time for a costume change, dear. And then I think we should go home," I say with a wink. Keagan's face brightens up behind his disguise when he realises my idea. We reach the third verse where all the men spin their partners towards the centre. There everyone comes in with raised hands, only to pull back out and repeat the step two more times. Then we rush next to each other and create a long circular arched bridge. Everyone is jolly and full of laughter. I try to laugh my best as well and enjoy myself, but it's a bit difficult when there's someone in the room who wants you dead.

The people to the right of us go through the shrinking tunnel one by one until it's our turn. Taking each other's hands, we crouch down as we shuffle through the bridge of hands. Twisting out my belt and giving it a snap, my costume begins to change as we move closer to the end of the tunnel. I glance at Keagan just as his outfit turns a deep blue, like my costume just was. Keagan is taking off his false moustache, and I notice that the wig I'm wearing is turning red as the curls fall down to my back. My beautiful blue dress catches the purple of a jester's costume as it becomes simple, along with a cream embroidered apron. If Damon still recognises us after this, then he's insane for sure.

We make it out of the tunnel and the dancing continues, but instead of joining we quickly slip back into the crowd. That momentary pass of the other couples hid us from the majority of the guests and gave us a small window for escape. Boy, I wish I had had a chance to see the stupefied look on Damon's face and that of his men. I bet it was priceless. *Now we must find Lori.* But as we bounce from one room to the next, I can't seem to find the geisha anywhere. "What were the other costumes for Tabitha again?" I ask Keagan.

"Uh…a French aristocrat and a farm girl?"

"No, those were mine."

"A geisha, an Italian Renaissance countessa, and a Dutch dancer," a voice says from my left side. "I'm surprised you can't remember, Sissy." I turn to see Lori in a green and brown dress with embroidered tulips. She even has her hair braided up in blond Dutch-style knots. I look past Lori towards the doorway and take note of a pair of harlequins sweeping the room with their eyes.

Not waiting a moment longer, I hook my arms around Lori and Keagan's before pulling us towards the door. "Say goodbye to the baroness," I whisper. Without a backwards glance, Keagan walks ahead of us as the three of us stroll towards the front of the house. He manages to find the baroness just as we make it to the doors, and they exchange kisses on the cheek. Keagan bows to her and makes his way towards the door where we are. I feel Lori tugging on my sleeve again, and I now see that from the adjacent room the Crusaders are stolling our way. I feel a terrible shiver run up my spine when I see them drawing near, their eyes locked on us.

Keagan makes it to us faster than they do, and we politely dart out the door to the nearest alleyway across the street. The second we're in the dark, I look behind us to see that the men are out looking everywhere. But when we turn to run, I knock over a rubbish bin, catching our enemies' attention. Keagan helps me up before we start to run at breakneck speed down the damp dark rabbit hole, Lori and I hoisting up our skirts to run properly. By the time we're at the end of the alley, we see a row of taxi carriages. Lori and I rush inside of one as Keagan instructs the driver where to go. The second he closes the door to the carriage, the driver whips the horses into a swift gallop, causing Keagan to accidentally barrel in on top of us before he can take a seat. Apologising, he takes a seat across from us.

He should be able to see out the back window above our heads. "Keagan, does it look like anyone is following us from the window?"

"Possibly. There are a couple of other carriages on the road, but none of them seem to be gaining spe... No, wait. There's a very large shiny dog outside that seems to be running our way, but it's at the very end of the block. Rather odd—it doesn't appear like it's a real dog by its speed."

I peer through the window above me and see for myself just what Keagan means, then I see that the metal hound is gaining speed relatively fast. "I had a run-in with the governor at the party," I say. "He said he has a 'new toy' for us to play with. I imagine this is it."

"Something about it looks rather familiar, don't you think?" Lori adds, joining me at the window. Focusing on it a bit more, I begin to recognise its legs—there *is* something familiar about them. Going back into my memories, I realise where I've seen them before: Damon's secret little warehouse in the river. That was the skeletal invention they were working on.

We tell our driver to lose the dog behind us, and with a swift turn on a corner, our carriage nearly topples over. Racing down the streets, we begin to feel the error of that order now that we have to brace ourselves against the walls of the carriage on our journey. We finally make it to the theatre, where we practically throw our money at the driver, telling him to keep going for a few more blocks while we race down the dirt alley to the back entrance. We have a quick greeting before we go to change behind single dividers. Keagan tells Tamrin all about the night and how he and Miss Masie would have adored it. But our visit with Tamrin is short-lived when a rapping at the door and the calls from policemen announce their arrival.

Our costumes are off; however, we stumble out of our changing stations half-dressed with stressed expressions. I have only my split skirts on, and a corset brazier with an under-blouse; Lori has her ruffled pantaloons on but no skirts and just her undershirts, not even a corset; Keagan is in only his undershirt and trousers, and his suspenders aren't even strapped on yet. Stuffing the rest of our clothes in prop carpet bags, Tamrin pretends the locks are jammed until we leave the back door area. As we frantically dance around the stage, looking for a way out, we can hear the sounds of the men and barking dogs from the back room.

"Up there." Keagan points up to the skylight as he rushes to a ladder and we follow behind. The moment Keagan opens up the skylight, however, is when the angry shouts of the men call out from below. Lori and I are only halfway up the ladder when we hear them, causing us to scramble up the rest of the way. Once we're within reach, Keagan hoists us up onto the rafters one by one before sending us up through the skylight.

I'm the first on the roof when the men enter the stage, and

the thing that leads their way makes me do a double-take as I help Lori out the window. The huge mechanical dog is running across the stage with them.

"Oi! Up there! Someone's going through the skylight!" One of the men catches sight of us pulling Keagan up. In a flash, their lantern lights are projected in our direction, but we don't wait to see how this scene ends. Pulling the rest of Keagan through the window, we grab hold of our carpet bags and race off over to the nearest building. *We should be safer up here, since those new bloodhounds should have trouble jumping from one building to the next, like we can.*

We make it to the ground a few buildings over and rush home, but we can still hear the sounds of artificial barking in the distance. After taking a detour through a small river in the park to lose our scent, we finally make our final steps back home through the shadows. Pauline lets us in and is quickly accompanied by Thomas and Uncle George in worried cries. I must admit, we're looking worse than we did when we first arrived here. At least then we were fully clothed. But we barely notice, as we can't stop talking about the events of the evening to them.

Pauline helps Lori and me change out of our soaked clothes, just as Keagan changes behind two Oriental dividers near the fire. Lori and I take turns ringing out our dripping hair in the kitchen sink. As I'm talking about the papers I found, I suddenly find myself with a cup of tea in my hands and a blanket wrapped over my shoulders, although I barely noticed Pauline leaving and fetching them.

"Thomas, I don't know about you, but I'm getting bits of stories here and there," Uncle George interjects into our squabbling, giving me a chance to down my cup of warm black tea. "Does any of this make sense to you?"

"Nope, I'm with you, but I think I'm starting to understand," Thomas replies, crossing his dark arms over his chest.

"Well, then pray tell, fill me in on what I'm not getting."

"Uncle George, Governor Damon from Currlion was at the baroness's party tonight," Keagan explains fervently. "You know, the one who wants to see us dead so he can reopen the slave trade for his skinning business."

"He found us tonight at the party, despite our disguises," I add. "He and his men nearly caught us."

"He even has these new mechanical tracking dogs," Lori adds as worry lines begin to paint her face in the firelight.

"The ones that look like real dogs but have twice the amount of scent accuracy and speed?" George asks excitedly, leaning forward in his chair. "Those must have been the test models you were chased by tonight, then. Even Scotland Yard has yet to use them on patrol. What were they like?"

"Terrifying, to say the least," I say, putting away my teacup on the tray. "You seem to be missing the point, though, Uncle George. They nearly caught us. I will say this, they do look and perform in a mesmerising manner. I would've loved to inspect them further if we hadn't been running for our lives."

"Well, you won't believe what I heard tonight," Lori chirps. And so our talk of the night goes on to the wee hours of the morning, including the ultimatum the governor gave me concerning Thatcher. Something tells me we will lose lots of sleep over this matter.

RESTLESS SEARCHERS

KEAGAN

I t's been two days since Aspen had her run-in with Damon at the ball, and we still haven't been able to figure out what to do or where to find Thatcher. We've had our partners search every location they've seen Damon go since he's been in the city, yet not one sign of Thatcher has been found. Aspen, Thomas, Lori and I even spent five hours last night trying to look for him ourselves throughout the city. We were nearly caught by Damon's dimie watchmen and hounds three times as well. *Now he knows we're trying to find Thatcher.* I'm starting to wonder if the whole thing is a bluff and that Damon is just trying to trick us out of hiding.

"Wicked old man," I mutter to myself, laying on the fireside chair in the laboratory as I rub my eyes. We've cleared most of the tables to lay down maps and lists of places that could be hiding him. I look over in the adjacent armchair and see that Lori is curled into a ball, fast asleep, the condition most of us should be in right now. Next to her, on the side table, Pauline has left us a plate of scones and meat pies, and a now empty tea kettle thanks to Aspen. Even Lori has red bags under her eyes. *If she looks like that, I can't imagine what I look like. Not to mention I've been messing with my hair nonstop from nerves; I must look a fright.*

Scouring map after map is getting us nowhere. I look back over to the desk where Aspen is staring at the white lily. Thomas is right next to her and has his head down on the desk where another map is. *We can't just fail him like this. We've tried so hard to find him. None of us have slept since the night of the party, even Thomas, despite our commands to him to do so.* Slowly craning his head up from off the table, eyes still sleepy, Thomas opens his hand to Aspen and gestures towards the lily. She hands it to him before getting up to stretch and walk about the room a bit. Thomas begins to scrutinise it next to the lanterns on the table; behind him, I notice the clock reads six forty-five in the morning. Another groan emanates from my throat at the sight.

The sun is just now hitting the horizon, but from what I've seen of the clouds and fog earlier, there's no way we'll see its rays. Poor Thatcher probably hasn't seen the light of day since he came to London with Damon. *He may not even be in London! He could be held out in the country for all we know. He could be in Ireland right now and we wouldn't be the wiser.*

"Hey, there's something weird about this flower," Thomas mumbles, bringing myself out of my head. "There's words on it."

All at once, Aspen and I shoot up in attention, waking up Lori in the process and scuttling our way back over to the desk, where Thomas is holding the flower close to the lanterns. Crowding around him, we see he's right; letters are forming in a rather yellow-brownish colour, gradually bringing up the words *"sounds of men."*

"Invisible ink," Aspen surmises. "It can be made with a

number of things—lemon juice, honey, vinegar, wine, saliva, milk, even onion juice. It could help us narrow down where he might be by seeing what it's made of."

"I think we can remove the possibility of wine, though, since you also need baking soda for that," I add. "That would be hard to get your hands on if you were a prisoner."

"Milk or lemon juice would be the easiest to use, but of course if it were saliva then that won't help us really." Aspen takes the flower and holds the other petals to the flame excitedly.

"How can we determine which it is, then?" Thomas asks.

"We need to get Uncle George. I'm not that knowledgeable about invisible ink when it dries; I just know what you can make them from, really."

"Seriously? Your uncle is a closet chemist and he didn't have you practise with them?" Thomas makes a funny face.

"Ironic, isn't it? He thought as long as we knew how to make it and told us how to have it reappear, it would be enough. We just didn't take the time to practise with all the different combinations," Lori yawns out as she stumbles her way to the desk.

Taking the time to hold each petal carefully close to the lantern's flame, we see that the flower finally reads:

The sounds of men above always. In a cellar, many bottles.

But on one single petal in large letters he wrote,

Jail.

"He's in some cellar or dungeon-like place, huh?" I scratch my neck, trying to think of the jails in London.

"Well, since there are a number of cellars here in London,

is it possible that he could be in a jail that also holds wine?" Lori says.

"What kind of jail would have their own winery?" Aspen looks up at her sister through her heavy eyelids.

"I'm just trying to come up with options here," Lori snaps back.

Just before we get into a spat about jails with wineries, there is a knock at the door, right before it bursts open. It's Pauline—and to our surprise, Cousin Harry and Isola as well, with Isola's head and whole purple body covered in a dark coat and scarf. They rush inside. "I must speak to you all," Isola says, unwrapping her scarf. "It's a matter of urgency."

"Tell us quickly, then." Aspen walks over to her.

"Do you remember that pub, the Viaduct Tavern, that Ghedi and Samuel followed Damon to?"

"Yes," I yawn out. "Their report said he rarely if ever visited, and when he did he only had a half-pint, talking to the bartender and then quickly off again. No one was able to get word out of the bartender about what Damon was doing there, even after a bribe."

"Well, I know a dimie around the area who does the produce deliveries to a store two doors down. He told me he saw the governor going into the pub around five this morning. When he passed by with his load of wares he saw the two men—Damon and the old bartender—go downwards behind the bar counter, but not crouch or bend over to pick up something. It looked as if they were going down a set of stairs situated somewhere in the floor." Isola is quite excited for someone at seven in the morning. Then I remind myself that she probably got sleep last night, the lucky girl.

"And you're positive it was behind the bar counter?" I ask.

"Positive," Isola and Harry reply in unison. Cousin Harry

hasn't said a word till now. Instead of wandering around and fidgeting with various items like usual, he just stands still and stoic. They both seem very sure of this information; they must trust that dimie who gave them this intel very strongly.

"All right, then," Aspen says. "Tonight after we've finally rested, we'll create a plan to check the place out. I wish your friend had come back with more evidence that Thatcher is truly hidden there."

"He's got to be." Harry puts a tightly gripped hand on her shoulder.

"And he probably is," a voice from the doorway echoes through the room. Uncle George, in his battered robe and pipe in hand, comes walking in with an air about him as if he were Sherlock Holmes and had just cracked the case. "Back in the sixteenth century, that tavern used to be a jail. It's rumoured there's still a dungeon area beneath the tavern floor. It would be highly improbable that the entire jail cellar was filled in, since that would be the optimal place to safely store wine and produce for meals. Since it was once a jail, there are probably some cells and shackles that can still be used. It would be the perfect front for Damon to keep a dimie where no one could find him. Also, he seems to have a trustworthy accomplice in this bartender who won't give out any information to anyone."

"You know, this does fit perfectly now," Lori says, holding up the flower and describing the note we found on it "If that doesn't fit the description of a hidden jail under a tavern, I don't know what does."

"Not to mention the words 'the sounds of men above always,'" I add. "You and your company were always commenting on how loud the tavern was during each visit.

Thatcher must be able to hear them from underneath the floor."

"All right, then, tonight we rescue Thatcher." Thomas takes another bite out of his scone. I give him a look that says, *yes, but not with you.* He doesn't seem to like it by his pout.

"Isola, whomever that dimie was who told you, please thank him for us in discretion. We may have finally found Thatcher." Lori takes Isola's paws tenderly in her hands.

"I already have, but I will again, this time with a bottle of wine for his loyalty," Isola says happily before looking closer at Lori's face and then the rest of us. "My word, have you been up all night? You look positively dreadful."

"Thank you, Isola," Aspen says in a clipped tone as she walks over to the blackboard.

"Forgive me, I just meant—"

"Don't mind her or the rest of us, Isola," Lori quips. "She gets like this when she's stayed up late and hasn't had her sixth cup of tea yet."

"It's my fifth, I'll have you know," Aspen pipes up, holding an empty teacup on her finger in the air whilst scrawling down new schemes on the chalkboard with her other hand.

After a yawn and a polite goodbye to Isola and Harry—Pauline promised to take them back outside safely—we decide it's time to rest. Lori takes Aspen's arm in hers as she slightly pulls her away from the chalkboard, though Aspen still stretches out to write a few more words before finally laying the chalk down. I take the job of picking up the newly sleeping Thomas after finishing off his half-eaten scone for myself. After tucking him in his bed, I do the same for myself, thankful for the good news of Thatcher right before I fall asleep as my head hits the pillow.

We finally wake up around six in the early evening. Uncle George is surely happy when we do so, telling us how he's gotten used to our company during the day and how strange it feels not having us around.

Pauline makes a delicious dinner of shepherd's pie, green beans and buttered rolls for us. We eat heartily as we discuss how we can get Thatcher. Lori suggests that she and Aspen or I could inquire about a job; or that they could flirt with the owner and servers, leading them to the back room, giving me the chance to get Thatcher behind the counter. But we quickly rule it out, along with five other ideas we came up with, since none of them are stable enough to work. Besides, I'd rather not have Aspen flirting with anyone, especially if they're working in league with Damon.

"There has to be something that could occupy not only the bartenders and servers but also the customers, so that no one will notice us going behind the bar and then taking a massive dimie out the door." Lori takes another bite of her shepherd's pie.

"Well, what were some of the ideas you had when you were trying to sneak away from me back in Currlion when we were out shopping? Maybe those tactics could work," I suggest smugly as I take another sip of wine.

"There were a few, but I think we're going to have to use the one we never used." Lori looks at her sister.

"Which is?" Aspen bites into another slice of lamb.

"Cause a fight—a big one that will involve the whole tavern."

"I think I can handle that," I say. "I was in the boxing club back at university." I rub my knuckles with an eager grin on my face.

"Yeah, and I could help out too," Thomas says with bright eyes. "I've been training every day like you've taught me."

"No, not you, Keagan," Aspen says. "Or you, Thomas." With that, she quickly shuts down our pride. "Our new team can help on this. Anthony, Samuel, and if we need another, Ghedi, can start the fight, allowing us three to find the trap door behind the counter. Keagan will go with me below, so we have a better fighting chance in case there's someone guarding Thatcher, and Lori will stand watch just outside the trap door. Ghedi will be in charge of pushing people further into the fight, including the bartenders, so that we can get behind the counter first. Then he can help Lori as a lookout. If we find Thatcher—"

"*When* you find Thatcher," Uncle George corrects Aspen abruptly.

"*When* we find Thatcher, you, Lori, can make sure we won't get caught."

"What can I do?" Thomas asks, raising his hand like a schoolboy.

"I'm sorry, Thomas, you can't come with us tonight," Aspen says with an apologetic expression. "We don't want you to get hurt, or seen as a part of our group if we do get caught. We don't need any more unnecessary injuries."

"Who says I would get injured? I've helped you for the past two days trying to find Thatcher. I even ran all over the city with you, despite the governor's men following us. Keagan, please?" Thomas looks at me with wide pleading eyes. *Egad, that's a hard face to say no to. How do the ladies do it so easily?*

Looking away from Thomas, I stare back at my plate and say, "I'm sorry, Thomas, but the girls are right. There's a high possibility you could get gravely hurt or even killed tonight, regardless of how good you've been during training."

"Augh! I never get to go anywhere anymore."

"Well, we'll just have to change that now, won't we?" Uncle George says. "Thomas, this next week is projected to be clear and sunny for once. What do you say starting tomorrow we do all your lessons in the park? That way I can teach you more about horticulture and survival skills as well."

"For Pete's sake, George, it's a park in London, not the Congo," Pauline interjects, filling his glass of wine again.

"You never know—he could go there someday," George points a fork at Pauline. "With how quick Thomas is with his lessons and inventions, he could find himself anywhere he wishes by the time he is Keagan's age." He ruffles Thomas' dark curly hair. He continues to frown, but I can see the edges of his mouth curl up a few times.

"I want to go, though! I want to see Thatcher as much as you do. He was my friend as well. I helped with the home-coming day and I even opened the portal. I can help, and you know it." Thomas says evenly to Aspen.

"Well…he could stay outside the bar, you know," I suggest whilst playing with the food on my plate. "What if he was with Andrea in a safe place where we could meet them with Thatcher? She could be at the ready as our nurse for anyone who gets wounded."

When I look up, Aspen's unamused gaze hits mine and I shrug my shoulders. Thomas again pleads, "Please, Aspen, I'm almost fourteen. I'll be fine."

"None of us are 'fine' on our missions, and we have years more experience than you do," Aspen says matter-of-factly, which only seems to make Thomas even more annoyed, crossing his arms over his chest and leaning back in his chair.

Aspen takes a long look at him, spinning her butter knife in her hand before placing it down with a great exhale. "I guess staying in the alley with Andrea wouldn't be such a bad idea. That way I wouldn't have to worry about you getting hurt."

"You're letting me come?" Thomas sits up.

"Aspen?" Lori exclaims after Thomas.

"You may come, but it's up to you to watch Andrea's back. She can fight, but not as well as you yet. I'll let you bring whichever weapon you're currently most adept with."

"Are you sure that this is—" Lori starts.

"A good idea? No, I don't, but we have to start involving him in jobs again sometime."

"He helped tremendously on New Year's Eve," I add. "Let's face it; we've been too afraid to let him out because we're no longer free to go out ourselves. He proved his worth; it's time we ease him back into the game." Lori gapes at the idea, obviously too scared still to let him get involved.

"Now, there's one important thing we haven't discussed yet," Uncle George says, bringing us back to our main conversation. "How do you plan on getting him out of there? I doubt people will miss his sheer size if you try to smuggle him out. After all, that's a humans-only bar; they don't even have dimie servers or delivery dimies, from what the group has told us."

"You know he's right." Lori takes a bite out of her buttered roll.

"What if we were to dress him up with a big coat and a low-brimmed hat?" I suggest. "That way it'll look like us and a large person wanting to escape the brawl. Uncle George, Thatcher is close to the size you were the last time I was here, before you lost the weight. Do you have any clothes left we could use?"

"Why indeed I do, and you'll be proud to see how much

I've been able to keep off since then. Use any of the clothes that you think will help you." He takes a gulp of wine. "This reminds me of my reconnaissance missions in Spain. Ho ho, what a great amount of trouble I got into then!"

"I want to hear about that later, but sadly we have to prepare for tonight," Aspen says.

"No problem, my dear. Now off with you four. The sun will be setting soon."

We don't wait to be told twice, standing up and making our way upstairs just as Pauline comes in to clean up our cleared plates.

After we've successfully dressed in our dark day cloaks and low-brimmed hats, we pack our weapons and head over towards the winery. After explaining the plan to our partners, we prepare until midnight comes and then set out on our mission. We decide to make our way there on foot, since the later the fight occurs, the better the chances of drunks pitching in and causing more chaos.

Around one thirty in the morning, we make our way to the Viaduct Tavern. Andrea and Thomas are hidden behind some barrels in the nearby alley. No rogue would be able to see them in the shadows where they lay. Samuel, Anthony and Ghedi walk ahead of us by a couple of yards. Waiting from the outside of the building, we peer into the windows above the fogged line of glass. Ghedi and Samuel have already taken a seat at a table in the centre of the room and start to act a bit drunk, right as their drinks arrive. After a few sips of their ales, they start to get a little louder, spilling their drinks on the floor and splashing them on the patrons around them.

The head bartender by now has noticed, and by the look on his face he's a little more than slightly annoyed. When I notice the bartender start to roll up his sleeves, I decide the charade's been going on long enough, and that it's time to get down to business. Aspen and Lori are resting against the wall. Tapping Aspen on the elbow for the signal, we head inside. Strolling in towards the bar, we walk by one of the metal support pillars. Taking a coin out, Aspen taps the coin to the metal once; the ring in the air is clear.

At the sound of Aspen's signal, Samuel throws his nearly empty glass of beer to the floor, causing it to shatter. "You damn bastard, you deserve to rot for that!" he bellows, followed by Anthony pushing away his chair into another patron just before he throws himself towards Samuel. Men from other tables try to separate them. As others begin fighting, we shift our way closer to the walls, and Ghedi finds his way to us.

"I helped by pushing in more people and shaking them up for more fighting," he says, coming up beside Lori in her trench coat and low-brimmed hat.

"Wonderful, now we just need to wait until…"

Right on cue, the bartenders behind the counter get involved in trying to break up the fighting. The four of us slip behind the counter, keeping our heads down, looking for any signs of the trap door. But there is no handle on the floor, rug to hide it, or signs of a cut-out lid anywhere. I look up only to see a bottle flying through the air, zooming towards us. Covering Aspen's head and mine, I pull us to the floor. Not a second later, the bottle shatters right behind Aspen. Releasing her, we look at where it broke and notice that it hit what appears to be a special vintage case, but is actually a *trompe l'oeil* painting. When we push on it, a few floorboards begin to sink into the ground just below Aspen and me, causing the shards of glass to glimmer as the boards slide away, exposing stair steps going down to a dark cellar.

"We'll call if we need backup," Aspen says directly to Lori, as Ghedi peeks his head over the counter at the sound of the fight becoming an uproar. Cracking our light sticks to give us some illumination, we tread carefully through the cool damp area. We see that this hidden place really is like a jail—I guess Uncle George was right. Looking in every cell we pass, we see that the first three are filled with goods for the pub—milk and eggs, beer and mead, bottles and bottles of wine, similar to what Thatcher described. This makes me think he must be near.

Turning around, the faint glow picks up something in the back corner of what at first glance seems to be a cell filled with rubbish. But the moment I see something shift, I push my arm holding the glow stick through the bars, and end up seeing Thatcher. They don't even have a guard on him, but I think I can see why; he wouldn't be able to put up much of a fight even if he tried. I can see his ribs through his brown filthy fur where he rests on a pile of hay. There is no food around for him, only a bowl of water that two rats have claimed for themselves. Not too different from how we found Gertrude in the warehouse. *What were your true intentions with the two of them, Damon?*

"Psst!" I hiss out, grabbing Aspen's attention as she views the contents of one cell over. After a bright flash in that cell, she comes over to me eagerly. I reach for the door, but before I can try to pick the lock, Aspen covers the keyhole with her hand. Looking up in bewilderment at why she would want to stop me at this point, she simply pulls out a hair comb from under her hat, and in the dim light I see her pull out some type of cartridge from a slot and point it at Thacher before snapping it shut. The glaring light that follows has me stumbling back a bit in shock. By the time I can see again, Aspen has picked the lock on the cell and I follow her inside.

Approaching our friend, we exchange looks of concern. He hasn't stirred once since we've arrived. "Thatcher? Thatcher, it's time to wake up," I say, but he doesn't seem to hear me.

Aspen reaches out and holds his shackled paw gently with one hand as she rubs his arm with her other hand. "Thatcher, it's Aspen and Keagan. We're here to rescue you. It's time to wake up." She speaks louder this time as she shakes his arm.

I begin to fear the worst as I reach for his neck to check his pulse. But the second my hand touches his throat, he takes a sharp inhale. My hand shoots back from the sudden shift between him being stagnant to now lethargically flailing his arms, saying, "No more, no more!"

"Peace, Thatcher, it's Aspen and Keagan. It's us. Look at us," I say, trying to hold his arms steady.

Even in his weakened state. he still has strength beneath it all. "No!" he roars in my face, finally opening his eyes. The second recognition returns to his face, tears begin to well, threatening to spill over. "You found me," he whimpers as I hug him tightly.

I can hear Aspen unlocking the shackles that bind his wrists behind me. "That's right, and now it's time to go. We're going to get you back on your feet in no time."

"You found me." He sounds so far away in his voice. I have to practically carry him so he doesn't fall, as Aspen makes sure the way is clear to the exit and then dresses him in civilian clothes.

With the sounds of the quarrel rising to dangerous levels from above, Aspen and I decide it's time to leave. We know it's only a matter of time until the bobbies come to stop the fight. Once making it back up the steps, after having issues balancing Thatcher between the two of us, we see a motionless employee on the ground with Ghedi crouching over him as he rubs his knuckles. Lori, however, is completely starry-eyed, gazing at him like he's a knight in shining armour.

"What happened?" Aspen and I ask in unison.

"Ghedi saved me from one of the workers when they were coming this way. He hit him so hard in the jaw that he was knocked out cold."

"Lori, you could have knocked him out in at *least* twelve different ways on your own and you know it," Aspen reminds her sister as we make our way out.

"It's the thought that counts," Lori says, giving her sister a tight-lipped look.

"Some other time, ladies," I remind the girls as I'm still bracing up Thatcher. "We need to get out of here before things become too violent."

"Too late for that, *mon amie*," Ghedi says, looking over the bar counter. We see Samuel and Anthony duking it out with a few men. Every now and then they are pulled apart by the bar owner. Poor man; his wrinkled face is lobster red, with veins bulging out of his temples.

"Let's go," Aspen says as she begins to pull at my and Thatcher's sleeves, nudging Lori towards the door. Before we're totally gone, I shut the cellar door, being careful not to cut my hands on the glass covering the ground. We pass right by the whole kerfuffle without a second glance, but as we're about to walk out the door, I notice a fresh plate of untouched food some chap must have ordered right before the fight commenced. I quickly slip out of the tavern with the plate in my left hand and holding Thatcher with my right arm. *Wasn't that kind of that customer to feed a starving dimie tonight?*

By now, Ghedi has already signalled Anthony and Samuel to cease fighting and leave the bar. Once we make it a safe distance at the end of the block, we crouch down in the shadows behind some crates in an alley. Andrea and Thomas emerge and immediately begin to look Thatcher over for any wounds that need attention. I hand Thatcher the plate of food, which he makes quick work of.

"It's so good to see you, Thatcher," Thomas says, holding Thatcher's large arm so Andrea can assess him better. But Thatcher is too busy eating to respond yet. With every bite, he seems to become more aware of what's going on.

Lori walks out of the alley we're hiding in and tips her hat in the direction from whence we came. The men must be coming our way; they'll be here soon to help us out. Thatcher is already finishing off the rest of his loaf of bread and licking the remainder of the plate. By the time he downs the canteen of water that Aspen offers to him, our valiant fighters have arrived and quick introductions are made.

"So you're Thatcher, huh?" Anthony says, taking Thatcher's arm in the traditional Roman handshake. "We've had some trouble finding you, mate."

"I don't remember you from Myrack Manor," Thatcher mutters.

"No problem, mate, we're new to the team."

"If it wasn't for these men and the rest of their party, I'm not sure we would've found you at all," Aspen says soberly.

"That's hard for me to believe, especially coming from you, Miss Wolfe." Thatcher smiles through his cracked and bleeding mouth. I take a long look at our poor friend and realise I didn't see all the cuts and bashes he received till now.

Andrea is currently tallying them up, it seems, and taking note of which need the most attention.

"We sure are glad to find you, Thatcher, but my God, what did they do to you?" Thomas asks.

"I'm afraid that is a question that must be answered later," Lori says, jogging away from the opening of the alley. "A pair of constables are headed towards us right now. We need to get to an actual safe place."

"Agreed," Aspen says. "Since we're closer to your safe house, Anthony, let's go there, and then we'll plan how to handle everything."

"Yes, ma'am," Anthony says with a short salute before helping to carry Thatcher's right side.

"You got yourself a real shiner, didn't you, mate?" I say, looking at his swelling left eye.

"Blame the bartender. He was so put out that he sucker-punched both me and Samuel. Sorry to say, but I suspect we won't be welcomed as patrons there anymore." At this, Andrea, Ghedi, Aspen and Lori begin to laugh.

"I don't understand what you're laughing about," Samuel protests. "He nearly made me black out. I thought he was about to kill us, to be honest."

"Well, we got what we came for, so that's what matters," I say, laughing as we race through the shadows. *We've got you, Thatcher. I promise you that you'll be safe from now on.*

WHAT'S IN A NAME?

LORI

Andrea takes her time making sure that she finds every possible wound on Thatcher as Issac and Isola prepare him a large meal. Thomas doesn't leave Thatcher's side as Keagan, Aspen and I tend to the wounds that Anthony and Samuel received amidst the bar brawl. Now that we can see Thatcher in better lighting, it's obvious how malnourished he is. It's like they've been feeding him once every two days. *I can't wait to see Damon again. I have a special punch saved specially for him.* We opt not to move him to Uncle George's place just yet, but instead to have him sleep and eat here till he's in a more stable state.

I listen to him talk to Isola and Issac in his native tongue. They're a few years younger than him, so I have a feeling they learned their native language from other older dimies in this dimension instead of their own. Every now and then, when I pass by a kitchen or a butler's pantry in the nice houses we visit, I will hear the dimies speak in a language I can't place. They're so strict about when to use it and who hears it as well.

Words must be very important if it's the one thing you can hold onto from home, aside from your memories.

Anthony and Samuel are all patched up now as they leave into the next room. Issac and Isola remain by Thatcher, however. Sitting near his bedside on the ground, I begin to hear him and Isola hum. Once they're both at the same tempo, they begin to sing.

I watch death's beginning as it falls like gold rain from the heavens in the sway of the wind.

Come dance through the colours of the whirlwinds.

Come rejoice before the fast approaching night, before the doors are shut up tight.

Observe the creation of wonder in the bareness of crystalline slumber, as the earth dreams of rebirth in its awakening.

Though it dreams away there are still creatures at play that delight in frolicking over the blanket that was laid.

For who could deny a gift such as this?

However, change comes again with budding jewels of fragrance and a flowing green sea.

Go through its waves, for you will find its treasures.

For you will find rebirth.

Then all can relax in the rays of warm splendour where you will find peace and mirth.

Now here we are each to his own, some live in warmth some live in cold.

Where is it that you find your home?

"And I say it here and now, with you humans I take off my hat for my home is here with you. For that is good and true," Thatcher adds in alone.

"I don't remember that verse," Isola says with a confused look on her face.

"That's because I made it up just now, and I mean every

word of it. Keagan, Lori, Thomas and Aspen. You are where I find my home, and I would like to stay with you if you will let me."

"You don't wish to go back to your own dimension?" Issac asks.

"It's not home anymore. Home isn't just a building or a place; in my culture, home is with the people you love and care for, and who care for you in return."

"But there you have a chance to be truly free," Aspen says gently, eyeing his wounds. "You won't have to worry about being chained up again or tortured."

Thatcher takes a deep breath before speaking again. "The only hope I had to start a new life in a new environment was when I had Winona. We were going to start it together. We promised one another that we would hold each other up and guide each other through every struggle we faced. But now, I don't think I could bear going there without her, when I've pictured us there so much already. I don't want those pictures to shatter. Besides, you still need all the help you can get when it comes to aiding the dimies."

"You wouldn't be completely alone though," I chime in. "You'd be around your kind,"

"I know, my dear, but I would constantly be thinking about all of you whilst I am there, knowing that you're risking your lives to save more of my kind when I decide to leave. I would detest myself for giving up just because things got rough. I've never been one to stand aside, as you well know. And I feel there is still a great deal I can do to help my kind. I feel so compelled to stay and fight, no matter the cost. So with your permission, once I am back to my full health, I would like to be of aid to this cause."

"Thatcher, we will always be indebted to you for saving us

on the ship," Keagan says, taking Thatcher's paw. "We'll make sure Damon pays for what he's done to you, and every dimie like you as well."

"And for that, if or when you choose to go back home, we won't stop you," Aspen adds. "I promise you, we'll get you in better shape than you've ever been! As for you wanting to help us, well, how could we say no to that?" She throws her hands up with a smile. I'm glad he's staying with us; he's such a good friend to have, and his loyalty knows no bounds.

"Hey, Thatcher, what was your home like before you knew about humans?" I ask, but the moment I do, I fear it may be too painful a question to answer. A pause breaks through the room, and it feels suffocating, knowing I caused it.

"Oh, strap yourself in for a story, Lori. My village was a proud tribe of fierce warriors like my father. We were a healthy and bountiful tribe with dimies of all kinds. In my dimension, some tribes like to have exclusivity in their kind."

"You mean like only bird dimies to a tribe?"

"That's right. Anyway, I remember when the humans came, after a bright light followed by an eruption of sizzling sounds through the air. After the commotion, my village became still. Everyone was looking in the direction of where the light had come from. Some of the men like my father were readying their weapons. Then one by one, out from the trees, the humans came with arms out open and shiny sticks strapped to their backs. They didn't try to give us any offering or many greetings. They found our chieftain quickly, since he came out from his hut to see what was going on. His name was Culpernea. The humans sat and talked with him in his home for a long time. The homes here in your world look very different to what ours are like; ours are made of thatched woven roofs. Some have stone and mud walls that become domed roofs for the smaller rooms. You have to take steps down to a lower level when you enter inside, too. And there can be many small rooms made with tunnels, like hallways." We listen with wonder in our eyes. No dimie has ever told us about their land, and the books that were being used to record their lives are supposedly destroyed.

"But I digress," he continues. "I remember my younger brother being excited and curious about one of the men who was carrying a long shiny stick with him. Little did I know then that it was a rifle. The man glanced at my mother before picking up my brother and putting him in his lap to pet his maroon fur. My brother was touching all over his arm, probably curious as to why he had so little fur. I wanted to go see the man too, since he made my brother laugh by accidentally tickling him, but my mother held onto me tight. I could feel the rhythm of her heart and I knew she was scared. We'd never seen creatures like these before, with no fur or feathers save the patch of hair on their heads. We almost felt sorry they didn't have fur, since they had to cover themselves up in strange materials of the same style and colour. I'd find out later that these were soldier uniforms.

"The men were everywhere in the village, trying to communicate with us. Some were giving away their watches or necklaces for tools or food we were making. When the men came out of Culpernea's home, they did not look happy. Culpernea came out as well with his arms raised and announced to us in our language, "Never speak your true name or the name of your tribe to these creatures or any like them." With a serious face, Thatcher stretches out his arms slightly with his palms towards us in a commanding stance.

"The men who talked with him were now pointing their rifles at him, but they didn't shoot him when he spoke. The captains of the soldiers told their men to *begin*—I remember those words even if I didn't understand them at the moment. If only we knew what they were about to do, things might have been different. When the commander of the soldiers gave them the order, all the men, including the one holding my brother, came together in the centre of the village. They all held children in their arms. There were outbursts and cries of alarm all around the village. Both the men and women began to advance towards the soldiers to take back their young, but the men made a barrier with the children stuck behind them in a tight circle as they aimed their guns at my people. The first to try and push through the barrier was shot; not fatally, but that certainly did the trick. There were screams and wailing all throughout the village. Everyone began to scatter and run away as others advanced on the men." Thatcher's whole demeanour changes from a storyteller to someone who looks like they should be in a doctor's chair.

"My mother was one of them—she picked me up and ran as fast as she could into the jungle. We ran so far and deep into the brush that we were nearing the border of our tribe's territory, a place I was told to never venture past. After my mother hid me under a Laponta berry bush, she told me to wait for her and to stay put no matter what. She promised she would return with my father and little brother. So I waited like an obedient son. I waited and tried to ignore the booming gunshots and the terrified screams of my tribesmen and friends. After a while, that strange exploding sound followed by the bright light came back, and everything soon became quiet." Thatcher pauses to take a swig of water. *That sound must have been the rift gate opening and closing.*

"I stayed there under that bush, eating my fill of the Laponta berries; hours had gone by, and night was coming in fast. That night I heard footsteps coming my way. I remember the swelling in my heart, thinking that my family was safe and we'd be together again. After being so scared and thinking the worst was over, I burst out of the bush in leaps and bounds when a bright light hit me, and all my fear returned. The only light we can produce at night is the warm light of fire or from glowing flowers that grow in our caves, but this was not a warm red or glowing blue, but rather a blinding white. Behind the light I heard the voices of excited soldiers. I turned to run but someone quickly tackled me down to the ground and put cold hard restraints on my wrists and ankles. I would soon become familiar with these chained shackles." Thatcher rubs his beaten-up wrists.

"I cried out for them to let me go, but they didn't understand me, nor would they have cared even if they did. They brought me back to what was left of my village where others were shackled in a line, waiting for something, it seemed. Come to find out it was the portal to take us to this dimension. My last memory of my home was seeing it torn apart, the huts and waggons ablaze or trampled on the ground like our food and weapons. There was a row of my people laying in the dirt. I called out to them, thinking, *How could they be sleeping right now?* I soon realised they weren't sleeping...they were dead. I remember what our chief had warned us about: to never tell these strange beings our true name or our tribe's name. I would come to associate our names with death, because that's what I thought killed my tribesmen who were laying in the dirt. Now everyone who remembers that day is around my age and older. We know better now, and yet we still do not share them, because we do not wish them to become subjective like our given name, 'dimie.' So you must promise to keep this name only for the ears of my kind that you can trust."

I lay my right hand over my heart and raise my left. "I solemnly swear I will tell only your kind whom I can trust, never a human, or may God strike me down where I stand." Aspen, Keagan and Thomas follow in suit.

Thatcher gives us a nod of approval. "My birth name is Reuel of Nephtali, and Winona's name was Merari of the Lotan tribe."

"She never told me that," Keagan says, looking rather hurt.

"She almost never told *me*. It was something she was very protective about, and for good reason."

"He's got a point," I shrug. "Maybe she didn't want Charles to ever hear her name and use it on accident in front of people other than Keagan and the household."

"You know, that could be right," Keagan ponders aloud. "If that was the case, I'm glad she never did, because then even the governor would know what to call her and the dimies."

"Do you have names for the different species, like how the bears and birds have different names to describe themselves?" Thomas asks curiously.

"Yes. All together, dimies have the title 'esuas,' in a similar way to how you call yourselves humans. But I would be known as a 'tolen' and Winona was a 'tola.' The birds are 'arodis' and 'eranis,' the monkeys are 'xueles and 'xolas.' The otters are known as 'chilecks' and 'chanties.' Also, whenever an esua is born into this human world, the mother gives them a true name, as we call it, that we keep to ourselves. Then she allows the humans to give the youngling a working name. Whether or not this practice has kept going is purely up to the mother, so not every esua in this world has or might even remember their true name, sadly."

"You're lucky to remember your true name, Thatcher. Issac and I don't remember our own," Isola says somberly.

"Perhaps I could give you your own later?" Thatcher smiles.

"I would very much appreciate that," Issac says with a big grin on his beak. Isola nods her head as well.

"Obviously, we can't use these names with just anyone, or any random dimie as well?" I guess, taking the conversation again.

"You would be correct. You can use them when it's just us talking; besides, that way, if any human were to overhear us, they would think we were talking in some kind of code."

"Brilliant!" Aspen says. So many new schemes are cooking in her head right now, there's practically steam coming from her ears.

"Thank you for trusting us with this information, Thatcher, and I'm sorry your story had to be as sad as it was...well, is," I add.

"Thank you, Lori. Let's hope the rest of my story is not so sad."

I truly hope it isn't either.

LOVE AND WAR

ASPEN

It's been a few days now that Thatcher's been back in our lives, and it seems Lori has been in a daze since. All she ever does is spend time with Ghedi; he's even become a frequent visitor at the house. Which is fine, of course; however, I don't like how he acts. Lori practically coddles him, the way she fetches anything from the kitchen he wishes, always making sure he's cosy on any couch with extra cushions. Never letting him lift a finger, as they both eventually laze about for hours. Lori's never been like this with any man —she's always wanted to go out on the town to every bakery, shop or attraction for enjoyment. But staying inside each and every day on the couch with Ghedi? That's not my sister.

I've even overheard them talk about this subject as I've strolled by the parlour. "Couldn't we go to the theatre tonight?" Lori will say. "They're supposed to be performing *Romeo and Juliet*. It's my favourite."

"Ah, Lori, there's no need for that," Ghedi will then reply. "Besides, I'd rather have you all to myself. What would I do if some gent came along and swept you away from me due to your beauty? I think I'd die of a broken heart."

"Ah, well, we can't have that, now can we?"

"No, my perfect one. Now, come here. I miss you already."

I think I might vomit from it all. *Who is he to manipulate the conversation and my sister like that?* I've decided it's high time for me to talk to Lori about the state of her relationship. Frankly, since we're working professionally with the gang, which includes Ghedi, this love affair shouldn't have happened in the first place.

After dinner, Ghedi finally goes home, and I ask to talk to Lori alone in our room. Happy as always, she bounces up the stairs as if nothing is the matter. Once we're alone, I sit down at the small table we have in the centre of the room. "I'd like to talk to you about Ghedi," I begin. "I heard from Isola that he's talked with you about possibly eloping?"

"Well, you don't waste time, now do you?" Lori arches one brow.

"Have you ever known me to?"

"Fair point. But I'm positive Ghedi means to traditionally marry me, so you can rest easy if it's the elopement part that has you worried." Lori places a reassuring hand on mine just before attempting to walk towards our door.

"What exactly did he say?" I take hold of her hand, preventing her from leaving.

"Well, I mean, there were a few other people around, and he invited them to come as well. He's asked me to come along with him when they leave London. He wants to go and see the world. Isn't that romantic?" Lori looks at the floor but quickly looks back at me with a hopeful gleam in her eyes. *Even she is unsure.*

"So he didn't ask you specifically to get married?" I say in a measured tone.

"Well, I—uh—"

"I'm just a little worried, since you've always told me you want a house filled with children and your loving, handsome future husband. Not wander the world like a vagabond with a man who has no thoughts of marriage."

"Who says he has no intention of marrying me?"

"Don't you think he would've at least entertained the idea with you by now? You've been spending so much time with each other, and he's your favourite topic these days whenever we're alone. Be honest, Lori. Do you really think he's the type to keep a respectable distance from you whilst you are unmarried and travelling together? I've seen how hungrily he stares at you; it's unnerving, to be honest."

I give her hand a squeeze, but she quickly snatches it back. "Why? Is it because Keagan never looks at you that way?"

I'm stunned for a moment at her uncharacteristic attitude. "Actually, it was Keagan who brought it to my attention. And for your information, he's looked at me that way plenty of times."

"Well, you know we've been travelling all around with Keagan for months. He has surely kept a more than respectable distance from you for the majority of it as well. Has he once brought up the idea of marriage with *you*?"

"That's different! We were living with him first, and technically he's our guardian."

"You'll be turning nineteen in a month. You'll have no need for a guardian then. The only difference I see between Ghedi and Keagan is money. Keagan also has travelled all over the world, and also has been with many unmarried women on his travels. Ghedi's poor and hasn't had the chance yet to travel like Keagan, but I can give him that chance." She stands up and crosses her arms over her chest.

"Wait, are you saying what I think you're saying? Are you going to spend your inheritance on travelling with him?" My chair scrapes the floor abruptly when I stand up.

"And what if I am? It's my inheritance to do with as I please."

"Lori, listen, I'm just trying to say that this whole relationship you have with Ghedi seems a little unhealthy. From what you say and from how he acts when you're around him, I just can't help but feel you're putting in so much more than he is. You're always paying for the outings, or at least the few you actually go on. You're always defending him, but when has he defended you? When you came home late on that rainy Valentine's Day, you arrived at the door wet and cold, then he left before you were even inside. Did he even offer to give you his coat? What kind of man does that sound like?"

"Don't talk about him like that! If anything, you're just jealous, since I get to go out on the town instead of being bolted up in this nuthouse day in and day out. You resent me and my newfound freedom."

"Oh, yes, Lori, I am immensely jealous," I say with dripping sarcasm.

"I think you are." She points at me.

"If I am, it's not for the reasons you think. When we were under the guardianship of Aunt Mae, she practically never went after you, and the few times she tried to, I protected you and took the punishment instead..." I can feel the fumes of my own words billowing around my head. "But where were you when I was getting yelled at, punished and beaten? Why did you always have to be so perfect and charming that she never laid a hand on you?" I swat away her finger.

"You're the one who never liked acting like a lady. You never made any real effort to get Aunt Mae to approve of you. If just once you had acted the part—"

"You mean put a broomstick up my arse before Aunt Mae could put one there herself?"

"Well, even if you did, you still wouldn't have come close to how *'perfect'* I was at it. Or at least how perfect I could've been if you had just let me be," Lori spits out, but the instant she does, she clasps a hand over her mouth. The room begins to buzz with white noise. I just stare at her with the urge to tear her apart. "I didn't mean that," she continues with her hands up.

I scoff. "You would've been dead if it weren't for me and Pearl. Perfect? Please. If a skeleton is what perfection is these days to our aunt, then yes, Lori, you were pretty damned close."

Lori's arms immediately come up, before flopping back down and hitting her sides with a thud. "Why am I the one under the magnifying glass right now? All I want is to be with Ghedi. I feel so strongly for him."

"Yes, and he wishes to feel you strongly as well, but not with his heart, I'll tell you that."

"Aspen!" She looks at me with an expression of disgust on her face. "You know what? I might as well just skip out on the plans for the mill, then. Since you obviously don't care to even be around him or me right now."

"Oh, you better be there, Lori. How would that look to the rest of the group if you weren't? Besides, you know how important this is to us."

"To us or to what we think Father would've wanted? Be honest, Aspen. Are you still living for him? Are you still holding on to that idea of him? I've finally let that image go. I want to live for myself now, not him. What about you?"

"I—"

"Well?" She looks at me expectantly.

"Be at the mill, Lori. Not for me, or you, or Papa. Be there because this is important for the lives of the dimies. That's what this whole thing is about—what it should have been about from the very beginning. And for your own sake, take a good look at Ghedi and how he treats you. I'm warning you because I love you." I reach for the door handle.

"You didn't answer my question, Aspen!" Lori calls out. But I race out of the room and slam the door behind me because...I'm afraid. I'm afraid of myself and the fact that I haven't let go of the idea of who I thought my father was. Finding the trick board in the wall, I open the secret door to the roof and blurrily stumble up the stairs through the tears in my eyes. The truth is, I don't want to let go of that image of him, and I hate myself for that. I don't want to let go of this perfect picture of my father, even though it's burning at the edges these days, so that the twisted photo of who he really is underneath is becoming what I see. And I try to put the flames out, as I collect its ashes because that's who I wish for him to be. But I know it isn't right.

"It's not right," I cry out before collapsing on the gravel rooftop in a heap. A loud slam verberates through the house, and it even echoes out on the street. Making my way over to the edge of the building, I look over the side to the street below to see Lori running off in the direction of the gang's safehouse. A tug in my heart tells me I need to go after her, to protect my little sister, but I know it would only be a mistake if I do. She wishes to be free from this life we're living, but where we are right now as wanted criminals, there's no way she could live in the empire as a truly free person. Without the queen's pardon, we'd have to go to some desolate place in America, or perhaps even Australia. That is where we used to send our worst criminals, anyway; why not us?

Lori, please come back.

THE MILL OF MISERY

LORI

Scaling this place wasn't the easiest job in the world, since we had to walk sideways up the wall for the most part, using ropes. The buildings near the mill are only one or two stories; the mill itself is five. I still can't believe this place is so thorough that they even use special thin long windows at the top of each room that only a child could squeeze through. So we climbed to the very top where it was evident that pigeons are regulars here.

Standing atop the mill, we peer over the sides to the ground far below, and I can feel tingles in my hands as fear tells me to get away, to jump. *My word, this place is so much larger in person, compared to the pictures of the blueprints we were viewing.* I mean, I know they made this place to be like a maze to trap the dimies inside, but it's utterly gigantic. As long as the walls inside don't move whilst we're in, we should be good—all of us have memorised every floor of this building. We've even tested each other with scenarios where we have to go around obstacles while people chase us from one floor to the next. I felt like I was going through boring lectures every night, though, and after every lecture, Aspen and I somehow found a way to fight each night on our way home. I hate it. We've never been in a disagreement for so long with one another.

Planning for tonight has taken up practically every second of our time for the past few days. I know Aspen and Keagan must have planned everything so it would keep me and Ghedi apart. I just want this to be over already, so I can spend real time with him again. Go in, get out, and be done with it. That's what I want.

We've tracked the vent systems, the exits, even the habits of the workers, with the help of Samuel and Anthony going in as a guard and a businessman separately. The gang even surprised us last night with a couple of large covered waggons that normally transport livestock from in and out of the city. Two tarped caged trailers await us at the loading dock near the wharf, with Harry and Uncle George as the drivers both in disguise. Everything is set, and I know that with this much preparation into our heist—unlike the one we made at the market in Currlion—there's little chance we'll mess up.

Taking our time oiling the edges of the vent's lid, we slowly pry it off, and Aspen anchors her grapple into the side of the brick building with the men holding on to it for good measure. After checking that the coast is clear, she gives the rope a tug to let us know it's our turn. The moment I set eyes on the fifth floor, my stomach drops and I can immediately see I was wrong before. The fifth floor is supposed to be where the dimies are, but this floor only has rows of desks and a fogged-glass side office. Obviously the owner's office. "Ren, when was the blueprint dated?" I come up right next to her.

"Four months ago. They must have made changes to the order of the rooms, though they'd only be able to make changes to two or three of them."

"They must have switched floors," Anthony says, pointing below.

"Exactly, since it wouldn't make sense to move all those expensive mills from one floor to the next," Andrea surmises. "Besides, they're too heavy and valuable to do a stupid move like that."

"Good work," Aspen says. "Now, let's get to the third floor. And remember, avoid guards as best you can, but if you can't…" She points to her wrist where her sleeping darts are held. The rest of the team salutes in acknowledgment. I'm a bit nervous about supplying everyone with sleeping darts, even after letting them practise shooting them, including Harry. One wrong move or bad aim and one of us could be put to sleep, becoming dead weight.

Heading down the curved and short hallways is a fairly easy task; there's no one guarding the top floor. The floor below us, however, is a different story. After finding the hidden staircase through a sliding panel in the wall, we make our way down to the fourth floor. The staircases in the building are one flight each, so no dimie could make a straight shot to the bottom, I guess. Each night guard paces the hallways with a rifle and a lantern. And to top it all off, they're partnered off, probably to keep each other from falling asleep on duty.

After darting around the four men on duty on the fourth floor, we take a peek inside the doors that hold the mills. Large, spindly machines that look like giant spiders sleeping in the dark lay all about the shadowy room. We all take turns looking inside through the slightly cracked door. But we don't dare go inside, since there are even more watchmen and even dogs in this room, prowling between the machines and checking the windows.

Just looking at those machines sends a shiver down my spine. It makes me wonder how many dimies have lost their fingers, limbs or lives to those contraptions. I've only heard stories about them, but I know they're lethal if you're not careful enough. There is a tall and rather long dark pillar near the end of the room that frankly appears to be out of place. *Why would there need to be such a large support beam there of all places? I don't remember that on the map.*

Sneaking down to the third floor through another set of hidden stairs, I already want out of this place. The next floor better be the one where the dimies are held. Darting past the guards on this level, we have Ghedi and Anthony stand watch outside. Aspen slowly slides open the door as silently as humanly possible. By moving her hand back and forth in a horizontal motion, and then curling one finger in the air, Aspen relays to us that there are no guards in this room, but the two fingers under her eyes means to be on the lookout.

Standing up and sliding her head in, she takes a long look around just before opening the door the whole way for the rest of us. "Let's get to work," she says calmly just before going into the mass of single tall black cages in perfect alignment with one another. The only light we currently have is supplied from ourselves until we find a switch along the walls that lights up two dim but adequate bulbs overhead. At the sign of the light, a few sharp inhales sound in the air, and the dimies slowly begin to rise from their beds. But the few out of the hundred or so that must be in here who are awake manage to lay their squinted eyes on us, only to stare in surprise.

Each cage allows enough space for a cot—some with bedding, others not—and about two feet of floor space for them to stand up. Isola and Issac walk in front of us to speak to them and assure them that we're here to help. The more they talk in their native tongue, the more dimies awaken.

Soon enough, we're unlocking the cages with the sleeping guards' keys and having other dimies help us wake up the few heavy sleepers left. There are dimies of almost every age here, even one little bird dimie with green feathers who tells me he's four years old as I free him. Each one looks confused, scared, or grateful when they look at us. A few need to be greatly encouraged here and there, but after Isola and Issac along with the others persuade them, they practically bound out the door.

"Do you know the reason for the heightened security?" I ask a plum-purple otter dimie as I unlock her cage, trying to keep my mind occupied with anything except the ungodly scent of the room.

"A few of us managed to escape a few months ago," she says in a high-pitched voice. "We never saw them again, so we have no way of knowing if they made it out or were shot."

"Do you know how they did it?"

"They learned to pick the locks to their cages with materials they found when most of us fell asleep. The few who stayed awake watched and learned. I was awake sometimes, but my eyes are bad, and I couldn't see too well as to how they did it from here."

"Clever, but it's a shame they didn't help anyone else." I'm starting to feel a slight pang of guilt in my stomach, other than the one from the stench. *Who knows when the last time they had a bath was, or their clothes were cleaned, let alone the floors,* I think as I see the filthy stained floors with questionable markings. Then I notice that the cells don't have bed pans for when they need to go to the bathroom at night. *How could anything living be treated so horridly?*

"They were about to help us when the guards came from the hall. They had to crawl their way out. There was no chance for the rest of us to escape without being seen."

"I see." That nauseating pit in my stomach just gets deeper and deeper. Cage after cage, we let each of them out. Some are such heavy sleepers that we have to let their friends wake them up, much to their surprise. I go to one of the last cages at the edge of the room where a red-furred monkey dimie with curled horns looks as if she's about to jump out of her own skin. "We must leave right now," she says, gripping the bars with all six and a half of her fingers.

"Don't you worry, we'll get everyone out in time." I fit the key into her lock.

"No, you don't understand, the guards come and check on us every night—"

"We've already taken out the guards on this floor. There's no one coming to check on you now."

"What about the lift?" She points to the dark pillar at the end of the room in the same location the other pillar was on the fourth floor.

"Lift?" *That wasn't on the maps either. How many other changes have been made that we don't know about?* "Ren," I call over to her, but she doesn't hear me. There are more dimies being freed and embracing one another as they come together in the centre of the room.

"They come around this time every night. I always wake up to the sounds, but everyone else sleeps through it."

"How long have they been doing these checks from the elevators?"

"This past week, once we were moved here."

"Does it go to the bottom floor?" I ask, hopeful for a good answer.

"Don't remember what the bottom floor looks like. I haven't seen it since I was sold and brought here. All I know is that it goes down at least one floor and up at least one floor. Those three floors are the only ones we're allowed on. We're never allowed in the halls unless being escorted to the medic or bathroom."

"What if we were to use the elevator? It might go to the bottom floor after all."

"We can't; only certain guards are allowed to operate it with a particular key and code. I know the code, but no one can get the key." She shifts her gaze from the lift then to me.

"Which guard has the keys?"

Just then, the churning and roaring sound of a motor sounds off, and the empty cage for the elevator quickly comes down. The long doors part, and there stands at least ten men, all armed. After a moment of staring at us in pure shock, they begin charging out at us. One has a key he's stuffing back in his pocket. Immediately everyone scatters, and a few darts land on three men as they slump to the ground. Three extension-magnet restraints are flung through the air and land on one man's wrist and another's gun just as they begin to aim at us. The magnets activate, and from the expressions of the men's faces, a painful connection happens before being dragged back to the elevator only a few feet away. The man whose gun is now stuck on the elevator was the one with the key. Seeing Aspen and Keagan's groups of dimies and the few men chasing them run off, I decide not to get behind all of that.

Taking my grappling hook, I aim and shoot the man who has the key straight in the gut as he gets off the ground, only to make him crumple down again. Rushing over, I rifle through his pockets as he throws a slew of slurs my way.

"Let's move, now! Everyone in, right now!" I don't have to repeat myself, as the remainder of the hiding and cowering dimies flood the elevator with Isola, Andrea and myself inside. Managing to hold the key into the slot myself, the monkey who informed me of the lift puts in the code before nearly smashing the down button. Despite the protests of the guard who is stuck to the outside of the elevator shaft, the doors close on us, and I can feel us descending. It's so tight in here that it's nearly impossible to breathe.

Tears well in my eyes in the pitch-black box as it slowly stops. "Ready yourselves; there are probably guards on this floor too," I tell Isola and Andrea, whom I have never been closer to. "Everyone, do *not* panic. Lead one another to the doors. Don't doubt yourselves, not now." Once the doors open and the figures of a guard and their dog are in sight, I lob over a tear-gas grenade. Andrea and Isola toss a few of their own in another direction the second we step out of the elevator. Flashes of bright lights and pillars of smoke fill the room, along with the sounds of furious men and whining canines. Letting the majority follow Isola in the lead and Andrea in the middle, I head out with the tail end of the group to watch out for the fallen, running through the smoke and dodging confused men.

I halt a moment at the side of one mill when the sound of a small cry following a thud sounds out behind me. Isola and Andrea are already at the open doorway, and through the smoke I can see that they're looking back at me, waiting to make it, with worry in their eyes. I'm picking up the dimie who has fallen when I call out, "Take the front of the group and make it to the rendezvous point. I'm right behind you." The second I turn around, I tumble over a dimie who was trying to stand up as well. I catch myself in one of the power looms, but my hand falls through some of the threads. The next thing I hear is the loud sound of an engine and a pulling on my arm. *One of the guards must have hit the power switch by accident.* Before I can untangle my arm from the fibres, my arm is sucked into the spindles of the machine. My hand and forearm disappear in the blink of an eye, and I instantly shriek due to the flesh-tearing, bone-snapping agony that is inflicted on me. It's blinding all of my senses—all I hear are my wails. I do notice when the hum of the engine turns off, but I can barely see what's going on through my blurred eyes. I clench my teeth together so hard I fear I might crack them as I moan.

I feel something tearing me away from that bloody nightmare they force these poor dimies to work day and night. Soft cloth enters my mouth mid-scream that I instantly bite down on, as tight binding is wrapped around the biceps of my torn arm. I look down as I scream into the cloth to see two green paws tying a white cloth splattered dark red around my arm before twisting the knot ever tighter.

The sound of a gunshot blazes through the air, and I can see flashes of coloured paws tending to my arm, before a scarlet red bear dimie quickly picks me up and runs down the hallway, along with the others who look terrified. My vision begins to fog, but I can feel every step my carrier makes through the pulsating sensation in my arm. Every breath and bounce is excruciating. *Is this what Aspen felt with every scar and wound she's received?*

It feels like hours till we stop running and make it outside. The pain is becoming unbearable even through my disoriented state. *I feel so exhausted.* "Lori? Lori! Oh, my baby sister!" comes a familiar voice, saturated in terror.

"Bloody hell! Quick, this way. I know someone who can help," a man's voice says in haste—it sounds like Keagan.

"What about the slaves?" *I know that one too…Ghedi's here.*

"Take them back to where we planned originally, and do it fast; we have to take care of Lori." I try to figure out who's around me and whose face belongs to whose voice, but it feels like my eyes are being weighed down by bricks. They're so heavy I can barely stay awake. I feel the bitter cold of the night creep over me as the warmth from my body seems to come in waves and then seep away in an instant. *Is this how Aspen felt when she passed out on the beach from her wounds? Did she feel this scared, or this cold?* I try to fight my exhaustion and stay conscious as my carrier runs on, but all too soon I lose my senses, till I fall into a black numbness.

THE PRICE OF A DOCTOR

KEAGAN

This was worse than our heist in Currlion. I can still feel my ribs crying out from the hit that mountain of a man at the loading dock gave me. Nothing worked on him, not even our magnet restraints. He broke through them like they were rock candy. The fact that he was still partially conscious when Lori was brought to us didn't help either. Having to leave him before we could take him down I think was the worst mistake, even if time is ticking for Lori. If we had waited just a moment longer to finish the job, he wouldn't have alerted their "backup security". Even as the thought enters my mind, though, I'm appalled at myself for it. This is Lori we're talking about. Still, if we had, then we wouldn't be currently chased on two overcrowded stolen horse carriages by Damon's dimie watchmen and those bloody hounds of his. They must have been patrolling the area when they heard the alarms.

Gaining on us in leaps and bounds, they gnash their razor teeth at us every few feet. Gripping onto Lori tightly from the inside of the carriage, I wish so badly that Aspen had chosen to hold her own sister and let me deal with the hounds. But there's no stopping her as she spouts out orders to us. Besides, I'm the only one who knows the way to my friend's place. So I have to give directions to Samuel as we race through the streets. Harry should easily be on his way to the safehouse without any issue, since the rest of us are acting as decoys to drive the hounds off the scent of the dimies. Obviously, these hounds have been made to catch us first and dimies second.

I still can't believe my eyes when I saw Samuel and Anthony come racing down the loading zone with two taxi carriages. I bet my best hat that Samuel stole those from his job at the station, but were they a godsend at the moment we were racing away, since we could see the hounds running down the street.

"Take a left at Shepherd's Street!" I roar out the window before settling back inside, only to see the look of disgust on Ghedi's face as we pass by a streetlamp. It's just a glimpse, but I can see his eyes directly on Lori's arm. He didn't even try to hold her or get near her when she was brought to us. *This bastard never truly cared about her after all, did he?* I feel the urge to stop everything, just to fight the coward. I feel like I'm looking at myself from just a few years ago—self-centred, never actually caring for the women I was with, so full of myself. It's exactly what I now see before me. No wonder I always disliked him.

The sight of Isaac's eyes landing on mine, full of fear, snap me out of my toxic thoughts. My gaze shifts back to Aspen on the other carriage. I recall her odd behaviour from before, how she cut off the remainder of Lori's blood-soaked sleeve just before hopping on the back of the second carriage. She's now wafting it dangerously close to the hound's nose right as we hit the turn, as Anthony's carriage with her on it keeps going forward. "What is Anthony doing?" I mumble absently as the scene before me begins to freeze. *Why aren't they following us? Aspen, you reckless woman, don't do this right now. I can't bear the thought of losing you both in one night.* Then I understand; the hounds have stopped chasing us and are now only chasing *her*. They could jump right on the carriage now if they wished.

Before jumping off the back of the carriage, Aspen shoots out her grappling hook towards a building at the end of an alley, and throws a restraining bracelet at the hound jumping towards her. It easily wraps around the mechanical beast's mouth and shoots it off towards the nearest lamp post. It was only a glimpse, but when she looked back at the carriage with Lori and me in it, I could see the fire in her eyes, right before they pointed back at the hounds. *If those dogs chase her long enough, I'm certain she'll dismantle them till they're just nuts and bolts.*

The dimie watchmen are a few seconds behind in a carriage of their own, but end up following only Anthony as well. *She could've at least told me, and any of our team could have fought with her. Does she really think she still has to handle everything alone? That she has to carry the burdens of everyone else alone?* I try to convince myself I'll be able to scold her later, but one look back at Lori's ashen complexion makes my whole being begin to shudder.

After one more turn, we end up at the right house, and we all begin pounding on Dr Price's door. If he's still the same man he was when I was in school, I know he'll be awake at three in the morning. Finally the door swings open to an astounded green bird dimie butler and Dr Price himself in his favourite charred and stained chemistry shirt. *He must still experiment as he used to,* I think as I rush in towards him with Lori. Staring at me for a second, he says, "Keagan Myrack?"

right before pulling me inside his operating room on the right side of his house.

Placing Lori on the examining bed, he races to the sink and washes his hands as Andrea runs in, flinging off her mask, hood and gloves before washing her own hands. "I'm a nurse. How can I help?" I hear her say to the doctor.

"Clean the wound and ready the bone saw as I prep her for cauterization," he orders professionally. "I have to prepare a blood test for her transfusion."

"A blood test will take too long, won't it?" she questions as she suds her hands.

"Not with my methods."

Cauterization...bone saw? I stand by Lori in dread. How could this happen to her? "Do you truly have to take it?" I ask.

"Only if you want her to live. Now, outside," he says, tearing me away from someone I view as my little sister. A ghost's hand pulls me out of the room just before the doors are shut in front of me. One more person goes into the room, but I don't recognise the man. The whole world is ringing in a sharp tone, voices are muffled, and the sight of people are like blurred photographs—undetailed and hard to make sense of.

"Not...worry.....Price's resident assistant....you see," a baritone voice says to me as I am led further away from the door. *Aspen, where are you? I feel as if I'm about to fall through the floor. I'm supposed to be your guardian, your and Lori's protector, and I've become the biggest failure to the both of you in less than a few minutes.* I sink into a chair and stare at my bloody hands.

Every so often I think I hear someone, but I'm not sure. Not until I hear her voice. "Where is she?" Looking up finally, I see Aspen, her clothes torn with minor cuts here and there, covered in mud and grease. She looks like she just won a war in Hell, and I don't doubt for a second that it was anything less. It takes me a moment to realise that Anthony is right behind her, looking less ragged but still not well-off, and with a swelling lip at that.

"You can't see her right now, ma'am," the butler dimie who pulled me out of the room says to her. "Besides, we should clean you both up at the moment as well. You look rather worse for wear."

"You think I care about myself right now? Where is my baby sister?"

"My friend Dr Price, his assistant, and Andrea are trying to...they're taking care of her right now," I say. "But they're right, Aspen. You're too unsanitary right now to see her when she's in such a critical condition. Besides, I think it would only upset you more to see what's going on behind those doors." I stand up and stroll over to her, gesturing to the three small blue-feathered dimie maids who are failing at hiding themselves as they spy on us. They all gasp and shuffle back out of sight just before one comes from the hallway. "Can you please help my friends here get cleaned up, and show us a place where we all can?"

"Yes, sir, there's a place in the garden where everyone can get clean if you wish. Unless you require a bath—that will take slightly longer." She doesn't look directly at me or Aspen, but just gestures to the way to the garden.

That's right, the gardeners' sink station. "No, that won't be necessary. The garden will be fine, thank you."

"Yes, sir. We'll bring down towels and soap for you. Please follow me."

"Oh, I know the way, thank you." I walk past her briskly, taking Aspen's hand and motioning for the rest of our party to follow.

"Uh, yes, Sir," she mutters.

Going to the back of the house and through the hallway that leads to the kitchen, I take us to the garden door. When I open it up, I notice some new plants since the last time I was here, and others I remember but that have grown so much. Many are beginning to bud and bloom. We walk absently to the covered deep stone sinks the gardeners use to clean up. I remember how the sinks always supply so much water. This is what our size of a group needs right now.

Turning on the sink, the maids bring us soap and towels. Aspen just sits on an overturned bucket, arms on her knees and head sunken down as the belladonna above her head waves in the breeze. The mud on her looks like it's beginning to dry, but her cuts aren't, and the one on her shoulder I fear may need stitches from the doctor later. I feel exhaustion cover me, but not so much as I see on her right now. The blue-bird dimie maid from before comes to Aspen's side, sitting on the ground as she gently takes her right arm that has the most mud on it. As she cleans her, Aspen doesn't fight back, talk, or even move.

The other monkey dimie maid with tan fur and small wings looks over Anthony and helps him clean his fat lip and the few scrapes he received. I think I should ask him what happened later, instead of Aspen. After washing my hands thoroughly, and checking the small shattered mirror that hangs beside the sink, I see that my face is also smudged with blood. Even though my clothes are black, I can see the shine and discolouration of Lori's blood on them as well. *My God, please, tell me why? Why like this?*

Once we're thoroughly washed up and have checked each other over, the gang goes back inside with the monkey dimie. I decide to stay with Aspen a while longer and relieve the other maid of her cleaning job. She had just finished giving Aspen's hair a quick rinse and wring, even cleaning and patching up most of her cuts and scrapes, but she hadn't yet gotten to her face. Kneeling before her, I push my fingers through her hair and away from her face. Even when her hair has been knotted up and gone through the mud, a good wash makes it as soft as ever. I gently bring my fingers to her jawline and drag them down to her chin. Once there, I pull her face towards me. Her head is heavy, and she keeps her eyes closed tightly. I can tell she's clenching her teeth even before I bring up the cool wet cloth to wipe the dirt from her beautifully pained face.

"You hate it right now," I say. "You wish you could go back in time, even switch places. You wish the entire world would just go away. But we must keep charging on right now. There will be time to scream, cry, and wish everything that happened hadn't, but not now. You do such things when you're alone." Aspen still doesn't move. "That's what my father told me the night my mother died. It was possibly the last time I was thankful for his words." She opens her eyes just a bit, and tears instantly fall to the earth. "We don't know what will happen yet, but now is the time to keep marching on. You could be talking to her again tomorrow, so don't you cry too hard just yet." I try to sound commanding and confident, like she is to us on our missions, but I can hear the hitch in my voice as my throat begins to close up.

Wiping her eyes with the cloth before she stands up on her own, she goes to the sink to splash her face with the freezing water. Letting out a small yell, she wipes her face and turns to look at me with the look of a tigress. There's my lady.

How long will it take to get an answer? Every thirty minutes we check back to hear how she's doing, but Andrea always says "wait a bit longer" or "too soon to tell" through the closed door. Aspen will have created a trench in the floor from her constant pacing by the time we can go in. The crystal bottle of brandy looks incredibly tempting right now, but deep down I know that would be the worst course of action. Besides, I don't feel all too thirsty right now, and I've lost all sense of appetite. Ghedi, Issac and Samuel have begun to play a card game whilst Anthony and Isola curl up on the chairs and have fallen asleep. It will be morning in a few hours and there is still no word for me to give to Uncle George and Pauline. They were so distraught when I called them about what happened, I can't bring myself to talk to them without a good answer. I can't even imagine a tomorrow at this moment.

The swift opening of the operating theatre's door grabs the whole room's attention, and everyone freezes in anticipation. Andrea and Dr Price rush out of the room and down the hallway, followed by the sound of two more doors opening and closing at the far end. Then I hear an unknown male's voice ringing out, saying, "Keagan, is it? May I see you?" I don't recognise the voice but it's reassuringly placid.

"What about me?" Aspen demands.

"Are you her guardian?"

"I'm her sister," Aspen says impatiently.

"All right, then both of you, please come in."

Rising from my seat, we make our way to the room. "I am Dr Price's assistant, Mr Doyle," the man says. "I'm relieved to tell you that Lori is alive. We managed to save her in the nick of time. She's still in a very critical and fragile state, however, so you may not touch her, and don't try to wake her up. We're currently still working on stabilising her."

A great breath escapes my lungs before I feel tension released from my shoulders and back. "Please, I must see her," Aspen begs.

"Yes, of course, but I must warn you, Miss—"

"Aspen."

"Miss Aspen, I need you to prepare yourself for what you're about to see. Keagan, have you told her the extent of the injuries yet?"

I sigh. "No, I haven't." This is the final straw for Aspen, as she pushes Mr Doyle away from the doorway and rushes in, only to stop in her tracks a moment later. I stand right outside with the doctor, feeling like the great coward I am, the shock emanating from Aspen as she looks at her sister. Step by step, I walk into the room whilst she gets closer to the red-stained bed. Lori has been stripped of her shirt, and her chest and shoulders are wrapped up tightly. Her chest is covered by a splattered blanket, thankfully, but we can see Lori's arm outside of the sheets—well, what's left of it. Her hand and forearm are missing from her left side, and yet she lays there as if she were in a deep slumber, unknowing of what she's lost. Aspen doesn't touch her, though her hand lingers towards her missing limb as she takes a seat next to the bed on a stool.

"If this was what you meant when you said we could get hurt, I'm rethinking my joining." Samuel's voice rings in my ear as he and the rest of our team join us near the doorway.

"Samuel!" Isola scolds him as Aspen's hands clench into a fist.

"What? They were the ones who told us that they will do whatever it takes to free the dimies, right? You three said that you knew what you were getting yourselves into."

"Do we need to take this outside?" Aspen says, slowly

rising out of her seat. "Because I will gladly do so in a heartbeat."

"Miss Aspen, I don't think—"

"Don't think what? That I shouldn't take offence to what he just said? Well, I do, and I'm really in the mood to put someone in the hospital! You had the brass to say that, then let's go outside and I'll show you just how much I care, so *come on!*" she yells as she slams Samuel into the wall, then plunges her knife into the wall's panels, right next to his head. We flinch at the sight of the blade and the thunderous slam it makes.

Samuel seems to be muttering something as he tries to get his bearings straight. He is visibly sweating and turning red. I look down and see that Aspen has lifted him up to the tips of his toes.

So this is what she's like when she's furious. I should consider myself lucky after the secret fireplace incident. To think, I thought she was angry then.

"What do you say?" Aspen whispers.

"I—I'm sorry. That was the wrong thing to say. It—it won't happen again," Samuel manages to let out in a quivering voice.

"You're damned right it won't. Get out," Aspen orders as she releases both him and her knife from the wall in one fluid motion. Samuel nearly slumps all the way to the floor, and he clutches his chest. "None of you deserve to be in this room. *Get out.*" Once the door is slammed shut, everything becomes quiet again. The energy in the room feels like a poison that slowly seeps into every corner, filling the atmosphere with a terrible taste of aggression and fear. Mr Doyle quietly slips out of the room himself with a wide-eyed expression.

Seeing Aspen's rapidly breathing form still facing the shut

door, clutching the knife in her white-knuckled fist, makes me tense up again. It's as if she's turned into a wounded beast. I'm almost afraid to approach her, except for the fact that I know that's exactly what she needs me to do right now. Slowly, I make my way over till I'm right behind her. *She hasn't moved an inch. Does she feel the need to guard the door? Perhaps she's just too afraid to face me or look at Lori.*

I look down at the dagger she's still gripping in her left hand. "That has to go now," I say as gently as I can before I brush my hand over hers. Gradually, she lets go of the knife, and I take it from her palm and place it away on a side table. Pulling her from the doorway one step at a time, I can hear her breathing quicken. I move in front of her so we can face each other, and get a quick glimpse of her reddened, petrified face before I envelop her in a hug. I don't squeeze her tightly or anything, but simply hold her, so I can be whatever she needs me to be. A friend, a shoulder to cry on, or even a punching bag. I really hope it's not the latter, though; my ribs are screaming enough as it is.

In a flash, her arms wrap tightly around my shoulder blades as she sobs into my chest. I know where I've felt this pain and fear before. A memory appears in my mind's eye, me sitting outside my mother's bedroom just so I could sneak a glimpse of her whenever the doors would open. I wasn't allowed to enter her room because of the plague, but one night I snuck in with a handkerchief tied around my face to go and see her. She looked so pale.

Even when she was as sick as she was, she was a light sleeper, and she quickly woke up. "Keagan, my sneaky little boy, what are you doing in here?" she said weakly.

"To see you, Mum. No one will let me see you." I walked closer to her bed.

"Stop where you are, Keagan. There's a good reason you haven't been allowed in. Just the same, I'm happy to see you again."

She wouldn't let me come close to her, so I just sat on the floor with a pillow from the couch and a spare blanket. We talked for so long that night. I talked her into sleep, and when I was sure she was out, I snuck back out the door, but I remember I felt the need to guard it. When I woke up, Winona was shaking me. She managed to send me back to my room before my father or the rest of the house found out I had been there. She also managed to berate me the entire way back to my bed. *That was fourteen years ago. That was my last memory of Mum.*

"God, Winona, Mum, please let us keep Lori," I mumble unintelligibly. My eyes begin to water, but no tears fall. I do feel sad, but I feel more numb than anything else. Then a feeling of anger floods through my veins. Now I have the urge to kill someone, like Aspen did a moment ago. No wonder she wanted to fight so bad. I have half a mind to go release everything that's so pent up inside.

The simplest sound rings in the air, a small light moan, but it doesn't come from my Aspen who is quivering in my arms. No, it's coming from behind her. Looking over my shoulder, I see Lori stirring ever so slightly. She looks very uncomfortable, though. Dr Price still is preparing the pain medication—it won't be a pleasant awakening for her without it. I use the energy of my anger to fuel my actions, as I release Aspen and refocus her attention to her fidgeting sister. She quickly goes back to her aid as I run out the room, past the shell-shocked group of simpletons we call partners, and towards the back door. If my memory serves me correctly, the doctor has an apothecary in his garden in the guise of a greenhouse. He used to brag about it for days.

When I enter the garden and turn the corner opposite to where we cleaned ourselves, the old greenhouse light is partially hidden among larkspur and poppy flowers. I can just make out Dr Price's silhouette, pouring and mixing vials by the looks of it. "Dr Price!" I rush through the greenhouse fogged-glass door. "Lori is beginning to stir. I think she may wake up soon."

Without wasting a second, he hands me a bottle of alcohol and a large mug. "Fill it up halfway," he orders as he shakes a large canister vigorously with both of his hands wrapped around it. I do as he says right before he hands me the bottle he was just shaking. "Keep shaking like I was until I tell you to stop, and not a moment sooner." He takes a fresh syringe and fills it with a yellow concoction in the graduated cylinder. Recapping the syringe, he trots out of the greenhouse without another word.

I continue to shake the canister whilst I look around at all the hanging dried herbs and vials with pharmaceuticals in them. Makes me wonder if he still tutors chemistry like he did for me. He always loved to show me and the other students his garden and greenhouse. Just before my mind wanders off entirely to the past, I notice a fat open drawstring sack with something black inside. Moving closer to the work table under the lantern light, I see there are tiny black seeds, poppy seeds to be exact, and there is a scooper still half buried in the bag. Next to the bag, a pot simmers over a flame, emitting the familiar smell of vinegar. *Am I making black tar opium right now?*

Speak of the devil, I hear the courtyard door close once again, and Dr Price enters without the syringe he left with. "I just gave Lori an injection of the fastest-acting painkillers I could make in the time I had. She will feel pain and be aware of it, but it will be bearable; it's the best I could do at the moment. What you're mixing there will help more; however, it is much more addictive and should be regulated."

"May I ask what it is I'm helping you make?"

The doctor steals a glance at the open bag of seeds near my side. I can detect the slight smirk on his face underneath his black moustache. "I'm curious to see if your knowledge about pharmaceuticals has gotten any better. What do you think this is?" he says, flipping out his pocketwatch to check the time.

"Opium...for black tar," I say rather reluctantly. I know first-hand the effects of opioids after trying them during my travels in the Orient, but I also recall the withdrawals and addictive tendencies I went through. I finally weaned myself off the stuff last year. Thinking about giving it to Lori makes me nervous, despite her current condition. I don't want her to go through the same battle I did to get over it. Neither do I like the idea of it being so temptingly in reach of myself.

"Indeed it is, my boy. But don't fear. If it's regulated properly with the correct dosage, Lori should not experience addiction." Dr Price assures me.

"Where did you even get such a large amount?"

"I have my connections, much like you have yours. Which reminds me, your payment for Lori and her treatment. It'll be one hundred and fifty pounds, plus I need you to fetch a special powder for me from a merchant who's coming into port this Saturday eve. I need you to get me eight ounces of a certain yellow powder. It's from Thailand and has special healing properties, but the merchant is very sly. He never sells to people he doesn't know, only to regulars, friends and family."

"So how do you propose I get it?" I say as I continue to shake the canister.

"That's up to you. Beg, barter, steal or gamble. You were great at them all when you were my student." Taking the canister from my hands, he pours it out through a strainer to catch the poppy seeds over a bowl.

"And if I can't get the medicine? What then?"

"Then I'll have to charge you eighty more pounds. And if anyone were to ask what happened tonight, I might just mention you and your friends' names." *Blackmail, eh? He really hasn't changed a bit. He's always kept up the public appearance of a good doctor and helper, but he's really just an opportunist eager to make a buck, and loyal to few.*

"You haven't changed, Dr Price," I say, taking my leave from the greenhouse to get back to Lori and Aspen.

"Thank you. However, you, my boy...you've changed immensely." I pause in the doorway, due to the strange tone in his voice. When I turn back to him, though, I see only a genuine look of pride in his eyes. He holds the gaze for only a tick before blinking, then continues to work on the poppy tea. I walk my way back to Aspen and Lori with a lighter feeling in my heart now. As I walk into the operating room and see Aspen resting next to Lori, I can't help but smile a bit as I think of what he just said . *So this is what it feels like for someone to be proud of you.*

Father never gave me an expression like that in his life. Seems like there was an unending road of things I had to do to get his attention, let alone his approval. Ever since Winona died and Charles betrayed all of us, I've never really thought about how much it means to have someone older than you be proud of you. Now that I think about it, that wasn't the first time Dr Price has looked at me that way either. Back when I was his student and would help him in the garden or mix pharmaceuticals correctly, I remember seeing the pride in his eyes. *Maybe that's why he thinks I can also get that untouchable powder for him. Dr Price was able to look at me like that so easily. So why was it so hard for my father?*

BABY SISTER

LORI

After waking up in Dr Price's operating room last week, I wasn't able to grasp what he was saying to me at first. The room was still spinning, and I had never felt so terrible in my whole life, even after my first hangover. It didn't help that Aspen was crying in my ear half the time, and I didn't even know what for. I hated staying at his house in that white room for so long with nothing to do but rest that entire week. I wouldn't accept anything anyone was trying to say to me; I kept telling myself that I'm in a long nightmare and I'll scare myself awake any second now. However, today, waking up back at Uncle George's house, my hand grazes over my empty sleeve, reminding me that this is my new reality.

Hard to believe I've been in this position more than once, except last time I had both arms. Aunt Mae would always tell me how stunningly beautiful I was, except for the length of my waist and my weight. She would go on and on about how important a perfect figure is to the opposite sex. "You will always have a pretty face, Lori, but if you don't stop eating so many sweets, no man will want you. Men don't appreciate fat women." I would hear that so often, I finally lost all appetite for…well, any food. She controlled how much I ate and when I ate. I still reach for the measuring tape after meals sometimes, just like she insisted on back then, making me think that if I were just a little thinner, I would truly be perfect. Every day I looked to Aunt Mae for approval, but my shrinking waist was never enough. The weakness I feel now is comparable to when I became sick in my bed. Aunt Mae's words still ring in my ears: "It's just a cold; no need for a doctor, my dear. You know, Lori, I believe you're almost at your ideal weight. We should check your measurements in a little while." But I was too tired to get up to look in the mirror, no matter how much I wished I could.

Oh, the surprise I had that night when Aspen snuck into my bedroom with Pearl far past curfew. I miss Pearl. She was such a wonderful dimie handmaid. "She's trying to starve you to death, Lori." Those were Aspen's first words to me.

"What? No, she's trying to prepare me to find a suitor."

"Lori, we've been trying to get to you for days," Pearl said, unwrapping a plate of steaming food that made my mouth water. "Every time we get near your door, or even look upstairs, Aunt Mae threatens us." Putting the plate on my lap, I just stared at it, remembering what she told me. *I'm so close.*

"It's no secret that she hits me," Aspen added. "Thanks to the household, I've been protected long enough to piece things together and get back in the right headspace. However, you, Lori, she's trying to starve out. Do you remember how Father left us a will but it was never found? Well, until we find it, Aunt Mae is our guardian, and she seems determined to make sure that if and when the will is found, we'll already be dead. That way we can't possibly lay claim on any of the inheritance."

"But she's family; she wouldn't—"

"Miss Lori, look at yourself." Pearl shoved my hand mirror towards me in the candlelight. The sunkenness of my eyes was what scared me first, and then how pale I looked. The rosy cheeks I once had were gone, and had become skeletal in comparison. For the first time in over a month, I was able to see clearly what was actually going on.

"Lori, we're going to help you," Sissy reassured me. "We're going to help each other find that will. We have to know what it says."

So I began eating each and every day. It became harder for Aspen to come and see me, but each time Pearl came to help bathe or change me, there was another dimie in the walls where the servants moved unseen, bringing me food. Each time they came, I had a full meal, and they made sure I would eat every last bite.

One night, Aspen came to me with a new bruise on her arm and a sad smile on her face. "I can't find it. None of us can find it, Lori. And Aunt Mae figured us out as well." Her glistening eyes betrayed her. The feeling of lost hope surrounding her was too much.

"We said we would help one another, right?" I said, slowly standing up and putting my hands out open to her. The sight of me being able to stand on my own again took all her tears away, and that beaming clever smile I love so much came back as she took my hands. "So let's help one another. If nothing else, let's get out of here, even if we have to make her throw us out."

"When you get better, let's go to our cousin's home. We can finally start back on what Father was never able to finish."

I put my forehead to hers and closed my eyes. "You sure do miss tinkering, don't you, Aspen?"

"...Very much."

Almost two years have passed since that awful time in our lives. And yet somehow we find ourselves in a similar situation, except there's been nothing stopping Aspen from leaving my side this time around. No matter when I wake up or what I need, she's there to help me. *And what have I done to deserve it lately? Nothing. I even threatened to leave her for Ghedi. And yet I wonder if that could've been a better way to go,* I think as I rub the fabric of my hollow sleeve between my fingers. *Ghedi, where are you? Why haven't you come? Are you afraid to see me now?*

But my thoughts of him are cut short when I hear the shuffling of the sheets in the bed next to mine. Our beds are so small, it's rather hard for both of us to sleep in one, so Aspen pushed her bed next to mine to remain close. Stirring more and more, she finally wakes up. "Morning, Lori bird," she mumbles, still sounding groggy. Her brunette hair is in a messy braid, with curls poking out from every angle. When Aspen looks like that, it almost always means she had a good night's sleep.

"Morning, Sissy."

"How's your energy?"

"Still lousy."

"Hmm. Need your tea or the opium pipe?"

"No, it doesn't hurt too much right now. I'd love some breakfast, though; I'm famished." I reach for the cord next to my bedside, which rings a bell downstairs to let Pauline know I'm awake. She's so wonderful at bringing meals up. She even puts flowers on my platter. This time, though, she must have been waiting just outside for me, because she comes in ridiculously fast compared to when I usually pull the cord.

"Muffins, fresh orange juice, and two boiled eggs this morning for the both of you," chirps Pauline.

"Thank you, Pauline. And thanks for the flowers every morning. You really go above and beyond with the little things."

"Why, Miss Lori, he hasn't told you?"

The moment I hear *he*, my ears perk up and my heart skips a beat. "Has Ghedi been leaving these for me? Is he still here?"

I start to shuffle off my sheets and try to stand up, but Aspen is quick to my side. "Hold on, Lori. Ghedi isn't the one leaving you flowers. Thomas has been picking and buying them. I bet he'll keep doing so until you feel better."

I have no words right now. "Why hasn't he seen me yet? I'd much rather him give me the flowers himself."

"Oh, Lori, you haven't seen him, but he's seen you," Pauline explains. "Every time he's come to see you, you were already asleep. He's so afraid for your well-being. When we received the call from the doctor a few days ago, we were all so worried. Thomas wouldn't talk to us; he just tried to shut himself up in the laboratory until you came home. Aspen has since told him to help George finish the war balloon model for the queen."

"I can't believe he's the one who brought them. And Aspen, you really should be the one to finish the aircraft; honestly, I'm not going anywhere."

"I don't know if I'd say that. You just tried to jump out of bed at the thought that Ghedi could be in the area. Someone's got to make sure you get your bed rest."

I want to argue with her that I'm fine, but I feel light-headed just from my quick action of trying to stand up. Laying back down, we start breakfast. Since it's muffins this morning, Aspen doesn't need to feed me. I hate the feeling of being that helpless. Though I love the idea of being waited on like a lady, I just wish I had the energy to enjoy it.

Finished with our muffins and halfway through my egg, I ask Aspen if she could have Thomas come see me whilst I'm still awake. "No can do," she replies. "The doctor said there can be no visitors for at least one more day. Besides, you look like you're ready to go back to sleep now." Pauline slips Aspen's skirt over her head. Her day clothes consist of navy skirts and a cream-coloured ruffled blouse with a silver embroidered navy vest. She looks like she's ready for the sea with colours like that. "Andrea has been asking for updates on your condition each day to make sure everything's fine. Right now, she and our team have their hands full with feeding and helping the ill dimies we saved last week. She said that if you felt the least bit poorly, she'd be over like lightning to help treat you. Isn't that sweet?"

"That is indeed. It's handy having a real nurse on our side for once." Though I say it with a smile, I wish it was Ghedi who'd been asking all about me and threatening to break down the door just to be by my side. "Don't worry, I'll keep resting, though I see you've been keeping yourself busy during my sleep, Aspen. Your new journal has been bursting at the seams with how many ideas you've been putting into it. Tell me your most delicious one."

"They're just ideas for new inventions, and ways for us to meet the queen whilst staying out of trouble. I've probably created twenty new ideas and schematics for new inventions, though I'm at a loss for a good way to meet the queen. It's not like we're used to meeting royalty. It doesn't help that she shall meet us cross-dressed as men the first time around, either."

"Hmmm, what about Ghedi? Has he come at all to see me? I wish to see him very much."

Aspen and Pauline give each other a look I catch, as Pauline is leading Aspen to the vanity for her hair. "No, he hasn't come. But I'm sure if he truly cares about you, he'll be here any day now with a whole cart of flowers and chocolates."

"Pauline's right, Lori. He could just be keeping his distance since you can't have visitors. If he truly cares for you, he'll come. And in doing so, prove me wrong for what I said about him before." Aspen smiles halfheartedly. We haven't spoken once about that night, not this whole time, and I'm actually afraid to bring it up now. I don't want to cause any more trouble than there already is at the moment between us. With Ghedi, though, I can tell that they don't think he'll come. *If he comes. If he cares.* I know he cares, and I know he'll come for me. *I would come for him, so why shouldn't he come for me?*

SAYING GOODBYE

KEAGAN

Now that Lori has been certified as stable by the doctor during a quick home visit, Harry has been coming by daily to see how his cousin is and bring her fresh flowers, much like Thomas. I often think of how many wealthy pockets he must be picking as of late, seeing all the different bouquets of flowers he brings in. I always make sure to check that Uncle George and my wallets are untouched during and after his visit. A sad precaution but one that must be done. I'm so grateful when Andrea has an hour to spare every now and then from the dimies to come and look at Lori. It sure helps when Thomas and I relieve her and the others of their post every other day as well, so they can get out once in a while.

Three days into Lori's recovery, our teammates reach out to us by sending a letter through Harry as the delivery boy. Coming in with a fresh bushel of blue delphiniums, we both go up the stairs to see Lori as Pauline excuses herself to prepare the tea. When we come into the room, she is awake and Aspen is feeding her creamy potato mushroom soup with Thomas at the table working on his schooling. Probably history, the way his brow is furrowed. He never does that when it's mathematics or science.

One look at Lori and I can tell she's still rather feeble compared to her normal hale complexion; however, the sight of Harry and his flowers always puts a soft smile on her face. "Hey, Aspen, why don't you let Harry help Lori for a bit? There was something Uncle George wanted to see you about," I suggest.

"I'm coming too; I need a break." Thomas jumps out of his chair.

"No, I think—"

"Whatever he needs me for, it's probably something he'd want Thomas to see too," Aspen says. "George only asks for us when it's over a mechanical or a brilliantly convoluted matter."

"Indeed, it's true." Thomas races out the door with Aspen after she sets down the half-eaten bowl of food. Following them out, I have to jog down the hall to catch up, right as they reach the stairs. Putting my arm out in front of them, I hold the note up. "Okay, I lied, Uncle George doesn't need to see you. Harry brought this along with him. I haven't read it yet."

"Go on then, let's all hear it." Aspen nods at the note.

Opening it up, I read the scrawly writing and can only think it's Isola's. "They're asking what the next move with the dimies is. They say they're quickly losing room and food for the rescued in their hiding place. They're asking for more food, money and bedding. The dimies are beginning to question whether leaving the mill was a good decision."

"I need at least a full day to figure out if we should send them home just yet," Aspen replies. "I still want to send the teams out to different cities first, to get a headcount of where we should go next concerning dimie population."

"Yeah, and to challenge Damon. Don't even try to hide that part of your plan from me. I can see right through you."

"Smart aleck."

"I love you too," I say, kissing her on the cheek. She purses her lips, trying to hide her smile. How adorable. Looking down at Thomas, I see him trying to sneak his way down the stairs. "And where do you think you're going?"

"Oh, I thought you two would just want a little space is all."

"Thomas," Aspen and I echo.

"I'm taking a break. Please? History can be so boring."

"That just depends on how you read it. Go on back to the books; it's the last thing you have for today, anyways."

"Ugh! Fine, but afterwards can I go and see kids on the block?" He trudges back up the steps.

"Be my guest, but don't forget your false nose." Aspen pokes his nose with a little smile.

"Deal." And he's off, back to the bedroom and his book. Slipping my arms around Aspen's back, I pull her in for an embrace. "What's this for?" she asks.

"I just feel like you needed a hug. This is the first time you've left Lori's side in three days. I know you're scared for her, Aspen, but you're not alone, and she'll be okay."

"I don't think...well, that this is the best time to talk about it."

"Why not?" I say, pulling back, cupping her face in my hands.

With a slight smile, she gently holds onto my wrists for a moment. "Because I need to go back in there, and I don't want to walk in crying, because I won't stop, not for a long time." I hear the hitch in her voice right before she starts to pull away a tad.

"Maybe that's what you need. We both know from experience that penting it up never helped anyone."

"I do realise that. Just not right now, not whilst she is smiling again. But perhaps tonight when she's asleep. I honestly don't know how long I can hold it in."

"Tonight, then," I say, putting my hands in my pockets, releasing her to tend to her sister once again. As she walks off, I have half a mind to scour every inch of London to find that rascal Ghedi. Disappearing on Lori, who so devoutly adores him, is ridiculous. Practically abandoning her after a life-threatening injury makes me want to throttle him.

The constant banging on the back door at ten o'clock at night causes the whole house to stir. My only thought is that Thomas is back with something important, or one of the gang members for the same reason. Aspen and I reach the back kitchen door just as Pauline checks the peephole and swings it open to let in an unnerving sight.

"Thomas!" we both cry out before rushing towards his limp body. Harry comes hobbling in carrying Thomas, who is dishevelled and has a few gashes on his shoulder and brow. The closer he comes, the more dirt I can see on him. He must've gotten in a rough fight—was he mugged?

Taking him upstairs to our room, Pauline gets towels and clean water for him. As we are on our way, we pass by Uncle George and Thatcher walking down the hall. "By jove, what happened to the lad?" Uncle George exclaims.

"It's a hell of a story," Harry says, but he doesn't smile. His furrowed brow and downturned head shows a very serious side that hasn't shown up all too often yet.

Making it up the stairs, we head away from Lori and Aspen's room and over to ours. Setting him down, the mud is already smearing on the back of the chair when Harry pulls back his sleeves. Thomas grunts and holds his stomach in one hand as Pauline holds his other arm to look at his torn shoulder.

"Thomas, who did this to you?" Aspen says, flames almost visible from her mouth due to the heat of her words, and I can tell I'm just as mad. "Sailors, thugs, robbers? I'll tear 'em apart with my bare hands,"

"Count me in as well. What happened?" Thatcher says, hobbling his way in on a cane.

"I went out to find Ghedi to bring him here so Lori could see him, but things got a little heated."

"That's an understatement," I say.

"Why don't you tell us the details, hmm?" Uncle George suggests, looking peeved as Pauline strips off his ruined tan shirt to assess the damage better. His dark torso has a few bruise marks beginning to show, and I bet by tomorrow they'll be fully visible.

"Well, I found him coming out of a pub near the wharf close to their hideout, and I followed him into the alley. I told him how much Lori misses him and that it would help her health and spirit if he came to see her. He didn't agree. He said something like, 'I won't be coming to see Lori anymore. At one point Lori was perfect. But now that she went and got her arm torn up and amputated, she's now only *part* of a perfect woman. What man in his right mind would want to hold a metal hook instead of a flesh-and-blood hand? Also, what news on the slave relocation? We're getting mighty cramped at our place.' That really made my blood boil, and I couldn't help myself, I ran straight at him and jumped on him.

I tried to beat him, but he threw me off in an instant. The second I got up to attack him again, he kicked me in my stomach, straight into a wall. I managed to land a hit or two on him, but he definitely got more on me. All of a sudden, he grabbed my shirt and raised me off the ground, but before he could do anything else, I heard a cracking sound right before I landed on the ground again. When I opened my eyes to see what happened, I saw it was Harry who was then punching Ghedi's face into the ground whilst shouting obscenities."

Keagan and I give Harry a look. *Did you really have to go that far with language when Thomas was around?*

"Heh, I may have gotten carried away, but that pig deserved every bit of what he received," Harry says, crossing his arms over his chest and not making eye contact.

"What exactly did Ghedi receive?" Aspen asks in a put-out tone. It's hard to tell if she is mad at Harry or at what Ghedi said.

Harry pauses before saying, "Some broken teeth, a busted nose, and last I saw him he was unconscious in the alley I left him." His eyes aren't willing to meet Aspen's deadly stare.

"What alleyway did you say you left him in?" Aspen replies in such a hungry tone that I realise, if she so much as sees Ghedi again, she will kill him.

"Aspen, why don't we focus on mending wounds right now, instead of making more?" Uncle George says gently, turning her head towards Thomas's bruised body. In an instant, her demeanour changes back to one of worry.

"I still think he deserves more," Thatcher grumbles as he slowly sits himself down on my bed next to George.

"Thomas, whatever compelled you to go out and find him by yourself at night in the first place?" Pauline starts to clean the dirt off his face with the wet towel.

"I just wanted Lori to be happy again. She's been asking twice a day if Ghedi has come by at all, and nothing any of us do seems to cheer her up anymore, not even the flowers. Everyone else has been tied up taking care of Lori and getting parts ready for her arm. So I thought if I could find Ghedi and bring him here, she'd get better faster, because she'd be happy." Thomas winces as Pauline cleans the cuts on his shoulder.

"Ah, kid, you really are the best of us," I say. "However, you were still wrong to go and look for anyone, whether it was Ghedi or not, when it's this late out, especially without us knowing. What if there was a killer tonight just looking for his next victim?" I suddenly realise I'm sounding like a parent. Hopefully I sound like an older brother to Thomas instead of a father.

"Harry, how was it you found Thomas and Ghedi?" Aspen asks.

"Actually, I was on my way to see all of you, to make sure Lori was all right. But I got lost on the way again, when suddenly I recognised Ghedi and Thomas's voices in the alley. I started to come their way until I figured out what they were actually talking about. I stayed behind in the shadows to hear if her condition had gotten worse, because that might prepare me for when I actually made it to you all. But the things Ghedi said, I thought my ears had become broken. I couldn't believe how he described Lori, after lovingly talking about her for days on end before the accident at the mill. And before I knew it, Thomas was jumping on Ghedi, and soon Ghedi was beating Thomas just like the kid told you. He was able to direct me back here, thankfully, before he dozed off in my arms."

"I see…" she says, thinking so hard that I can hear the gears in her head turn.

"Thank you, Harry." Thomas says, looking slightly dejected —I guess he thought that he was ready to handle himself in a fight.

"No thanks needed, kid. I'm just glad I was there to see things for myself."

"This will hurt our relationship with the gang for sure, if it's not addressed and mended at once. Harry, were you planning on staying the night or going back to the safehouse?" Aspen asks.

"I'm at your disposal, cousin, as long as I can see Lori first."

"That will be fine, but I'll need you to deliver a letter to your group. We need to all meet up to address the grievances from tonight. Two people on both sides have been hurt by the other, and that insults both sides as a whole. The only way we can continue to work with them is if we come together and apologise."

"But I was—"

"Not you, Thomas. I need to apologise for my own behaviour. I haven't exactly been the kindest to them when giving orders over the past few days. I yelled and bossed them around like a slave driver."

"No, Aspen, you weren't that bad," I say, trying to reassure her as she plops down at the writing desk. "You got them working faster, that's for sure, and you showed an ample amount of assertiveness, but you were no cruel slave driver. In the circumstances, it was only natural that you were so passionate. Besides, the way they were acting, I think they deserved a little scare to whip them into better shape."

"Regardless, when we meet up, I still feel the need to apologise," she says, twisting the tip of the fountain pen just as the bell in Lori's room goes off. Aspen stands up in a flash, causing the chair she was sitting in to tumble backwards. Harry stands back up with her and rushes to the door.

The second they leave, I turn my attention back to Thomas. "I think we should wait just a short while till we tell Lori what happened tonight. It would be better for her health."

"But what am I to tell her when she sees my bruises?"

"Leave that to Aspen and me. We'll say you didn't dodge a blow or two from us during sparring practice, since you've been worried." Thomas nods his head, but he still looks at the ground with his puffy lower lip. "Rest easy, Thomas," I add. "I would've done the same thing as you in the situation."

"We all would have," Thatcher says.

"Believe him," Pauline says matter-of-factly. "He was in enough fights during boarding school."

"Thank you, Pauline. If Ghedi, or anyone for that matter, had talked about either of the ladies the way he did, I would have started a scrap as well with the bloke."

"Do you really think he'll apologise? To Lori, I mean?"

"That's what the better man would do, even if the jackass doesn't mean it," Uncle George says in a huff. "But there seems to be some people with an actual brain in that group, so they should be able to get him to apologise sincerely."

I'm still angry at Ghedi, though, and just like Aspen, I have half a mind to go seek him out tonight. But we shouldn't add to the apology tab any more than we already have. "Hang on, I'm going to get a drink of water for you." Pauline is already beginning to dress him in a clean shirt as I head out the door.

The moment I enter the hallway, I see Aspen and Harry, staring down at a parchment. Hearing my footsteps on the floorboards, she looks up at me with a deadly serious face that causes me to stop walking. "It's time to send them home," Aspen announces.

"Wait, what about Lori? Don't you think she should be there to see it?"

"No, she needs to rest. Besides, we have the larger lens, the generator, the safehouse and the dimies, and this time we're not going to spread the word about it. No need to waste any more time; we're completing this homecoming tonight. Keagan, get the generator. Harry, you stay here with Lori and make sure she gets anything and everything she needs. Can I count on you?"

"You know you can," Harry says without hesitation.

"You're right. Keagan, the generator. Let's go. There's no time to waste now. This way, no one will be expecting it or know about it. This large group of dimies will officially be safe." Aspen snaps into action, rushing downstairs to the lab.

"All right, but what about the whole apology thing you were going to send them?"

"I'll just deliver it myself in person. Let's go." She puts Gear Heart and the new lens in its protective carrying case Uncle George gave to her.

I feel the same amount of adrenaline and nerves pumping into me, just like the first time we tried this back in Currlion. I place the generator in its carrying case and strap it to my back securely, like Aspen does, as we fix our masks to leave. Aspen takes a handful of tools, and we both reload on extra grenades and sleeping darts. As we make our way down the stairs to go out the back way, Pauline goes out first as usual, to check to make sure the coast is clear. After a quick "godspeed" from her, we race down the alley and up to the rooftops.

The twenty minutes to the hideout is filled with silence, since we're running and jumping incessantly from one building to the next. Luckily, most of London seems to be in for the night at eleven-twenty. Not to mention there's a new moon tonight, so the sky remains dark aside from the stars.

Not a sound is to be heard when we make it to the wine cellar, or when we head through the giant barrel secret door after giving the signature knock. A groggy and rather grumpy Samuel answers our knock after the third try; looks like he fell asleep on guard duty yet again. "What are you two doing here at this time of night?" he says with squinty eyes. "We weren't expecting you, and there's no more room for any more dimies."

"We know," I say. "We're sending them home. Wake up everyone."

"But we aren't ready for that. Shouldn't we postpone it because of your sister's injury?"

"It's been postponed until now, and we *are* ready. We have everything we need. Now go, there isn't a second to lose!" Aspen orders with the same power in her voice as the night Lori was injured.

Samuel jumps a bit before rushing off and beginning to yell into the rooms, waking the occupants up. Our partners slowly come to us in the middle of the largest room, where we are setting up Gear Heart and the generator. Everyone except Ghedi is here. "What's the idea of coming here in the bloody dead of night to wake us all up?" Andrea asks in a sour tone, to which I answer in one of my own.

"You told us in your latest letter that you couldn't house any more dimies, that funds and food stock were low. What did you expect us to do? Supply you with more food and money?"

"Well, I mean..."

"Wrong. This group's homecoming has been postponed long enough, and tonight they go home. Just make sure they're ready and are in an orderly line, women and children first." The loss of drowsiness in their dumbfounded expressions says it all; they've been expecting us to house them for who knows how long. Makes me wonder how much money they've wasted on themselves, and how much food actually went to the rescued dimies' bellies instead of their own. "What are you waiting for? A kiss on the cheek?" I say snidely.

The gang does as they're instructed and begins lining up the dimies, with a child in between each two adults. There have been a few times I've returned home to Currlion in the past by ship to see immigrants coming and going off boats much smaller than mine. Here now, seeing the dimies' worn and tattered clothing, carrying all they own on their backs, they remind me of those immigrants I used to pass. Though sometimes I've felt that the only difference between us is our finances, going to a brand-new place to live that doesn't quite feel like home is something we have in common.

Starting up the generator, the bright zap and glaring light booms out and fills the entire wall with the entrance to the portal. Everyone gazes at the night scene of a tropical place with a dark purple sky dotted with yellow stars. There's a breeze in the strange curled trees with their long blue leaves, along with warm lights off in the distance that flicker like fire, not uncontrolled like wildfire but appearing to be contained. The dimies who made it a few months ago must have begun to build a new village. I wish to go inside and find them. Eli is in there; I wonder if he misses playing card games or if he prefers a simpler life. Gertrude's words still ring in my ears, how this isn't what they want. We're sending them to a place they're not used to anymore. But this is a place where they're free. That doesn't come without hardships and hard work.

"Keagan?" I hear Aspen's voice at my side as I feel her hand slip into mine. Turning, I see her stepping forwards, watching the dimies in the room slowly slip through the folds of the rift back to their dimension. "Looks like they made it after all." Her back is to me, but I can see something shimmering from the light as it falls in front of her. *She's crying?* This whole spontaneous whim was to distract herself by getting work done, wasn't it? I can't blame her for doing it. Besides, this is the most productive thing she could've done to distract her from Lori's condition.

I don't say a word; instead, I come to her level and slowly turn her my way by wrapping her up in a hug. The job we've been working so hard at is finally being completed the right way this time, with no sabotage, surprise guests or imprisonments. I wish I could say this is how it should've been, but it's still incomplete without the people who are lost and hurt. We should be celebrating. Though much like Aspen, I can't bring myself to feel much joy, if any, at this moment. One by one, the long line of dimies walk their way back home to freedom. I wonder what awaits them. *Will they make a new tribe or will they join their old ones? At least they now have a choice to do so.*

TRUE LOYALTY

LORI

It's been almost two weeks now since the incident at the mill. I can walk around just fine, and the doctor will come over soon to change out the bandages and see if I'm healing well. We've been so careful about everything that it should be fine. I should be grateful to be alive, but I'm not. Ghedi still hasn't come to see me, and if he won't have me now, who in their right mind would? I don't recall ever seeing a woman who's been damaged from the plague and has prosthetics get married. I've certainly seen plenty of bed warmers with missing limbs, though. I can't help but fear that a life like that is what awaits me. I'm still so tired that all I want to do is sit by the windows in our bedroom. *Why did it all go wrong?*

"Lori? How are you feeling today?" I hear Thomas say. Turning, I see him standing in the doorway with a bouquet of flowers, just like every morning. Thatcher is by his side as well, with a stack of playing cards in his hand. "Feel like a game of poker, Lori?" he inquires, leaning on his cane a little.

"I'd love to after lunch, Thatcher."

"All right." He smiles as he walks off, leaving Thomas and

me alone. I take a long look at him and realise how much he's grown since the first time we met in Currlion, both taller and stronger.

"Thomas, please come here," I say, holding out my one hand. Trotting over, he sits down on the footrest beside me, laying the flowers down on the dresser on the way. "Thomas, you living with us was never supposed to be a permanent situation. We've even been looking for a new family here that Uncle George could introduce you to. We want to make sure you will be comfortable. You'll be fourteen soon, and though you're not yet an adult, you're probably as smart as Aspen was when she was your age." That compliment makes him smile a little through his growing frown.

"Thomas, the choice is yours. We can help you find a real family here, a good one that can provide for you and give you a proper education. Or you can continue to live with us, but you know we can't offer you many good things. Not a proper education, and for a long time not a proper permanent home either. If things don't work out with the queen, we could very well be incarcerated or killed, and you could end up in an orphanage. We want to make sure you now know what kind of world you're getting into."

"I'll follow you anywhere, Lori, and will always help you," Thomas replies, looking at me with a similar expression that Keagan had for Aspen that night we came down the stairs in our dresses to meet Timothy, pained but full of longing.

"Hmm, can you pass me that album in the drawer behind you?" Once he gives it to me, I flip through Aspen and my memories of our family. Most are just plain family portraits; however, a friend of our father's came over once with a special quick amateur camera he wanted to try out, so we were able to take more candid shots. There are some of Mum tickling Aspen and me on our bed when we were five and four. There are others of us in the garden, picking flowers, and then one of us putting them in Mum and Papa's hair. By the looks of them, the experiment in a "casual camera" was successful.

"This is what I believe a family should look like," I say, pointing to my family sitting together for a photograph on the steps of our house. "You have your parents and the children, and you love and live with each other through the good and the bad. I want you to have the chance to have a relationship with a mother and father."

"But are we not a family as well?" he asks in confusion. "If I had the choice, I'd choose to live with you three over total strangers any day."

"Yes, but with parents you could have a future. With us, you could become a wanted criminal."

"But you're not bad people."

"Yes, well, society thinks we are. And if you think it's easy to rebuild a reputation after it's shattered so greatly, you are sadly mistaken."

"I don't care about reputation. I was a gear master's grandson; I already don't have any money or prospects aside from the amount you've been putting aside for me. I can build my own reputation any way I wish, since I don't have one to begin with."

I have to admit that's a fair point, but it's still a hard thing to do with us around. "I just don't want to drag you through the mud with us is all."

"It's starting to sound as if you want me to leave. Is that what you want?" He sounds hurt.

"Thomas, I would never wish that. I just want you to be happy and have a future of opportunities."

"I'm happy here with you, and it's with you that I see my future."

I have the strangest feeling he's talking directly to me, and not referring to our whole group anymore. Looking back at the album, I slip out a photograph of my mother and father carrying me as we lay in the grass. All of us are as happy as can be. "See this? This is what I wish for. I'm sorry for being pushy. But I just want you to experience this kind of happiness. This is how I picture myself with Ghedi."

"What if he doesn't, though? What if he doesn't come?" Thomas huffs out, sounding annoyed.

"He will, and when he does, then know that I may not be around much longer."

"Lori—"

"No, Thomas, don't try and talk me out of it. When he comes, then I'll know he truly loves me." But even as I hear the words come out of my mouth, I don't believe them, and I know Thomas doesn't.

"Lori, um, Samuel came by last night to deliver a message. Aspen wanted me to wait so she could be here with you, but I think I should tell you now." I can hear the underlying gravity in his voice, and my heart slowly begins to sink. "Ghedi and Samuel have decided to split from the group and play their hand in Europe. Issac decided to leave with the rest of the dimies when the portal opened two nights ago, but Isola remained with us. They thank us for the indescribable experience and wish us all the luck in the world." He pulls out a sheet of paper and starts reciting from it. "If we are ever to cross paths in the future, we would be happy to help you once again. We wish we could have stayed long enough to see that Lori is okay, but we feel it best to leave. Your teammates, Samuel and Ghedi.' The rest of our teammates remain here, ready for our next orders. However, Aspen has only told them to lay low, at least until we speak with the queen."

"There's nothing directly from Ghedi to me, then? No words of goodbye or when we'll meet again?"

"I'm afraid not, Lori. But cousin Harry has decided that he wishes to stay with us directly, and we all agreed that would be fine, so he's living here with us now. Isn't that nice—to have more of your family close?" I know he's trying to make the matter lighter than it is, but it doesn't help. I feel like I could crumble right to the floor. Seeing this, Thomas's whole demeanour changes. "I really don't know what you saw in him. He treated you terribly, and controlled where you went and how long you were there. He doesn't deserve someone as radiant as you."

Thomas's heated words ring in my ears. The thoughts of Ghedi's actions as we were courting play out in my head, and I realise that they were slightly peculiar. "He was just a particular person. You didn't know him like I did."

"Believe me, I know exactly who he is and what he would have done to you if you ever crossed him." He raises his voice slightly, with a hand covering his shoulder as he stands up. What's gotten into him?

"You barely said two words to him, Thomas. You're speaking about him as if he were some kind of thug," I say, sitting up from my chair, my brow furrowed now. I can't believe we're even quarrelling about this right now.

He shoves his hands in his hair as he growls. "Maybe that's because he didn't have to say much to show his true self to me. Let's just say that I think I got a good taste of who he really is. You can take my word for that."

At that moment, the door opens to Pauline and Aspen laughing as they come in. Thomas quickly stuffs the letter into his shirt before Aspen can see, but I only wish I could put away the feelings painted on my face as well. Aspen was always so much better at hiding her emotions. I wish I shared the same talent. "Lori, you look frightful," Pauline says as she comes rushing to my side. "Are you feeling worse? What do you need?" Thomas looks at the floor and Aspen seems to notice. Looking down at myself, I see the paleness of my skin beside my white night dress and shawl. Along with the light from the bright overcast day, I can tell I must look like a ghost to everyone. Funny; that's just how I feel right now. "Thomas, did you say something upsetting to Lori, perchance?"

"...I might have."

"Thomas—"

"It's all right, Aspen, I was going to have to hear it eventually," I say with a sigh. "Besides, now I know the truth: Ghedi is gone. You should be happy. You were right; you always are."

"No, I'm not."

"Yes, you are. You knew he would leave, that he never really loved me."

"But I was still wrong about one incredibly important thing. The mill. I thought that this time we were prepared, that we finally had it all planned out and had the upper hand. But again we were blindsided. I know we're used to going into these things together, though I almost wish you had run off with Ghedi, and then I could have run after you and the mill would never have happened. Sure, we would fight, but at least you wouldn't have gone through all this." I hear the trembling in her voice as a thump sounds from something hitting the floor. I look over to see her on the ground, covering her face with her hands. "No matter what I would've done, you would've ended up hating me and getting hurt."

At that, I give Thomas the photo album, stand up from my

chair, and walk over to Aspen. Crouching down, I get on her level and wrap her in a one-armed hug. The words that should have been said long ago finally come. "I don't hate you, Aspen, I love you. I blame myself for everything, and…" My voice cracks as tears flood my eyes and my throat begins to close up. "I forgive you, Aspen, but can you forgive me? I was about to leave you for my own selfish stupid reasons. I—I was blind to what I have now."

"If it wasn't for me, we would have a normal life instead of being wanted by the Crown," Aspen cries into my good shoulder.

"If it wasn't for you, I'd be dead. If not by this, then by Aunt Mae. I didn't mean what I said before, I didn't mean it." We stop speaking; all we can do now is wail and cry. Everything that's been tearing us apart starts to be washed away by our tears. I feel a pair of hands on my back that aren't Aspen's, and I remember that Thomas and Pauline are in the room as well. They don't say a word; however, they do offer a handkerchief that I use liberally. We cry for what seems like forever. We don't move away from each other, though, almost as if we're afraid to let go.

I want to take back all the fighting words we said to one another, all those bad thoughts about how I thought Keagan and Aspen were just jealous and were trying to stop me from being happy. *Take it away, take it all away.* As the tears begin to slow down, the exhaustion begins to set in, and I feel like I did the first day I woke up after surgery. Aspen and I are led to our beds and tucked in, only to fall fast asleep.

Waking up, I see Aspen is already awake and looking over our photo album next to me. Noticing my stirring, our eyes meet. "Hi there, Lori bird." She smiles softly.

"Aspen, why do you call me that?" I realised I've never asked that.

Without answering, Aspen flips through a few pages of the album, and slips out a photo from its slot. Handing it to me, she says, "I guess you don't remember, but we once had a laurel tree in our garden back at home. It used to grow these beautiful strands of cream flowers. Mother loved the word 'laurel' so much, she decided to name you Lori. We were three and four when she told you about it, and for the rest of that year whenever you saw a bird fly into the tree or hop around it, you would point at it and call out 'Lori bird, Lori bird!' We all thought it was so cute that we started calling you that. See here, how you look like you're dancing under the tree?" She points to a different photo in the album where my hair is bouncing in the air as I look like I'm dancing around the base of the tree in my little dress.

"Yeah."

"You used to do that when there were a bunch of birds in it singing. You would dance around the tree, singing 'Lori bird'. I think you thought that the more birds there were in the tree, the more special you and your name were."

"That's a fair assumption," I say, looking at the photo of when I wasn't even a metre tall yet. I can't help but feel a twinge of pain in my stub where my elbow used to be at the sight of me with two arms. All that's left of my arm is my bicep and shoulder. "Could I have the opium pipe? I think I could use it now."

"You've already had your smoke this morning. We don't want you to get addicted, remember?"

"Right." *I still want more, though.* Keagan sat and explained to me before about the addictive properties of the medicine I've been taking. When I can feel the need of wanting more, that's when we need to be the most careful, since withdrawals are likely to occur once the medicine is gone. He confessed that he was once addicted to opium and how it was a struggle to get off it. *Keagan really has been through a lot. I wonder how he's been mentally lately? I know that I for one am still worse for wear.* "I haven't been hearing any commotions as of late, except for a few loud bursts at random times. Is Keagan doing better with his outbursts?"

"Those were probably Uncle George and Thomas, or me in the lab. We've had a few hiccups and—ahem—explosions concerning the airship. Our mad scientist sides are beginning to show a lot more these days. Keagan, however, has been doing better, as far as I know. He's currently gone for the day; he said he has some business with the doctor to deal with. But he did have another bad dream last night, and the night you got hurt...but nothing's happened during the day, so I think that's an improvement. He and Uncle George have been talking more and more to each other about what troubles them, and it seems to be helping them both. I join in sometimes as well. Helps me with how I see Father and what I went through with Aunt Mae."

"That's wonderful. Glad George hasn't set either of your hair on fire through all of this, you know. I was so worried he'd end up killing us when we first came here. You never seemed too worried, though," I say, feeling in better spirits.

"You're right," she says, smiling. " I guess when I met him, I started to see more of my eccentric side in him. I felt a kinship towards him for that reason. I could tell he wasn't completely crazy and that he wouldn't hurt us on purpose.

Though I knew to be careful around him as well, because if he's anything like me, he can be a bit reckless."

"A bit?"

"Oh, tish tosh," she says, making me smile as we go back to looking at the old photos. Yet I still have a bit of uneasiness about me. "Hey, this is weird. Look at this picture."

I lean over and look at a large photograph of our entire extended family. "What's weird about it?"

"It appears thicker than the other photos," Aspen says, starting to play with its edges. I help with another edge, and when mine pops out first, I see there are papers underneath. Aspen slowly slips them out and lights a lantern by our bedside. "Lori, we found it."

"Found what?"

"The will Father left us!" She shuffles her sheets off and stands up on her bed.

"What? Let me see." She comes back down to my level, laying out the three papers before me. After taking time to read them carefully, I realise Aspen is right. They were finalised two weeks before his passing, and even have his special seal on each page.

Aspen reads over each page faster than I can. "If I'm reading this correctly, and I believe I am, we're to inherit almost everything. Father's siblings will receive a few items that belonged to Grandmother and Grandfather, such as Grandmother's pearls, and Grandfather's deed to an old mine."

"The abandoned one?"

"The one and the same." Aspen smiles. "We should get Uncle George and Keagan to look these papers over; they have more experience with wills. We can't do anything about the claims to our inheritance until we're pardoned by Her Majesty."

"Do you really think this will work, Aspen? This whole idea of proving ourselves to Her Majesty?"

"Honestly, no. But doubt has never stopped me from trying the impossible, and it's obviously worked for us in the past...somewhat."

I don't respond, and instead what ensues is an awkward feeling of silence between the two of us. "Um, Aspen, are things settled now, between you and me?"

"You forgave me, and I forgive you, I don't see why they wouldn't be." She takes my hand and gives it a squeeze. A genuine smile grows on my face, not the fake one I've been putting on every day so everyone wouldn't worry about me. It feels good.

PLACE YOUR BETS

KEAGAN

Stretch, warm up, practice jabs and prepare the gauze for after the bell. Thanks to Anthony, I finally managed to find a place where we can make the money for Lori's arm in one night. It may be a poor choice, but after training for so long, I'd say I have a fair shot. Anthony said the Lamb and Flag Pub holds bare-knuckle boxing matches, winner takes all. James, I, and a few of our old schoolmates would go to places like this to bet on the men, but they would never let us in on the fighting since we were too young. Once we made it to university, however, that's when things became a real whirlwind.

I didn't do much to hide my appearance today besides making myself look dirtier. If I had put on a false nose, wig or eyebrows, they could easily get knocked off, and then I'd be seen as even more suspicious. Besides, places like this are where all walks of life rub elbows, from wanted criminals to rich men. Apparently there's a rule that the only person who can call the coppers is the owner, so no one can be turned in even if they're recognised. Even dimies are allowed to fight here for money, though it's quite rare to see dimies fighting humans, or at least that's what Anthony told me. He was wary of me coming here, since it was easy for him to understand why I would come to a place crawling with desperate men. Good thing he joined me today; I'm actually slightly relieved for someone to have my back.

Eventually it's my match against a man named Victor. Anthony already has his bets on me and gives me a pat on my back before shoving me towards the ring. The crowd starts shouting the moment I enter the walled-off ring. I hear people taunting and insulting, although whether they're for me or my opponent, no one can tell. Victor enters the ring the same time as I do, and by the looks of his brawny physique, I have my work cut out for me. Both of us are shirtless, and nothing covers our hands. This really does feel foreign to me, since I'm so used to being covered up in my night-running gear during real fights.

Meeting in the centre, we briefly shake hands then back up. There is a smile painted on his face and I can tell by the look in his brown eyes that he thinks I'll be easy to beat. I'm slightly shorter than he is, and he's certainly larger than me in regards to muscle mass; but if I can play with him for a while, I bet I can eventually surprise him.

He makes the first advance, and I quickly dodge and slip behind him. Spinning around, he attacks me again, and this time I block before jabbing his shoulder. Staggering away, he readies himself and looks me up and down now. His smile has begun to fade, and with each failed advance he only becomes angrier. However, after knocking him hard enough with a left hook to his ear that he's forced to take a knee for a moment, he comes shooting at me with a fierce speed I wasn't prepared for.

He lands a shaky hit in my ribs, and as I'm doubling over he attempts to uppercut my chin, but only grazes me. Now I'm the one on the ground, pretending to be hurt, as he stumbles around the ring a bit. He's feeling the effects of my hit to his ear. The crowd half-cheers for Victor and half-boos for my sake, though the loudest cheer is coming from Anthony, who has a determined look on his face. Picking myself up and running to Victor's side, I clock his left ear before he can fully block me. I immediately give him a left hook right to that vulnerable spot on a person's temple. He falls straight to the dirt and the crowd both cheers and hisses at me. "Sorry, chap," is all I say to him before his unconscious body is hauled off and the cheering crowd grows louder as they go to get their winnings.

The next round of men enter the ring as I head out to cool off for a spell. Anthony goes to collect his bets and make new ones as women begin to tail me, along with angry and excited men who lost their wager. But soon, those who won start to fend off the sore losers; one is kind enough to lead me to the counter and buy me a pint. Taking a swig from the frothy glass, I look over the crowd and back into the dirt-floored ring to get a good visual of my opponents. One has a mechanical arm, a metal one at that, which extends his fist out, giving him an unfair advantage with his range. Anthony takes a glance at me, and I see that his former determined look of assurance almost completely dissolved. I raise my glass to him and give him a knowing expression, to which he immediately nods his head and smiles nervously.

"Are prosthetics really allowed?" I ask the black-bearded man with squinty eyes who bought me my pint.

"I'm afraid so, son. That there is the current champ for the last two months. He makes a killing, and so do I, by always betting on him. Name's Brutus."

"Am I allowed to bring anything into the ring with me, since he has that enhancement?"

"No. These are bare-knuckle fights, and his knuckles are indeed bare, whether they're flesh or metal in nature."

We watch as Brutus knocks out his opponent. I notice that he steps before he punches, and he favours his side with the metal arm, but in doing so he leaves open his ribs and chin on the other side. "Do yourself a favour, mate. Bet on me this time." I take another swig of my beer before clapping a hand on his shoulder. The man just laughs as I walk back towards the ring.

The bell rings and we begin. He is faster than I care to admit and has great balance, since he's had to get used to his metal arm's weight being shot out by a spring and back, hidden by a hollow cylindrical brass container. As we fight, I lay a critical blow to his chin, causing him to grab the edge of the wall to steady himself as I advance again. I can't help but think about how much Aspen would love to look over his arm. Perhaps she and Uncle George, or a prosthetics specialist, can create an attachment like that for Lori.

I get wrapped up too much in my thoughts and miss a block, and his normal arm swings out in a right hook and lands a jab in my side, causing me to hunch over before he manages to punch me in the right ear. My senses discombobulate for a moment, and I stumble away as best I can from my opponent's next blow. By the sound his metal fist makes as it swings through the air, it could've easily been a knockout punch.

When my eyes finally settle on Brutus again, he's not the opponent from before. My blood is now boiling. I've never wanted to fight someone more in my life. Ears still ringing, I now see that backstabbing old dog, Charles, in front of me now, dancing around the ring and laughing at me. I practically leap off the ground, yelling; my arm is already raised and lands straight on his face. His taunting attitude has quickly disappeared, and he now realises I'm serious. *Go ahead and be scared, Charles. You should have realised the mistake in crossing me and everyone else, far before you made the choice to.*

He tries to back away from my blows, but I don't let him get away that easily. Backing him up into a corner, I manage to get around his blocks and land critical hits to his torso and jaw. Backing up to catch my breath, he wipes his mouth and tries to come at me once more. He lands one more hit to my temple that sends me back to the ground. I can feel the dirt on the floor caking my back. "Keagan, get up. Get up right now!" I hear Anthony's voice amidst the thunderous crowd. But no worries; *we aren't finished yet.*

Again and again, I knock him down just as he does to me, until he hits me too hard and my vision turns red with rage. The next thing I know, my fist makes contact with his jaw and he is falling to the floor. The second I see his body hit the dust, my hands go towards his neck. However, before I can choke the traitor, Charles's face disappears from the man on the ground and what's left is Brutus. *Charles was never here, then.*

The ringing in my ears dissipates, and I hear an overwhelming roar of the crowd surrounding me. Taking a look about the makeshift pigpen-like ring, I expect to see more angry faces since I just downed the two-month reigning champ. But instead there is full-out excitement amongst the men, women and dimies alike. I can see how a champ could get used to this kind of admiration and the winnings that come with it, though I doubt he usually has to fight this hard every time against a normal opponent. Taking a look down at myself, I notice the blood dripping from cuts on my stomach as well as the stinging pain from the blows I received.

Anthony leads me out of the ring and sits me back down at the bar stool, where the shell-shocked bearded man sits with his empty pint. Instead of fighting further, I decide to see what our winnings are and call it a day.

"Your lady is going to kill you when she sees your condition, you know." Dr Price glances up at me from his work on my stomach. I remember the bad feeling I had about my stomach when I tried to patch it up myself after the match. Anthony tried to pour some alcohol over it, since he's seen Andrea do that, but it became a very unpleasant matter. Even with the gauze covering it, it wouldn't stop bleeding. The cut isn't deep or long, but it still needed stitches. *Getting cleaned off when I get back home will be the best feeling,* I remind myself as I think about all the dirt still covering my skin.

Sadly, the doctor has four patients waiting for him that I just jumped in front of when he found out I was here. He told me that if he had more time, he would offer me a bath as well. And after having to put my clothes back on right after the fight whilst drenched in sweat, blood and dirt, I would have taken anything he offered. Even the light cleaning of my cuts he did was satisfactory for me. If only there wasn't such a small window of time to find that crummy merchant, hands down the most impossible man I've ever had the displeasure to do business with. I don't regret any of the threats I threw at him; those were probably the only reason he was willing to sell me the powder in the first place.

"Aspen has seen worse," I respond. "When she sees that we have enough funds for Lori's new arm, I think she'll let me live."

"Wishful thinking indeed. But bravo for winning double the amount you were originally fighting for," he chuckles.

"That was just pure accident, if you ask me. I didn't know that if you beat their champ, you win a special amount on top of your other winnings. And with Anthony betting highly on me as well, it helped out tremendously." I try to laugh, but it hurts too much to do so.

The doctor reports that by some miracle, I didn't break any ribs during the fight, but did sustain plenty of bruises and busted skin. I wince again as he sews another stitch in my skin, and ask him, "By the way, how did you create that blood-testing formula?"

"Can't tell you, or even my assistant for that matter. I haven't had a chance to patent it yet. Also, there are a few more tests I need to do to make sure that it's a hundred percent accurate for medical use."

"Wait, are you saying there was a chance you could've given Lori the wrong blood type?"

"Sadly true. But with her need for blood being so great, we had to go with it."

"You're still as shady as ever, but you get the job done, I'll give you that." I clench my teeth.

"Thank you, my boy." He stands up, all finished with my stitches.

"Don't thank me. It wasn't much of a compliment." I tip my hat to him as I get off the examining table.

"So were you able to come up with the money for her prosthetic? I mentioned Lori's case to my specialist friend. He's been working on prosthetics ever since the beginning of the plague, one of the best in his line of practice. He can even design something to look more delicate and feminine for Lori if you would prefer."

"Could he make it look real?"

The doctor doesn't answer right away; his normal cocky attitude has turned sombre. "If he could, do you think there would be so many people on the streets with garish-looking prosthetics?"

"No, I guess not." I feel my heart sink a bit hearing this.

"The best thing would be a flesh-coloured sleeve. He's unable to make something look and feel like real skin as of yet, sadly."

"I understand."

"So, tell me, how did you convince the merchant to sell you the medicine?" Dr Price looks at me inquisitively

I just stare at him and smile for a second before saying, "Can't tell you. Trade secret among renegades." His arms slump at my play of cruel irony, but he doesn't stay unamused for too long, as his moustache lifts slightly once more whilst he turns away. I can hear him chuckle slightly as well when he walks out the room with his sutures and topical medicines. He didn't even seem the slightest bit fazed when I arrived at his door earlier, Anthony holding me up by the shoulder as one hand covered my bleeding side and the other his medicine. I almost wish that Aspen will be as nonchalant as Dr Price, but then that would hurt my pride even more than the punches did. Egad, the day is only halfway over and I'm already drained. What else awaits me?

By the time I come home and change out of my clothes, I feel a sharp pain in my stomach. Looking down, I unwrap my bandage only halfway and see blood beginning to appear. *Great, I broke the stitches.* Not bothering with a shirt, I head downstairs to the laboratory, since it was the last place I saw our medical box. Uncle George or Aspen must have burned or cut their hand again when working with metal, I think as I trump down the stairs. The house is strangely quiet and it makes me wonder if Aspen has shut herself up with Lori again, possibly along with everyone else in the house for that matter. I thought we had agreed that Lori's condition was stabilised and that the doctor will be by later to see her. Aspen was just starting to get back to work, and I know she's trying to contain herself whilst keeping a constant watch over Lori this past week. We both know she was actually chomping at the bit to get back to inventing as usual.

Well, no need to worry at the moment, since the lab is empty and I can redo my own stitches myself without any fuss. At least now I don't have to try and hide the pain. Unwrapping my bandages completely allows a trickle of blood to seep out of the cut. Preparing the needle under a flame and threading it, I steel myself for the first stitch. The burning makes me groan and grit my teeth, but just as I pull the needle and thread, the door to the lab opens, and staring back at me is Aspen.

"What happened to you?" she cries out, rushing over to me. "My word, you're covered in dirt and blood."

"Don't worry, it's not mine. Or, well, most of it isn't, at least," I claim, though she probably knows I'm lying.

Grabbing the pitcher of water, bowl and rag that are kept by the window, Aspen rushes back over to me. Standing in between my relaxed legs, she starts to clean me off as I finish the last broken stitch. I relish the feeling of the dirt coming off my skin, and yet I wince each time she accidentally rubs over one of my sore areas. I know that even she must still be sore from the wounds she received fending off the dimie watchmen. Her stitches will be coming out soon enough, though. She is trying to focus on the task of being a nurse, but I can tell from the small exhale through her lips that she's examining more than just my wounds. By the slowing of her hands and the parting of her lips, I happily blame myself for making it hard on Aspen to concentrate on her task.

"Were you jumped by the dimie watchmen, men, or the hounds?" Aspen asks as I light my pipe.

I finally realise how exhausted I am when I try to explain the events of the day to her. My memory becomes foggy as I recall how the fight went, pipe now resting in my hand on the table. "Aspen, you would've loved what I saw. My opponent had a metal arm, and his fist would shoot out at least two to three feet in front of him before it recoiled." I decide to leave Anthony out of the recalling, so she doesn't become angry with him by association.

"Really? What did the chamber for the recoil look like? Was it bulky? That man must've been strong if he could handle something like that."

"Yes, he was," I say, gingerly putting my fingers up to my temple the doctor taped earlier. "But it really didn't look all that bulky." The more I explain my opponent's metal arm, the more stars shine in my Aspen's eyes. She looks so intrigued and beautiful, I barely notice that I'm beginning to ramble, until I'm just sitting there staring at her with a smile on my face. I can see her cheeks blush.

"Can we all stop getting hurt so much? Our meeting with

the queen will be coming sooner than I'd like. I was hoping we'd be in better shape in case we need to escape the palace."

"Do we still have time for Lori to get her new arm?" I ask.

"Absolutely. And if a wrench gets thrown into the works, then we'll become adaptable for her." I lay my head on her chest, feeling the weight of the day come crashing down on me. "Thanks to you, of course, winning that money gives Lori a chance at having an arm again." She pauses to give me a kiss on the back of my neck and brushes her soft lips down my neck to my shoulder, making my eyes shoot wide open. *I could get used to thank-you's like this.* "Now we can stop looking for so many parts to make one ourselves. I still like the idea we had for her, hollowing out parts of the arm so she can store makeup and weapons in different hidden compartments." She wraps her arms around me to clean my back.

"I bet if you show the specialist your ideas, he can work something like that out. Fighting that metal-armed man tonight made me realise it's possible. And if he can't, then I know that between you and George, it can certainly be done."

She hits a sensitive spot, making me shudder for a second. "I hate seeing you like this." I raise my head and meet her sad eyes as her arms rest on my shoulders.

Taking one of her hands, I place it over my heart and hold it there as it beats. Feeling the quickening of my beating heart makes Aspen's blushing smile even redder than it already was. "Gee, I thought you'd enjoy seeing me undressed like this. But if you don't, I guess I'll just put my shirt back on."

"Keagan, you know what I mean. I'm serious. I hate seeing you get hurt and being so worried that you could become crip-pled or—"

Before she can finish her train of thought, I stand back up and pull her into a kiss. When I pull away, it's only to lead her straight to my chest, where her head rests just below my chin. "You care so much about so many people, and stress about things that may never happen. I'm just glad I'm one of them. I'm not going anywhere; I thought I've made that clear by now. You can believe me when I say that only the grim reaper himself could take me away from you and everyone else at this point." I glide my fingers through her brown locks. I enjoy the feeling of being so close to her, as well as the peace that comes with it.

"I love holding you like this," I say deeply in her ear.

"So you promise not to do those fights anymore?"

"Okay, Miss Aspen, I'll stop fighting."

"You were going to stop anyway, weren't you?"

"Perhaps…"

Then the tiniest whisper makes it to my ear: "I love you too."

Who knew this would become one of the best days of my life?

MENDING SCARS

ASPEN

We have to take Lori to a specialist, since he needs to perform the surgery with all of his equipment. Even Dr Price is present in the surgery room. It makes me feel better, to be honest, knowing we have someone we can trust in there with her when we cannot. Our entire household, even Isola, Andrea and Anthony, are here with us in the waiting room. Our teammates even bring Lori a few goodies from the local bakery. I hope that will cheer her up when this is all over. We were told to come in the back way, and the specialist made sure to close up the front of his building early today for us.

Much to our surprise, Timothy showed up early to see the doctor, Uncle George informs me as we wait. Apparently, as I was finishing the last five rather difficult inventions that had taken Timothy months to figure out, he came up with special parts to add onto Lori's arm. He hasn't said much except "I only wish I could provide more" and "Thank you, Miss Wolfe, you have helped me tremendously." I know he had to swallow a lot of pride to utter those words. It's good to see that his whole demeanour has become much less arrogant than the last time we saw him. Thomas has been holding onto something wrapped up in brown paper since we left the house; he hasn't let anyone see what it is either.

After a few hours of painstaking waiting, Dr Price and prosthetics specialist Dr Avery come out of the surgery room. "Lori performed wonderfully during the whole thing. A few tears were shed, but even the strongest of men cry during the process."

"Remind me again why she couldn't have any anaesthetic?" I rub my temples. Lori must have hated this entire process. Those baked goods will come in handy for sure.

"We needed to make sure throughout the surgery that the arm would continue to work at each stage, as her nerves and muscles were connected one by one to the machine. When there are occasional malfunctions or accidents during surgery that must be addressed immediately, the patient must be awake and able to move their appendages to know that all is right and if something needs to be corrected."

"Sounds like a pretty sensitive procedure." Uncle George puffs his pipe with a worried but inquisitive look.

"Indeed, Mr Adlene, it is; however, know that everything is fine. We've already administered some painkillers and she should be fine to leave after we've conducted a few mobility tests."

"Oh thank the Lord," Pauline says, clutching her chest. All of us seem to take a deep breath of relief now that we know she's okay, but my anxiety to go and see her is heightened. I have only a vague idea of the measurements and the material of her arm. I almost wonder if Thomas knows more than I. He's been asking so many questions during the past few days to me and Uncle George about Dr Avery's design for Lori's arm. But whenever we asked why he cared so much, he would just play it off or change the subject.

Going in to see Lori, we see her sitting up in her bed in a surgical white gown. I get a flashback to when I was in the exact same position not three months ago. That bottomless pit of fear and worry I had for her two weeks ago comes back to me again. We have to be positive for her, and by the pursed lips and furrowed brow on her face, we may need to be extra careful on how we go about it.

Her arm is covered up by a white sheet, and once we're all in, Dr Avery walks over and slips it off to reveal Lori's brand new arm. It appears as slender and feminine as Dr Price said Dr Avery could make it. The silver steel is attached to the majority of her bicep and looks nice and clean next to her porcelain skin. Where her skin is attached to her new arm, however, is currently red, and I can bet it will be bruised and sore for a while. The rest of the arm looks plain and simple, with gyroscopic balls as replacements for her elbow and wrist sockets. With something like that, she should theoretically be able to do a 360-degree rotation of her arm and hand, much like a ship's propeller. Her fingers look whole and slender, and you can see the gears in between her fingers at her knuckles.

Giving us a quick demonstration for now, Lori makes a fist, and then one by one unfurls her metal fingers. "That was excellent, Lori," Dr Avery says in a kind manner. "I think I'll let you all talk for a short time as I prepare the mobility room. We want to make sure everything works as it should, Miss Wolfe. After that and a quick one-on-one discussion with me, you should be good to go." He and Dr Price leave the room, closing the door behind them.

"This looks incredible, Lori," I start.

"Indeed, I've never seen such a graceful prosthetic arm as this," Isola says kindly.

"Agreed," Uncle George says approvingly. "I was afraid it would be heavy and bulky, like most of the brass ones we see people on the streets wearing. But this must be a very special design."

"You think so, do you?" Lori says with a sarcastic grimace. "Because I'm not so sure." She rips off her sheets and stands up out of the bed. She takes my right arm and raises her metal one, putting the cold steel next to my skin. "I don't know about you, but this seems like a pretty big difference. One is living, warm and soft. The other is cold, hard and unfeeling. I didn't ask for this!"

"You think anyone ever would?" Pauline says with her hands on her hips.

"Of course not, but why did it happen to me? I've gone through hell without any major scars. And now I have only one real arm." Lori's voice raises in her fury.

"Lori, I know you're still processing everything, and it's scary, but you're not alone in this—"

"How am I not alone when everyone here still has all of their appendages? Look at me, Aspen! Who would take me as a wife now, with such a grotesque thing as this attached to me?" Lori yells in my face as tears stream down hers. "*What self-respecting man would marry a woman with a cold mechanical arm?*" Lori screams at the entire lot of us now. The look on her face reminds me of when she and I found out the secret Keagan tried to keep hidden in the fireplace.

"'What man', she says," I spit out, pulling off my thick navy shirt and beginning to loosen the ties on my corset before practically tearing it off of my waist.

"Aspen?" Keagan's voice is barely a whisper, but I can hear

the confused concern in it. I know what they're thinking. *What is she doing? Is she so worked up she's having trouble breathing?* But I don't care about hiding them anymore. And I don't care if I have to show everyone in this room to prove a point.

"You really think you're alone in this situation?" I say, turning around and lowering my chemise whilst clutching my garments to cover my bare chest. The room stands silent, aside from Lori's shuddering breath. "Or have you forgotten that I'm broken and yet loved as well?" I'm so fired up at the moment that I don't even feel embarrassed to show my marred back to the men and women in the room. I let them have a good look of what I've only seen in a mirror, a maze of white and red scars carved into my pale back. As the coolness of the room reaches my skin, I recall the pain I once felt for my newest and largest scars, connecting from one shoulder blade to the other and still a bright red.

Slipping my shirt back on, I turn around and walk to Lori. She doesn't make a move. "You will meet the same type of man who would love a woman as beaten and scarred as I. And this one right here is a prime example of that type of man." I point to Keagan's reddened wide-eyed face. I see now that Thomas, Uncle George, Isola and Anthony all have their backs turned to me. Andrea and Pauline just look on with a sombre expression. "The same kind of man who would want me will want you, Sissy. He will love every part of you. Just wait. He may even be an inventor and think your new arm is magnificent." I lace one finger around Lori's metal one, and it curls around mine.

"How did we even make it this far, Aspen? We aren't who we once were at all," Lori mutters as tears still fall.

"Quite true, but I think that we've changed for the better. We've changed to survive," I say softly now.

"I don't want to just survive, though. I want to live and be loved."

"And who says that you won't?" Uncle George pipes up. "There was a time in my life when I felt like all I could do was fight to survive in a terrible environment. Finally, once I was out, I realised the difference between surviving and living, and let me tell you, I am living now. Whether you marry or not is another matter, but with all of you in my life, I feel loved and am satisfied in knowing that. You best believe you'll find somebody wonderful. They'll probably love you even more because you're that much more interesting with this new part of you. It's a great story to have, and the right man will see your strength and beauty shine out of you from over-coming such a harrowing event." He comes over with a handkerchief and dries Lori's wet eyes as he speaks. Lori in return gives him a long hug whilst he is careful not to touch her new arm. Pauline comes over to me and helps lace back up my corset.

"Lori, I for one think your arm is very interesting," Thomas says with a small voice. "I made something for you I've been wanting to give to you."

Lori pulls away from Uncle George to take the gift Thomas offers to her. Sitting back on the bed, she unwraps the brown paper to reveal two ornate cuff-like pieces of brass on top of polished steel. The pieces are engraved with vine leaves that curl and wrap themselves in a maze of foliage.

"Oh, Thomas, this is..." Lori begins tearing up at the sight of it, but Thomas comes next to her and begins to fix them onto her plain metal arm. The design fits perfectly—no wonder he was so focussed on the measurements of the prosthetic design. Just by adding the cuffs to her bicep and forearm, it looks like a completely new design. Lori covers her mouth and nose with George's handkerchief as everyone comes around to marvel at its new look.

"You made this? How old are you again?" Timothy gapes, but Thomas ignores his question.

"You did an incredibly detailed job on this, Thomas," Uncle George beams as he scrutinises the cuffs. "When did you do it? I never saw you working in the lab."

"That's because for the past week I've been Jack the Riveter's new roommate, you could say. I took a lot of my metal-working tools and used the fire from the furnace to make it. By the way, Jack still twitches every now and then. Nearly stopped my heart the first time it happened." Thomas points at Aspen before Lori brings him into a hug. She's still crying, but with the new arm design, she doesn't have as much of an expression of hopelessness on her face. Andrea and Isola present Lori with gifts as well, a collection of her favourite desserts, bringing such a grand smile to her face.

"How did you know I love sweets?" Lori asks.

"Lucky guess, you could say," Anthony says, glancing at Keagan.

See, Lori, things aren't always as bad as they seem.

Turns out there's much more to Lori's arm than we knew about at first. The new hidden attachments are quite incredible. Each of her fingers is able to perform a different task; her index finger is a knife, her middle a lighter, which she can flick like a little flamethrower just with her mind alone. Her ring finger is hollow and can stretch out like a spyglass, which will help immensely for transporting small things. Her thumb has its own special safety trigger, and for good reason. Uncle

George and I met with the doctor specially last week to help make this piece for Lori. It holds a similar power source as Jack the Riveter's, and when concentrated and flexed out, she can deliver fifty thousand volts of electricity.

Her pinky is a special gift from Timothy, which he slipped to the doctor before surgery. A special adaptable pick that can fit any keyhole. I loved seeing the sparkle in her eyes when she found out I provided a compact mirror making up a slim portion of the top of her hand. Her forearm on the inside has a flat hollow waterproof compartment for carrying her fan, sleeping darts, jewellery, or whatever else she may wish to carry. She even has a safety latch for her entire hand, to keep her gizmos dormant whenever needed, like sleeping.

Dr Avery warned us sternly that, though we can add onto the original design of her arm, we shouldn't mess with the inner wiring on our own. He even made us sign an agreement promising that if we want to replace or remove one of the gadgets she already has, we will consult a doctor who's proficient in arm prosthetics and gadgetry. But we're all quite satisfied with what she has now, so it will be some time till anything is replaced.

Lori, through each demonstration and mobility practice, is beginning to look at her new arm with less disdain. She doesn't seem completely happy with it, to say the least, but she at least appears as if she doesn't loathe it anymore. This transition will take time, but I just pray that one day she'll learn to at least accept her new arm.

ENTERING THE LION'S DEN

LORI

Dressed up in at least three layers of clothes and all wearing gardener outfits, Keagan, Aspen and I go towards the servants' entrance. There we are let in by the guards, thanks to the worker's passes given to us by Timothy. We decided early on not to just walk in with all of our precious inventions, and instead have Pauline bring them the night before and help Timothy put them in a secure place under lock and key. Apparently Pauline is still allowed in the palace's weapons room, after years of loyalty working for the queen, unlike Uncle George. And it's no wonder why; after looking after Uncle George for so long, she's practically a trained agent herself, under the queen's service to continually keep him in check.

Walking through the garden, we three find a secluded area and take off our gardeners' clothes to reveal our suits underneath. Now we look like we could be classy engineers for the queen's armoury, with our tailored moustaches and tweed grey and black suits. For good measure, we even wear our knife-proof chest plates, for Aspen and I to have a more masculine physique. Not to mention the stubble makeup—anything to hide our appearance more. Timothy gave us a map of the garden and told us to meet him by the Italian cypress trees that shoot straight up to the sky. We were able to see them from far away by how tall they are. The queen sure has some rare and strange-looking plants in her garden.

It's been two weeks since I received my new arm, and I've gotten fairly used to it regardless of how it moves. However, it can be rather sudden at times when I'm practising my strength and changes in motion. I've already broken half the teacups, three bowls, a porcelain kettle, and a metal spoon. At least the hole in the wall wasn't too hard to patch up. I just wish I could've learned to control my arm sooner before meeting the queen. It doesn't move as fast as I'd like sometimes, and at other times can be much too fast and hard to control. But at least I haven't electrocuted or burnt anyone with one of my fingers, though I threaten to use it whenever Uncle George and Harry decide to tease me a bit.

Seeing Timothy come out of the trees, he motions us to hurry. It's thirty minutes till we meet the queen, and we want to make sure everything is up to par. Hurrying along, we follow Timothy through the garden, dusted with fresh morning dew and the golden rays of sun that stretch out over the edges of the palace walls. This takes me back to our garden back home. Aspen and I would play so many games as children, dancing through the long grass with our mother and tackling our father every chance we got until they tickled us into submission. It makes me want to wander away in this garden for hours, and just forget where we are now.

But I know that's my cowardice and anxiety talking. I'm tired of running and hiding; we have to face this now. Earlier, Aspen even tried to reassure me that we'll be okay one way or another as she was filling the hidden container on my forearm full of sleeping darts and smoke bombs. I could tell even she was nervous about today. There's no guarantee we'll walk away from this one. In fact, this may turn out to be the worst idea we've ever had, but it seems to be the only one we have to save our names and lives at this point. I always wanted to be the princess who needs rescuing; I guess some things have changed since then.

Once Timothy enters the code to the door, we go into the armoury and walk through a hallway with wall-length windows. We can see that the room is filled with all different inventions. Some appear as if they've exploded or simply fallen apart, whilst others fill up a whole corner or hang from the ceiling. Many are small hand-sized ones that cover the work tables. Bumping into something straight on, I pull back only to see my drooling sister gawking at all of the machines. Looks like she's found her heaven.

"Aspen, you'll love this next room," Timothy says at the end of the hall where a door is. Aspen practically sprints down the hall to get to the door as I trail behind her.

"Where are the other workers?" Keagan asks, walking in first.

"Out. Most of them like to get a cup of tea in our break area before starting work; Actually, we're a bit early for anyone to usually start working." Timothy continues to lead us over to his area, where underneath his desk he slowly pulls out a mass wrapped up in old sheets. *Jack.* The next thing he pulls out is from his wide lockable drawer. Pulling out the tip of our deflated airship, my heart skips a beat. *They're both here and untouched, oh thank God.* He pulls over a cart with a curtained bottom area. Slipping Jack into the bottom where he is slightly curled up, we put the airship atop the cart and inflate it. Once the airship is ready to go, we cover it with a lightweight tarp, then we're off. Our time with the queen should be happening soon, so we all wheel it over to the queen's privy chamber.

"The queen had this chamber made exclusively for the viewing of new inventions," Timothy says. "It comes with a seating room, where plenty of people can remain in the everyday regal furnishings, whilst looking through a tempered-glass window into a testing room. This way the Crown remains comfortable and safe, as there have been issues with new inventions backfiring during their demonstrations, as well as the death of at least one inventor." We begin to look at one another at the mention of this, and I can't help but think that this really is an inappropriate way to help bolster us before we're about to show these sensitive inventions to Her Highness. He seems to have a knack for putting his foot in his mouth, as I've gathered from all of our past encounters.

Waiting outside of the doors to the privy chambers, the guards stand tall and stoic. The hallway is tall and very wide, the ornate stained glass windows at the end of the hallway shining speckled colours all the way to us in the middle of the corridor. The opposite wall from us is covered in old photos and paintings of Parliament, and a few battle scenes. I feel like each pair of eyes we pass can see right through our disguises, threatening to call us out. We don't have to be anxious for long, however, since a single knock on the double red doors causes the guards to instantly open them up.

We all enter, Timothy in front and the three of us behind, pushing in the heavy cart. There's plenty of room, just as Timothy told us; currently there are three men in a back corner conversing over papers, two of them in grey suits with their backs turned from us, the third listening to the other two. The queen is currently speaking to an older man who must be her advisor, Sir Conroy, since he's dressed to the nines in his official regalia. There must be something important before or after our meeting with Her Majesty, because she herself is dressed in fine jewellery of emeralds and pearls, with a white and gold-trimmed forest-green dress covered in elaborate designs. There are even pearls sewn into the fabric. *What if this is just a part of her daily clothing, and she has other outfits even more ornate? What a wardrobe. It almost makes me swoon.*

"Your Highness, I must express the greatest of gratitudes to you for taking time out of your salient schedule to come and see what I and my associates have created for you," Timothy begins. "Might I add that you are looking radiant as always today, my Glorious Queen." *Sucking up a bit hard there, don't you think, you twit? I hate that he has to take the credit right now. It's Aspen who made the majority of it; she should be the one who should be talking.*

"Ah, yes, the wonderful invention you have been so generous as to remind me regularly of," she says, scrutinising each of us individually. "As for you and your helpers, I'd like to hear what they have to say." I feel myself begin to sweat, and I pray that my moustache stays in place.

"Yes, your excellency—"

"Not you, sir. You two, speak." She points to Aspen and me. My heart sinks. I was able to fool a few guards once with my voice, but I practised a bit before I did.

"Your Majesty, I can attest that this machine will truly be a wonder for you." Aspen bows and speaks cooly in the deepest tone she can muster. However, it sounds like she just woke up —it's deep but not deep enough to sound fully like a male's voice, I'm afraid.

The queen lifts her head slightly, then turns her eyes

towards me in expectation. "Um, indeed, my queen, what my associate says is true," I stumble out. But the queen doesn't look convinced, and I don't blame her. I feel like a ball of nerves.

"These three accomplices of yours, that you claim have been working with you on your machine. I have never laid eyes on them in my life, and neither have my heads of weapons and engineering departments. I did a look of everyone's files a few weeks ago, after we let go of my worst workers. These faces were not amongst the files I received. And I can guess by your heights and builds alone that two of you are female, yes?" Heat rushes to my face as panic floods my very core. *How did she see through us so easily?* We were even able to fool Thomas and Pauline this morning by showing up at the front door in our outfits (and nearly got slapped by her as well, when we tried to come in without showing who we really were). There's no way she figured us out so easily on the spot like that. "Governor Damon has informed me of the possibility that you three would come to me eventually. Seems he was correct, considering all the evidence. Isn't that right, Mr Keagan Myrack, Miss Aspen, and Lori Wolfe? You *are* familiar with Governor Damon, I presume?" Her Majesty nods to the back of the room.

"Good morning, Miss Wolfe. You know, moustaches really don't suit you," I hear from behind me. Turning around, I catch the eyes of the one man I truly despise right before he rips off my moustache, exposing me to everyone in the room. As my upper lip burns, he quickly acknowledges us all with a nod and a serpent's smile before bowing to the queen.

YOUR HIGHNESS

KEAGAN

"Your Majesty, if you would allow me to explain," I begin; however, the queen quickly cuts me off.

"No need. I trust Governor Damon of Currlion to be a devoted member of society, whilst the three of you have proven yourselves time and again to be menaces to the empire with your renegade behaviour. I'm almost curious to hear of your tales of rebellion and why I should believe you, instead of believing in a faithful member of government who has served the empire from before you were even born." Her words lash out at us like knives, cutting our hopes to pieces with every syllable, and yet Damon's smile broadens ever more. "Now that we all are acquainted, tell me, where have you been residing?" But we just stand there silent as statuary. Lori and Aspen have begun to take off their disguises, and after some silence I take off my false glasses and moustache, stuffing them in my pockets.

"Your queen asked you a question," Sir Conroy presses.

"We don't wish our host any harm," Lori pipes up. "He's

just a kind man who was scared of us enough to house us."
Aspen clears her throat, and I know she's said too much.

"Is Mr Pembrook here?"

"No, ma'am," he responds rather quickly.

"Someone else who possibly works for the Crown, then?"
Sir Conroy asks.

"No, Your Highness," I say.

"Well, then it must have been someone who used to, or
else you would've had to do a great deal of digging to even get
into contact with Mr Pembrook. That is, unless you've known
each other for some time."

"Yes, my queen," I say. "Mr Pembrook and I went to school
together."

"Is this true?" She addresses Timothy, to which he nods
fervently.

"It amazes me how differently people can turn out despite
having the same education," Sir Conroy scoffs. The queen just
stares us down, regarding Sir Conroy, and he nods back to her.

"Sir Conroy, get me Sir George Adlene and his household,"
the queen orders, and in a flash Sir Conroy exits the doors and
orders the guards to do the queen's bidding. They are on their
way to George's house. *Thomas and Thatcher; what will it look like if
they're found? A practically emaciated dimie and a boy who was reported as
kidnapped a few months back, after the charge of us murdering his family.*

"Who?" Aspen looks at me, obviously trying to play off not
knowing him.

"Your Majesty—"

"Silence. "The queen raises her hand. "And don't try to act
ignorant. This isn't the first time he's tried to harbour enemies
of the Crown. It would be no surprise to me if he's done it
again. Not to mention that the governor has brought it to my

attention that Sir Adlene is a family member of a dear friend of yours from Currlion. It would make perfect sense to use his home as a place to stay."

The first thought that comes to my head is the image of all of us hanging by the yard arm. My second is that George never told us he was knighted. My shoulders slump in a feeling of despair. *What will become of us now? She has us pegged perfectly. This isn't good. What about her spies that lurk among the crowds? Have they seen us? And if they have, how much do they know?* My eyes turn towards that iniquitous Damon; he's made our lives even worse than before, it would seem. Damon must feel my ragging stare, because he turns to me and smiles under his peppered moustache and three-pointed beard. "Oh, come now, young Keagan, don't give me that look," he says. "I'm the queen's guest for this day. She told me she was having a very special meeting with one of her engineers. He said he's created the perfect war balloon with his aides, which she's been eagerly awaiting. Take heart, though; it wasn't until you entered that I figured out who you were. However, I did take the opportunity of warning the queen earlier of you three possibly coming to her to beg for a pardon. Don't hate me for your bad timing, boy." He sneers. I could tear his groomed beard right off, and from the tension I sense on either side of me, I can tell the ladies are having even worse thoughts.

"What's going on?" Sir Conroy asks as he enters back into the room.

"The governor was kind enough to enlighten us on the means of him being here today," Aspen says, maintaining her composure.

"Yes, Governor Damon was quite generous in supplying Scotland Yard with his new invention, the tracking hounds," the queen explains. "I've seen them work in a demonstration this morning, and they are frightfully marvellous."

We've seen them too, first-hand, and they are anything but marvellous.

"Well, Your Majesty, we have two gifts of our own to bestow upon you," Timothy says. "One is something you've been wanting for quite some time, and the other is something your weapons department has lost."

The queen ponders this whilst gazing at the cart for some time. "All right, I'm curious enough to see what you have to show. However, before you bestow anything upon me, since this now concerns my top weapons engineers, I would like for them and the captain of the weapons department to be here to attest that it was indeed lost." She nods to the human attendants at the door, and they leave the room. However, when they leave, a man steps into the room and whispers something to Her Majesty that causes her eyebrows to raise slightly. "Until they and the Adlene household arrive, you may wait in the hallway; I require privacy at the moment."

What did that man say to her? I wish Aspen had created a listening earpiece of some kind that isn't as noticeable as today's ear horns or bionic ears. Then I'd know how bad off we are currently. If we live through this, I'll let her know about my idea later. Even though we may not have such machinery as that, I notice a large fly come from Aspen's coat pocket and land on the top of the back of the door without any of the attendants paying any mind. Even in our most grave moments, Aspen thinks of something. I can't believe she had her Fly On The Wall with her, though.

As we wait to re-enter the chamber, guards with bayonet guns line the ends of the hallway, boxing us into a secluded area just outside the door that also has two guards in front of it. It's somewhat hard to take them seriously with their tall black fuzzy hats, though I don't find anything worth laughing about right now. Not with Damon being in such close proximity to us, and us unable to do anything to him but talk.

Aspen and Lori take off their coats and begin to roll up their sleeves, looking a bit more feminine in doing so, despite wearing men's trousers. Timothy just walks off towards the end of the hall, raking his hands through his hair and muttering to himself. The stained-glass windows have stopped displaying patterns of colour along the floor, the hall instead is overcast in a whitish blue glow. Damon, I just realised, has a thick coat draped over his arm. The outside is a deep chestnut brown and looks like mink, but as it slips down a little, he adjusts it in his arms, and that's when I notice the telltale yellow-tan fur.

"That's a new coat, is it not?" I say, surprising everyone by talking to him so cordially, but I stare straight at the yellow fur that lines the collar and seems to make up the lining of the inside as well.

"Ah, yes. You remember Gertrude?" Damon says, causing me to give a shocked look, which only seems to rile him up for more conversation. The guards are too far down the halls to properly hear us, so I don't find a problem with it.

"Why did you have her help you and show she was in your group if you were just going to skin her in the end?" Aspen asks with a sneer.

"What better way to taste betrayal than from the one you're trying to save?" He gives us all a smug side glance that makes my blood boil. "To be honest, I never cared much for her, even when she was just my household slave. She was always a snitch. I knew I couldn't truly trust anyone like that, so she was useful to me for finding you three out. Once she figured me out and got scared, that's when I found out about the note. And then I thought to myself, 'You know what you could use, Louis? A new fur-lined coat.'"

None of us speak immediately, but I can feel the anger rising uncontrolled from all of us. "What did you do with Winona's body?" I blurt out, walking closer to him, surprising myself.

"Go to the bottom of Currlion Bay, and you'll see for yourself. She was shot where it showed, so we couldn't use her anyway." Damon looks me squarely in the eye. The thought of Winona getting killed by a bullet reels through my brain as my vision turns red, and I see my target before me. I throw myself atop Damon, slamming him into the ground, but the guards are on me before I can land a single blow. We're ripped from one another despite how resistant we both were to that action. Even Damon tries to lash out as we're being pulled away from one another. I know he wants to fight me just as badly.

"Do you want to hit me, boy? Go ahead, I'll give you the first shot!" the governor hollers with a smile as he's taken away.

"I'll be doing more than that the next time we meet. You can bet on it, you monstrous bastard," I spit out.

"Ahem. The queen is ready for you to re-enter her privy chamber. Do compose yourselves," an attendant with an upturned nose says, entering the hallway. Aspen pushes through the guards and helps straighten me up a bit by fixing my shirt and my dark strands of hair. The guards let me go, and I shake off the feeling of their vice-like grip on my shoulders and arms. Feeling a hand on my face, I finally look someone in the eye again, and it's Aspen. The look in her forest-green eyes shows pride and concern at the same time. I never thought I'd see a look like that from her. "I'm sorry," I say sheepishly.

"Don't be. You just beat me to what I was about to do." She smiles before taking my hand and walking back towards the doors.

Once we are all back inside along with Governor Damon, we stand there in silence for an uncomfortable amount of time. "Your Majesty, please let us—" I start, but the queen raises her hand, silencing me.

One of Her Majesty's attendants enters the room and whispers to her, putting sparks in her eyes. "Very good, send them in," she says in a light voice. Uncle George, Pauline, Thatcher and Thomas are led in the room. *Lord, why does Thomas have to be here? The queen has a reputation for disliking children; he may hurt our case even more, just by being here!*

Once they're all inside, Uncle George goes right ahead and speaks to the queen as if she were an old friend. "Victoria, how radiant you look. How are you on this fine day?"

"Annoyed, to be perfectly honest, *Sir Adlene,*" she says, stressing his last name as she looks down at him over her long nose. He seems to get the point—to my surprise—and just nods without another word. Turning to the four men on her right, she introduces them to us. "This is my head engineer, Mr Oxley, and captain of the weaponry, Captain Thorne." She does not, however, introduce the other two men. She says nothing else, but instead just sits in her raised chair, looking expectantly at us.

Aspen gets back into motion, and Timothy follows, aiding her by lifting off the cover for the airship. The second they do, we look to Her Majesty who gives it a quizzical expression. "Haven't seen a model quite like that one, have we?" She turns to Mr Oxley.

"No, Your Majesty we have not," he replies, striding towards the creation. I get a nervous feeling from how close he scrutinises it, though he doesn't touch it. Aspen, meanwhile, has pulled something out of her pocket that she's quickly cranking up as everyone talks. "This is by far the largest model that's ever been exhibited. It looks sound. Note the way the turbines are curved to take in the air on the sides. How do you power it?" he says to Timothy alone. "I'm guessing electricity."

"I, um...I assume it is, sir."

"You assume? You mean you don't know for sure?" Captain Thorne walks over towards Timothy.

"That's a surprise for later," Aspen says boldly, earning herself a cynical glare from Mr Oxley. "We would like you to see it fly first,"

"Indeed, sir, you must see it fly first," Timothy adds.

"Well, then, let's see it," Captain Thorne says, looking intently at the front of the airship.

Carrying the airship into the testing room, we step back outside, and Aspen stops winding up the device. It looks similar to the controls on the radio transmitter she made for us for the first homecoming. One button, when pressed, makes a small lightbulb flicker on. Then there are the two controls; one moves around in four different directions, and the other is gyroscopic in design. Flicking the gyroscopic ball, the balloon flies up, with the insides of the machine lighting up in the process, the propeller-like turbines on the sides of the machine that take up half of its middle cavity spinning so fast that you can barely see them. With a turn of the knob, the airship turns to the left in the air and sails about the room in a circle. I turn back to see that there's not one unpleased face in the audience, except for Governor

Damon. The queen herself has a wide smile covering her face.

"What about avoiding enemy bombings or turbulent weather?" Captain Thorne asks.

"The outer lining is very durable," Aspen elucidates, "and though it's slightly flexible, it's very strong. We've tested it thoroughly, and not even eight hard strikes of a hammer is enough to break it. This model will be an exact replica of the real thing."

"How big were you planning on the real thing being?"

"About four hundred metres, to accommodate enough soldiers and ammunition onto the aircraft where it can still fly with ease," she says as she shows us an extreme flight pattern where the airship flies with sharp turns about the room at a surprising speed. She explains that this is how quickly the ship can be turned if they ever needed to do so. "The airship could even be turned upside down, provided everyone on the ship secured themselves at their stations first."

"My word," the queen says, looking legitimately astonished. "I must say, this is a very impressive invention. But you have failed to explain how it works. What does this use for fuel?"

In the covered area under the cart we rolled in, we five (including Thomas) slowly pull out Jack and gently lay him in the centre of the room. The moment we step away with the tarp, Mr Oxley and Captain Thorne both step up and stare deadpanned at the thing they had lost months ago. "Is that ghastly thing what I think it is?" Her Majesty asks.

"Indeed, Your Majesty, this here is none other than—"

"Jack the Riveter," Mr Oxley says meekly.

At the sound of that name, the queen's guards begin to surround her in a barrier of protection. "Where did you find this? Did you destroy the inside?" Captain Thorne demands, pointing to Jack.

"No, sir," Aspen replies. "He's still fully intact, though he's currently neutralised. If you open up his chestplate, I'd be happy to show you how we were able to make this possible." However, no one takes her up on the offer.

"How did you catch him in the first place?" Mr Oxley breathes out.

"Well, after he chased, attacked and nearly killed us, it was actually a random person's love of music that saved us. Music triggers a resting state in him, where his kinetically stored energy is processed—"

"Yes, I know how he works. I helped build him," Mr Oxley snaps.

"Then why didn't you make him more stable?" I ask. The queen, much to everyone's surprise, starts to laugh a little. Her eyes are on Mr Oxley. He, however, doesn't look amused and keeps his head down.

"I must thank you for making him the way he is, though, or else we never would've found the perfect fuel technology for the aircraft," Aspen says rather boldly.

"The aircraft model uses a similar power source and processor for its motor that Jack here uses."

Frantically, the remaining engineers that were talking in the corner earlier with Damon, along with Mr Oxley and Captain Thorne, rush over to Jack and nearly rip off his chestplate. They take their time examining his insides. Of course, the clamps are still on it in the most vital areas, but we hope they're not too proud to mess with them.

"What have you done to him?" Captain Thorne stands back up and points squarely at Aspen.

Aspen just smiles for a second as the rest of the room turns their attention to her. "It was a group effort to be sure, but we managed to neutralise Jack without damaging any of his interior. Luckily for us, we were able to do it in a way that allowed us to study him further. The model airship you see flying is powered almost the same way as Jack; however, we've enhanced it. It's a continuous flow of kinetic energy. Once it's created and used, the more the turbines move, the more energy is made. It can go on for much longer and be more resilient than Jack, you see."

The engineers' faces turn bright red and some look angry whilst others keep their heads down in embarrassment. I guess if you're a glorified "genius of the Crown", it'd be a hard thing to swallow to have a young woman fix your rogue invention. I felt something similar when both of the ladies used to beat me in fights all the time—at least now I'm winning half the time.

"Miss Wolfe, I find it hard to believe that you could design and invent this aircraft all on your own, let alone a multidimensional transporter, regardless of what Mr Damon has told us of you," the queen finally says. "And redesign such a sensitive thing as Jack's fuel supply processor. That being said, there's only one person I can think of who would aid a group like yourselves and who has connections to me, and that is you, Sir Adlene." She looks at the aircraft model still flying around the testing room, then back to George.

"You flatter me, Your Highness." He smiles at her; however, she still doesn't look amused. "Your Majesty, you are right that Aspen did not do those things alone; however, I will say that she did indeed create the majority of all the things you speak of. Thomas here and I aided her wherever she wished us to, like the making of the turbines on the sides, or the placement of the core for the fuel. Our addition to the machines were minor, though, compared to the blood, sweat and tears she's poured into this."

"I see."

"However, Victoria," he says more gently, "you must realise there's another reason they've presented themselves to you today."

"Don't tell me," Sir Conroy scoffs. "They wish to have their status as criminals be pardoned? After all they've done? I just received word that there are dimies and lower-class citizens rioting together in the streets, and now there's no doubt a rebellion is on the rise after that little heist these people perpetrated a few weeks ago. They began a catalyst against the Crown, and yet you ask Her Majesty to pardon them? How dare you, Sir Adlene."

"They can be of use to you, since they in fact were aiding your subjects, both slave and working class. They wish to help the poor to get their jobs back by freeing the dimies. I've seen them working first-hand at making the impossible possible, my queen, such as the making of Gear Heart, the capture and neutralisation of Jack the Riveter, and the creation of a working airship. All of it to help you and your subjects, not to start a revolt. Your Majesty, if you only hear the reasoning for their cause, maybe you will see the truth in it." George looks pleadingly to the queen.

"I once had a profound respect and trust in you, George," the queen replies in a melancholic tone. "But this, I must say, is pushing the limits even for you. I never took you for an extremist."

"Victoria—"

"You will address Her Ladyship as Your Majesty or Queen Victoria. Is that clear, Sir Adlene?" Sir John Conroy snaps at

Uncle George in a booming voice, causing some colour to drain from Uncle George's face.

"Yes, sir," Uncle George replies weakly.

Governor Damon takes this opportunity to speak freely instead of reading the room. "Honestly, Your Majesty, this group is nothing but a pack of thieves, waiting for the opportunity to plant a bomb that could destroy the entire empire. It seems as if they already have, by how the plebes are acting right now. Why, they've already stolen a child, and practically all the slaves in Currlion—"

"Yes, we managed to *save* the ones you hadn't already massacred on your ship in an unauthorised mass shooting," Aspen interrupts. "You know, right after you discussed reopening the portal to start up the slave trade again for your dimie-skinning fur business."

"You were the one who reopened the portal and let the slaves run away," Damon says to the three of us pointedly.

"More like swim away with their lives on the line as you shot at them from your ship!" Lori snaps back. "Go ahead, Your Majesty. Ask the witness, Thatcher, whom we saved. He's right here with us, and a policeman—"

"Silence, wench!" Damon says, cutting Lori off as he fronts her with a raised, shaking backhand, as if he's about to strike her. I move in front of her immediately and stare that beast straight in his black eyes. I can see his shell chipping away more and more, the further truths we tell. There's a dark madness that begins to show in his eyes.

"Peace, Damon. You can show a little more decorum than that," Sir Conroy orders, hands coming away from his back and out to his sides in clenched gloved fists. "Enough of this. Apprehend them and take this model to the rest of the engineers. We finally have a design to work with."

"I have a patent that makes me the legal owner of this aircraft and everything it's made of," Aspen retaliates as the guards come near us.

"It's true, Your Majesty, I have a copy of it with me here," Uncle George says, allowing Pauline to take it up to the queen.

"You just admitted that you created it with a piece of machinery that already belongs to the queen," Captain Thorne shouts.

"Wrong. I studied the machinery that belongs to Her Highness and made an enhanced version of it that is totally of Uncle George and my creation. We simply made it our own after being inspired by yours. If you take it from me, that's considered stealing, and last I checked that's against the law." Aspen smiles smugly.

"She is the queen. She *is* the law."

"It might be smart to have them near, to make sure the airship is built soundly," the queen ponders with a finger to her chin.

"Your Majesty, we don't need them to recreate this airship. We can do it ourselves," Mr Oxley says reassuringly.

"That's where you're wrong, my queen," Aspen says with a confident tone to her voice. "Would you really trust these men who already failed at creating the *ever-so-reliable* Jack that lies before you here? And then to recreate an even more advanced machine, which they don't know the first thing about? Or would you prefer the original inventors to be there to make sure it's safe and that no lives will be lost in the process of creating such a sought-after rare invention?"

"Oh yes, break the law even more, for the sake of your own skin. That's what this is really about, anyhow," Damon says.

"You're one to talk," Lori snaps at him.

"Sir Conroy is proposing breaking the law to steal someone else's possession to make it his own," I snap. "If word gets out—and it will—I can assure you very few inventors of any rank would try and aid the Crown again."

"Hold your tongue, boy." Conroy wags his finger at me, inspiring a strong desire in me to break it.

"That's enough." The queen stands and addresses the entire room. "Line them all up before me, including Governor Damon." Everyone freezes at the sound of her voice, but against our wishes, we're placed one by one in front of Her Majesty. Much to my chagrin, Damon is placed kneeling next to me.

Her Majesty stares down at us with her hands resting on her sceptre. "Now where do we even start with the lot of you?"

BY ORDER OF THE QUEEN

ASPEN

The queen looks at each of us until her eyes land on Thatcher. "You there, bear dimie. Pray tell, what was your name again?"

"My name is Thatcher, Your Majesty. What do you wish of me?"

"No doubt you heard Miss Lori Wolfe's little outburst, saying you were a witness to a supposed massacre dealt by Governor Damon."

"Your Majesty, you can't seriously trust the words of a slave?" Damon interjects.

"Silence," she snaps so fiercely at Damon that my breathing catches. "Under oath of your own sacred religion and the oath of your people, tell me and my two most trusted members of Parliament here what it is that you witnessed."

"By the honour of my people and my god, I swear to tell you the whole truth." Thatcher's fur is for the most part covered by his normal cream day shirt and trousers. But I bet if he took off his shirt for everyone to see, that would be evidence enough to prove what Damon has done is more than just a crime; it's a multitude of sins.

Thatcher explains every detail of what he saw, and what he's been put through since. He offers up things he hadn't even told us about yet, like how he was a witness to Keagan and me being caged on the ship, and the treatment we were given along with everyone else. The one that sends a chill down my spine, though, and seems to greatly disturb Her Majesty as well, is when the governor decided to have a paid tanner skin Gertude in front of Thatcher and make him watch. At this last account, the entire room looks horrified.

"Your Majesty, if I may, look at the inner lining of the governor's coat," Keagan suggests. "It's the same colour fur as the late Gertude whom he skinned."

"How do you know of this, Mr Myrack?" The queen looks sceptical.

"He showed it off to us in the hallway as we were waiting, Your Highness."

"Sir Conroy, if you would, please."

Sir Conroy immediately takes the fur coat that Damon has shamelessly tried to hide behind his back. Taking it, he opens it up to the queen only. "My queen, I know of a scar on her fur," Thatcher says. "It was long and resembled a tree." At this, the queen takes a long look at Thatcher's eyes just before calling over her unnamed members of Parliament. It's no wonder we couldn't identify them before; they're wearing plain clothes today, not their usual robes when in session. The three scrutinise the fur and pause near the hem at the bottom. They exchange looks before they release the coat.

"My Queen, if you would, just look at these photographs taken right before we rescued Thatcher from Damon," I say, pulling out the small photos I took that night. "They should be enough to show his mistreatment of dimies." Luckily, the film turned out clear and bright. One of the men from Parliament takes the photos, and the looks of disgust on all three of their faces says enough. However, the man does not give them back, or the coat, once they finish scrutinising them.

"Thank you, that will be sufficient," the queen says, visibly disturbed. "And you, young boy, Damon mentioned you are the kidnapped child. What do you have to say about your captors? And remember to swear in."

After swearing in, he stands up and addresses Her Majesty directly. "It only appeared as if they were kidnapping me, but the people who reported it thusly were actually the ones who killed my grandfather when raiding my family's shop. If it wasn't for the Wolfe sisters and Mr Myrack, I would probably be dead as well. They've even been providing me an education, and I've been able to become a greater metalsmith thanks to Aspen."

"Miss Wolfe has been your teacher?"

"Indeed, Your Majesty. She and George...er, Sir Adlene, have taught me mainly, but they've all helped. I've been learning history, mathematics, physics and literature, but my focus is on metalsmithing and mechanics. The ivy cuff on Lori's arm is an example of my work." At this, Lori sheepishly rolls back up her sleeve, allowing the metal to glean in the light.

Mr Oxley comes over and, placing his monocle in his eye socket, looks very closely at the design. "Beautifully done, and for someone of your age as well."

"Thank you, sir," Thomas beams with pride.

"That is all," says the queen. "Thank you, Thomas..."

"Brimstone, my queen," Thomas says, taking off his cap and bowing to Victoria before kneeling before her again. I notice that he missed the part where we were the cause of them raiding the place in the first place, since we were hiding slaves there. He's learned well from us on how to tell a story, and I don't know if I should be worried or proud.

"Your Majesty, I must speak, please." Damon raises his palm.

"Very well, speak," the queen says plainly.

"In my defence, I was simply on my way to see you with the entire cargo hold full of slaves that these young rogues stole from practically every home in Currlion, as well as these criminals here, who have been charged with numerous crimes besides the ones already addressed, might I add. I wished to propose a new foundation for the slave trade to re-open again, but also for the use of their fur. All I was trying to do was please the Crown."

"And how were you so sure you would? Damon, what you've done has greatly displeased and discomforted me. Did you not realise that my order would be needed for the skinning of dimies? That is if I would even seriously entertain the idea? Or the mass killing of them on your ship? There was no need for that. You could have contained them, but you shouldn't have killed them. At this point, I'm almost afraid to hear what else you've done."

"He tried to steal my multidimensional transporter as well. He succeeded in stealing my father's journal with the plans for it," I point out, feeling rather childish as I speak.

"Aside from Thatcher and Mr Brimstone here, I feel as if I should lock every last one of you up for what you've done, starting with you, Damon. You have lied and defied the Crown on multiple occasions, and not in a light way, it would seem. You have truly committed atrocities that even the dimies do not deserve. And what's worse, you assumed I would approve of such cruelty after bribing the Crown with new inventions created under false pretences. Not the first time, either, I've now found out. While you were out of the room, my spies informed me they have 'found enough dirt on you', to use the American phrase, to dig your own grave." She pauses, looking down at him, with her members of Parliament standing behind her. He looks as if he's received a death sentence with how pale he has become, his mouth just hanging open in shock.

"And you three." She pauses to gesture to the rest of us. "I've heard many tales and rumours about you three phantoms. You certainly seem to have a talent for seeing your plans through despite the odds and dangers." Her eyes rove over us, only to rest on Lori's metal arm. Lori notices and unravels her sleeve as she keeps her head down. *Oh, Lori, please don't let her make you feel that way.* "But you also have a nasty habit of causing quite a bit of trouble. I've been aware for some time of the rumours of an uprising, calling for the end of the dimies' slavery. But due to your last heist at possibly our most successful mill, there is not one household in all of England who is not talking about you or the end of the dimie workforce." I have the urge to thank her since I take that as a compliment, but I know better.

"Your Majesty," I say, "even if you were to imprison or kill us, it wouldn't stop the growing crowds that talk of change. I can honestly say, however, that revolt is not what we wish for. We want to take care of the dimies and help our fellow man, not cause chaos in the streets. We knew we had to do this despite the strict laws against the reopening of the portal. So I rebuilt one. Gear Heart is what I've named it."

"Miss Wolfe, if your cause is so important, why did you not ask for permission from Parliament or the Crown?"

"We've tried, Your Highness, over and over. It's been near impossible to see anyone, let alone you." I gesture to the model of the airship. "Even with the airship, the odds were against us seeing you personally."

"It seems that long odds have never stopped your actions before, Miss Wolfe." She doesn't look angry anymore, only inquisitive. The wrinkles on her aged face are more noticeable when she looks down at me from a high angle like this.

"To be honest, Your Majesty," I reply, "we've never had much luck when it comes to the odds. We can almost always count on roadblocks for everything we try to accomplish. But because we have the strength of each other, and our combined wit, we've always been able to make it through. I for one know I could never have gotten this far without my family by my side."

"Something still doesn't sit right with me about this airship," Sir Conroy murmurs. "How do we know for sure that you didn't just buy your way in here whilst Mr Pembrook created the machine himself?"

"Actually, Sir Conroy, Miss Wolfe and Mr Adlene are responsible for creating the majority of the machine, from the design to its own working engines..." Timothy corrects him. Uncle George and Keagan clear their throats, and he hastily finishes, "...and for fixing my last seven assigned weapons."

"Don't forget, she also built Gear Heart herself, Your Highness," Keagan adds, making me start to feel embarrassed. He knows Thomas helped.

"Is this true, Miss Wolfe?"

"Well, not entirely, my queen. My father and I built Gear Heart together, but then it was destroyed. I re-built it myself, with Thomas creating the outer shell elements and soldering wires where my own hands wouldn't fit."

The queen's eyebrows raise. "Mr Brimstone, can you attest to this?"

"Everything Aspen has said today is true," Thomas responds with a perfect poker face, but he sounds earnest enough to seem honest.

"Hmmm," Her Majesty muses as she nods her head slowly. She seems to be thinking something through, since there is a long drawn-out silence yet again. "Governor Damon, at this point, if what they have said against you is true, then you are no less guilty in your endeavours than they are. And on top of it, it seems they were trying to prevent you from going further. That being said, Keagan Myrack, Miss Aspen and Miss Lori Wolfe, to repay your debt to the Crown, you have three choices. Be hung and made an example of for the empire; hand over your estates and inheritance, as well as serve extended prison sentences for your crimes; or act as my special service ambassadors to our fellow nations, while being my eyes and ears to what they might be conspiring in their political agenda."

"What!?" both Sir Conroy and Governor Damon echo. "Your Majesty, is that really wise?" Sir Conroy questions.

"Indeed it is. We all know by now the rumours of war that have been growing in our neighbouring nations. I need people like the three of you, who know how to gain the trust of slaves and humans alike. I want you to stop this war before it begins."

"You can't be serious, Your Majesty," Damon speaks up again. "They'll bring you nothing but ruin."

"You, Governor Damon, will be sentenced to prison, for the killing and skinning of dimie slaves without permission of Parliament or the Crown. Your title and estate will be revoked from you as payment, unless you wish to serve a death penalty as well."

I'm speechless, but Governor Damon is not. "Your Majesty, you can't do this. I was trying to supply the nation with a new trade, and reopen the once prosperous slave industry. I was trying to help, truly."

"Yes, with an illegally made invention that you stole from this group, whom you also tortured."

"That's not—"

"On top of that, Mr Damon," she continued, holding up her hand, "you were the person who discovered the portal in the first place that fateful night years ago. Though it did make our nation prosperous, the scales have fallen from my eyes. What was once a godsend will eventually be our downfall, now that both the slaves and the poor are becoming volatile and talking about revolt. Heaven and Earth, Damon, are we to fall and be made examples of, like so many failed regimes before us? I think not. You're dismissed."

"Your Majesty, wait—" But he is quickly dragged out of the room by two guards, all the while trying to defend himself. I wish I had a camera right now; I'm enjoying this moment tremendously.

When the doors close, the queen's attention comes back to us. "It appears as if you three are a package deal, so I will take you all. As for the Adlene household..." She pauses and the entire room stares. "Seeing how many times you have secretly aided my weapons department by fixing their machines, I will pardon you as well, after my men have searched your house for any other weapons."

"Oh, Your Majesty." George actually looks more unnerved now than when our lives were on the line.

"Now off with you. No time like the present, you know." I

can feel my cheeks begin to burn, since I just realised they could easily find all my weapons and claim them for themselves. Once they leave the room, the queen returns to her throne and sinks into it with a sigh. "Do you need time to make your decision, or shall we have it now?" she asks us.

I look at Keagan, who has his natural smirk on his face, and then to Lori, who looks slightly worried but musters a smile for me. "I always thought we would make pretty good spies," I admit, smiling.

"We would be honoured to serve you, Your Highness," Keagan says, lowering his head as he is still kneeling. Lori and I do the same.

"The Crown accepts. You will serve me until I see that you have done your job justly. Only then will you receive a full pardon. Sir Newberry, my spymaster, will have you ready for the field in a fortnight. Miss Wolfe, we will discuss the details of that patent for your machine later. For now I have other engagements I must attend to." I can hear the smile in her voice and I feel unnerved as she and her attendants, along with Sir Conroy, walk towards the door. I suspect we've gotten ourselves into something possibly greater than we can handle. *Let's see where this line of work takes us now,* I muse to myself as I think of all the gadgets we'll get to use, the secrets we'll get to learn, the dimies we'll get to save, and all the future trouble we'll get into.

"Oh yes, and one more thing," the queen says with a level gaze just before turning to walk out of the double doors. "If any of you step out of line or double-cross me in any way, you can forget about that pardon, and about your lives as well." My mischievous imagination slams to a halt until a new feeling comes over me, as if we are in a game of poker.

Deal. I love a good challenge.

For Reading My Book!

I really appreciate hearing all of your feedback.

I need your input to make the next version of this book and my future books better. Every review matters, and it matters a *lot!*

Please take a minute to leave me an honest review on Amazon or wherever you purchased this book letting me know what you think of the story. Or click this link for more exclusive book content such as:

- New secrets and stories
- Official art of the characters, scenes and cities
- Aspen's inventions

Thanks so much!

Michelle R Young

ACKNOWLEDGMENTS

Soul Cogs was a riveting adventure for me, to say the least, since it did not come to me in a dream as *Gear Heart* did. This book gave me the chance to grow and experiment as an author more than ever. I was amazed to see how many aspects from my life and world events were able to mix perfectly into the story. I want to give a solid thank you to my bestie and soul sister, Hannah Stanley, for being my favorite writing and late night talk buddy. (I can't wait to read your own book when it's ready!)

I grew up hating to write anything for school, or anything in general, due to my disabilities: Dysgraphia and ADHD. I was always thinking up poems and story ideas in my head, but never truly writing them down unless it was an assignment... until *Gear Heart* came along. I haven't been able to stop writing since. I highly encourage people with disabilities to dismiss your doubts and go ahead and try anyway.

I'd like to thank my beta readers: Hannah Stanley, Carter Hannah, and Katelynn Pizzio--you women are incredible and are loved so much! The editing journey for this book has been crazy. I'm grateful for my wonderful family and friends for believing in me and supporting me during the whole writing process.

I cannot thank my wonderful launch team enough. I would not be where I am today without your awesome support: Lauren Olvera, Sydney Symes, Ranee Samaniego, Kayla

Painter, Jet Parker, Amanda Figueroa, ew Hudson, A.J. Hutchinson, Kat Lapatovich Healy, Samantha Peacock, Jared Chapman, Cidell Rosipal, Brittany Parsons, Victoria Kamilar, Theresa Bello, Shayla Alexander, Lauren Mayfeild, Rae Mojica, Claire Randal, Chelsea Pigao, Rene Vrhovec, Deirdre Stokes, Tricia Toole, Tricia Griffin, Michael Collum, Faith Upton, Hannah Diaz, Rhonda Grosser, Mackenzie Luttrell, Mike Bessette, ea Bessette, Dalene Young, Pierce Young, Malley Nelson, Leslie Wilson, Regina Cummings, Kara Burton Barr, Stephanie Van Den Heuvel, Isabella Venegoni, Amber Wagshal, Chris Erler, Alli Hydeman, Cassie Larsen, Jim Lewis, Jayme Deville, Jessica Cosgrove, Alexis Besch, Sara Hinkle-Morrison, Victoria Wykoff, Adrian Murphy, Tiara Koren, Margaret Whitaker, Rachel Hugo, Anissa Howell

ABOUT THE AUTHOR

Michelle Young is an artist, writer and social media specialist that helps businesses with their networks. When she isn't writing, she can be found painting, hanging out with her friends, or simply marveling at nature. Texas born and bred, she has a positive outlook on life and where God has planned for her next. You can see more of her creations and stay tuned for her next book by visiting her and our heroes at www.My-pureart.com/

DISCLAIMER

*Disclaimer: Soul Cogs is a work of fiction. Names, characters, businesses, places, events, locales, and incidents are either the products of the author's imagination or used in a fictitious manner. Any resemblance to actual persons, living or dead, or actual events is purely coincidental or twisted for the purpose of the different fictitious world the characters live in.

9 781735 942124